James Frey is originally from Cleveland, Ohio. He is married and lives in New York. His first two books, *A Million Little Pieces* and *My Friend Leonard*, were bestsellers around the world.

Praise for *Bright Shiny Morning*:

'Frey writes with pace and energy' *Times Literary Supplement*

'A sparkling narrative, which doesn't shrink from exposing the city's seamier side but ultimately is a huge celebration' *Daily Mail*

'An absolute triumph of a novel. In fact it's so good that it makes Frey's real-life resurrection from crooked biographer to great American novelist far more impressive . . . Frey, a natural novelist to his fingertips, hits the deeper truths with this honest, vibrant and tender portrait of Los Angeles and the American dream . . . It can be no exaggeration to say that *Bright Shiny Morning* amounts to the literary comeback of the decade . . . James Frey is probably one of the finest and most important writers to have emerged in recent years' Irvine Welsh, *Guardian*

'An intriguing novel peopled by characters whose presence lingers once reading has ceased' *List*

'A compulsive piece of popular fiction . . . He's an excellent entertainer . . . Frey can tell a story and has a fine eye for the variegated economic milieux in which his characters travel. So what if, by the end, you come away thinking the novel superficial and lacking in original insight? This is Los Angeles, baby. And in LA superficiality has its own integrity' *The Times*

BRIGHT
SHINY
MORNING

BRIGHT
SHINY
MORNING

James Frey

JOHN MURRAY

First published in Great Britain in 2008 by John Murray (Publishers)
An Hachette UK Company

First published in the United States of America in 2008 by
HarperCollins*Publishers* Inc.

First published in paperback in 2009

2

A CIP catalogue record for this title is available from the British Library

B-format ISBN 978-1-84854-047-7
A-format ISBN 978-1-84854-049-1

Printed and bound by Clays Ltd, St Ives plc

John Murray policy is to use papers that are natural, renewable and recyclable
products and made from wood grown in sustainable forests. The logging and
manufacturing processes are expected to conform to the environmental
regulations of the country of origin.

John Murray (Publishers)
338 Euston Road
London NW1 3BH

www.johnmurray.co.uk

Nothing in this book should be considered accurate or reliable.

Following the light of the sun, we left the Old World.

—CHRISTOPHER COLUMBUS, *1493*

On September 4, 1781, a group of forty-four men, women and children who call themselves the Pobladores establish a settlement on land that is near the center of contemporary Los Angeles. They name the settlement El Pueblo de Nuestra Señora la Reina de Los Angeles de Porciuncula. Two-thirds of the settlers are either freed or escaped African slaves, or the direct descendants of freed or escaped African slaves. Most of the rest are Native American. Three are Mexican. One is European.

They can see the glow a hundred miles away it's night and they're on an empty desert highway. They've been driving for two days. They grew up in a small town in Ohio they have known each other their entire lives, they have always been together in some way, even when they were too young to know what it was or what it meant, they were together. They're nineteen now. They left when he came to pick her up for the movies, they went to the movies every Friday night. She liked romantic comedies and he liked action films, sometimes they saw cartoons. They started the weekly outing when they were fourteen.

Screaming, he could hear her screaming as he pulled into the driveway. He ran into the house her mother was dragging her along the floor by her hair. Clumps of it were missing. There were scratches on her face. There were bruises on her neck. He pulled her away and when her mother tried to stop him he hit her mother, she tried again he hit her mother harder. Mother stopped trying.

He picked her up and carried her to his truck, a reliable old American pickup with a mattress in the back and a camper shell over the bed. He set her in the passenger seat carefully set her and he covered her with his jacket. She was sobbing bleeding it wasn't the first time it would be the last. He got into the driver's seat, started the engine, pulled out as he pulled out Mother came to the door with a hammer and watched them drive away, didn't move, didn't say a word, just stood in the door holding a hammer, her daughter's blood beneath her fingernails, her daughter's hair still caught in her clothes and hands.

They lived in a small town in an eastern state it was nowhere anywhere everywhere, a small American town full of alcohol, abuse and religion. He worked in an auto-body shop and she worked as a clerk at a gas station and they were going to get married and buy a house and try to be better people than their parents. They had dreams but they called them dreams because they were unrelated to reality, they were a distant unknown, an impossibility, they would never come true.

He went back to his parents' house they were in a bar down the street. He locked the doors of the truck and kissed her and told her she would be fine and he walked into the house. He went to the bathroom and got aspirin and Band-Aids, he went into his room and pulled a video game case from out of the drawer. The case held every cent he had $2,100 he had saved for their wedding. He took it out and put it in his pocket he grabbed some clothes and he walked out. He got in the truck she had stopped crying. She looked at him and she spoke.

What are we doing?

We're leaving.

Where we going?

California.

We can't just up and go to California.

Yes, we can.

We can't just walk away from our lives.

We don't have lives here. We're just stuck. We'll end up like everyone else, drunk and mean and miserable.

What'll we do?

Figure it out.

We're just gonna leave and go to California and figure it out?

Yeah, that's what we're gonna do.

She laughed, wiped away her tears.

This is crazy.

Staying's crazy. Leaving's smart. I don't want to waste our life.

Our?

Yeah.

She smiled.

He pulled out turned west and started driving towards the glow it was thousands of miles away, he started driving towards the glow.

Drawn by plentiful water, and the security of an established community, El Pueblo de Nuestra Señora la Reina de Los Angeles de Porciuncula grew quickly, and by 1795, it was the largest settlement in Spanish California.

Old Man Joe's hair turned white when he was twenty-nine. He was drunk, it was raining, he was standing on the beach screaming at the sky, which was eternal, black and silent. Something, or someone, hit him in the back of the head. He woke just before dawn and he had aged forty years. His skin was thick and dry and it sagged. His joints ached and he couldn't make fists with his hands, it hurt to stand. His eyes were deep and hollow and his hair and his beard were white, they had been black when he was screaming and now they were white. He aged forty years in four hours. Forty years.

Joe lives in a bathroom. The bathroom is in an alley at the back of a taco stand on the boardwalk in Venice. The owner of the taco stand lets Joe stay there because he feels sorry for him. As long as Joe keeps the bathroom clean, and lets customers of the taco stand use it during the day, he is allowed to use it at night. He sleeps on the floor next to the toilet. He has a handheld television that hangs from the doorknob. He has a bag of clothes he uses for a pillow and a sleeping bag that he hides behind a dumpster during the day. He washes himself in the sink and he drinks from the sink. He eats leftovers that he finds in the trash.

Joe wakes every morning just before dawn. He walks down to the beach and he lies down in the sand and he waits for an answer. He watches the sun rise, watches the sky turn gray, silver, white, he watches the sky turn pink and yellow, he watches the sky turn blue, the sky is almost always blue in Los Angeles. He watches the day arrive. Another day. He waits for an answer.

In 1797, Father Fermin Lasuén establishes the Mission San Fernando Rey de España on the northern desert edge of the San Fernando Valley.

Traffic starts in San Bernardino, an agriculture and trucking city in the desert just beyond the eastern edge of Los Angeles County. They're on a sixteen-lane highway, the sun is up, they're both tired and excited and scared. She's drinking coffee and staring at a map she speaks.

Where we gonna go?

Anything look particularly good?

This place is huge. There's too much to even look at.

Los Angeles County is the most heavily populated county in America.

How do you know?

I know shit, woman, I paid attention in school. You should know that by now.

School, my ass. You saw it on *Jeopardy!*

Maybe.

Maybe nothing. You did.

Who cares. All that matters is I know shit. I'm Mr. Know-Shit.

She laughs.

Okay, Mr. Know-Shit, if you know so much, tell me where we're going?

West.

She laughs again.

No shit.

We're going west and when we get where we're supposed to be, we'll know it.

We're just gonna stop?

Yeah.

And see what happens?

Yeah.

And we'll know it when we know it.

That's how life works. You know it when you know it.

They're nineteen and in love. Alone except for each other. Jobless and homeless, looking for something, somewhere, anywhere here.

They're on a sixteen-lane highway.

Driving west.

In 1821, the Treaty of Córdoba establishes Mexico's independence from Spain. Mexico assumes control of California.

Putt Putt Bonanza. It sounds good, doesn't it. Putt Putt Bonanza. Just rolls off the tongue. Putt Putt Bonanza. Looks great on a sign, great in an ad. Putt Putt Bonanza, Putt Putt Bonanza.

***

Seventy-two holes of championship caliber miniature golf (the US Mini-Open has been held here four times). A go-kart track built to mimic three of the turns in Monaco. A bumper boat pool with crystal blue water. A video and pinball arcade the size of a football field, a clubhouse with ice cream, pizza, burgers and fries, the cleanest and safest bathrooms of any attraction in Los Angeles County. It's like a dream, spread across four acres of land in the inappropriately named City of Industry, which is primarily '70s-style ranch houses and mini-malls. It's like a dream.

***

Wayne's official title is Head Groundskeeper, though all he really does is pick garbage out of the holes and the water traps and the sand traps. At thirty-seven years old, Wayne is absolutely ambitionless. He likes to smoke weed, drink cream soda and watch porn. He has an office behind the clubhouse, it's a four-by-six room with a chair and television. He keeps a stack of magazines and a digital camera with a high-powered zoom lens hidden behind the television, he uses the camera to shoot pictures of hot moms who are at the Bonanza with their kids. He can only do it when the boss isn't around, and he always tries to frame the kids out of the shots, at the moment he has 2,345 of them. Wayne lives in a broken-down house in a broken-down neighborhood in the broken-down port town of San Pedro, which is twenty minutes away. He lives there with his mom, who is seventy-three years old. He doesn't believe in God, but every night before he goes to bed, unless he's hammered and forgets, he prays to God to take his mom away.

***

TJ has big dreams. At twenty-four, he has played in the US Mini-Open three times. The first year he finished 110th out of 113 competitors. The next year he finished 76th. The third year he finished 12th. TJ wants to win this year, win every year after, and ultimately become known as the greatest mini-golfer in the history of the game. TJ grew up in the City of Industry. His earliest memories are of the Putt Putt Bonanza sign, which is bright blue, yellow and white, and sits on two poles 75 feet in the air. When he was five he traded rooms with his younger brother so he could see the sign from his window. When he was twelve he took a job as Wayne's unpaid intern so he could play for free. When he was fourteen he won the Junior Nationals, and he won three of the next four, the last on a seemingly impossible shot through a windmill, across a bridge, and along a rail that ran over a waterfall. TJ plays mini-golf for six hours a day. He works nights as a security guard at a car lot. He's hoping to join the mini Pro Tour next year, which supports about ten full-time players. He knows if he finishes in the top five he'll be able to join the tour. Top five isn't good enough. TJ has big dreams. He is chasing history.

***

Renee works at the sundae bar in the clubhouse. She fucking hates it. She's seventeen and all she wants to do is get away. Get away from Putt Putt Bonanza, away from the City of Industry, away from her father, who works at a missile plant during the day and gets drunk in front of the TV every night. Her mother died when she was six. She was in a car wreck on the 110 near Long Beach. Her father never recovered from it. Sometimes, when he thinks he's alone, Renee hears him crying. Renee doesn't remember much about her mother, but she never got over it either. She doesn't cry, she just wants to get away, as far as she can as fast as she can, get away, away.

***

His given name is Emeka Ladejobi-Ukwu. Emeka means "great deeds" in the Igbo language of southern Nigeria. His parents immigrated in 1946, when he was four. They came to California because his father loved fruit, and he heard that the best fruit in America was in Los Angeles. The family lived in Hollywood and his father worked as a janitor at a department store. He had four other brothers, Emeka was the youngest. When he was six, his father started calling him Barry, and changed the family name to Robinson in honor of Jackie Robinson, who had broken baseball's color barrier the year before. All four boys were raised believing that anything is possible in America, that it truly is the land of opportunity, that they could become whatever they wanted to become. One became a teacher, another a police officer, the third owned a convenience store. Emeka, now Barry, had a different dream: he wanted to bring joy and fun to the middle class at affordable prices. He was eleven the first time he told his father of his dream. The entire family was having Sunday dinner. Barry stood, said he had an announcement to make, and asked for silence. When silence arrived, he said Family, I have discovered my dream, I want to bring joy and fun to the middle class at affordable prices. There was a moment of dense quiet before the room exploded with laughter. Barry remained standing and waited for the laughter to end. It took several minutes. When it did, he said I will not waver, I will make my dream a reality. Barry struggled in school. He got one A over the course of his entire academic career, which came in eighth-grade gym. When he graduated from high school, he took a job on a construction crew. Unlike many of the men on the crew, he did not specialize in one particular field. He learned carpentry, roofing, painting, electrical, plumbing. He learned how to lay carpet, how to pour cement. He saved his money. He drove a beat-up twenty-year-old Chevy, he lived in a one-room apartment in Watts the bathroom was down the hall. Every night before he went to sleep he lay in bed and dreamed, lay in bed and dreamed.

In 1972 he found the land. It was located on a major street equidistant from the 10 (the San Bernardino Freeway) the 605 (the San Gabriel River Freeway) and the 60 (the Pomona Freeway). City of Industry was a solid middle-class community surrounded by other solid middle-class communities: Whittier, West Covina, Diamond Bar, El Monte, Montebello. The land was flat and clear. The owner was going to build a mini-mall, but decided there was too much competition.

He designed all four courses himself. He wanted them to be entertaining for adults, challenging for children. All seventy-two holes would be different, there would be absolutely no repeats. He made doglegs in every direction. He made ramps and hills, traps of every conceivable kind. One of the courses had a zoo theme and life-sized animals were an integral part of every hole. Another course was based on the famous holes of real golf courses. The third was based on famous films, the fourth was called The Spectacular!!! and involved all of his wildest ideas. He laid them out himself. He poured the concrete with friends from work. He laid the Astroturf, did the painting. He made sure everything was perfect, built to his exact specifications. Every spare minute away from his job was spent working on the courses. It took him two years to finish them.

He opened for business on a Thursday. There was no clubhouse, no arcade, there were no go-karts, no boats, no parking lot. There was no sign. Just a card table and cashbox at the entrance, with Barry sitting in a folding chair smiling and shaking everyone's hand. He got nine customers. He made thirteen dollars and fifty cents. He was thrilled.

He sat there day after day. More and more people came. He saved every cent he made and planned for the future. After three months he had enough to build a small shack that replaced the card table. After eight months he put in a parking lot. He lived in the same place, drove the same car. He wore a collared shirt that said Putt Putt Bonanza on the back and had his name on the front.

Word spread amongst the population of the local communities. People loved the courses and loved Barry and knew good, affordable entertainment when they saw it. Eighteen months after opening, he put in the track, which was followed by the arcade and the bumper boats. In 1978, he built the clubhouse, which was as nice as many of the clubhouses of local country clubs. He considered it his crowning achievement.

The '80s were the "Boom Years." Putt Putt Bonanza was packed seven days a week, 365 days a year. Video games became a cultural phenomenon, led by Space Invaders, Pac-Man and Donkey Kong. Putt Putt Bonanza was featured as one of the primary settings in one of the most popular films of the decade, *The Kung Fu Kid*, which led to an explosion of popularity in mini-golf and the park itself. Barry held races at the track, had family discount days, established a special section of the clubhouse for birthday parties. The money coming in often went to upgrading or maintaining the facilities, though he was able to build a decent-sized nest egg. For Barry, the '80s were a dream come true, a time when his vision became a complete reality, and when it was celebrated by the throngs of middle-class customers that flocked to his attractions.

When the '90s arrived, it was like someone flipped a switch. People stopped coming as often, and those that did come seemed unhappy. Kids wore black T-shirts and scowls, they openly spit, swore and smoked cigarettes. Parents seemed depressed, and they kept their wallets in their pockets. Wrecks, usually intentional, became much more common on the track, little kids started getting in fights at the boatpond, most of the new video games involved guns and death. Barry figured it was a cycle, and that good times would return.

The Bonanza made enough money to stay open, but maintaining Barry's high standards required that he dip into his savings. As the decade dragged on, and things didn't seem to change, his savings ran dry. In 1984 he had moved from his one-room apartment to a small rancher a couple miles from

Putt Putt Bonanza. He took a second mortgage on the rancher to maintain the course. There was a brief return to glory with the boom of the Internet, but it was fleeting. And the kids, they just kept getting worse and worse, louder, ruder, more unruly. Occasionally he would catch some of them drinking alcohol or smoking marijuana, occasionally he'd find a couple of teenagers fooling around in one of the clubhouse bathrooms. Barry still goes to work every day, still takes great pride in Putt Putt Bonanza. He knows, however, that his dream is almost dead. He's closing the go-kart track and the bumper-boat pond at the end of the year because they've become too expensive to insure, and he knows a lawsuit would ruin him. He can't bear to go into the arcade because it's all weapons and death, explosions and noise. His staff takes no pride in their jobs, the turnover is so high that sometimes he can't open the clubhouse. Some of the concrete in the holes of the courses is cracking, he can't keep up with the weeds, he finds urine in the water traps at least twice a week. His savings are gone so he can't do renovations. He can stay open, but that is all.

A developer came to Barry and offered to buy Putt Putt Bonanza. The developer wants to level it and build a mini-mall. The money would allow Barry to pay off his house and retire in relative comfort. Barry's brothers tell him to do it, his accountant tells him to do it, his sense of reason and his brain tell him to do it. His heart says no. Whenever he allows himself to hear it, his heart says no, no, no. All day long, every day, his heart screams no.

Before he goes to bed every night, Barry sits in bed and looks through an album he keeps on his nightstand. It's a pictorial history of his life at Putt Putt Bonanza. It starts with a picture of him shaking hands with the seller of the land the moment they closed on the sale. It follows him through the planning, most of which took place at a table in his parents' house, the building of the course, which he did with many of his old friends. There is a shot of him on opening day, sitting and smiling at his card table, there are pictures of him during each of the expansion phases, pictures of him with smiling happy customers, laughing children, satisfied parents. About halfway through the album, there is a picture of him with the stars of *The Kung Fu Kid*: an old Chinese man, a young Italian-American teenager, and a blond ingénue who would go on to win an Academy Award. They are standing at the entrance of the park, the Putt Putt Bonanza sign glows behind them. Barry was forty-two years old when the photo was taken, at the height of his career, his dreams had come true and he was happy. When he gets to the photo, he stops and stares at it. He smiles, even though he knows it will never be like that again, even though he knows the world no longer wants what he has, what he loves, what he has devoted his life to building and maintaining. He lies in bed and stares at the photo and smiles. His brain says let it go, sell it. His heart says no.

His heart says no.

Because of the long and difficult nature of its original name, sometime around 1830, the settlement of El Pueblo de Nuestra Señora la Reina de Los Angeles de Porciuncula became known as Ciudad de Los Angeles.

Amberton Parker.

Born in Chicago the scion of a great midwestern meatpacking family.

Educated at St. Paul's, Harvard.

Moves to New York lands a starring role in a Broadway drama in his first audition. The play opens to brilliant reviews and wins ten Tony Awards.

Makes an independent film wins a Golden Globe.

Makes an action/drama about American corruption in the Middle East. Film grosses $150 million, get nominated for an Oscar.

Dates an actress the biggest!!! actress in the world. Dates a model who goes by one name. Dates a debutante, an Olympic swimmer the winner of six gold medals, a prima ballerina.

Stars in a series of action films. Stops terrorists, mad scientists, bankers intent on ruling the world. Kills an Eastern European who possesses a nuclear weapon, an Arab with a virus, a South American temptress with the most addictive drug the world has ever seen. If they're evil, and are threatening America, he kills them. Kills them dead.

To prove his versatility he does a dance film, a mob film, a sports film.

He wins an Oscar playing a principled explorer who falls in love with a luscious squaw and leads a ragtag mixed-race rebellion against a corrupt king.

He marries a beautiful young woman from Iowa. She is a minor movie star who, after the marriage, becomes a major movie star.

They have three children, they shield them from the public.

He starts a foundation. He does the talk-show circuit. He dedicates himself to peace and education. He speaks eloquently about the meaning and need for transparency and truth in our society.

He writes a memoir about his life, his loves, his beliefs. It sells two million copies.

He is an American hero.

Amberton Parker.
Symbol of truth and justice, honesty and integrity.
Amberton Parker.
Public heterosexual.
Private homosexual.

In 1848, after two years of hostilities between the United States and Mexico, the Treaty of Guadalupe Hidalgo makes California a United States territory.

Her parents were fifty feet across the border when she was
born her mother Graciella was lying in the dirt screaming her
father Jorge was trying to figure out how to keep them from
dying. Jorge had a pocketknife. He cut the cord, pulled the
placenta away the baby started crying, Jorge started crying,
Graciella started crying. They each had their reasons. Life pain
fear relief opportunity hope the known the unknown. Crying.
They had tried four other times to make it over. They had
been caught twice sent back twice, Graciella had gotten sick
and was unable to continue twice. They were from a small
farming village in Sonora that was slowly dying, the farms
disappearing, the people leaving. The future was to the north.
Jobs were to the north. Money was to the north. Someone in
their village told them if their child was born on American soil
that the child would be an American citizen. If their child was
an American citizen they would be allowed to stay. If they
could stay there might be a future.
They were cleaning her off when Border Patrol pulled up, one
man behind the wheel of a jeep, a pistol on his hip, a cowboy
hat on his head. He stepped out of the truck looked at them
saw the child, saw the blood running down Graciella's legs,
saw Jorge petrified. He stood and stared at them. No one
moved. The blood ran.
He turned and opened the back door of the jeep.
Get in.
No hablamos inglés.
Usted aprende mejor sí usted desea hacer algo de se en este
país.
Sí.
Get in.
He motioned towards the backseat, helped them inside, made
sure they were safe, closed the door, drove as quickly as he
safely could across the desert. Jorge shook with fear he did not
want to get sent back. Graciella shook with fear she couldn't
believe she held a child in her arms. The baby screamed.
It took an hour to get to the nearest hospital. The jeep pulled

up to the emergency entrance the man helped the new family out he led them to the door. He stopped before they entered looked at the father spoke.

Welcome to America.

Gracias.

I hope you find what you're looking for.

Gracias.

They named her Esperanza. She was small, like both of her parents, and she had a full head of curly black hair, like both of her parents. She had light skin, almost white, and dark eyes, almost black, and she had exceptionally large thighs, almost cartoonishly large, as if her upper legs had somehow been inflated. She was an easy baby. She constantly smiled and giggled, rarely cried, slept well, ate well. Because of complications related to her birth in the desert, which had partly been caused by her giant thighs, Jorge and Graciella knew they would never have another child, and it made them hold her more closely, carry her more gently, love her more, more than they thought they would or could, more than they imagined was possible.

The family drifted through Arizona for three years, Jorge worked as a picker at citrus farms tangelos, oranges and nectarines, Graciella, who always had the smiling, giggling Esperanza with her, cleaned the houses of the wealthy white upper class. They lived simply, usually in single-room hovels, with only the bare necessities: a bed they shared, a table, a hotplate, a sink and a bathroom. They saved whatever they could, every penny nickel and dime was coveted, every dollar counted and kept, they wanted to own their own house, make their own home. That was the dream, an American daughter, an American home.

They drifted north into California. There were always citrus farms, there were always houses that needed cleaning. There were always communities of Mexicans in the same position, with the same dreams, the same willingness to work, the same desire for a better life. Two more years and they went to East

Los Angeles, which is the largest Hispanic community in the United States. They lived in the garage of a man whose cousin was from their village. They slept on a mattress on the floor, went to the bathroom in buckets that they poured down the sewer. It would be temporary, they hoped, they were ready to find their house. They didn't know what they could afford, if they could afford anything, how to buy, where to begin looking, all they knew was that they wanted, they wanted a home, they wanted.

They didn't have a car, so they took the bus all over East LA, looked through Echo Park, Highland Park, Mt. Washington, Bell Garden, Pico Rivera. There was nothing they could afford, they went to Boyle Heights, which at the time, in 1979, was the most dangerous area of East LA, and they found a small dilapidated house with a ramshackle garage, the previous owners had tried to light it on fire because they thought it was possessed by a demon. It didn't burn, they tried three times and it wouldn't burn, so they changed their mind and thought it might be protected by God. Either way, they were scared to live there and wanted to get rid of it. When they saw Esperanza, they marveled at her thighs, which were almost adult-sized, and they were charmed by her smile and her giggle, and they proclaimed her to be a child of the Lord and Savior, and sold the house to Jorge and Graciella for $8,000, which was every cent they had to their name. As they walked out of the house, after agreeing on final terms, Jorge fell to his knees and started crying. American daughter. American home. American dream.

They moved in a month later. They had their clothes and a couple of worn blankets, Esperanza had a doll she called Lovie. They didn't have any furniture, no beds, no plates, knives, cups, pots or pans, no means of transportation, no radio, no TV. On their first night in the house, Jorge bought a can of grape soda and some paper cups, Graciella picked up a Hostess fruit pie. They had soda and pieces of the pie. Esperanza ran around the house asking what they were going to do with all of the rooms, she wanted to know if it was a house or castle. Jorge and Graciella sat and smiled and held hands. They slept on the floor of the living room, the three of them under one blanket, father mother and daughter, together under one blanket.

On February 18, 1850, Los Angeles County is formed as one of the original twenty-seven counties of the Territory of California. On April 4, 1850, the City of Los Angeles is incorporated. On September 9, 1850, California becomes the thirty-first state of the Union.

Dawn fades with the rising sun. No answers for Old Man Joe. There never are, never have been, he wonders if there ever will be, he'll keep coming every morning until either the answers arrive or he's gone. He gets up brushes the sand from his legs and arms walks back to his bathroom, which he will vacate, except for the facilitation of necessary bodily functions, for most of the day.

After he's organized and hidden his belongings, he eats breakfast, which is usually leftover Mexican from the night before, though he often trades food with other homeless men who live near dumpsters belonging to a pizza parlor, a Chinese restaurant, a burger joint, and every now and then a hot dog stand (sometimes the dogs just aren't edible after twelve hours in the open air). After his breakfast, he gets a cup of coffee, which a man who runs a coffee stand gives him for free in exchange for advice on women. Even though Old Man Joe is single and has never been married, he considers himself an expert on women. Most of his advice to the man revolves around the idea that if you ignore a woman, she will like you more. Occasionally, of course, this tactic backfires, but it works often enough to have provided Old Man Joe with free beverages for several years.

With his coffee in hand, Joe walks south for fifteen blocks to the Venice Pier, which sits at the end of Washington Blvd., and denotes the border between Venice and Marina Del Rey. He walks to the end of the pier, which juts two hundred yards out into the Pacific, walks in a circle, and walks back to the boardwalk. Occasionally, he stops at the end of the pier and watches surfers, who use the wave breaks on both sides of the pier, which crash against its pylons. When he walks, he tries to empty his mind, find some peace, think one step, one step, one step until he's thinking about nothing. It doesn't, however, usually work, and he finds himself thinking about the same old shit: what will I eat today, how much money will I get from the tourists, when will I start drinking?

After his walk, Joe heads out to a bench along the main

section of the boardwalk and sits down. Once he is comfortably seated on the bench, Joe begs money from tourists so he can afford to get drunk.

In 1856, Mexican nationalist Juan Flores attempts to start a revolution intended to liberate Los Angeles and return southern California to the control of the Mexican government. He was caught and hanged in what was then downtown in front of 3,000 spectators.

The Second Amendment of the Constitution of the United States reads as follows—*A well regulated militia being necessary to the security of a free State, the right of the People to keep and bear arms shall not be infringed.*

***

It's an ugly building. Nondescript and drab in Culver City. It's surrounded by deserted factories, warehouses, empty parking lots, auto-body shops. There's razor wire along its perimeter. There are two doors at the lone entrance and exit, one is made of steel bars, the other is made of solid steel. There are security cameras along the roof that record everything that happens along the boulevard, everyone that comes in and out of the doors. The exterior walls are made of aluminum siding, and behind the siding there is a two-foot layer of concrete to prevent a vehicle, almost any type of vehicle except a tank, from driving through them. Parking is on the street.

***

Larry's a hater. A mean-ass motherfucking hater. He hates everybody. He hates blacks, Latinos, Asians, he hates women and gays, he hates Jews and he hates Arabs, he really fucking hates those Arabs. Larry is white. Unlike most white racists, Larry is not a white supremacist. He hates whites too, hates them as much as he hates anyone, sometimes more because he's one of them. When asked about hating whites, Larry says—If I was given the choice between shooting a white motherfucker and some motherfucker with pigment in his skin, I'd line 'em up back-to-back so I could shoot 'em both with one bullet. The first time his mother heard him make the remark, she commented on how intelligent she thought he was. He told her to shut the fuck up, that he hated her too.

Larry is a gun freak. An avid believer in and defender of an individual's right to bear arms. Larry owns more than 400 of his own guns. He owns handguns, hunting rifles, shotguns, assault rifles, machine guns, sniper's rifles. He keeps his guns in a fortified room in the basement of his house, which is a few blocks from his shop. The armory, which is what he calls the room, is also stocked with more than 10,000 rounds of ammunition, and booby-trapped with plastic explosives.

Larry owns the building, rebuilt it to his own design after he acquired it in the early '80s. He also owns and is the proprietor of the gun shop housed within it. Officially, on the papers he filed with the state for both his business and gun dealer's licenses, the shop is called Larry's Firearms. Unofficially, Larry calls the shop—the place where I sell shit to kill people.

There is no doubt, in Larry's mind, as to the motivations of his customers. Whether the killing is done in self-defense, or as the result of some form of aggressive action, is irrelevant to him, the result is always the same, a sad dead motherfucker going to the morgue. Though he hates almost all of them for one reason or another, Larry makes no distinctions between his customers. As long as they are not convicted felons, and as long as he is legally allowed to sell them a firearm of some kind, be it a pistol, a rifle or a shotgun, be it revolver, single shot, or semi-auto easily converted to full auto, Larry will take their money and give them what they want.

Once they leave his shop, what they do with the weapons is none of his business. He knows, however, and takes a certain joy in the fact, that if used properly, the weapons will do their job, they will kill human beings, kill motherfuckers that he hates, rid the fucking world of them. He doesn't care about their race, religion, gender or sexual orientation. He hates them all equally. He sells things that kill them.

***

She is twenty-six years old. She is originally from Indianapolis. She has lived in LA for nine months, she moved here to become a publicist, her family did not approve. Three weeks ago she was walking through a parking garage, it was late at night, she had been on a first date, she had had two glasses of wine with dinner. Her date had wanted to walk to her car, but she liked him, really liked him, he was a year older, an entertainment attorney, someone who wanted, like her, a career and later a family, and she knew if he walked to her car he would try to kiss her. She wanted to take it slowly, try to engage in as old-fashioned a dating process as possible. She said she'd be fine. He said he would call her. She smiled and said she looked forward to it. She walked away.

She had been in the garage many times, her office was down the street, it was in Santa Monica, which is a safe, wealthy, stable community. The garage was fairly empty. She took an elevator to the fourth floor. She got out and started walking towards her car, which was on the opposite side of the garage. She immediately felt uneasy. She started walking more quickly something was wrong wrong she was suddenly terrified absolutely fucking terrified something was wrong. She was twenty feet from her car, fifteen, ten she reached for her keys ten feet away as she reached for her keys she was terrified. He stepped out from between two cars, came at her from behind, she was five feet away, her keys in her hand.

***

A sampling of customers at Larry's Firearms on an average day:
Angelo. Age 18. Purchases a .30-30 rifle. Also purchases a scope.
Terrance. Age 21. Purchases a 9mm Glock semi-automatic handgun.
Gregory. Age 22. Purchases a .357 Magnum revolver.
Aneesa. Age 19. Purchases a 12-gauge pistol grip shotgun.
Javier. Age 21. Purchases a 9mm Luger Parabellum handgun.
Quanda. Age 18. Purchases a California-legal AR-15 M4 assault rifle.
Jason. Age 21. Purchases a 9mm Beretta semi-automatic handgun.
Leon. Age 19. Purchases a .30-06 rifle.
John. Age 24. Purchases a Colt .45-caliber handgun.

Eric. Age 26. Purchases a Smith & Wesson .38-caliber handgun.

Lisa. Age 21. Purchases a 9mm Glock semi-automatic handgun.

Tony. Age 18. Purchases a California-legal AR-15 M4 assault rifle.

William. Age 21. Purchases a 9mm semi-automatic handgun.

Troy. Age 21. Purchases a Remington Derringer.

Andrew. Age 21. Purchases a .50-caliber Desert Eagle semi-automatic handgun.

Clay. Age 21. Purchases a 9mm Browning semi-automatic handgun.

Tito. Age 18. Purchases a California-legal AK-47 assault rifle.

Tom. Age 19. Purchases a California-legal AR-15 M4 Flat Top assault rifle.

Carrie. Age 19. Purchases a California-legal Bushmaster AR-15 M4 assault rifle.

Jean. Age 22. Purchases a .357 Magnum revolver.

Terry. Age 20. Purchases a California-legal AK-47 assault rifle.

Phillip. Age 21. Purchases a 9mm Glock semi-automatic handgun.

Gus. Age 22. Purchases a 9mm Beretta semi-automatic handgun.

Stanley. Age 18. Purchases a California-legal AK-47 assault rifle.

Ann. Age 19. Purchases a California-legal AR-15 M4 assault rifle.

Alex. Age 18. Purchases a California-legal AK-47 assault rifle.

Doug. Age 19. Purchases a 12-gauge pistol grip shotgun.

Daniel. Age 22. Purchases a .357 Magnum revolver.

Peter. Age 22. Purchases a .50-caliber Desert Eagle semi-automatic handgun and a California-legal AK-47 assault rifle.

Carl. Age 18. Purchases a California-legal Bushmaster AR-15 M4 assault rifle.

***

Ricky hasn't had a job in four years. He used to work at a

printing shop, but it closed due to advances in printing technology that allowed small businesses to do their own printing. He went on unemployment, it ran out, he couldn't find another job, printing shops all over the city were going under. He liked sitting at home watching television and drinking beer all day, so he stopped trying to find another job. He needed money, was trying to figure out how to get it, when a friend, a convicted felon, called him and asked him to buy a gun (felons can't buy firearms in California). He went to Larry's Firearms with the friend, bought a 9mm semi-automatic handgun and a California-legal assault rifle using the friend's money. When he got home with the weapons, he filed off the serial numbers. He charged his friend, who needed good weapons for his work, five hundred bucks.

That felon told another felon who told another felon. Ricky started making money. Under California law, he could only buy one handgun a month, but there was no limit on the number of assault rifles, and if needed, he could always go to Arizona or Nevada to circumvent the California law. He bought a set of files and some hydrochloric acid to make the serial numbers disappear properly. At this point, not one of the 300 firearms he has bought for convicted felons has been traced back to him.

He's in Larry's today with a man named John. John just got out of prison for manslaughter and wants an assault rifle. Ricky doesn't ask why, but John makes several comments about an ex-wife, a former business partner, and some missing money. Larry is showing them AKs and AR-15s, weapons that can be easily converted from semi-automatic to full automatic. Ricky, as per John's instructions, buys one of each. He also buys the parts that allow the conversion from semi-auto to full, and a book with instructions on exactly how to do it. Ricky will have to wait a day to pick up the weapons, and will need two more days to get rid of the serial numbers. At that point, he will turn them over to John, and if asked, will deny ever meeting him, speaking to him or having anything to do with

him. What John does with the weapons is none of his business.
None.

**

He held a gun to her head, made her drive into the hills above
Malibu, made her park at the end of a remote fire lane. He
raped her in the backseat. He pistol-whipped her. He threw her
into the dirt and drove away.
It took her four hours to find help. She went to the hospital,
filed a police report. The incident was reported in the papers
and on the local news. There were no fingerprints. There was
no DNA.
She didn't tell her parents or her coworkers. She didn't want to
hear I told you so, she didn't want any pity. She took her
vacation and she stayed at home in bed and cried for two
weeks. She called the detective working on her case twice a
day, there were no leads.
When she went back to work, she was a different person, she
no longer smiled, laughed, she ate lunch alone, she left at
exactly five and never went out with her coworkers. The man
she had dated that night called her and she never called back
he called three more times she never called back. She saw a
therapist it didn't help. She saw a rape counselor it didn't help.
She saw a pastor it didn't help. She joined a support group it
didn't help. She started drinking it didn't help.
She recognized him when he took her order at a fast-food
restaurant. He had worn a mask and she didn't see his face,
but she knew his voice and she knew his eyes. He smiled at her
as she ordered. He asked if they knew each other from
somewhere. He asked her name. There was no mistaking the
fact that he knew who she was, and he knew that she
recognized him. He touched her hand as he passed her order
over the counter. As she walked away, he smiled at her and
said I hope to see you again.
She never went back to her job. She stopped leaving the house
she was scared. She didn't pick up the phone or use her

33

computer. She stared at the ceiling, at her pillow, at her wall. She never looked in the mirror.

This morning she woke up and she showered and, for the first time in months, she put on her makeup and did her hair. She looked beautiful, like the girl who had arrived from Indianapolis with dreams, with a future, with a life ahead of her. She went out for breakfast with two of her friends from work. She called the man who had taken her on the date and apologized for not calling him earlier. She sent e-mails to friends and called her parents. She told them all that she loved them.

When she was done she drove to Larry's Firearms. She bought a brand-new Colt .45. She submitted the information necessary to acquire the weapon. She left with a smile. Tomorrow she's going to pick up the weapon, bring it home, load it. At that point, she will make the decision, find him and shoot him in the face and kill him, or put the gun in her own mouth and blow the back of her head away. Either way, she will think of him just before she pulls the trigger, think of him touching her and smiling at her, think of him standing behind the counter knowing that she recognized him. Either way, her life will be over. She is going to think of him touching her and smiling at her. She is going to pull the trigger.

**

Larry closes the shop goes home eats dinner and drinks a six-pack of nice, cold American beer. He sleeps without a care.

In 1852, the first Chinese immigrant arrives in Los Angeles. By 1860, Chinatown is established and flourishing. By 1870, it is one of the largest communities in the city.

Amberton wakes up on one side of his house, a thirteen-bedroom mansion in the hills of Bel-Air, his wife and children are on the other side. There is a young man in his bed, as there often is, the young man's body was purchased through a service, $5,000 per night, all inclusive. The young man is tall blond and muscular, and he is extremely accommodating. He is one of Amberton's favorites. He doesn't talk much and he leaves through the back door without a word.

Amberton gets out of bed, takes a shower, walks through his house to the kitchen, which is made of Carrara marble, brazilwood and steel, and cost $400,000 to build. He says hello to his wife Casey, who is tall and thin with black hair and green eyes, and is regularly listed among the best-looking and best-dressed women in the world, and he kisses her on the cheek. Away from the paparazzi's cameras, and away from the eyes of his adoring public, he has never kissed her anywhere else. As he pours himself a cup of coffee, which was prepared, along with his breakfast, by his chef, he speaks. He uses his private speaking voice, which is soft and lilted and slightly fey, a dramatic difference from his public speaking voice, which is strong, direct and forceful.

Good day today?

Casey speaks.

Yeah.

Where the babies?

They don't like it when you call them babies, Amberton. They're seven, five and four, they've sort of outgrown it.

I don't care, they're my babies, I'll always call them that.

She laughs, speaks.

They're at gymnastics, and then they have riding, and then they have art.

Busy day.

Very.

And what are you going to do?

I have a meeting with my agents to talk about this film in England. They're going to come over here for lunch.

What's the film?

It's about a poet who falls in love with a doctor who gets killed doing charity work in the Congo. She struggles with her work and contemplates suicide but pulls through and wins a huge award. It's a really smart piece.

You'd be the poet, I assume?

No. I'd be the sister that helps her learn how to heal. It's a great role. I might be able to get a best supporting nomination out of it.

He giggles.

Very nice. Very very nice. We like nominations.

She giggles.

We do. What are your plans?

Work out, lie by the pool for a while, maybe do some online shopping.

Who was the guy last night?

How do you know there was one?

I could hear you.

He looks shocked. In a fake dramatic way.

No.

Yes.

Please tell me no.

She smiles.

Yes. You were loud. Or maybe he was. I couldn't really tell. It was that blond boy. The expensive one. We were both making noise. We make such sweet love we just can't help it.

Try to keep it down. I don't want the kids to hear.

Just tell them I'm working out.

She laughs.

And in a way it's true. I'm working out.

She stands.

I'm going to yoga?

Here?

In the studio?

Can I come with?

Sure.

They go to their rooms, change, meet in their yoga studio, which is in the deep recesses of their backyard, a hundred yards from their house, built beneath two massive cypress trees. It is a simple building, the floor a light maple, the walls plain and white, two small windows on each of the walls. When they arrive their teacher is there, sitting cross-legged on the floor, quietly waiting for them. They spend the next ninety minutes doing yoga, assuming strange and difficult positions, the teacher gently guiding them and adjusting them. When they finish, they take showers, sit in shaded chairs by their pool, each of them reads a script for a film they've been offered. As they read their scripts, they talk, laugh, and have fun with each other. Though their marriage is a sham, and their public image a wild distortion of reality, they truly are best friends. They love each other, trust each other, and respect each other. It makes the charade easier, and makes their most important roles, those they play on red carpets and in interviews, easier to perform. Shortly after noon, Casey goes to her room and gets dressed. Amberton takes off his shirt and lies down on a towel at the edge of the pool. Their housekeeper sets a table and their chef prepares lunch. Casey comes back with a glass of champagne and sits down at the table, a few minutes later, her agents arrive. Two of them are gay men in their forties, one of them is an attractive woman in her early thirties, all of them wear expensive, custom-tailored black business suits. There is a fourth agent with them, a junior agent, a twenty-five-year-old former college football player. His suit isn't as nice, and he lacks the accessories of his bosses, the shoes, watches, rings, designer glasses, the subtle touches that denote wealth and power. He also walks with a slight limp as a result of the knee injury that ended his football career. He's six foot five, weighs 230 pounds. He has black skin, short black hair, black eyes. Amberton waves to the group yells hello. He lies back and pretends to close his eyes and he stares at the football player, stares. As his wife and the agents start their lunch, Amberton falls in love, he falls in love, falls in love.

In 1865, the population of the city reaches 14,000 people.

They drift, drift through neighborhood after neighborhood, sometimes it's hard to tell the good from bad, the safe from dangerous. They start looking at cars in driveways, figure European cars mean nice neighborhood, American cars mean okay neighborhood, shit cars mean shit neighborhood. Their theory holds until they hear automatic gunfire on a street lined with Mercedeses and Cadillacs.

Unlike most major American cities, there is no logic to the streets of LA, no easy grid to follow, there was no foresight in the construction of its transportation system. As the city grew, often at exponential rates, roads were built, highways were built. They go where they go and sometimes they make sense and sometimes they don't. For two kids who grew up in a small town in the middle of nowhere, it's daunting and intimidating. They're looking for something, looking for somewhere. Maps won't help them, so they drive, they drift. They sleep on the mattress in the back of the truck. In order to save money they eat popcorn and saltines for breakfast, lunch and dinner, they drink water from the sinks of public bathrooms. After three days they find the beach. They park in a mammoth lot in Santa Monica, they lie in the sun, swim in the ocean, sleep on the sand. They splurge and buy hot dogs and ice cream cones on the Santa Monica Pier, which is like a county fair built over the water with rides, a merry-go-round, games, and sweet, cheap, greasy food. They pretend they're on their honeymoon. They forget about their past lives and forget about the prospect, or lack thereof, of their future life. They lie naked beneath a blanket. Their bodies warm the sand, they kiss each other, hold each other, say I love you to each other. The waves break twenty feet away. The moon spreads itself across the blackness of the water. For now, at least, they have found it. Whatever it is. They have found it. For now.

In 1869, City Marshal William C. Warren founds the Los Angeles Police Department. He hires six officers, and pays their salaries using funds collected from violations of city laws. He is also given $50 by the City Council to furnish Police Headquarters, which is in his house. He subsequently charges the city $25 a month in rent. In addition to being police commissioner, Mr. Warren is the city dog catcher and tax collector. He is later shot by one of his own officers and dies.

Esperanza started school, Jorge got a job on a landscaping crew, Graciella started cleaning houses again. Over time, they furnished the house, buying most of their belongings at secondhand shops and church auxiliaries. When they could afford it, they bought a television, which they watched together in order to improve their English. They also wrote to their relatives in Mexico, told them about their house, their good fortune, their life in America. When they could, they sent them money.

Esperanza was a good student. She was quiet and shy and well suited for school. She loved to read, loved to work on math equations, she helped her teachers at every opportunity. She was not a popular girl. The other students resented her intelligence, and her willingness to help her teachers, and her thighs, which grew with her, gave them plenty of reason to tease and harass her. As she got older, it got worse, with each passing grade, the taunts and insults became more pointed, more obscene, more vicious. Outwardly, she was impervious to their taunts and insults. She smiled at her tormentors and did her best to ignore them. Inwardly, they tore her apart. She wondered why they hated her, wondered what was wrong with doing well in school, wondered why she had been cursed with her giant thighs. She had never done anything to any of them. She actually liked most of them, and did her best to be kind to them. It didn't matter, they tore her apart.

As the years passed, relatives started moving up from Mexico. None of them had any money or anywhere to live, all of them had entered the country illegally. Jorge and Graciella took them in with the understanding that once they found work and had some form of income, they would find somewhere else to live. No one ever left. There were two cousins four cousins seven. A sister, a brother, an uncle. Four children. Three more. The house, originally three small bedrooms, expanded. Jorge did the work himself, with the help of his invading relatives, and none of it was done legally or within the building codes of the city. He added a side wing, a lofted bedroom, he put a kitchen and a bathroom in the garage, he added a wing to the back, built a second loft on top of it. Lumber and supplies were scavenged from construction dumpsters, abandoned buildings, burned-out buildings. Furniture often came from the side of a road, paint and wallpaper from wherever it was cheapest, or from wherever they could find it. The result was that different wings were different colors, one bright red, one yellow, one purple, the main part of the house was light blue, the garage bright green. There was no sense or real plan to any of the construction, additions were added where it was thought they might fit, the family sawed, banged and painted like mad until somehow it did fit or until it was sturdy enough not to collapse. When they were finished, the house and garage had a total of nine bedrooms, six bathrooms, two kitchens, an outdoor shower and two living rooms. It housed a total of seventeen people.

Regardless of how crowded the house became, Esperanza always had her own room. It was the only room in the house that had a real paint job (pink with yellow and blue flowers) and had furniture purchased new from a store (bed, dresser, bookshelf, desk, also all pink). The first thing Jorge told everyone who came into the house, whether they were there for a few minutes or were moving in, was that Esperanza's room was off-limits unless Esperanza invited you in, and that when her door was closed, she should not be disturbed.

Behind the door, Esperanza read, listened to music, dreamed. She dreamed for hours, lying on her bed with her eyes closed, or staring out the window. She dreamed about boys, about her prom (someday?), about being one of the popular kids, about dating an actor on her favorite television show, about someday marrying the actor. Although she loved her family, she dreamed of escape, of living away from her sixteen roommates, of living alone in her own house, her own big house, a house where her parents could visit and have an entire wing of rooms just for themselves, the wing would have a phone that did not accept calls from Mexico. The dream she went to most often was about her thighs. The older she got the more she hated them, and the more she realized that they were truly odd, and the more she dreamed of life without them. Day after day after day she dreamed that she could make them shrink, disappear, deflate them, that she could wake up with normal-sized legs or have some kind of surgery to reduce them, that she could have her thunderous thighs cut off and replaced with some sort of small electronic thigh. Nothing ever came to be: she did not become popular, she did not go to prom or on any sort of date at all, she never got away from the house, her thighs remained as large and outsized as ever. She kept dreaming.

Esperanza did well in high school, she graduated with honors and received a scholarship to a local community college. It was the proudest moment of Jorge and Graciella's life, and they decided to throw a huge party for Esperanza. For several days before the party, Jorge paraded around, and justifiably so considering his own background and educational résumé, like a proud peacock. Graciella sewed herself a new dress and had her hair and nails done at a salon in Montebello, a middle-class Latino neighborhood twenty minutes away. They spent three days cooking a feast, they cleaned and decorated the entire house, they planted flowers in the yard. Every member of the household chipped in, and because Esperanza hadn't had a quinceañera, a traditional Latino party announcing a girl's womanhood that usually occurs at age fifteen, they wanted to make her graduation day extraordinary.

The day arrived. Esperanza wore a specially tailored pink dress that hid her thighs as much as possible. Her aunts and female cousins doted on her and did her makeup and hair. When they were done, she looked in the mirror, and for the first time in her life, she thought she was beautiful. None of what she experienced over the past years, the teasing, the taunting, the loneliness, the insecurity, the pain, mattered to her. She looked in the mirror and she thought she was beautiful. It erased everything.

The guests arrived, started eating and drinking, one of them brought a guitar and started singing traditional Mexican songs. The yard was packed when Esperanza made her entrance. There was clapping and cheering, hooting and hollering and whistling. Guests who had known Esperanza her entire life were shocked by her transformation, those who didn't know her commented on how lucky Jorge and Graciella were to have such a lovely and intelligent daughter. As she worked her way through the crowd, saying hello to and thanking all of the guests, men flocked to her, crowded around her, vied for her attention, fawned over her. She was smiling, glowing, becoming more beautiful and confident with every passing moment, reveling in all of the attention. As the crowd around her grew, men began jostling for position and pushing each other, throwing subtle elbows and knees into each other's sensitive areas. Within five minutes, a fight broke out.

The fight started between two men who had both, unsuccessfully, been searching for a wife. Both were in their early thirties and felt their time was running out, one was known all over East LA for his terrible breath, the other for his awful body odor. They had, over the years, pursued the same women, failed with the same women, and blamed each other, instead of the odors they carried around with them, for their failures. As they pushed their way towards Esperanza, they confronted each other. When the man with the breath got in the face of the man with the body odor, a punch was thrown. It was returned in kind. Neither punch hit its mark, striking other men instead, who reacted by throwing more punches. The violence, as it always does, escalated very quickly, and within ten seconds, every one of the twenty men surrounding Esperanza was involved.

Esperanza tried to get away, but there were too many men, all of whom were now more concerned with their own safety than with hers. One of them stepped on the edge of her skirt. Another fell against her. She got knocked over, and as she went down, her skirt tore at the waist. There was almost immediate silence, immediate calm, an immediate end to the hostilities.

Esperanza lay spread-eagled on the ground. Her thighs, which no one, aside from her parents, had ever seen unsheathed, were on open view. There was silence, dead heavy silence. And then it came: clapping and cheering, hooting and hollering and whistling, and above them all, laughter, laughter, laughter.

In 1871, the Farmers and Merchants Bank is founded by John G. Downey and Isaias Hellman. It is the first incorporated bank in Los Angeles County.

It takes Joe between five minutes and three hours to receive the donations necessary to purchase his daily dose of alcohol. If it's summer, and the hordes of tourists are swarming, and there are sometimes as many as 250,000 per day on Venice Beach, the money comes quickly. In the winter, when the number dwindles to as few as 25,000 per day, it might take longer. There is also a fair amount of luck involved. Sometimes Joe will get a twenty-dollar bill right off the bat, sometimes it's nickels and dimes for hours. Regardless, the goal is always the same: acquire the cash necessary to purchase two bottles of nice, cold Chablis.

Joe considers himself a connoisseur of Chablis. If the bottle costs less than $20, he's tried it and has an opinion on it. If it costs less than $10, he can expound at length about it. If it costs less than $6, he can recite both the front and back labels verbatim, can opine on the wine's strengths (at that price there are few) and weaknesses (many), and can most likely identify it by taste and smell. Joe likes to think that there isn't a Chablis in America that he hasn't tried at some point, and there isn't one under $10 that hasn't made him vomit on multiple occasions. Whenever he is asked about his drinking habits, he smiles and recites a verse of his own composition— Chablis is for me, from sea to shining sea, it sets me free, Chablis Chablis Chablis, Chablis is the drink for me. Poet he is not, connoisseur of mediocre wine, undoubtedly.

Joe first fell in love with Chablis when he was a child. He grew up in New Jersey with his mother, his father showed no interest in him beyond the moment he was conceived. One afternoon, as his mother was getting ready to receive guests, he heard her say the word, *Chablis*, and he loved the way it rolled off her tongue. He asked her to say it again, *Chablis, Chablis, Chablis*, and he knew, whatever Chablis was, and at that point he had no idea, he was in love with it. Even though he could barely read, and wasn't out of the first grade, Joe started searching for mentions of Chablis in books, on television, as he listened to the radio. The first nonfamilial reference came from television, where he saw a washed-up, overweight film director, who was once the most heralded auteur in the world, expounding on the joys of a particularly wretched California Chablis during a television commercial. For days he walked around imitating the man's voice, and saying—Chablis, for all your special moments! He said it over and over again, his mother finally had to threaten him with no dessert for a month if he wouldn't stop.

His next encounter with Chablis came when he was eleven. A girl in his fourth grade class, a mean little girl who never came out of her biting, hitting, spitting and scratching phase, was named Chablis. Joe became infatuated with her as soon as he heard the name. He followed her around, carried her books, gave her his lunch (she was also extremely overweight and capable of eating four or five lunches), wrote her love letters. She responded by biting him, hitting him, spitting on him and scratching him. Their love affair ended when she was sent to a school for children with special needs. Joe cried for a week.

At thirteen, Joe discovered the true meaning and power of Chablis. He was at a friend's house and was helping his friend take out the garbage. There were several bottles in one of the bags, Joe slipped as he was carrying the bag, the bottles came tumbling out. Joe started picking them up, there were three 40-ounce bottles of malt liquor, six Pabst Blue Ribbons, two bottles of Boone's Farm Strawberry Hill, and a bottle of Chablis. There was a small amount of yellow liquid left in the bottle of Chablis, some of it undoubtedly wine, some of it most likely saliva. He picked up the bottle, smelled it, it didn't smell very good, he didn't care. He brought the bottle to his lips, drank the yellow liquid as fast as he could, it hit his stomach and started burning, it hit his head and started buzzing. *Chablis*, it was as if the Sirens were calling him to the rocks. *Chablis*, like a runaway train heading straight into a brick wall.

Since that day, that fateful day, Joe has not gone more than eighteen hours without a taste of Chablis. As a kid he stole bottles from his friends' parents and stockpiled them in his room, sneaking sips before he went to school, when he got home, when he went to sleep. When he was sixteen he got a fake ID and bought bottles at low-end liquor stores, he kept them hidden in his mother's garage. When he was eighteen, and he was graduating from high school, in the space beneath his picture where he was supposed to list his life's ambition, he wrote—Spend my life drunk on Chablis.

He left home two days after graduation. He had a backpack filled with six bottles of Chablis and a toothbrush, he had no money, no change of clothes, no idea where he was going. He started walking west. He went through Pennsylvania slept in the weeds on the side of the highway, begged for money at truck stops, took rides when he could get them. He drifted into Cleveland and stayed for two months, sleeping outside of the old Municipal Stadium and feeding his Chablis habit by selling predictions on the games (they were always the same: the Cleveland teams are going to lose, lose, lose). He drifted south into Kentucky and Tennessee (fuck that Jack Daniel's shit) and ended up in New Orleans, where he slept in the streets outside of the jazz clubs for three years. From there he wandered through Texas, where he got beat up and called names on a regular basis (men who love Chablis aren't really welcome in Texas), he worked his way through New Mexico and into Nevada, where he lived on the Strip in Las Vegas for a year, eating gourmet buffet food out of casino dumpsters and playing the occasional slot or video poker game in low-end gaming houses. He left Las Vegas when he started hearing voices in his head. The voices said—walk west, Joe, walk west, walk west, walk west, Joe. Initially he thought somebody might have given him a quarter or a dime soaked in LSD, which he then absorbed through his fingers. The voices continued long after a dose would have worn off, so he thought maybe he knocked some of his brain wires loose when he fell down after consuming eleven bottles of discontinued wine he purchased at a wine close-out sale. He smacked himself a few times with his hand in the hope that he could get the wires properly realigned, but alas, the voices continued. He finally decided that he was insane, and that there was nothing to do but obey the voices. He started walking west. The voices stopped. He kept walking west. They did not return. He walked west until he reached the ocean, and walking any farther would have led to his death by drowning. As he stood on the sand staring across the ocean he heard one word—here here here. And so it was, here.

In December 1871, the Los Angeles Fire Department is created. It consists of three fire engine companies, two hook and ladder companies and three hose companies. Each company consists of no more than sixty-five men and no less than twenty-five men, all of whom are over the age of twenty-one. Membership in the fire department is on a volunteer basis.

They spend six days living on the beach. On the sixth day, their truck gets robbed. The driver's-side window is broken, the radio is gone, their stash of money, $1,500, is gone. They have what is left in their wallets, about $150. The $1,500 had been hidden in a crevice beneath the steering wheel. He had hidden money there in the past, it had never been found. They weren't in Ohio anymore.

They wave down a policeman on a bicycle. There are policemen on bicycles all over Santa Monica. Because of the traffic and the crowds and the pedestrian walkways that line the beach and the overhanging bluffs, it is easier and faster for police to ride bikes than it is to drive. The truck is in a crowded parking lot. The policeman looks at it, looks at them. He speaks.

How long's it been here?

Six days.

You move it at all?

No. I didn't think I had to.

Thieves walk around this lot looking for cars that haven't moved. They figure the cars are either deserted, or the owners are putting them in here because they don't have room for 'em anywhere else. They're easy targets.

I didn't know that.

What's your name?

Dylan.

What's her name?

She speaks.

Maddie.

Like Madeline?

Yes.

You have ID?

They both say yes, hand the officer their driver's licenses. He looks at them.

Long way from home.

Maddie is nervous, Dylan speaks.

Yup.

53

You on vacation?

We're trying to get settled, find a place to live.

You come out here to get famous?

Nope.

The officer laughs.

Two kids from small-town Ohio move to LA and don't think about becoming movie stars? Right. I believe that.

He hands them their IDs.

You can file a report if you want, but there is almost no chance of finding whoever did this, and your money's gone. I'd recommend finding somewhere else to park.

There any cheap places to live around here?

The officer laughs again.

No, there aren't.

Any idea where we might find one?

Go somewhere in the Valley. You'll find something there.

Where's the Valley?

Buy yourself a map. You'll find it.

The officer rides away. Dylan and Maddie get in the truck. Dylan cleans out the broken shards of glass before they sit down. They drive to a gas station, buy a map. They get on the 10 and drive to the 405, get on the 405 and head north. They are almost immediately stuck in a massive traffic jam. Dylan looks at Maddie, speaks.

Holy shit.

Indeed.

You ever seen anything like this?

Nope.

We get eight lanes on each side of the road. A sixteen-lane parking lot.

We're moving a little.

He looks at the speedometer.

Three miles per hour.

How far away is the Valley?

Like ten or twelve miles.

She laughs.

Nice four-hour drive. Concrete and car horns and the smell of exhaust. Welcome to California.

Traffic picks up as the 405 enters the canyon between Brentwood and Bel-Air. On the Bel-Air side there are mansions built into gray stone slopes, on the Brentwood side is the looming, white marble behemoth of the Getty Museum. It takes ninety minutes to get through the canyon and into the San Fernando Valley, which is 260 square miles of overdeveloped desert surrounded by mountains on four sides, home to 2 million people. It's primarily middle class, but there are sections of extraordinary wealth, and sections of extraordinary poverty. Dylan and Maddie pull off the exit for Ventura Boulevard, stop at a light. Dylan speaks.

Where do we go?

No idea.

Right or left or straight?

If we go right we drive into a big rock hill.

He laughs.

Choose something else.

Straight.

He nods.

That's how we're gonna do it from now on. You tell me when to turn and where to turn and we'll drive around till we find somewhere to stop.

We need money. We need to find some way to get money.

At some point today, I'm gonna stop and rob a bank.

Seriously?

No.

I'd help you if you were.

Seriously?

No.

Dylan smiles.

The light just turned green.

Maddie smiles.

Go straight.

He drives straight turns left, right, right, drives straight

straight straight, turns right, straight. They drift, turn, get lost, roam. There's no radio so Maddie sings softly, she has a light, clean voice, sometimes she hums. Neighborhoods have clean streets well-kept lawns children on sidewalks mothers with strollers. Others less clean, no grass, fewer children, no mothers. There are long desolate stretches lined with battered steel warehouses. There are golf courses and baseball diamonds they're unnaturally, perfectly green. They see Warner Brothers, Disney, Universal, they're behind thick walls, guarded gates. They drive for six miles without seeing a home only gas stations, mini-malls and fast-food restaurants. They find palm-lined avenues mansions on both sides, they find what appears to be a war zone. The hills along the southern rim are wild, and overgrown, houses are built on stilts, carved into the side of the rock. There are apartment complexes that hold more people than live in their old town, some are gorgeous, some decrepit, some look livable, some don't. They stop in a grocery store. Everyone is beautiful. The people who appear unattractive would probably not be considered so in other parts of the country. Coffee shops are full, outdoor cafés are full, traffic is relentless, it seems like no one has a job. The sun is always up, shining, the heat ebbs and flows, the more with concrete, the less with green.

The day slides away, they take it in remember it, forget it. As the truck runs low on gas Dylan pulls into a motel. It doesn't look good, doesn't look bad, most people probably drive past it without noticing it. It's brown and yellow, there are two floors, a railing along the second, a mostly empty parking lot. It has a neon sign that doesn't glow it says Valley Motel and Motor Lodge, Weekly, Monthly. Maddie speaks.

Why are we stopping here?

I think this is the place.

What do you mean?

For us.

To live?

Yeah.

How are we going to live here?

I have a plan.

What?

Let me go inside and check a couple things out.

You're going to leave me here?

It doesn't look bad.

It doesn't look good.

You'll be fine. I'll be right back.

He kisses her gets out of the truck walks into the lobby. He talks to a man behind the reception desk. The man is thin and his hair is thinning and he has a patchy mustache that his friends laugh about behind his back. Maddie watches Dylan talk to the man, the man nods continuously he nods when he talks he nods when he doesn't talk it's like a nervous tic nodding, nodding. Dylan reaches out, shakes his hand, the man nods. Dylan walks out of the lobby gets into the truck.

Our new home.

Maddie shakes her head, looks distraught.

No.

What's wrong?

This is not what I thought we were coming here for.

What do you mean?

This is California. I thought we'd live in a beautiful place near the ocean and we'd be happy.

We're nineteen. We don't have any money and we don't have jobs. This is the best we're gonna get.

Where are we?

North Hollywood.

This is Hollywood?

North Hollywood. The guy said real Hollywood is worse.

I'm scared, Dylan. I want to go home.

This is our home.

No it's not. This will never be my home.

We can't go back. We can't go back and live our parents' lives. I'd rather die.

I'm scared.

We're gonna be fine.

How are we gonna pay for this? How are we gonna get jobs?

He motions to a used car lot across the street, a sign says—we pay cash.

I'm gonna sell the truck. A room here is $425 a month. We'll stay till we can afford something better. It can't be any worse than it was back there.

Promise me this won't be our life.

I promise.

Maddie smiles, nods. Dylan starts the truck, pulls out, drives across the street. He sells the truck for $1,300. It's worth more, but he takes it because he knows he's in no position to haggle. They walk back to the motel. He pays the man behind the counter two months rent. They go to their room it's at the far end on the second floor. They go into the room the carpet is stained and worn, the bedspread is stained and worn, the television is old, there's no clock. There are two threadbare chairs near the window and there is a sink and a microwave, there are orange and brown curtains hanging at the window they're stained and frayed. Dylan sits on the bed. Maddie looks around, shakes her head, looks like she's going to cry. Dylan stands and walks to her puts his arms around her.

I promise we'll find something better.

I'm scared to touch anything.

This is just the beginning.

I know.

She looks at the bed, starts to cry.

Don't cry. I don't want you to cry.

I can't help it.

Is there anything I can do?

I'm scared to touch anything.

In 1874, the Point Fermin Lighthouse is built in San Pedro, which is now the site of the Port of Los Angeles. In 1876, the Southern Pacific Railroad connects Los Angeles and San Francisco. In 1885 the Sante Fe Railway connects Los Angeles to the transcontinental railroad.

There are seventy-five residences in the Palisades Heights Trailer Park. They are spread across eight acres of land on the bluffs above the Pacific Coast Highway, and were originally built, if that is even the correct word, to be a form of affordable housing in an upper-class community. For years they were the butt of jokes, they were sneered at, mocked, demeaned, the people who lived in them ignored by the rest of the community. When the real-estate boom of the late '90s and early '00s hit, they boomed at a greater percentage than the rest of the country did, and more than the surrounding area, where mansions sell for as much as $50 million. At that point, some of them were sold, some upgraded, some expanded, some went unchanged. The largest is a triple-wide on a double lot, the smallest is a 170-square-foot Airstream Bambi.

***

Tammy and Carl moved into the park in 1963. They were from Oklahoma and both grew up, on opposite sides of Tulsa, dreaming of a life at the beach. They met in their freshman year at Tulsa State, they were both studying to be teachers. They married a year later, had their first child, Earl, a year after that, Tammy dropped out to stay home with him, Carl stayed in school and got his degree. Two days after graduation they got in their wood-paneled station wagon and drove west. When they got to LA, Carl started looking for a job and they started looking for a place to live with a view of the ocean. They looked up and down the coast, from Ojai to Huntington Beach. Carl applied for seventy-four jobs, they couldn't afford anything that was habitable. They lived out of the wagon for a month, parking in the lots of public beaches, cooking hot dogs on a small hibachi.

The job came first. It was teaching science to eighth graders at a public junior high school in Pacific Palisades, an upscale ocean community that lies between Santa Monica and Malibu. It was a good school, and the pay was good for a teaching job, but it was not enough to live in the Palisades or in Santa

Monica or in Malibu. They found the trailer park, which was on the edge of the Palisades. They bought a double-wide for $3,000.

They had two more children, a boy named Wayne and a girl named Dawn, and they lived together as a family in the trailer. It was crowded, but the lack of space brought them closer, forced them to live in peace with each other, made the good times better and the bad times shorter. They would walk down the hill to the beach every weekend, and every day during the summer, and they would play in the sand, in the waves, the boys both learned to surf, they continued cooking hot dogs on the hibachi. The kids went to the public schools, which are among the best in the state, all of them did well and went on to college. Carl continued to teach science, and became the football coach, at the junior high for thirty-five years. Once a year at Christmas they went back to Tulsa, where their relatives looked at them like they were aliens. Once a year, at spring break, they drove down to Baja and rented a bungalow on the beach and spent a week eating tacos, playing Frisbee and surfing. The years drifted by simply and easily and wonderfully. Aside from the fact that they lived in a trailer park, the family had a quintessential California beach life. The kids are gone now, grown and on their own, Earl is an entertainment lawyer in Beverly Hills, Wayne is a college English professor in San Diego, Dawn is married with children in Redondo Beach. Carl is retired and he and Tammy spend their days walking along the beach, sitting on the patio in front of their trailer reading history and mystery books, playing cards with their neighbors. They see at least one of their kids every weekend, usually at the trailer, and their grandchildren, there are seven of them, love visiting them. Earl, who makes an absurd amount of money, has offered to buy them a house but they don't want to move. They love the park, they love the trailer, they love the life they have led and continue to lead. They want to stay until they're dead and gone, until they move on to what they believe will be their next life. Tammy and

Carl, like hundreds of thousands of people a year, came to Los Angeles to make their dreams come true. Sometimes it happens.

***

Josh bought his trailer three years ago. It's a small standard in the back of the park. It's in good shape, is relatively new (ten years), and was sold with its furnishings, which are simple and tasteful.

Josh is a television producer. His specialty is dramatic one-hour police shows. He comes up with the ideas for the shows, finds writers to execute his vision, sells the shows to networks, supervises their production. He has had three make it on network prime time in the last five years. One of them was canceled, two are still on, and one was recently syndicated.

Josh is thirty-six years old. He is married and he has three children. He lives with his family in a seven-bedroom Spanish mansion north of Sunset Blvd. in Beverly Hills (most of Beverly Hills is wealthy, the ridiculously wealthy live in the hills north of Sunset). His net worth is just past $75 million. Fifty million of it exists on paper in the United States, $25 million of it is in untraceable bank accounts in Monaco and the Caribbean. He hides the money because he believes it is his money, and his money alone. Should his marriage end in divorce, and he loves his wife and is not planning on it ending, though he would also not be surprised if it happened, he does not want her to be able to get at everything he's earned. He doesn't give a shit what the laws of the State of California say, it is his money, his alone.

Josh bought the trailer with overseas money. His wife does not know about it, none of his friends know about it. He uses it to sleep with actresses who want jobs on his shows. He meets them all over town, at casting sessions, in restaurants, in clothing stores, everywhere. Those he likes, and he likes them young, fresh and unspoiled, sixteen at the youngest and twenty at the oldest, he invites to the trailer. Nothing, except a private meeting, is ever explicitly offered. Once the girls are in the

62

trailer he offers them liquor and drugs. Sometimes they take it, sometimes they don't, and it doesn't really matter either way. Usually the girls are impressed enough with his success, his money and his power to sleep with him willingly. When they aren't, he tells them he'll make sure they never work if they don't change their minds and spread their legs. Now and then, he has to force himself on them. When he's done he orders them a cab. He tells them to call him, that he'll take care of them. Unless they're spectacular, and he plans on seeing them again, he gives them a fake number. Those that he sees again are used until he's finished, and then they're discarded.

***

Betty is three and three-quarters years old, which she takes great pride in telling everyone she meets. She is thirty-seven inches tall, weighs thirty-four pounds, has blue eyes and curly white hair. She moved into the park with her mom, who is a nurse at a hospital in Santa Monica, when she was two. She calls the park Trailer-Land, and she calls herself the Princess of Trailer-Land. Her favorite activities are riding her tricycle and playing with her doll, whose name is Dollie.
Betty's mother, whose name is Jane, inherited the trailer when her aunt passed away. Although she loved her aunt, and was truly and sincerely saddened by her death, she believes the trailer was a gift from God. Jane's husband was an alcoholic who beat her on an almost daily basis. At various points in their relationship he had broken her nose, eye socket, both of her arms and six of her fingers. He hadn't seriously hurt Betty yet, but he had started abusing her as well, slapping her when she made too much noise, pinching her on the backs of her arms and legs when she did things he didn't like, kicking her away if she came near him when he was in a bad mood. He told Jane if she went to the police he would kill her and kill their daughter, if she left he would find them and kill them. She believed him. If she tried to do anything, she believed he would kill them.

Jane prayed to God for a solution. Every day, three times a day, she got down on her knees and prayed please God help us we need a way out please God help us please. She did not go to church, she did not claim some sort of false conversion, she did not scream hallelujah to the sky; three times a day she got on her knees and prayed, three times a day. The abuse continued. He knocked out three of her teeth. She kept praying.

She was at work when she saw him. She worked as an ER nurse he came in on a gurney. He had been in a bar during lunch he was drunk he followed a woman into the bathroom and tried to force himself on her. Her boyfriend came into the bar heard her yell opened the bathroom door saw him pulling her hair and trying to bend her over the sink. The boyfriend slammed his head into the mirror above the sink. The mirror shattered and shards of glass went into his eyes.

They operated, but they couldn't save them. He would never see again. Later the same day, the aunt died. When Jane got home from work, she kissed Betty, thanked God she got down on her knees and thanked God over and over again, and she cried herself to sleep. There were no tears for him.

Jane filed for divorce the next day. The day after, she and Betty left the house with a few bags of clothes and some toys and they drove for two days to the Palisades. He was in the hospital for a week and released. He had a new white cane. He went to his mother's house. He hated his mother but she was the only person who would take care of him.

When they arrived, the trailer was in perfect condition. There were two small bedrooms one for each of them, a small yard with a flower garden. Jane switched jobs at the new hospital, went from the ER to pediatrics, she found a babysitter to watch Betty while she worked. They built a life, a new life, one that revolved around each other. They play at the beach on Jane's off days, they watch the sunset when she gets home from her shift. They grow tomatoes in the garden and have barbecues in the yard, they've been to Disneyland six times. Betty becomes more adorable every day, more outgoing, she skips and smiles and laughs through her days, she plays with her toys and reads her books, she never asks about her daddy. She has become friends with almost everyone in the park, young old rich or poor everyone loves her, loves her silly little giggle, her crazy hair, her best friend Dollie. She tells them all she's the Princess of Trailer-Land. None of them disagree with her.

***

Emerson hit his peak when he was nine years old. He was in three films, two of which were massive hits, he made two million dollars, and he was nominated for an Academy Award. He didn't win the award, but he was the youngest nominee in history. He went to the ceremony with his mother and he got a blow job, his first, from a thirty-four-year-old blonde in the bathroom.

Emerson is now twenty-nine years old. The intervening twenty years have not been kind to him. His movie career was over by the time he was twelve, he dropped out of high school to pursue an ill-fated dream of rock superstardom, most of his hair had fallen out by the time he was twenty-two. At this point, the only area of his life which is not in a state of disrepair is his financial life. He invested well and spent frugally. He has four million bucks in the bank.

He moved into the trailer park when he was twenty-four, a year after giving up on his rock-star dreams and a year before he decided to rededicate himself to the craft of acting. He no longer has an agent or a manager, and he hasn't had a paying job in fourteen years. He still, however, has the dream, and he believes that if he was nominated once, it will happen again. He spends his days taking acting classes and consulting with acting coaches. He spends his nights reading plays and doing theater at small playhouses around the city. He spends his weekends at the beach reading gossip magazines and dreaming of the day he'll be on the cover with the words COMEBACK KID beneath his name.

He doesn't date and he doesn't socialize, unless he believes it will somehow help his career. He wants it again. His name in lights. That feeling when he walked down the street and people stared at him, pointed towards him, called out his name.

***

Leo and Christine moved out from Chicago twenty-two years ago. They had both worked forty long years at a car factory and had dreamed of the sun and the sand and lawn chairs and endless bridge games. They had been married for thirty-six years when they retired, had raised three children, had scraped and saved and planned. They're in their late eighties now. They've had all the sun and sand and bridge they wanted and needed to have and they're ready. They will miss their children, and their grandchildren, and their soon-to-be three great-grandchildren. They will miss their lawn chairs, where they sit every day and chat and have coffee and read the paper. They will miss staring into each other's eyes, even after all these years they still love staring into each other's eyes. There is much they will not miss. They go to bed together every night knowing they're ready. That it might be their last. They're ready.

***

Twelve acres of land adjacent to the park is being developed into a high-end gated community. The houses will have between six and ten bedrooms and will range in price between four and nine million dollars. The views from their living rooms will be the same as the views from the living rooms of the trailers.

66

By 1875, Los Angeles had separate and distinct communities of Africans, Spanish, Mexicans, Chinese, and white Americans, easily making it the most diverse city in the country west of the Mississippi. There was little intermingling between the communities, and the Los Angeles City Council passed a law allowing whites to discriminate against all non-whites.

Amberton sits in his home office. He also has an office for the production company that he and Casey own together, but he rarely goes there. That office is for the employees and for his public persona. This office is his and his alone. It is very safe, very secure, very private. It is where he keeps his deepest secrets: his journals, pictures, videos, mementos he keeps from his favorite lovers his records of their time together.

He is naked in his chair his feet are on his desk he is wearing a headset. He dials the agency. A young woman answers.

Creative Talent Management.

Kevin Jackson please.

One moment please.

He smiles. Kevin Jackson. The thought of him. Oh, the thought of him. A deep thick male voice answers.

Kevin Jackson.

Is this him?

Yes it is.

Why don't you have an assistant?

Who is this?

And you don't recognize my voice. That hurts.

Who is this please?

Should I use my public voice? My talk-show, movie-star voice? Amberton's voice becomes deeper, more masculine.

Hello, Kevin.

Mr. Parker. How may I help you?

He reverts back to his real voice.

Did you just call me Mr. Parker?

Yes, sir.

Oh my God. Did you just call me sir?

I did.

My name is Amberton. I have other names, but we don't know each other well enough for you to know them.

How may I help you, Amberton?

I would like to have lunch with you today. We can go anywhere you like.

I'm sorry, Amberton, but I have lunch plans today.

68

Cancel them.

I can't do that.

Amberton laughs.

I make your agency millions and millions and millions and millions of dollars a year. I have friends all over town, good friends, and some not so good, who do things for me just because. I am an international superstar, as bright as a supernova. I highly doubt whomever your lunch is with is as important as me.

It's my mother.

Really?

Yes.

How wonderful. I'm coming.

Excuse me?

I'm coming. Where and what time?

I'm not sure . . .

Amberton interrupts him.

No argument. I am coming.

Kevin laughs.

We're going to Soul by the Pound. It's on Crenshaw.

Amberton giggles.

Is that really the name?

Yes.

Amberton gets the address hangs up the phone goes to his room to get changed. His closet is ridiculously large, 800 square feet of perfectly organized high-end clothing, most of which he gets for free from designers and clothing companies who hope he's seen in their garments. He struggles with what to wear. He wants to be impressive but not too impressive, casual but not too casual, handsome, but in an effortless way. He tries to coordinate the outfit with his hair, he has trouble deciding whether he should or should not wear gel. He walks in circles around the closet runs through the options in his head: suit, slacks and a shirt, jeans, shorts (Wow, that's casual!). It wasn't like this with his other targets. He decided he wanted them, he pursued them, he got them. It was simple and predatory, there was almost no thinking involved, he relied on instinct and desire. Now, with this football player, this tall, beautiful black football player, he was losing his edge. He sits down, takes several deep yoga breaths, tells himself to focus, focus, focus. When he feels focused, he puts on a pair of black slacks and a black button-down and black loafers. He puts gel in his hair. He looks in the mirror and smiles and says—yes, you are the biggest star in the sky, yes, you are.

He starts driving towards the Crenshaw district, where Soul by the Pound is located. He drives his Mercedes. It's a black sedan with darkened windows. The windows are darker than is allowed by law, but Amberton had them done after someone saw him in his car, got excited, drove into a telephone pole, and subsequently blamed Amberton for the accident and sued him. Even though he could have won the suit, Amberton settled it. He decided he'd rather pay the person off, even though their case was baseless and their motives despicable, than deal with going to court for two or three years. The next day, he had the windows in all of his cars (he has seven) darkened.

He drives through Beverly Hills down the fantasyland of Rodeo Drive to Wilshire Boulevard. He drives east on Wilshire both sides lined with glass towers overflowing with talent agencies, talent management companies, production companies, PR agencies, attorneys. He drives south on Robertson away from the wealth and shine of Beverly Hills into another one of the nameless areas of Los Angeles dominated by fast-food restaurants, gas stations and used car lots. He gets on the 10 heading east it's a parking lot. He turns on the radio listens to light hits radio sings along to several of his favorite love songs from the '80s. He hears a song he recorded for a film (it was a big hit!), he sings along at high volume. He remembers the boy he slept with during filming, a nineteen-year-old production assistant from Tennessee. He was tall and blond and he had a cute accent. He was nervous and embarrassed. He was a beautiful boy, and Amberton was gentle with him. By the end of the song, there are tears running down Amberton's face. He pulls off the Crenshaw Boulevard exit takes a right starts heading south. Crenshaw is one of the major thoroughfares of South LA. The district surrounding it is one of the largest black neighborhoods in America. In the '50s, '60s and '70s it was largely middle-class, in the '80s it was overrun with gangs and consumed by crack and became one of the most violent neighborhoods in the country, in the '90s it was devastated by the LA riots of 1992 and the Northridge earthquake of 1994. Though it has been partially rebuilt, Crenshaw Boulevard itself exists in a state of perpetual decay. It is lined with an inordinate number of fast-food restaurants, liquor markets and discount stores. There are storefront churches in mini-malls and car lots surrounded by razor-wire fences. Drivers of most of the cars have their doors locked and their windows up. Pedestrians, of which there are few, glance nervously around as they hurry along the sidewalk. The residential neighborhoods directly behind both sides of Crenshaw consist primarily of Spanish-style stucco houses and two- and three-floor apartment complexes. The streets are clean and the yards generally well kept. Despite its outward appearance, there is an air of menace that hangs over the area. People who do not live there, if they're willing to go there at all, drive quickly through it. Amberton is nervous as he looks for Soul by the Pound. Despite having lived in LA for many years, he's never been on Crenshaw, or in the neighborhood, and he's terrified. He tries to summon some of the bravery he displays on-screen as an American action hero, but it's nowhere to be found. Worst-case scenarios start running through his mind: he'll get carjacked, he'll get rammed, he'll run out of gas and get mugged (it doesn't matter that he has a full tank), he'll get shot in a drive-by, he'll be dragged from his car and scalped, he'll get kidnapped and fed to an angry pack of malnourished pit bulls. When he sees the restaurant, in the back of a decrepit mini-mall, he whoops with joy and cuts across traffic in a rush to park.

He finds a spot in front of the restaurant he gets out of the car turns on the alarm though he knows it won't make a difference if someone wants to steal it. He turns towards the door takes a deep breath the smell is magnificent some combination of fried roasted and baked food, doubtlessly and wonderfully full of grease and fat. He walks to the door, opens it, steps inside. The restaurant is small and crowded. There are about twenty tables, simple card tables with white paper spread across them folding chairs at each side of each table, all of them are full. The walls are covered with signed headshots of athletes, rappers, jazz musicians, politicians and actors who have visited, all of them are black. Amberton looks for Kevin, everyone in the restaurant turns and stares at him. Aside from being who he is, his is the only white face in the establishment. He hears someone say—Goddamn, it's a white boy—he hears someone else say—Look, man, it's that actor motherfucker. He looks for Kevin nothing. He looks for someone that might be Kevin's mother nothing. He thinks about leaving getting in his car and driving home as fast as he can when he hears his name.

Mr. Parker?

He looks around, can't tell who's speaking to him. A little louder.

Mr. Parker?

He looks but can't see, is someone going to shoot him, hit him, should he run, oh my.

I'm right here Mr. Parker.

He sees an attractive dark-skinned African-American woman in her mid-to-late thirties sitting alone at a table about ten feet away. She's wearing a black business suit and glasses, looks like she's a lawyer or a banker. She motions for Amberton to come over he walks towards her she's about ten feet away. He's nervous, almost shaking, he has to steady himself. He knows he has to be in character as the public image of Amberton, and leave the real one, the gay one, hidden.

I have a table for us. Kevin isn't here yet.

In his deep voice.

Great.

She offers her hand.

Tonya Jackson.

He shakes it.

Amberton Parker.

Nice to meet you.

You too.

They sit.

Are you Kevin's sister?

She laughs.

No, I'm not.

Cousin?

No, I'm not his cousin, Mr. Parker.

I assume you're related?

She laughs.

Yes, we're related. I'm Kevin's mother.

Amberton looks shocked.

No.

She laughs again.

Yes.

You look so young.

I'm not old.

Did you have Kevin when you were five?

Laughs again.

You're very charming, Mr. Parker.

Seriously. You're younger than I am.

I might be. I was a very young mother.

Don't mind saying how young?

I do if you're planning on judging me.

I'm just curious.

I was fifteen.

However old you were, you did a great job. Kevin is an
incredibly impressive young man.

She smiles.

Thank you. I'm very proud of him.

A waiter arrives they order drinks diet soda for both of them.

Without bothering to consult Amberton, which actually impresses him, Tonya orders lunch, fried chicken fatback and chitterlings, mac and cheese, red beans and collard greens, corn bread cooked in bacon fat. As she finishes the order, Kevin arrives, he's wearing a crisp black suit and a blue shirt and a conservative red tie. He leans over, gives his mother a hug and a kiss on the cheek, she smiles and says hello. He sits down, looks at Amberton, speaks.

You found it alright?

Amberton smiles.

I did.

And you found my mom.

She found me.

She smiles, speaks.

He was hard to miss in this place.

They laugh, start talking, Amberton starts asking questions about their life together, about how they survived. Tonya answers most of them, we lived with my parents until I was twenty-one and they watched Kevin while I worked and went to school, we moved into our own place when I could afford it it was across the street from my parents, I went to college at night and graduated when I was twenty-five, I got a job as a credit analyst at a bank. He asks about Kevin's football career, he was always gifted we could tell when he was seven that he was going to be great, he set high school passing records and got recruited by every college in the nation, we were thrilled when he was drafted #1 we were crushed when he got hurt. Amberton glances at Kevin when he can, tries to control himself. He wants to be closer to him, to touch him, to hold his hand. He stays in character, tries not to be obvious about how he feels, is extremely aware of the fact that everyone in the restaurant is staring at their table.

When the food arrives, Amberton is relieved to have a distraction from Kevin his lovely Kevin, and although he usually adheres to a strict nonfat, low-carb, raw-food diet prepared for him by his personal chef, he digs in. The food is heavy, rich, incredibly good. As they eat, Tonya starts asking Amberton about his life, he gives her his pre-prepared spiel, I'm married I love my wife we have three beautiful children together (all conceived in petri dishes). She asks about his work he says he's taking a break he wants to enjoy life for a few months, that his next film will be about a rogue chemist who develops a supervirus, it is Amberton's job, against impossible odds, to stop him.

They finish eating Amberton tries to pay Tonya tells him to put his money away. The manager comes over with Tonya's change asks Amberton for a picture to put on the wall, he will be the first white man to make it, Amberton says of course that he's honored. They get up leave Amberton walks behind Kevin watches him walk to the door Amberton is still hungry, still hungry. Once they're outside, he kisses Tonya on the cheek tells her it was a pleasure to meet her she echoes the sentiment. Amberton says goodbye to Kevin he shakes his hand it is the best part of his day a simple handshake. They get in their respective cars and drive away. Amberton turns on the radio station that plays love songs. As he drives down Crenshaw towards the 10 he feels no fear. He hears a song about love, true love he sings along at the top of his lungs. He is still hungry.

Between 1880 and 1890 the population grows from 30,000 residents to 100,000 residents. Land prices skyrocket until the market collapses in 1887, creating the first real-estate depression in southern California. With the population boom also came the first inklings of the entertainment industry as musical theater companies from the East began migrating to the city and opening their own venues.

Esperanza didn't leave her room for almost a year. She didn't let anyone, aside from her mother and father, come in to see her. All of her relatives tried to comfort her it didn't do any good. Her father and her cousins tracked down all of the men at the party who laughed at her and forced them to come to the house to apologize for their behavior, it didn't do any good. For the first two months after the party she stayed in bed and cried. Every time she tried to stop crying, or tried to get out of bed, she remembered lying on the ground, on what was supposed to be the best day of her life, her skirt at her waist, fifty men standing around laughing at her. Her mother finally convinced her to get out of bed, told her that they would try to deal with her thighs together. Even though money was extremely tight, they bought a number of exercise machines specifically designed for the thighs, the Thighmaster, the Thighrocker, the Thighshaper, the Thighsculptor and the Thigh dominator, but none of them helped. Esperanza tried all sorts of exercises, the inner-thigh press, hack squats, safety squats, rear lunges, walking lunges, hamstring curls and all manner of leg lifts, including the vaunted outer-thigh leg lift they were all useless. Once she gave up on the exercises she tried running in place it didn't work running in small circles around her room it didn't work jumping on a mini-trampoline it didn't work. They consulted a trainer he said that genetics were the main factor and no one could change their genetics, they consulted a doctor he said sometimes God gives us things we don't like and we just have to learn to deal with them. Esperanza was distraught. She went back to bed, crying all day long, cursing her thighs, cursing her life.

She came out of her room when one of her cousins died. He was a sixteen-year-old named Manuel who had dreamed of being a doctor. He came across the border with his parents at twelve, learned to speak perfect English in a year, was the best student in his class, stayed away from the gangs that dominated the neighborhood. He was a kind, gentle boy, one who had been taught to be a gentleman, to hold doors, give compliments, to help those who needed it. He was killed as he walked home from school. A stray bullet from a drive-by hit him in the back of the head. He was dead before he hit the ground.

Esperanza was crushed, felt guilty for not having seen her cousin during the previous year, was embarrassed to admit she had acted in such a ridiculous manner. She pulled out her nicest dress, did her hair and put on some makeup and left her room to mourn with the rest of her family. After the funeral, she helped her mother prepare food in the kitchen for guests coming to the house to offer their condolences, she served them, filled their glasses, cleared their plates. That night, she stayed up late with her surviving cousins, sharing their favorite stories about Manuel, laughing about his bookish ways, cursing the gangs whose culture killed him.

The next day, Esperanza found everyone in the house, all seventeen of them, took them aside and individually apologized to them. They all told her not to worry about it, that they were just happy to see her again. She went to church in the afternoon and prayed for guidance, gave her confession, lit a candle for her cousin. When she went home, she resolved to start living again, living outside of her room and her house, outside of her low self-esteem and self-hatred, outside of the image she had of her body. It was a slow start. For the first week she went out once a day, usually to church. Second week a couple times a day she went grocery shopping, went to a discount clothing store. Third week she started making phone calls and attempting to get back on the path she had left a year earlier. The scholarship she had was gone she was told she could reapply. The spot at school was gone she was told she could reapply. Her family didn't have any money she didn't have any money if she was going to go to school she knew she needed a job. She asked her mother if she knew of anything she asked her father if he knew of anything. They both asked their friends. Esperanza started going through the classifieds, walking through her neighborhood and talking to local business owners, she started filling out applications and doing interviews. Because she was still self-conscious about her thighs, she always wore oversized skirts that hid them. While she was looking for work, she occasionally went on cleaning jobs with her mother. Her mother usually did two houses a day, one in the morning and one in the afternoon. On Friday, she did one large home in Pasadena that took all day. The woman who lived in the home was in her seventies, extremely wealthy, had been born in and spent her entire life in Pasadena. Streets, parks and schools were named after various members of her family. She had a live-in staff for most of her life, but as she got older, she didn't like having people around all the time. When her children moved out, she had three daughters, all of whom married well and lived nearby, and her husband passed away, he was ten years older and died at seventy-three of a heart attack while playing tennis, she let the live-ins go and hired Graciella. After her third week working at the house with her mother, the woman asked Esperanza if she was interested in a full-time job. Esperanza said yes, the woman said her sister was looking for someone to cook and clean. Esperanza said she would like to meet her.

She had an interview the next day. It was in the morning she woke up early put on her best skirt she felt hopeful and confident if she could get a job she could go to school at night, she knew whatever the work was she could handle it. She took a bus into Pasadena, with traffic it took fifty minutes without traffic it would have taken ten. She got off the bus and walked to the house, it was another fifteen minutes the sun was up it was already hot she was starting to sweat. When she found the address she stopped in front of a gate and stared through black iron bars. The house was huge, looked more like a museum than a house. Two long wings spreading out on either side of a massive columned entrance. The yard was huge and perfectly green, split by a white stone driveway. As she stared at the house, a voice buzzed her from a small speaker discreetly built into the stone wall that held the gates,

Are you the girl that works for my sister?

She looked at the speaker. Her mother recommended that she speak some English, but not let her prospective employer know that she was fluent. It would allow her employer to feel superior to her, which wealthy Americans tended to like, and feel that they would be able to speak and communicate in their home without worry of eavesdropping, which they also tended to like.

Yes.

I'll open the gate. Come to the front door.

Sí.

The gate started silently opening, Esperanza walked towards the house it began looming over her the closer she got the more intimidating it became and as she started up the steps that led to the door, the door opened. A stern, seventy-year-old woman stood waiting for her. The woman had white hair and piercing blue eyes, she was tall and gaunt, had a severe jawline and defined cheekbones, wore an expensive flowered dress. Even though it was only eight in the morning, she looked like she had been up for hours and was ready for a dinner date at the club or some cards with her bridge group. She looked Esperanza over, which made Esperanza nervous and insecure. She spoke.

How was it getting here?

Okay.

No problems?

No.

I've had people get lost because they couldn't read the English bus and street signs that we use here in America.

It's okay for me.

Esperanza reached the top of the stairs, stood in front of the woman, who continued to look her over, everything she felt, nervous insecure self-conscious, felt worse.

My name is Elizabeth Campbell. You can call me Mrs. Campbell.

Esperanza looked at the white marble floor, nodded.

Your name is?

She looked up.

Esperanza.

Have you ever cleaned a home as large as this one?

No.

Do you think you are capable of it?

Sí.

Why do you think you are capable of it?

I work hard to clean.

You understand that in my home I make the rules and you do not question them?

Sí.

Are you sure you understand me?

Sí.

Mrs. Campbell stared at her.

Why don't you come in and I'll show you the maid's quarters.

Mrs. Campbell turned and walked into the house, Esperanza followed, she carefully closed the door behind her. They walked through the foyer, which had twenty-foot ceilings and a huge crystal chandelier and oil portraits in gilded frames of Mrs. Campbell's relatives, they walked past a grand staircase that curved gently up, they walked into a small hall past a laundry room to a small door. Mrs. Campbell never looked back assumed Esperanza was behind her. She opened the door walked down a flight of stairs into a concrete reinforced basement. There were laundry machines and a sink along one wall, a mass of cleaning supplies and mops, brooms and a vacuum against another, a small cot and a wardrobe next to the supplies. Mrs. Campbell turned around, spoke.

This is your area. Like the rest of the house, I expect it to be kept spotless. The wardrobe is for your extra uniforms, which I will supply to you, and for your formal uniform, which you will wear when I have guests. The cot is for the occasions when you have to stay overnight. It doesn't happen often, but if it's required, I'll expect that you do so without complaint. If I ever find you sleeping during the day, you will be immediately terminated. You will do all of the laundry down here, though I

will expect you to continue to work on other things while you
do the laundry. I do not like loafing. I pay you to work, not
loaf.

Esperanza looked around the room. It was gray, drab and
depressing. Like the dungeon beneath a palace. Mrs. Campbell
snapped her fingers in front of her face.

Did you hear me?

Esperanza looked at her, visibly hurt.

I want to know if you understood what I said about loafing?

Esperanza nodded, hurt.

And you understood everything else?

Sí.

I doubt it, but I guess we'll see.

I understand, Mrs. Campbell.

I'll show you the rest of the house.

They walked upstairs, walked around the house, it took over
an hour, they walked to the guest house, which was larger than
most normal houses, four bedrooms and four bathrooms it
took half an hour.

When they were finished, Mrs. Campbell walked Esperanza to
the front door.

When can you start?

When you like?

Tomorrow morning?

Okay.

You'll have to press and iron one of the uniforms before you
begin, and if it doesn't fit you'll need to take it home with you
and tailor it.

Sí.

Any questions?

How much you pay me?

I will pay you three hundred and fifty dollars a week. That's
good money for someone like you.

That's not enough.

Mrs. Campbell looked shocked.

Excuse me?

The house is very big. You must pay me more.

You are not to make demands on me, young lady, do you understand me?

Esperanza nodded again, by this time, she was a wreck.

Sí.

Do you understand me?

Esperanza recoiled. Wrecked.

Sí.

She stared at Esperanza. Esperanza stared at the floor.

How much do you think you deserve?

I don't know.

You'll get four hundred. Not a penny more. If you don't like it, I'll find someone else to do it. There are plenty of people like you in this city and it won't be any trouble.

Sí.

I will see you tomorrow then. And if you're late, your first day will be your last.

Gracias.

Esperanza turned and walked away, hurried down the driveway, whatever confidence or hope she had coming into the interview was gone, she just wanted to be away, away from Elizabeth Campbell, who she knew was staring at her from the doorway.

In 1892, Edward Doheny and Charles Canfield discover oil in a friend's front yard after noticing that the wheels of his cart were always covered with a wet, black substance. Doheny immediately buys a thousand acres of land surrounding the house, just outside of what was then Los Angeles proper and what is now the Echo Park neighborhood. He starts drilling and within a year has 500 oil wells. Within two years there are 1,400 oil wells in Los Angeles County. By the early 1920s, almost a quarter of the world's oil is supplied by the wells in Los Angeles.

Dylan walks up and down Riverside Drive, which, theoretically, runs alongside the Los Angeles River. The river is a forty-foot-wide concrete ditch that carries sewage and rain overflow into the Pacific Ocean. It rains an average of thirty days a year in LA and there is usually no rain between April and November, so it isn't much of a river. Dylan walks into every gas station every bodyshop every auto-repair shop he finds on the drive he fills out applications looks for work. After three days he finds a motorcycle repair shop that's looking for someone. The owner of the shop is a member of a biker gang (though he calls it a motorcycle club) called the Mongrels, he's six foot five, 320 pounds, has a braided ponytail that hangs to his waist, is probably the scariest looking human Dylan has ever seen. The man, who calls himself Tiny, looks at him, speaks.

How good are you at fixing bikes?

I can fix anything.

My wife's a fucking pain in the ass, can you fix her?

Probably not.

How good are you at fixing bikes?

I can fix anything with an engine.

Go fix that pile of shit over there.

He points to an old Harley in the back of the shop. It's covered with rust and the engine is in pieces on the floor.

What's wrong with it?

You said you can fix anything with a fucking engine, go fucking figure it out.

Dylan walks over to the bike, Tiny walks to his office, where he picks up the phone, dials it, and starts yelling at someone. Dylan starts looking at the pieces of the engine spread across the floor. He takes off his shirt, starts handling the parts, looking closely at them, when he needs to wipe grease off his hands, he wipes them on his pants. He walks to a large battered steel tool chest, casually picks up a couple tools, walks back to the bike. He quickly puts the engine back together. He tries to start the bike, nothing. Tries again, nothing. Makes a couple of adjustments, tries again, nothing. He takes the engine apart again, organizes it on the floor. The entire process takes three hours. When he's finished, he walks over to Tiny's office. Tiny is still on the phone, still yelling. Dylan stands at the door and waits for him, when Tiny sees him, he cups the phone, yells at Dylan.

What the fuck do you want?

I figured out what's wrong with the engine.

What?

It's an unfixable piece of shit and you should throw it away.

Tiny laughs.

I've sent four other dumbasses back there to look at that thing and you're the first one with enough sense to tell me what I already knew.

So I've got the job?

Hold on.

Tiny puts the phone back to his ear, speaks.

I gotta call you back.

He waits.

No. I gotta fucking call you back.

He waits.

Listen, shit-for-fucking-brains, there's someone in my fucking office and I can't fucking talk.

He slams the phone down without waiting for a response, shakes his head, speaks.

People are fucking stupid, man. Every day I'm amazed at how fucking stupid people are.

Yeah.

You better not be fucking stupid or I'll throw you outta here on your ass.

I'm not.

We'll see. You passed my test, but I ain't convinced yet. You might still turn out to be a dumbfuck.

Dylan laughs.

Hours are nine to five. Sometimes might be earlier, sometimes might be later. Just depends. Pay is six bucks an hour, I'll pay you in cash. Ain't no benefits 'cept you get to hang around me all day.

Six bucks an hour seems a little light.

I'm paying you in cash so you ain't got no taxes, and if you don't like it, don't take the job. Sooner or later I'll find me some illegal-immigrant beaner I can pay four an hour.

I'll take it.

There you go, you passed dumbass test #2.

Dylan laughs.

One other thing, maybe the most important thing.

Yeah.

Things happen here and are said here that are private, if you understand what I'm saying. You ever talk to anyone else about 'em, and you and whoever you care about will end up in a bad situation. You try talking to me about 'em and I'll hit you in the goddamn mouth.

Understood.

Good. Now get the fuck outta here. I'll see you in the morning.

Dylan turns and leaves, walks two miles back to the motel. When he gets to the room, Maddie is gone. There's no note, no message. He walks out to the balcony looks up and down the row of rooms, tries to listen for her voice, hoping he hears her in one of the rooms, terrified that she might be in one of the rooms, which are inhabited by an alcoholic couple in their seventies, a reformed, or so he says, bank robber, a meth dealer, two aspiring porn actresses who star in teen-themed films, a guy who calls himself Andy the pimp-ass motherfucker. He walks along the row of rooms listens starts to panic he walks downstairs walks along the row of rooms on the first floor he only knows one of the residents a former rock star turned heroin addict he doesn't hear a thing anywhere. He walks into the lobby asks the man behind the desk who watches a ten-year-old sitcom on a small color TV the man shrugs and says got no idea, man, I ain't seen a thing.

Dylan walks back to the room. He opens the door leaves it open lights a cigarette wishes he had something to drink tries

to figure out what to do, call the police, go walk around, she
doesn't have any friends in LA nowhere to go no one to see he
thinks about his neighbors which one, which one, she comes to
the door, speaks.

Hi.

He looks up. She's holding a bucket of fried chicken and a
bottle of cheap champagne.

Where you've been? I've been freaking out.

She walks towards him, speaks.

I went out to find a job.

Kisses him.

And I found one.

She smiles, does a little victory dance.

Where?

99 cent store.

He laughs.

Seriously?

Yeah. I'm a cashier. I'm getting a uniform and a hat.

He laughs again.

Awesome.

Since we're gonna have some money coming in, I got us a little
surprise.

She sets the chicken and the champagne on the table. Dylan's
still sitting on the bed.

I was really worried.

I'm a big girl.

There's a bunch of crazy people in this motel.

I know. That's why—

She reaches into her pocket, pulls out a small spray cartridge.

I bought some mace at the 99 cent store. It only cost 66 cents
with my new employee discount.

He smiles. She smiles.

Come over here and eat and drink some champagne with me.

He stands, takes a couple steps over.

How'd you get champagne?

Walked into a liquor store and bought it. Guy was staring at my boobs the whole time, never even asked me for ID.

You have nice boobs.

She smiles.

If you're a good boy and you eat your dinner I might let you see them.

He sits down, grabs one of the pieces of chicken, takes a giant bite. She laughs. They eat, talk, he tells her about his job, about Tiny, she tells him to be careful, he says he'll work there until something better comes along. As they drink the champagne, they both get happy, playful, neither were big drinkers at home, neither has ever had champagne. They end up in bed feeling, exploring, playing, doing all of the things they couldn't do in the backseats of cars and under the Ping-Pong tables of friends when they lived at home. She shows him everything he wants to see, gives him whatever he wants, takes from him whatever she wants. They stay up late they go again, again, they lie in each other's arms and say I love you they're nineteen and on their own and they're in love and they still believe in the future.

Next day they start their jobs, they wake up get coffee together stop in a donut shop. He has a Boston crème and she has a maple bar they kiss and go their separate ways. Maddie walks to the store it's four blocks away. She finds the manager, whose name is Dale, he walks her back to the locker room. He's in his late thirties, tall and thin his hair is falling out, he wears a thin, patchy mustache. He opens the door for Maddie, follows her in, closes the door behind him. The room has two walls covered with rows of metal lockers, benches in front of them. Along one of the other walls there's a sink and a counter with a coffee machine and a basket of snacks on the counter. Dale speaks.

We each get a locker. You keep your uniform in it, and your clothes while you're working. Can't have no drugs or alcohol in there, and you can't have no weapons. If I find any that shit in there I'll take it and keep it. If I'm really pissed I might give it to the authorities or some such person like 'em. On breaks you

can hang out in here if you want to. I tend to get out of the
store, but some people like it in here. And there ain't no
fooling around allowed with any of the other employees, unless
it's a girl and I get to watch, or it's me.

He smiles. Maddie speaks.

That a joke?

He laughs.

Sure is, little sister. Or maybe not. That's for you to decide.

He laughs again, a bit louder.

Do you have my uniform?

Sure do. It's in my office. I'll go get it for you. You can choose
a locker while I'm gone.

He leaves. She looks at the lockers, looks at the ones without
locks on them, opens one of them there's a pile of dirty socks
in it, she shuts it immediately. She opens another there's a bag
of half-eaten potato chips and an army of ants she shuts it. She
opens two more both empty but they don't feel right to her she
looks for one in a corner away from most of the locks. She
finds one, opens it, there's nothing in it. She stares at it, puts
her head inside of it, smells it. The door opens, Dale walks in
with a 99-cent-store shirt and visor, which are red, yellow and
orange with black 99s printed all over them. He speaks.

How's it smell?

She pulls her head out, blushes with embarrassment.

Okay.

You like smelling things?

Not really.

Here's your uniform.

He hands her the shirt and visor.

Thank you.

We prefer you wear white pants with it. Makes them colors
really pop.

Okay.

You got any?

No.

Get 'em with your first paycheck. And get some white panties too. If you don't, people be able to see what color you're wearing through your pants.

She blushes again, speaks.

Do you have a lock I can use?

Nope, but you can buy one. Guess how much it costs?

Don't know.

Ninety-nine cents.

He laughs, turns around, walks out. Maddie puts on the shirt and the visor, walks to his office. He shows her to an aisle, sets her up behind a cash register. It's the same model as the one she used at the gas station at home, so she knows how to use it. She spends the day ringing up cans of soup, ramen noodles, packages of candy, small plastic toys, soap shampoo and toothpaste, batteries. She tries to smile at every customer, make everyone feel better as they leave than they did before they checked out with her. By the end of her shift, she's exhausted, her feet hurt, her fingers hurt, her eyes, her mouth hurts. She punches out walks home. She picks up a bag of tacos on her way, watches TV while she waits for Dylan. She watches a daily entertainment show, it's about the private lives of celebrities, about their love lives, their parties, the houses they live in and the clothes they wear and the cars they drive. The show is produced a couple miles away, the celebrities live on the other side of the hill. She looks around her room, at the dirty walls, the shitty furniture, the bed she would never touch if she didn't have to, the stained carpet, she walks to the window draws the curtain sees two men in the parking lot yelling at each other, a woman stands between them she's crying and one of her eyes is swollen black. Maddie turns back to the television. A singer is buying a diamond watch in Beverly Hills. It's on the other side of the earth.

Dylan comes home he's covered in oil and grease he kisses her takes a shower. They eat their tacos, watch TV, fall into bed fall into each other they go to sleep two hours later sleep easily, deeply. They wake up and walk to the donut shop together. He has a Boston crème, she has a maple bar.

Their life falls into a routine. They work, eat dinner watch TV, get into bed and play, fall asleep, do it day after day, day after day. They don't enjoy their jobs, but they don't hate them. Maddie learns to ignore Dale, who hits on every woman in the store every chance he gets, Dylan does what he's told, speaks when spoken to, minds his own business. In his spare time, Dylan works on the old Harley in the corner, he scavenges parts, fixes others, he has it running in a couple months. He starts driving Maddie to work in the morning, picking her up at the end of the day. At night they go for long rides in the Hills, through the twisting ups and downs of small compact streets packed with cars, houses built into the rock houses on stilts houses built on top of each other the smallest of them probably costs a million dollars the largest ten or twenty. They ride along Mulholland Drive, a two-lane road that runs for twenty-one miles along the ridge of the Hollywood Hills and the Santa Monica Mountains. They pull into viewing vistas at different points along the drive, the vistas face east, west, north and south to the west they see the distant blue of the Pacific to the east north and south they see the endless sprawl of lights and cars and houses and people it stretches to the horizon lines the sprawl, it's terrible and beautiful the sprawl. They ride through Bel-Air and Beverly Hills. They move slowly along wooded, guarded streets they stare at the mansions try to imagine what it's like to live in one of them to have that kind of money. They ride along the Pacific Coast Highway they take off their helmets and scream at 100 mph with their heads back and their eyes open they're free and on their own and it's cold and dark and the wind is in their faces and they're in love and they still dream, still dream.

When they're at the motel they stay in their room, avoid the other residents. The bank robber leaves is replaced by a man convicted of manslaughter who leaves replaced by a rapist, the drug dealers are replaced by other drug dealers, there are fights in the parking lot almost every night, they hear screaming and crying coming from the rooms at night, in the morning, at all hours, screaming and crying. They try to save money. They want to move somewhere cleaner, safer. Most of what they make gets swallowed up by rent and food but they scrape, most of their meals come from the 99 cent store, they don't buy any new clothing. After two months they have $160 after four months they have $240. Maddie gets food poisoning from a fast-food restaurant they go to the emergency room, when they pay the bill they have nothing. The rapist leaves replaced by a child molester. Andy the pimp-ass motherfucker threatens to kill the child molester. The child molester leaves replaced by another rapist.

The Los Angeles Parks Department is created in 1889. At the time, there were no official city parks, though there were five pieces of land designated for the potential development of parks. In 1896, Colonel Griffith J. Griffith, a Welsh military officer who made a fortune in the California Gold Rush, donated over 3,000 acres of land in the hills above his Los Feliz Rancho to be used as a city park. The city purchased additional acreage to bring the total size of the park to 4,210 acres, or just over five square miles.

At any given time, there are between 100 and 300 homeless men and women living in the area of and surrounding the Venice Beach boardwalk. The population drops in the summer when there are swarms of tourists and police looking to promote a clean, safe image of the city and the weather is pleasant enough to live in other parts of the country. It rises in the winter when the sun is still shining and it's still warm and it's possible to sleep outside and there are still enough tourists to eke out an existence.

For twenty-five years, most of the homeless lived in the Venice Pavilion. The pavilion was an arts and recreation center housed in several buildings spread over two acres of beachfront property. It was built in 1960 and abandoned in 1974, when the plumbing, electrical and heating systems all failed due to poor construction. As soon as it was abandoned, the homeless moved in and took over. They built their own society within the fenced borders of the property. Alcoholics and different types of addicts, crack, heroin, and in the '90s meth, lived in different sections, buildings or rooms, and the various groups constantly warred with each other, stole from each other, and plotted against one another. Rapes, of both men and women, were common. Stabbings and beatings were a daily occurrence. It was one of the most violent communities in the country. At a certain point the LAPD stopped patrolling the pavilion and gave up trying to control what happened within it, their goal became containing it and not allowing its violence to spread. When the pavilion was leveled in the late '90s, during the renovation of the boardwalk, the residents scattered. Some took cover along the boardwalk itself. Some moved to Skid Row in downtown Los Angeles, a 10,000-person, fifty-square-block mini-city of cardboard box encampments and scrap-metal fortresses, which has a similar level of violence and depravity. Those that stayed started setting up boundaries and rules. The general division was that drug addicts and young alcoholics stayed on the northern end of the boardwalk, the older and mellower homeless, some alcoholic and some not, lived on the southern end. The community on the northern end was far more dangerous and violent, most of the residents of the southern end were content to live as quietly and peacefully as they could.

Old Man Joe is one of the pillars of the south end. Though he is only thirty-eight, because he looks like he's in his late seventies, and because of his heightened status as the resident of the bathroom, he is considered a wise and benevolent old-timer, someone who helps keep his section of the boardwalk, or at least the homeless community that lives around it, in order. Once or twice a month he mediates a dispute over a bench or a dumpster, helps settle issues of theft and violence, helps decide the punishments for such offenses. Because the police more or less ignore the homeless, the residents of the south end have their own system of justice. When one of them is found guilty of something, they're forced to either pay restitution, or compensate their victim by giving up a prime sleeping, eating or begging spot. If someone refuses to abide by the punishment, they are driven out. In the south it is understood that if the residents work together, and police themselves, and help each other, their lives, which can be grim and depressing, will be slightly better.

On the north end there is no such system, no sense of community. It is survival of the most brutal, most heartless, most fucked-in-the-head. Theft, rape and violence are still common. Disputes are settled with fists, knives, bricks and broken bottles. Women are considered property and are bought, sold and traded, newcomers are immediately sized up, and if considered vulnerable, attacked and abused. Because many of the homeless on the north end of the boardwalk look threatening and behave in menacing ways, tourists are much more reluctant to give them money or food. Their inability to make money panhandling or begging further fuels the violence and lawlessness of their culture. They do what they need to do to get money or get high or get sex, it doesn't matter what it is or who it hurts. They do what they need to do.

There is little or no interaction between the homeless residents of the north and south ends of the boardwalk. They are aware of each other, but choose to ignore each other. Aside from panhandling and occasional harassment, which is quickly and forcefully dealt with by the LAPD, there is little or no interaction between the homeless and the tourists who swarm the boardwalk every day of the year (between 50,000 and 250,000 depending on the season). Residents of greater Venice, parts of which contain movie stars and rock stars and their million- and multimillion-dollar homes, and parts of which contain gangs and crack-infested ghettos, generally ignore the boardwalk. Many of them live in Venice because the pace of life, even in the dangerous sections, is slower than the rest of the city, mellower. And unlike most of the rest of the city, people in Venice talk to their neighbors, walk through their neighborhoods, to their local stores, restaurants, schools and churches. The boardwalk is loud, crowded, dirty, parking is a nightmare, it smells like fifty types of food, almost all of them fried. It is a world unto itself, and the homeless population is a world within that world.

It's dawn and Old Man Joe is awake on the beach he's staring at the sky slowly turning blue, it's slowly turning blue. He came this morning with the hope that he would learn why, why but he hasn't learned anything it is as it is every morning he's learned nothing. It's already warm somewhere in the mid-70s. The sand is cold against the exposed areas of his skin, his hands, ankles, neck, the back of his head. There is a light breeze. The air is wet and clean and it smells like salt and tastes like the ocean he takes deep, slow breaths, holds them, exhales, takes another. He hears someone walking towards him he doesn't move they're closer doesn't move voice.

Joe.

Yeah.

I need your help.

Who's that?

Tom?

Six Toe Tom?

No, Ugly Tom.

What's up, Ugly?

I need your help.

Can it wait?

Don't think so.

What's wrong?

There's a problem behind the dumpster behind the ice cream store.

Which ice cream store?

The one next to Sausage Paradise.

What's the problem?

There's a girl passed out. Looks like she got the shit kicked out of her.

Call the cops.

I got warrants. I can't call the cops.

Have someone else call 'em.

That's why I came to get you.

I'm busy.

You're just lying there.

Yeah, I'm busy.

This girl is fucked up, man. You gotta help her.

Old Man Joe turns his head, looks back at Ugly Tom, who is indeed ugly. He's tall, though his legs are fairly short, he has patches of stringy gray hair. Three of his front teeth are gone, the rest are a deep yellow or brown, pockmark scars cover his face and neck. He is originally from Seattle, where he grew up in foster homes until he ran away at sixteen, drifted down the coast to LA. He's been on the street for two decades. He lives in the corner of a parking lot near Muscle Beach, sleeps in a sleeping bag, keeps his clothes at the bottom of it.

I guess you're not going to leave until I agree to come with you.

Nope.

Joe sits up.

There wasn't anyone else around?

Everyone else is still sleeping.

What if I was still sleeping?

You wouldn't be.

I might.

Come on, Old Man. Everyone knows you're down here every morning staring at shit.

Joe laughs, stands.

You think I stare at shit?

I don't know what the fuck you stare at.

He laughs again. They walk towards the strip of buildings that house Sausage Paradise, the ice cream shop, a bikini shop, a tattoo parlor, and three T-shirt shops. The buildings, like most along the boardwalk, are three or four floors high and were built side-by-side in the '60s and early '70s. The shops are on the first floor, there are apartments above the shops, some of the buildings have roof decks where the residents, almost always male, sit and drink and call down to female tourists and try to get them to wave, come up for a beer, take off their shirts.

Joe and Tom walk to the back of the buildings, start walking down Speedway Avenue, a glorified alley that runs parallel to and directly behind the entire length of the boardwalk. Speedway is lined with dumpsters, overflow from the dumpsters, single and double parking spots that usually belong to the shops or restaurants in the buildings. Many of the homeless, on both ends of the boardwalk, live on Speedway, they sleep there, eat there, buy and sell drugs there, get drunk there. Film crews often use it to shoot scenes that are supposed to take place in decrepit neighborhoods. On the side opposite the boardwalk, Speedway is lined with walk-streets, which are residential lanes with double-sized sidewalks instead of actual streets, there are no cars, the streets are lined with palm trees, wild hydrangea and multimillion-dollar homes, the residents, many of whom are artists, writers, actors and musicians, tend to avoid crossing over if they can help it. Joe and Tom stop in front of a large, battered brown dumpster. It doesn't have a lid.

It reeks of sour milk, and the remnants of old ice cream, now congealed into something resembling white and brown glue, streak its sides. Joe speaks.

Man, this is one foul-ass dumpster.

It's 'cause all the old rotten ice cream gets baked by the sun.

That's nasty.

Yeah.

Where's the girl?

Back behind there.

How'd you find her?

Sometimes I go in there and see if there's any good ice cream.

That's disgusting.

It's good sometimes.

You're gonna get sick sometime.

I got bigger worries than getting sick from ice cream.

Joe starts to step around the dumpster, sees a pool of blood, stops, takes a deep breath shakes his head. He steps all the way around the dumpster. There's a small teenage girl lying facedown in a heap. She's wearing ratty black jeans and a black T-shirt, her hair is blond streaked red with blood. Joe wonders if she's even alive. He steps closer, sees her chest rise slightly, he crouches down next to her stares at her for a moment. He can see the edge of one side of her face. What he sees is covered in dried, cracked blood, beneath the blood it's deep blue and purple. Joe turns around looks at Ugly Tom, speaks.

She's hurt bad.

I know. I found her.

She was just like this?

I don't know. I guess so.

She move at all?

Maybe a little.

Joe turns back to the girl. He puts his hand on her shoulder. He quietly speaks.

Young lady?

Nothing. He gently shakes her.

Young lady?

Nothing. He looks carefully at her hands, they're caked with
dirt, there is grit under her nails. He turns back to Ugly Tom.
What do you think we should do?
If I knew I wouldn't have come and got you.
She looks like a street kid. She's got street hands.
That's what I thought too.
There's a lot of them street kids around the boardwalk.
Not down here, though. They don't belong down here.
Ain't nothing we can control.
They always cause problems when they come down here.
Life's all about problems.
Yeah, I know. That's why I drink and live in a sleeping bag.
Joe nods, turns back to the girl, stares at her. She breathes
slowly, doesn't move. Her hair is streaked with red. The blood
on her face is dried and caked. He looks up at Tom.
You got any money on you?
Why?
I want you to go to the liquor store and buy me a bottle of
cheap Chablis.
I ain't got no money.
You know where I hide my extra bottles.
No.
If I tell you, and bottles start disappearing, I'll know it's you.
I don't like Chablis.
If it's got alcohol in it, you like it.
Yeah, you're right about that. But the only thing I like less than
Chablis is mouthwash.
You ain't got no taste.
Chablis ain't got no charge. I drink 'cause I need to get fucked
up. Chablis just ain't got no charge.
Go get me a bottle. I got two or three in the toilet tank in my
bathroom.
Just one?
Yeah, just one.
Okay.
Here's the key. Lock up when you leave.

Joe reaches into his pocket and hands Tom the key.

You mind if I use the toilet? I ain't used one in a while.

Where you go?

Usually just walk into the water.

Yeah, go ahead and use the toilet.

Thanks.

Ugly Tom walks away. Old Man Joe moves so he is sitting next to the girl, his back against the wall of the building. He looks up, stares at the sky, the sun is up completely, the sky is a perfect infinite blue. Joe stares, breathes, waits.

Thirty minutes later Ugly Tom comes back, gives Joe his key his bottle he heads back to his sleeping bag in the corner of the parking lot. Joe opens the bottle, smells the wine, takes a sip, holds it in and savors it, holds it until his mouth is saturated with its taste, swallows it. The girl hasn't moved. She lies on the concrete, her chest slowly rising, slowly falling. He drinks. He stares. The sky is blue and it's warm and bright and getting warmer and brighter. He waits.

In 1901, the first major wave of approximately 1,000 Japanese immigrants arrives in Los Angeles. They set up a community downtown, adjacent to Chinatown. At this point, each of the city's major ethnic groups, black, white, Mexican, Chinese and Japanese, has its own separate and distinct community. There is little or no mixing between the communities. What interactions there are often result in violence.

Sometimes she had money, sometimes she didn't. Sometimes she earned it, more often it was given to her she usually didn't know why.

She had known love.

Her heart had been broken.

She had lived on three continents six countries seventeen cities twenty-seven apartments, she didn't have a home, no home, no home.

Depression, self-hatred, fear they were all her friends.

Sometimes she slept for sixteen hours a day, sometimes not at all.

She ate steak rare, chicken fried, drank smoked ingested.

She drove fast in the rain, slow in the sun.

Security and peace came to her in brief fleeting moments. She never knew when or why she would stop regardless of where she was or what she was doing, she would stop and breathe slowly and deeply, stop and slowly and deeply breathe, experience security, experience peace.

She always sought ecstasy. Beneath women, men, on top of them in front of them inside of them inside of her. It was always physical. She heard there was more, some sought, she had heard, there was more, she had heard.

***

She didn't want to go. Another party in LA full of clothes and jewelry and irony and desperation. Her friend called six times before noon, said please come please come, I don't want to go alone please come. Her friend wanted to meet a producer or a director or an actor anyone with money and fame, take him to the bathroom and fuck him, move in with him and fuck him, leave him and sue him and fuck him. She had been trying for four years, had been to hundreds of parties, had seen plenty of porcelain, a couple big houses, not much else.

She calls again. Again. Again. She calls again.

Hello?

Please come.

Why?
I need you there.
No you don't.
I do.
Why?
Because I do.
It'll be the same as every other one. I'm sick of them.
It won't.
It will.
For half an hour. If you hate it you can leave.
I'm gonna hate it.
You won't.
I will.

***

In 1996 the drive would have taken fifteen minutes. In 2005 it
takes an hour. They move slowly past fast-food restaurants,
strip malls, auto-body shops. Her friend drives and smokes and
talks she never stops talking. The Hills loom over them on one
side. The Flatlands stretch endlessly away on the other. It's hot.
The air-conditioning is on high. She stares out the window.
The sidewalks are empty, as they always are, the sky is blue, as
it always is. Her friend keeps talking.

***

She's sitting on a couch in the backyard. Three men have
offered her their phone number, one offered to take pictures of
her, everyone she's met has asked what she does for a living.
She's drinking, trying to decide whether she's going to get
drunk, or how drunk, she thinks about doing some coke she
knows it's around.
Hi.
She looks up. Tall thin dark hair dark eyes. Pants too low,
purposely battered tennis shoes, a loose black T-shirt.
Hi.
You doing well?

Sure.
You don't remember me.
No.
He smiles. She looks at him. Nothing.
Do I know you?
Yes.
How.
He's still smiling. He turns and walks away.

***

She watches him. He flirts with other women. He laughs with
his two friends, one of whom is drinking, the other smoking
weed. He eats four cheeseburgers. He drinks domestic beer in a
can. He knows she's watching him. It doesn't seem to affect
him. She's trying to figure out where, when, if he's full of shit,
if she slept with him. She watches him. He flirts with other
women and laughs with his friends.

***

It's dark. She's on her fourth drink. She's inside the house,
sitting on a La-Z-Boy, which she has fully reclined. There is
another La-Z-Boy next to her, a nicer one, full black leather
with cupholders, a built-in television remote, shoulder and
lumbar massage systems. He sits down in it, twirls it in a half
circle so he is facing her. He speaks.
You lived in Indianapolis.
You from there?
Nope. You also lived in Barcelona.
I know you're not Spanish.
And you lived in Boston and Atlanta.
No accent, so you're not from either of those shitholes.
I'm from Albany.
Albany?
Where you went to school in first, second, eighth and ninth
grades.
I went to an all-girls school.

With my sister. I was a year older, I went to the boys' school.
Your sister's name?
He smiles again, gets up, walks away.

***

Her friend wants to leave. She wants to stay. Her friend says
there's another party. She tells her friend to go without her.
He plays Ping-Pong in the backyard. She watches him through
a sliding glass door. He plays well, has a nice spinning serve.
He knows she's watching him.
He leaves the table even though he hasn't lost. He walks inside.
She watches him, he smiles at her. She's sitting at a table with a
group of people she doesn't know. They're talking about agents
and auditions, friends who have become famous and forgotten
them. He stops in front of her.
Come out front with me.
Why?
Because I want you to.
Why?
He smiles takes her hand. He guides her from the chair. He
leads her to the door and opens it and they walk outside.

***

They have been standing beneath a light in front of the door
for twenty minutes. When they got outside he turned to her
and put his hands on her waist and leaned towards her and
gently kissed her. She didn't resist, couldn't resist, he felt right,
smelled right, tasted right. They kiss, their mouths slowly
opening, exploring, their hands slowly moving, their bodies
tense and relaxed, their bodies becoming closer, closer, closer.

In 1873, the city's first newspaper, the *Los Angeles Daily Herald*, opens. Despite best efforts, it is actually only published a couple times a week. In 1890 it goes bankrupt and closes. Several months later it starts again, publishing as the *Los Angeles Herald*.

They met when they were eleven. Both were in fifth grade, both had just moved to Inglewood, they started school on the same day. He came from Watts and she came from Long Beach. Their mothers, both raising their children alone, moved to find, if only slightly, better schools and safer neighborhoods. There were jobs in Inglewood, many of them at the Forum, the stadium where the Lakers and Kings played and which has since become a massive church, and Hollywood Park, a racetrack adjacent to the Forum, where middle-class gamblers came to watch the ponies, place bets and get drunk.

LaShawn was giant for his age, very tall and very heavy. His skin was extremely dark, and he could be, to teachers and other students, extremely imposing. People often assumed he was older than he was and that, because of his size, he had been held back in school. In reality, he was exceedingly intelligent, spent most of his free time reading, and was extremely gentle. His mother had taught him that with his size came a responsibility to be kind. LaShawn always listened to his mother.

Anika was his opposite, small and delicate, almost frail. She had skin the color of milk chocolate, pale green eyes, one of which occasionally drifted, she wore her hair in long, thin braids, which she usually kept in a ponytail. She was happy and outgoing, talkative and articulate, people often commented positively on her charm and intelligence. She was always the first to raise her hand in class, always offered to help students having trouble or lead them in group activities. While boys and other teachers adored her, some girls felt intimidated by her or jealous of her. They called her names, sent her nasty notes, bullied her when she was alone with them. Her mother had warned her that this would probably happen to her, and she told her to do her best to ignore people who mistreated her, and to, as Jesus said, turn the other cheek. Anika always obeyed her mother, and she always obeyed Jesus.

They became friends during lunch. LaShawn always sat alone the other children were too intimidated to sit with him. Each

day as he ate, he would hum, or sometimes quietly sing, songs
and hymns he had learned at home or at church. His voice was
soft and on the high side, he sounded younger and smaller than
he actually was. When she first heard him, Anika was
surprised. She had been scared of LaShawn, even though he'd
done nothing to scare her. As she listened more, she became
enchanted, almost dependent. She started sitting at the table
next to him so she could listen to him, if the table wasn't
available she'd find another near enough to hear him. When he
wasn't in school, which was rare, she became agitated,
annoyed, anxious. She'd wonder where he was what he was
doing she'd worry, get scared. One day, several months after
she first started listening to him, he sat down, started eating,
didn't hum, didn't sing, didn't make a sound. Anika wondered
what was wrong. He had a book with him he ate his sandwich,
drank a juice box, turned the pages. She stared at him, he
seemed oblivious to her. She stood up walked over to his table
stood next to him. She stood for a moment, two, three, he
looked up, smiled, spoke.

Hi.
She spoke.
Are you okay?
He nodded.
I'm good. You?
I guess. Why aren't you singing?
I'm reading a book.
But you always sing.
Not today.
Why?
Because.
Because why?
Just because.
You can't answer me that way.
Yes I can.
Just tell me why you aren't singing.
Because I wanted to see if you'd notice.

Stop playing.

I'm not playing.

Yes you are.

I'm not.

How you even know I listen to your singing?

I ain't no fool. I see you sitting near me every day.

That's just coincidence.

No, it ain't.

Yes it is.

Then why you standing here asking me about it?

'Cause.

'Cause why?

'Cause I feel like it.

Yeah, right.

He turned back to his book. She stood there. He took a bite of his sandwich, turned the page. She put her hand on her hip. He took another bite, kept reading. She spoke.

Fine.

He kept reading. She spoke again.

I said fine.

Kept reading. Again.

I said fine.

Reading. Again.

FINE. FINE FINE FINE.

He looked up.

Fine what?

Fine, boy, I like your damn singing.

He smiled.

If you want to hear it, you can sit here with me. If you don't sit here with me, I won't do it.

She turned, walked to her old table, picked up her lunch tray, walked back, sat down, spoke.

Okay, get to it.

He spoke.

Not till tomorrow. Today we'll just see if we like each other.

Stop playing.

My momma tells me you got to work for what you want in life. I'm gonna make you work.

Your momma also shoulda told you if you wanna have a good life, you gotta give women what they want or they'll drive you crazy.

He laughed, set his book down, started humming. She sat quietly and listened and it became a ritual day after day they sat together at lunch and he hummed and sang and she sat with him and listened. Their relationship did not initially extend beyond the edges of their lunch table. If they saw each other in the halls they did not speak. When they happened to share classes, they sat on opposite sides of the room. On the school bus home, Anika sat in the back with the cool kids, LaShawn sat alone in the front. Other children asked Anika why she ate with LaShawn at first she said it was because she didn't think he should eat alone, later because she thought he was nice. The children thought she was crazy, they were all still scared of him. He seemed bigger every day. He was bigger every day.

Several months after they started sitting together, they ran into each other at the grocery store. They were doing their Saturday morning shopping with their mothers, they turned on to the canned foods aisle at the same time, started walking directly towards each other, their mothers were behind them. As they neared each other, they started smiling, Anika started giggling LaShawn started humming. Something happened, it happened inside both of them, and they knew, without a shred of doubt, without any reservations and without any suspicion, they knew. From that point forward they started spending most of their time together. They shared a seat on the bus, walked side by side through the hallways at school, kept their lunch tradition, spent their afternoons at each other's houses, alternating every other week, they spent their nights on the phone for hours and hours they could talk about anything everything nothing they spent their nights on the phone.

Their mothers, both of whom watched their children carefully, approved of the friendship, though both stressed, due to the fact that they had each gotten pregnant as teenagers, that it shouldn't get physical, or if it did, it shouldn't go beyond holding hands and kissing. The mothers also became friends, both had grown up in dangerous low-income neighborhoods, both had had their children before they were out of high school, both had been abandoned by the children's fathers. When they weren't working, they sometimes spent weekends together, took the kids to the beach, the mall, to dinner and a movie, they took them into different parts of the city, some wealthy some poor some in the middle, so that they could see the world beyond Inglewood.

As they moved through school, they both had to deal with the temptations of drugs, gangs (many of which actively recruited LaShawn because of his size), had to fight against the idea that being good students and good citizens was somehow uncool. LaShawn started playing football, and because of his size, in tenth grade he was six foot six and weighed 300 pounds, in the twelfth he was six foot nine and weighed 360 pounds, and because of his strength and intelligence, he quickly became a star. Anika focused more on her studies, but was also a cheerleader. They both ran for and won positions in their school's government, on Sundays they taught classes at their respective church's Bible schools. Despite their love for each other, and their clear commitment to each other, they never moved beyond holding hands and kissing. They believed they had a lifetime, and there would be plenty of time.

As they neared the end of high school, they started seriously planning their future. Both had received multiple scholarship offers, LaShawn's were athletic, Anika's were academic. They wanted to go to school together, and if possible stay in Los Angeles, near their mothers and near their community. Having grown up during the Crack Age, and having witnessed the drug ravage Inglewood and many of the communities around it, through both addiction and violence, some of it gang-related and some not, Anika decided she wanted to study a subject that would allow her to come back and make their home a better and safer place. LaShawn wanted to use college as a springboard to the NFL, where he believed he could make enough money to guarantee them some form of financial security.

They decided to go to the University of Southern California, a highly regarded private school with 30,000 students located a couple miles southwest of downtown LA. It's a beautiful school, with neoclassical buildings and palm-lined walkways, surrounded by tough, low-income neighborhoods where most of the residents have income levels lower than the school's annual tuition. Anika enrolled in a pre-med program, LaShawn started going to the weight room. With one of the best football teams in the country, he believed if he continued to get bigger, he would stand out enough to get the attention he needed to play pro. After his first year he was on the starting offensive team, Anika was on the dean's list. Because most of the rest of the pre-med students had gone to more prestigious and more academically inclined high schools, Anika had to work hard to catch up to them, and work harder to keep up with them. Though he didn't get paid, and was also required to attend class, LaShawn spent all of his time working out and practicing. Between them, there was little or no time for anything but studying and football. Once a month they went on a date together, usually a walk through campus, a free movie at the school theater, dinner at an off-campus restaurant. The morning after the date, they woke up and went back to their routines.

During the summers, both went back to their mothers' homes. Anika volunteered at a local hospital, LaShawn trained for the upcoming football season. During the summer before his senior year, in which he was expected to be an All-American offensive tackle and enter the NFL draft, he got into a car accident while returning home from the local high school's track. A car full of gangbangers fleeing the scene of a drive-by ran a red light and slammed into the side of his car at sixty miles per hour. Both cars were decimated and three of the four gangsters died. LaShawn broke eight ribs and both of his legs, suffering a compound fracture of his right femur. Anika was at the hospital when an ambulance brought him into the emergency room. He was screaming and bawling, there were bones protruding from the meat of his thigh.

It took four surgeries to put his legs back together. His football career was over. Doctors were worried that because of his enormous size, and the weakened condition of his legs, even when healed, they would not be able to support his weight, and he would be unable to walk. He was transferred to the USC hospital for further treatment and to begin rehab, which, despite the fact that he would never play again, the school agreed to cover for him. It was a slow and grueling process. It took three months for the swelling to subside. The pain was excruciating, and he became physically dependent on painkillers, which he needed to take in enormous doses for them to have any effect. He dropped out of school, and because he had been so focused on football, wasn't sure what, if anything, he would do when it was time to go back. Anika spent all of her free time in his room, often slept in a chair next to his bed, studied while he slept, while he was at rehab. When he started detoxing from the painkillers, she stayed at his side, putting cold compresses on his forehead, holding his quivering hands, helping to clean the vomit from his clothes and sheets, comforting him when he started to scream. When the detox was over, the rage and depression arrived. He had had a huge career ahead of him, one in which he would have played in front of packed stadiums and made millions of dollars. It was gone, no chance of returning. All of his dreams were shattered, all of his hopes destroyed, all of his hard work wrecked by a car full of the people he had spent his life trying to avoid. He might not ever walk again, and he wanted to die, and when he didn't want to die, he wanted to kill someone. The year was long, brutal, Anika thought of walking away there were so many times she couldn't imagine going back to

LaShawn's room, even though it broke her heart every time she walked through the door she went anyway. He was reduced physically and mentally, lost over a hundred pounds, didn't recognize himself when he looked in the mirror, he said his confidence was gone, his sense of self-worth was gone. She did what she could to bolster his spirits, told him she loved him every time she arrived and every time she left, told him he would be okay, he just needed to believe, he would be okay. She knew she couldn't do anything more. He would have to do everything else on his own.

A break came in rehab, he was trying to bend his knee couldn't do it, he started bitching, whining and complaining. A few feet away, a former gang member, a man who had been shot in the spine and would never walk again, told him to shut the fuck up and quit being a bitch. LaShawn was shocked. The man said he knew who LaShawn was, that they were from the same neighborhood, that he had watched him play football since he was a kid. He said LaShawn was being weak, that whatever had happened, there are worse things in life than not having money and fame and the rest of the bullshit LaShawn was crying about, that he should be thankful he could still use his legs, still had Anika, still had an opportunity to finish his education, still had a chance at life beyond gangs, drugs and violence, which was more than many of the people in their neighborhood had, or would ever have.

Two months later he got out of the hospital and he was walking, though he couldn't go for more than a hundred yards or so. He attended Anika's graduation, she finished in four years with honors. The day after graduation, with a ring bought using borrowed money, he got down on one knee and proposed. A month later, at a Baptist church in Inglewood, they were married. They didn't have money for a honeymoon, but a wealthy USC alumnus, who also happened to be a huge football fan, offered them his beach house in Malibu for a week. After years of neglecting each other's bodies, they spent most of that week in bed.

Anika started USC Medical School in the fall. LaShawn went back to get his degree in education. To supplement their income, and make medical school possible, Anika worked as a graduate assistant in undergraduate courses, and LaShawn worked for the football team. Days were long and grueling, they were in class, studying or teaching for eighteen hours, they slept the other six, they were always tired, always tired. At the end of Anika's second year of medical school, and just before LaShawn graduated with his education degree, Anika got pregnant. They were surprised because, when they did have time to be intimate with each other, they thought they were being careful.

Both were thrilled, as were their mothers, who volunteered to watch the baby while Anika was in school. LaShawn, who had stopped singing and humming when he started playing football, started again, he would lay his head next to Anika's belly and softly serenade their unborn child. Anika joked that the child needed to have more of her genes than LaShawn's because a baby resembling him would never make it out of her body. Friends, fellow students and coworkers pooled cash and helped them get a crib, a nursing chair, a changing table, they moved to a cheaper, but larger, apartment and LaShawn painted one of the rooms yellow, pink and blue.

The baby was born in February, it was a girl, small and light like Anika. LaShawn cried the first time he held her, she was ten minutes old, he held her against his chest and his hands shook and his limbs trembled and he cried. They named her Keisha. She went home with her parents three days after she was born. Anika took a week off from school during which she still studied, still kept up on her reading, still graded papers for her undergraduate teaching assignment.

Anika is almost done with school, when she finishes she wants to do her residency somewhere in Los Angeles. LaShawn is doing duty as the largest stay-at-home father in California, he can still hold his daughter in the palm of one of his hands. When the residency is over, they're going to move back to

Inglewood, and at some point LaShawn wants to try to get a job teaching and coaching football at his former high school. He walks with a limp, and always will, every now and then someone recognizes him and asks for an autograph, which he loves and hates at the same time. Anika is going to train to be an ob-gyn, she wants to treat young single black women, help them live productive lives and raise productive children. Once a month the two of them go on a date, a walk, a movie and dinner. At least once a week they work on adding to the size of their family. They go to church with their mothers on Sundays. They thank God for the life they have together. They offer thanks for the dreams that have come true, they try to understand the ones that haven't, they pray for those they still have, the ones they think about at night, while they lie in bed together, their daughter asleep a few feet away.

In 1886, while on their honeymoon, Hobart Johnstone Whitley and Margaret Virginia Whitley decide to name their country home Hollywood. The home is built outside of Los Angeles, near the Cahuenga Pass. As more people start settling in the area around their home, Whitley, who had founded more than 100 separate townships around the country, buys large chunks of land and incorporates the entire area as the city of Hollywood. He later builds the Hollywood Hotel and sells all of his land to developers.

Jack and Dan sit at a bar in Culver City, a lower-middle-class, mixed-race community east of the beach, south of Beverly Hills, and west of Los Angeles proper, that is dominated by Sony Studios, formerly MGM Studios, which is set almost precisely in the middle of it, and huge numbers of hamburger restaurants, furniture stores and condo buildings built in the '60s and '70s. Jack and Dan are both in their early thirties. Jack is a counselor at a low-income public high school, Dan is a lawyer for the ACLU and works for the Democratic Party of Greater Los Angeles. They both grew up in the neighborhood, have been friends their entire lives, went to elementary, middle and high school together, went to college together at Cal State LA . Both are from lower-middle-class families and had to work their way through school, Jack in one of the college's cafeterias, Dan on a maintenance crew. When they finished, they got an apartment together, a two bedroom in a rundown condo building squeezed between a used car lot and a mini-mall. They have been living in the apartment for the last six years. Until of one them gets married, which will not be any time soon, they will continue to live there.

They come to the bar most nights. Sit and watch baseball or basketball and nurse beers. They check out whatever women are in the bar, sometimes they approach them, occasionally one of them gets into bed with one of the women. Both are good-looking men. Jack is tall and lithe he has blue eyes and black hair. Dan is slightly shorter, heavier because he lifts weights three times a week, has short black hair, brown eyes and creme-colored skin, his father was black his mother white. Neither of them has ever had trouble attracting women. Together it's fairly easy.

It's a quiet night. The bar is almost empty, the Lakers are on TV they're getting trounced by the Cavs. Both Jack and Dan are tired. Though the real-estate boom of the early twenty-first century affected Culver City in a positive way, and improved the level of student at his school, Jack still spends a large chunk of his time trying to keep order in the halls and common spaces of the school. Today he broke up three fights, one between Hispanic students and white students, one between Asian students and a group of black, white and Hispanic students, one between black students and Arab students. Dan spent the day in court fighting for the rights of illegal aliens. Jack speaks.

They should win tonight. For us. To make up for our shitty day.

Dan speaks.

I doubt they see it that way.

They should. We're their real fans, their base. Those movie-star motherfuckers who sit courtside are fair-weather. They just go to the games to get their picture taken.

They can pay for the tickets, though. We can't.

That's why they should win for us. The working man. The middle class.

You really think they care? They make millions every year. They could give a shit.

They used to care.

When?

When Magic played.

Those days are long gone.

They were good when they lasted.

But they are long fucking gone.

I wish I could have played basketball.

A white dude that's barely six feet tall? Playing for the Lakers?

Maybe if you grew up in Indiana. Here they wouldn't let you even try out for the high school team.

I tried out.

What happened.

I got cut at the end of the first day.

They both laugh. The door of the bar opens. An attractive blonde woman in her early 40s walks in, Dan glances at her in the mirror behind the bar. He starts to say something to Jack, looks back into the mirror, watches the woman walk to a table in the corner and sit down. He turns around, gets a better look, turns back to Jack, speaks.

That's Susanne Carter?

So what.

You know who she is?

Middle-aged blonde who was smoking hot nine years ago and is doing her best to age gracefully?

She's Thomas Carter's wife.

The congressman?

Yeah.

The guy from Orange County?

Yeah.

No way.

It's her.

Why would the wife of a congressman be in this shithole?

No idea.

It's not her.

It is.

Go talk to her.

What do I say?

Tell her you're an admirer of her husband.

Dan laughs.

Yeah, right.

Tell her you like her highlights, that the blonde streaks are subtle and disarming.

That's a good line.

Ask her if she wants a drink.

He motions towards her table, where a waitress is setting down a cocktail glass.

Looks like she got one already.

Just go ask her if she wants ten minutes in the bathroom and the time of her life.

She's probably got security somewhere. They'll come shoot me.

I don't see anyone.

I've got black blood in my veins. If she's anything like her husband, she's carrying a gun and she'll shoot me.

Just go ask her.

Dan looks over at her. She's sitting alone. She's nursing her drink. She looks lonely.

***

She smiles and says yes, they end up in the men's room. It's small and cramped, it has a toilet and a urinal and a sink squeezed into a space the size of a closet. He presses her against the door, their mouths are open, they're pushing, tangling, their hands are grabbing and seeking, one of his is in her shirt the other up her skirt spreading, squeezing, both of hers are working the buttons on his pants. He unbuttons her shirt unhooks her bra, starts sucking and biting. She drops his pants to the floor pulls his head away from her chest and gets down on her knees.

***

She comes back the next night.
She's missing over the weekend, comes back on Monday.
He takes her outside on Wednesday, they go into an alley behind the bar.
Thursday they get into the backseat of her car.
They do not speak to each other. They have never exchanged names or numbers. She just shows up and smiles and takes him by the hand and tells him what she wants.

***

She disappears for a couple weeks. Dan misses her, misses her smell and her taste, her hands lips and tongue, misses being inside of her. He watches the news and reads the papers, looks her up online, tries to track her as closely as he can. She's campaigning with her husband, who is running for his third term in Congress. He is a conservative who serves a conservative constituency, a born-again Christian who is anti-abortion, pro-gun, supports the war in Iraq and supports the idea of future aggression in the Middle East. He believes in creationism and prayer in public schools, believes that homosexuality is a curable disease and that all gays and non-Christians will burn in hell for eternity upon their death. His opponent is a moderate and has absolutely no chance of winning. Nevertheless, the senator raised a huge campaign fund and has run hundreds of ads on television, on the radio, and in newspapers attacking everything from his hair and clothing to his wife, children and marriage. The senator's justification for the ads is— God is going to judge him someday, I might as well do it now.

***

Jack and Dan sit at the bar. They're both drinking beer. Jack speaks.
Have you told her what you do?
Dan speaks.
No.
You think you should?
No.
Why not?
Because we never talk. And because it's irrelevant.
You really think that?
Yeah.
If her husband was a mortgage broker or an insurance agent would you be fucking her?
No.
Would you have even approached her?
No.
Then it's relevant.
Maybe to me, but not to her.
How about her husband?
It's probably very relevant to him. For a number of reasons.

***

She shows up the next night. Dan's surprised because he knows Congress is still in session. As he's sitting at the bar, she comes up behind whispers—let's go, right now—in his ear.
They leave. Get in her car. He wants to get a motel room he starts driving. She gives him head as he drives. When they find a motel, they park and she finishes him off. He gets out, goes into the lobby, gets a room. As he walks to the room, she gets out of the car and follows him into the room. He closes the door and

124

she's on him. When they're done they lie in bed. Her head rests on his chest. There is a streak of light coming through a crack in curtains. He speaks.

You've never told me your name.

She speaks.

Is there some reason you need to know it?

It would be nice to put a name to your face.

My face?

Among other things.

My name is Jane.

Jane what?

Jane Doe.

He laughs.

You think that's funny?

Sort of.

It wasn't supposed to be a joke.

Okay.

It's important to me that you know me as Jane Doe. I come to the bar. We decide where we're going, if anywhere. I let you do whatever you want to me. I'll keep doing it as long as you acknowledge me as Jane Doe.

I can't do that.

Why?

I work for the ACLU and the Democratic Party.

She sits up, stares at him. There is shock and rage in her eyes, spreading across her face.

You've gotta be fucking kidding me.

I'm not.

What do you?

I'm an attorney.

She stares at him for a moment, gets up, puts on her clothes, walks out. When she's gone, he stands and spreads the curtain and watches her walk to her car and get inside her car and pull out of the parking lot.

***

Jack and Dan sit at the bar. They're both drinking beer. Jack speaks.

Are you surprised?

Dan speaks.

Yeah.

Why?

There was something there.

Jack laughs.

You spoke to her once.

So what.

So there couldn't have been much.

I love her.

Jack laughs again.

You're fucking kidding me.

Dan shakes his head.

I'm not. I love her.

You're never gonna see her again.

Probably not.

That's why you love her. It's that shit that happens when you get dumped. Doesn't matter if you loved the person or hated them, if they dump you, you yearn for them and miss them and love them and feel all the shit you didn't probably feel when you were with them. It's stupid and crazy, but that's the way it is.

I know that syndrome well. It's not that.

What is it then?

If I knew it'd be easier. That's part of the problem. And it doesn't matter that we hardly spoke. When we were together there was that thing, that unexplainable thing, and I felt it, felt it very strongly.

And you think it's love.

I don't think. I know.

And it doesn't matter that she's married to the fucking anti-Christ.

Nope.

And that she'll never leave him.

Nope.

You're fucked, dude.
Yeah.

***

He watches the returns on the day of the election. Her husband wins in a landslide.

***

Five months later. Jack and Dan sit at the bar. They're both drinking beer, watching the Dodgers kick the shit out of the Giants. Jack speaks.
The Giants suck.
Dan speaks.
Yeah.
You think they'll ever be any good?
Hope not.
The door of the bar opens, she walks in, Dan sees her in the mirror. He smiles, watches her walk towards his stool, she's smiling. She stops behind him, whispers in his ear.
I've missed you.
He nods.
I tried to stay away but I couldn't.
He smiles.
I got a room at our favorite motel.
He turns around, stares at her. He stills feels it, whatever it is, still feels it strongly.
I want you to take me there and do whatever you want to me.
He stands, takes her by the hand, they walk out of the bar.

In 1882, the California Normal School of Los Angeles opens in downtown LA. Its mission is to train teachers for the population of the southern half of the State of California, and it is funded by the State Legislature of the State of California. It is later moved and renamed the University of California, Los Angeles.

The Malibu Colony is a walled, gated, guarded group of homes that sit on the beach next to the Malibu Lagoon and Surfrider Beach. It was the first land in Malibu to be developed, when, in 1929, the Rindge family, which owned a 13,000-acre, twenty-seven-mile oceanfront parcel, sold the land to finance a legal battle against the state over the building of the Pacific Coast Highway, which they did not want passing through their property. They lost, and the town of Malibu gradually formed on their land. Now, the homes in the colony, almost all of which are second homes to residents of Beverly Hills and Bel-Air, sell for prices between five and fifty million dollars. Casey and Amberton have a 15 million dollar glass, concrete and steel home built by a famous architect. They spend eight to ten weekends a year there, occasionally a holiday. The house has five bedrooms, six bathrooms, a gym, a roof deck, a pool and a full-time staff of three. Their neighbors are actors and actresses, heads of talent agencies and film studios, media moguls. Both are sitting by the pool. The kids are with their nannies. Casey is in a bikini she's rubbing oil on her legs. Amberton is nude. Casey speaks.

What are you going to do?

I don't know.

How many times have you called him?

Thirty?

Thirty?

Maybe forty?

You've got to be kidding me.

I'm not.

You've called him forty times?

Yeah. Maybe more.

Oh my God, you've got to stop.

I can't.

How many times has he picked up?

Twice.

And you had good conversations?

Not really.

What did you say?

I asked him to have his assistant hang up.

At least you remembered to do that.

And then I told him I couldn't stop thinking about him and had to see him.

What did he say?

He said he didn't think of me that way.

What way is that?

Amberton laughs.

The gay way.

I met him. He's gay.

See. That's what I thought too. Totally.

He's just hiding behind that football star, pillar-of-his-community thing.

It's a deep closet, I'm sure.

Not that we're ones to talk.

Our closets exist for marketing and PR reasons, my dear. His exists for another reason entirely. I think he's scared.

Scared?

Yes. Absolutely.

Casey looks down, Amberton is still nude.

Maybe I should call him. I could tell him there's absolutely nothing to be scared of.

They both laugh. She speaks.

Really now, what are you going to do?

I might go see him.

And do what?

Tell him I love him.

Are you sure?

Yes.

After one meeting, one lunch and forty unreturned phone calls?

Yes.

You sure it's not a case of a man with everything obsessing because he can't have something?

I have had men rebuff me before.

Not many.

That singer. In the boy band.

He slept with you.

Only once.

That's not being rebuffed.

He shrugs, they both laugh. They hear their children coming up from the beach, doubtlessly accompanied by their staff. Amberton stands,

I'm going to go shower and drive into town.

To see him?

Yes. I'm going to march into his office and shut the door and push him against the wall and start passionately kissing him.

What if he punches you?

He'll melt. I know it. He's going to melt.

He turns walks into the house upstairs to his bedroom, which, in the same manner as their other house, is separated from the other bedrooms. He goes into the bathroom looks at himself in the mirror is pleased with what he sees. His hair, which was recently enhanced with very subtle plugs, looks thick and full. His body is lean and taut, his skin, which he conditions daily, is soft and smooth he runs his hands along his torso he imagines they are Kevin's hands he smiles and feels a chill along his spine he imagines they are Kevin's hands.

He steps into the shower. He turns up the water lies on the floor lets it hit his chest it sprays his face sprays the rest of his body. The stream is strong it feels like someone is pushing down on his sternum with one hand and tickling the rest of his body with hundreds of little fingers he just lies on the black marble floor and lets the water drop, hit, flow, spread.

He sits stands. He lathers up using triple-milled French soap it smells like perfume he rinses it off, lathers again rinses, lathers again, rinses. He steps out of the shower stands at his sink marble shaves with a straight razor stainless carefully uses his comb ivory when he's done he stands and stares at himself he wants to air-dry so that the smell of the soap stays on his skin. A breeze drifts through an open window. The sun comes through another. Amberton stares at himself he likes what he sees he smiles, smiles.

When he's dry he walks into his closet he has a full wardrobe in the house, as does every member of his family, though his is not as extensive as the one in the other house. He tries to decide what to wear should he dress up, dress down, how far up, should he wear shorts and flip-flops. He thinks through his greatest outfits he has always been famous for wearing faded jeans Levi's and black boots snakeskin and a white linen shirt Italian. He feels strong in it, confident and secure, no one can resist him. He opens the drawer where he always keeps it he smiles.

He gets dressed. He looks at himself again he looks good damn good. He gets in his car a Maserati puts the top down drives along the PCH to Sunset Blvd. into Beverly Hills he knows as he drives he looks damn good. He pulls up to the valet at the agency looking damn good and walks into the agency looking damn good. As is often the case wherever he goes, even in places where people should know better, all heads turn to stare no words just stares part of the reason is his superstar status part of it is because he's looking so damn good.

The agency looks like an art museum. Everything is clean and white there are a million two-, three-, four-million-dollar paintings on the walls. The receptionists, both male and female, are dressed in black suits they're extremely good-looking. On one side of the building is the executive wing, where the high-level agents, department heads and partners keep their offices. Most of them have multiple assistants, their offices have windows, some of them have second rooms with bars and refrigerators and large-screen televisions, a couple have their own bathrooms. The other side of the building is for the younger and lower-level agents. Some have assistants, some don't, a few of the offices have windows, but most do not. The televisions, if there is one, are smaller, there are no bars. Amberton doesn't know where Kevin's office is, but knows,

because he's a relatively new agent, that he'll be on the lesser
side of the building. He starts walking through the halls heads
turn people stare actors who generate the kind of box office he
generates are rarely, if ever, seen in this part of the building.
He stops at a desk where a young woman with a bob haircut
and a black suit sits in a cubicle wearing a headset. Using his
public voice, with a bit of extra sexiness thrown in to match
his mood and his outfit, he speaks.
Hello, darling.
She looks up. Surprised immediately nervous, almost shaking.
Uhh, hello.
Are you having a good day?
Sure. Yes. Yes, I am, Mr. Parker. Thank you.
He stands and stares at her, she looks away, looks back, smiles
nervously, looks down, back up.
Can I help you?
Do you know where Kevin Jackson's office is?
At the end of the hall.
He continues to stare at her, watches her become more and
more uncomfortable. He loves to do this, to see how people
react to him, to see how his presence affects them, to feel how
much power he has over them. He reaches out, puts his hand
on her shoulder, it's shaking.
Thank you. And you're a beautiful girl.
He walks away, down the hall, towards Kevin's office, as he
approaches he can see him through an open door, he's sitting
at his desk staring at a computer, he's wearing a headset as
Amberton gets closer he can hear him talking.
He'd be great for it.
He nods.
He's got two films coming out, supporting roles. There's talk
he might get nominated for one of them.
He waits.
He plays a compulsive gambler.
Amberton walks past Kevin's assistant, an attractive young
woman in a black suit.

Yes, it's negotiable.

Amberton steps into the office closes the door.

Meet him. You'll see. Trust me.

Kevin looks up, Amberton smiles.

Set it up with my assistant.

There is no window in the office, the wall behind Kevin is covered with pictures and awards from his football career. There is a chair opposite his desk, Kevin motions towards it. Amberton sits down.

Great. Thank you.

Kevin hangs up, types something into his computer, Amberton stares at him. Kevin finishes. Looks up.

How can I help you, Mr. Parker.

Mr. Parker?

Yes. How can I help you, Mr. Parker?

We know too much about each other for you to call me Mr. Parker.

One lunch?

There's more than that.

I'm not sure what you mean.

Why don't you return my calls?

I didn't think it was appropriate to return them.

Amberton smiles.

Why not?

Because that's how I felt.

Amberton stands.

If you thought my approach was inappropriate, you would have called and told me so. I think you're just scared.

You're mistaken.

Am I?

Amberton takes a step.

Yes you are.

It's okay.

Another step.

I'm not going to tell anyone.

Another.

And, as you can imagine, I understand the situation better than anyone you'll ever meet.

He steps around the desk.

I can see, and I can feel, and I know in my heart, that you want me as much as I want you.

Steps towards him.

And I want to love you.

He reaches out to him.

And I'm not going to hurt you.

Amberton stares at Kevin, holds out his hand. Kevin takes off his headset, takes the offered hand, stands. Amberton smiles, Amberton smiles.

The Indiana Colony, so named because its founder was from Indianapolis, becomes one of the largest citrus groves in the United States. In the early 1890s it holds a competition for a new name, the winning entry is Pasadena, which means *of the valley* in the language of the Chippewa Tribe of Minnesota. The moneyed class of Los Angeles starts moving into the area in large numbers in an effort to escape the concentrations of immigrants, primarily Mexican, Chinese, black, and Irish, that are living in the city.

Dylan and Maddie lie in bed it's late the drapes are closed it's pitch-black in the room, though they feel each other their legs intertwined their bodies side by side the tips of their fingers touching they can barely see the other. Maddie speaks.

He did it again today. I was in the break room.

Alone?

Yeah.

I told you not to go in there alone.

I was with this girl Candi, who's a stocker. She had to go to the bathroom. I thought I'd be fine.

What'd he say?

Awful things.

Like what?

He said he wanted to eat me like a hamburger.

Dylan laughs. Maddie's annoyed.

It's not funny.

Okay.

It's not.

You're right I shouldn't have laughed. What else did he say?

That he'd nibble my nipple like a sesame seed.

Dylan laughs again. Maddie's annoyed again.

Come on, Dylan.

Sorry.

Seriously.

I said sorry. Keep going.

He said he wanted to cover my coochie in butterscotch and strawberry sauce and use his tongue like a spoon.

Dylan laughs again, this time louder and longer. Maddie moves beyond annoyance into anger. She pulls away from him, sits up.

It's not funny, you asshole.

Dylan can't stop laughing.

Stop it, Dylan.

He can't. She hits him on the shoulder.

STOP IT, DYLAN.

He calms down.

I'm sorry. I couldn't help it.

You could have.

I said I'm sorry.

It really sucks, Dylan. He totally freaks me out and makes me uncomfortable.

Are you scared of him?

Not really.

Do you think he'd actually do anything?

No.

He's a harmless weirdo.

Yeah. But he's really really weird.

And don't get mad at me, in a way it's pretty funny. I mean, what kind of freak tells someone he wants to eat them like a hamburger.

She giggles. He keeps going.

And nibble their nipple like a sesame seed.

She giggles again. Keeps going.

Imagine what must be going through his head to actually say that kind of shit.

He's a loon.

Although I do sort of like the butterscotch and strawberry line.

Another giggle, she speaks.

It won't work on me no matter how nice you say it, so don't even try.

He laughs.

What do you think he says to his wife?

Nothing.

You don't think he's got some specials saved up for her?

I met her. She scared the shit out of me. She's, like, the size of your boss, and could probably kick his ass.

Get her number in case I need her.

They both laugh. Dylan speaks.

I have a question. An important one.

What?

Are there any lines he could use that would work?

You've gotta be kidding.

I'm not.

Why do you want to know that?

So I can use 'em. Maybe get some before we fall asleep.

You don't need lines. You have other things that work on me.

She leans over starts kissing him it's pitch-black and they can't see each other but they can feel each other with hands and legs and lips the tips of their fingers feel.

Next day is the same as the last nothing changes week after week after week. They work, eat noodles and soup from the 99 cent store discounted to 66 cents, they go for long rides through the Hills, they watch TV play sleep. Dylan never calls home has not called since they pulled away, Maddie calls every few weeks her mother always answers. Maddie doesn't speak, just listens as her mother, who somehow knows that she is on the other end of the line, yells at her, tells her she's worthless and stupid, calls her a piece of shit, calls her a cunt and a whore, tells her she's a waste of space and would be better off dead. Sometimes Maddie hangs up on her, sometimes she doesn't, when she doesn't she sits and listens for two three four minutes eventually her mother gives up and slams down the phone. Her mother's hate doesn't always affect her she can walk away and forget it happened. Sometimes, though, she sobs for hours after it's over she lies on the bed and sobs. Her mother has been telling her the same things, calling her the same names, for most of her life. Maddie tries not to call but she can't stop herself. Part of her believes what she hears and part of her doesn't. She thinks that someday she'll either hang up stop listening never call back, or speak out and say I know, Mom, you're right, I am everything you say I am. Until that point, that moment, that decision, she'll keep calling, keep listening, keep thinking, keep sobbing.

For Dylan, life at the shop vacillates between moments of extreme boredom, occasional contentment, and extreme terror. Tiny is very particular about the motorcycles he will and will not allow to be fixed at his shop. He doesn't allow Japanese or European motorcycles of any type, any brand. He doesn't allow bikes ridden by people he considers RUBs (Rich Urban Bikers), individuals who work normal day jobs, often high-paying white-collar day jobs, and wear leather and ride motorcycles on the weekends. He doesn't allow motorcycles of members of other motorcycle clubs, though most aren't stupid enough to bother trying, and he doesn't allow motorcycles owned or ridden by members of law enforcement. The one time a cop's bike did end up in the shop, Tiny set it on fire and dumped it in the cop's front yard. Most of the bikes that come in belong to members of his club, or associates of members of the club. When a member's bike comes in, Tiny accompanies the member, who is usually between thirty and fifty, bearded, dressed in jeans and a black leather motorcycle vest, and terrifying, back to see Dylan. Tiny will stare at Dylan until he looks up. When he does, Tiny speaks.

This is one of my brothers.

Dylan will nod, speak.

Nice to meet you, sir.

He needs his bike fixed.

I'll do it right away.

Don't fuck it up.

I won't.

Use new parts and don't charge him.

Okay.

And if you fuck it up, we'll kick your fucking ass.

I won't fuck it up.

We'll kick your fucking ass like it ain't never been kicked before.

I understand.

You better. You fucking better.

Tiny and the member then go to his office, where they shut the door and laugh, drink, get high. The associates, who are usually less terrifying, and usually work or run errands for the members, are treated much worse. Tiny doesn't care what kind of parts Dylan uses for their bikes, doesn't care how well he fixes the bikes, and he charges them a fortune for the work. Dylan is amused by the interactions with both the members and the associates, and always does a sound job on the bikes, regardless of who owns them. When there are no bikes to fix, he reads copies of porn and gun magazines Tiny keeps in giant stacks in the back of the shop. Once or twice a week members of the club come in with people who don't ride bikes, some of them drive pickup trucks, some of them drive Mercedeses and Porsches, and Tiny tells Dylan to get the fuck out of the shop. Dylan usually walks up and down the street looking at vehicles in used car lots, trying to decide which one, if he could afford any of them, he would buy. There is a sky-blue Corvette in one, an old Chevelle convertible in another, a third that seems to have an endless supply of restored pickup trucks from the '50s and '60s. And as much as he may like those, there is a silver DeLorean, in all of its brushed steel, winged-door glory, that always brings him back. It sits in the back of a low-end lot, and from what he can tell, it never moves, and may not even have an engine, but he loves it, and dreams of rolling through his former town in it, seeing his father walking out of a bar and giving his father the finger. When he doesn't look at cars, or stare longingly at the DeLorean, he sits in one of the five burger restaurants within sight of the shop and eats French fries and vanilla milkshakes. When the visitors leave, he goes back to work. If there's nothing to do when he gets back, he reads magazines from Tiny's stacks.

When he walked towards work this morning, there were two Mercedeses in front of the shop, three Harleys. The garage door was closed, which it normally isn't, he assumed he wasn't wanted until the cars were gone and the door open. He went across the street. The closest of the burger restaurants, which served breakfast biscuits and scrambled egg sandwiches before 10:00 AM, was open he went in and ordered a biscuit and a coffee.

As he ate slowly and drank the coffee slowly and read the paper more bad news just bad fucking news, he thought about Maddie, about what she was doing, about her job and her ridiculous boss, about how badly he wanted to get her away from there, away from the motel, away from the desperation they both knew and felt but couldn't acknowledge. He thought about the promise he had made to her. They wouldn't live there forever, they would find a better life. He believed he could keep the promise he just didn't know how. There were no promotions coming, no other job prospects. They didn't have savings there were none coming. Though he never let her know it, he was scared of the other residents of the motel, and knew, if it really came to it, he probably couldn't protect her from them. Occasionally, he looked across the street. Nothing changed. He kept eating two biscuits one with bacon one not kept drinking three cups of coffee milk no sugar he read the entertainment section of the paper twice, goddamn those movie stars make a shitload of money he kept thinking about his promise, aside from Maddie herself, it was the only thing in his life with meaning. After two hours, and a large number of dirty looks from the restaurant's Bulgarian manager (#1 burger man from all of Iron Curtain!), he sees five Hispanic men get into the two Mercedes sedans, watches them pull away.

He gets up walks out of the restaurant the manager is happy to see him go the manager doesn't like the motorcycle men from across the street they're big angry and mean sometimes they call him a commie and tell him to fuck off sometimes they make fun of his accent and tell him to go back to Russia. The one time he asked them to stop insulting him, they rubbed a ketchup, mustard and pickle laden burger bun in his face.

As Dylan walks across the street he senses something's wrong. The garage door is still down there is no noise coming from behind it. The door next to the garage is open, swinging. As Dylan approaches the door he hears moaning his heart starts pounding as he gets closer the moaning is louder he's scared. He stands at the door. He can hear multiple voices, one is moaning another says help me the third says fuck. He stands at the door can't move he can hear the voices he can hear pain, helplessness, anger. He stands at the door his heart is pounding his hands are shaking he wants to run, he wants Maddie, he wants to be back in Ohio, he wants to call the police, he wants to run he can hear the voices.

He steps into the garage. It's dark there is a streak of light coming from the door another from the office, which is in the back. He can't see anyone. He starts walking towards the office he hears a voice in the shadows, it's faint, labored, hurt.

Kid.

He turns towards the voice.

Kid.

His eyes adjust.

Help me.

Tiny and three other bikers are duct-taped to folding chairs, their ankles to the front legs their wrists to the stems that hold the back. All of them are bleeding their faces cut and swollen there are open circular burn wounds along their arms and chest. Tiny and two others are conscious one of them isn't his head is hanging limply against his chest. Dylan stops, stares, he wants to run. Tiny speaks.

Kid.

Dylan stares at them.

I need your help.

One of the other men moans.

I need . . .

Tiny loses his breath. Dylan steps towards him, speaks.

What do I do?

There's a knife in my back pocket. Get it out and cut me free. Dylan reaches around, Tiny tries to lift himself off the chair can't do it. Dylan wriggles his fingers in the pocket feels a polished-wood pocketknife pulls it out. He flips the blade his hands are shaking.

What do I do first, your hands or your feet?

I don't give a fuck.

Tiny's breathing is labored there is blood dripping from his nose, his chin, running from a cut above his eye, the teeth on one side of his mouth are in shards, Dylan can smell the burned hair and flesh on his arms and chest. The other two

are staring at Dylan both are in the same condition, the last
one still hasn't moved. Dylan starts cutting the tape from
Tiny's wrist he frees one arm, steps around to the other. He
cuts it free the tape was wrapped three or four times around he
moves to his ankles cuts them free. When Tiny is free Dylan
stands. Tiny moves his legs a few inches away from the chair,
leans back takes a deep breath, the flow of blood changes
direction starts dripping from his cheeks, his ears. Dylan
speaks.
You okay?
Tiny leans forward, speaks.
No. I'm not fucking okay.
What do you want me to do?
He motions towards his friends.
Cut them free, you dumbfuck.
Dylan cuts the one next to Tiny free, the one next to him.
Both of them react the same way Tiny did, move their legs
slightly, take deep breaths. Dylan looks at the fourth man,
whose head is still on his chest. He doesn't appear to be
breathing. He looks at Tiny.
I think he's dead.
Tiny looks back, speaks.
You a fucking doctor?
No.
Just cut him free.
Dylan starts working on the tape, Tiny slowly stands he walks
over to the open door and closes it and locks it. The other two
slowly stand they're also covered in blood and still bleeding.
When Dylan cuts the fourth man free he slides from the chair
hits the floor in a heap his body is limp Dylan stares at him.
No movement, no breath, nothing. Dylan looks back at Tiny,
who is walking towards his office. Dylan speaks.
I think this guy's dead, Tiny.
Tiny ignores him walks into the office, looks around, starts
yelling.
Fuck.

FUCK.
FUCK.
Dylan is frozen. The other two men are dazed and appear to
be in shock, they're breathing heavily, looking at and gently
touching the wounds on their bodies. The fourth man still isn't
moving. Tiny picks up the phone in his office, throws it against
the wall it shatters he yells FUCK again, steps out of the office,
looks at Dylan, speaks.
Give me your fucking phone.
I don't have one.
I need a fucking phone.
I don't have one.
Find one.
I could call 911 from a pay phone.
We're not calling fucking 911. That's the last fucking thing we
need.
Don't you need an ambulance?
Find a fucking phone.
One of the other men looks at Dylan, speaks.
I think he has one.
He points at the man on the floor, who still isn't moving. Dylan
steps over and leans down he can smell burned flesh and blood.
He pats the man's pockets he doesn't feel anything. There are
two pockets he can't reach without turning the man over. He
looks back at Tiny, who is looking through his office, yelling
fuck. One of the men is sitting in a chair staring at the wounds
on his arms, the other is sitting on the floor he's coughing and
there are fragments of his teeth getting caught in his beard.
Dylan feels like he's going to vomit. He doesn't want to touch
the man beneath him, but doesn't want to deal with Tiny if he
can't find a phone. He gets on one knee puts his hands on the
man's hips and chest rolls him over. It's dead weight. He can
feel cold flesh through the man's chest. He wants to vomit.
He checks the man's back pocket finds a cell stands and walks
it to Tiny's office he can still feel the cold, dead weight he still
wants to vomit. He reaches the door, speaks.

Here's a phone.

He holds it out for Tiny, who steps over and takes it, steps away and starts dialing. Dylan looks at the office. The drawers of the desk are all open and their contents, papers, repair manuals, pens, a calculator, are spread along the desk's surface and on the floor. The phone line is cut, the fax machine destroyed. The paneling against the back is smashed, there are two safes, which were once behind the paneling, that are open and empty. Tiny puts the phone to his ear, waits, speaks.

It's Tiny. We got a situation.

He waits.

Some fucking spic meth dealers taped us up and tortured us. The safes are both fucking empty. We need a fucking doctor right fucking now.

Waits.

Just get the fuck over here.

He hangs up, looks at Dylan, speaks.

What the fuck do you want?

What do you want me to do?

Stand in the corner and shut the fuck up.

Can I leave?

Try and I'll put a bullet in your fucking head.

Okay.

Dylan stands at the door, unsure of what to do. Tiny starts looking through the mess on his desk. Dylan steps back looks across the room. The two men are sitting together staring into the distance even though there is no distance to see. Both are still bleeding, occasionally look at each other or mumble a word or two to each other. The fourth man still hasn't moved, and will never move again. Dylan is shaking and his heart is pounding and he still feels like he's going to vomit. He walks to the back of the shop, as far as he can get from the blood and the chairs and the duct tape and the vacant, wounded men and the motionless body and raging Tiny and whomever else is coming and whatever else is going to happen he wants to get away. He finds a dark corner moves a battered box of used

146

parts and a pile of rags there is grease and oil on the floor he
sits down anyway. He pulls his knees to his chest. He stares
across the length of the shop. The door is still locked, the
garage gate still closed. He sits and stares.

Thirty minutes later he hasn't moved. Tiny has been on the
phone the entire time rummaging through his office yelling
fuck. One of the remaining men has passed out on the floor,
though he is still breathing. Dylan hears motorcycles
approaching, the bikes that the club members ride are
extremely loud and can be heard from blocks away. He can tell
by the rumble there is more than one of them as they pull into
the driveway the garage door shakes, the windows shake. Tiny
motions to the one conscious man to open the door he stands
and slowly, gingerly walks towards it every step he takes looks
like it hurts, every movement he makes looks like it hurts.
Before he reaches the door there is pounding the doorframe
shakes yelling open the motherfucking door. He does not
change his pace. He slowly, gingerly and painfully walks
towards it, the pounding continues the yelling continues. He
reaches it unlocks it opens it. Huge bearded men stream into
the garage four five six seven eight nine of them. A smaller
man, without a beard and wearing slacks and a golf shirt, who
is carrying a black leather medical bag, comes in with them.
He immediately starts looking at the man who opened the
door, who motions to the two men on the floor. The bearded
men have spread out. Some are going to Tiny's office. Others
are crouching around the men on the floor they immediately
start calling Doc Doc, get over here Doc. No one seems to
notice Dylan, who sits in the corner, his knees at his chest, his
entire body shaking with fear. Over the course of the next two
hours he watches and listens as:

Tiny tells the men that he and their friends were doing a meth
deal when their Mexican partners pulled out weapons, taped
them to the chairs, demanded their cash, guns and drugs, and
tortured them until they revealed their locations.

The doctor pronounces the one man dead. And though he

knew it already, hearing the doctor say—This man is dead—is shocking, crushing.

One of the bearded men leaves and returns with an old Cadillac. The garage door is opened and the Cadillac is backed into the space.

Three men move a large steel tool cabinet, Tiny opens a floor safe hidden beneath it. They pull out two scoped sniper's rifles, two handheld rocket launchers, a machine gun, and four machetes.

The second man dies. He goes into convulsions before he goes, vomits blood, bites off part of his tongue. The doctor is unable to do anything to save him.

The trunk of the Cadillac is opened.

Tiny and the remaining man have their facial cuts stitched and the wounds on their arms and chests cleaned and dressed. Tiny is silent through the process, the other man alternates between moaning and screaming.

The weapons are dispensed.

The doctor is paid from a large bundle of cash hidden in the back panel of a refrigerator and the doctor leaves.

The bodies of the dead men are loaded into the trunk of the Cadillac. Tiny tells the driver, and two other club members who are going with the driver, to take the bodies into the desert and bury them. The Cadillac pulls away.

Tiny gathers the remaining club members and gives them the names of the men who tortured and robbed him. He tells them he thinks they're somewhere in or around Echo Park, a Hispanic neighborhood just northwest of downtown LA. He wants them found preferably in their homes. He wants their families killed in front of them, to be, if possible, hacked to pieces using the machetes. If it isn't possible, shoot them, blow them up, find some way to fucking kill them and send a strong fucking message to motherfuckers who think they can get away with fucking with him. Tiny gives them each a bundle of cash in case they need it, tells them paying off addicts and small-time dealers might help them find the men. The club members leave.

When they're gone, when everyone is gone but the two of them, Tiny walks over to Dylan, stands above him, speaks.
Get up.
Dylan stands he's stiff and it hurts to stand he's shaking.
I probably don't gotta say it, but if you tell anyone about anything you saw or heard in here today I'll fucking kill you.
Dylan nods.
And I'll fucking rape your girlfriend, and then kill her. And then I'll fucking find out where you're from and kill your fucking family.
I'm not gonna say anything.
You can't ever say shit. Not a week from now, not twenty fucking years from now.
I understand.
I need you to clean this place up. Mop the fucking blood off the floor and find a dumpster for the bloody clothes.
Okay.
Put the clothes in a bag and put a buncha fucking rags on top of 'em and climb into the dumpster and stick it right in the middle of all the trash. If you put them at the bottom they'll be at the top when they empty it. It's gotta go right in the middle.
Okay.
And then lock this place up. Make sure it's fucking locked.
Do I come in tomorrow?
Yeah. Business as usual. I gotta keep up a front. You should fucking know that by now.
Okay.
Tiny turns, walks out. Dylan hears him start his bike and ride away. Dylan goes to the cleaning closet, which is near where he just spent two hours huddled in the corner, he gets a mop, fills a bucket with bleach and water. He walks to the spot where he found the man taped, starts mopping dried blood. He moves to spots where the men died, and where the blood had dried in outlines roughly the size of their bodies, and mops the blood. He mops along the paths where Tiny walked, and where there were thick red trails. He mops in the area beneath the trunk of

the car, which leaked after it was filled. He cleans the mop. He cleans the bucket.

He walks through the entire garage, picking up rags making a large pile of them. He does it again picks up bloody clothing, soaked bandages, towels. He puts the clothing bandages and towels in a black garbage bag puts the rags on top of them. He puts the bag inside of another black bag, does it again. He walks through the entire garage to make sure he hasn't missed anything.

As he passes the refrigerator he notices the back panel is still open, just slightly, almost imperceptibly. He walks over to it opens it further there are still bundles of cash in it. He has never seen this much money in one place. He has no idea how much there is. All he sees are hundred-dollar bills. They're worn, beaten, frayed at the ends, held together by rubber bands. He reaches out touches a stack of them. He knows one stack would change his life. He knows one stack would get him and Maddie out of the hotel, give them a new start, provide them with a safer more stable existence. One stack. His hands start shaking for different reasons this time just one stack. One fucking stack. Change his life. Make Maddie safe. Maddie safe. If he gets caught he'll die.

There's no way anyone will notice, no way Tiny has any idea how much was in there earlier, how much is in there now, how much he used today.

Dylan's hands are shaking.

One stack.

Maddie safe.

One stack.

He'll die.

One stack.

There's no way Tiny will ever know.

His hands are shaking.

It'll change their life.

He reaches out his hand to touch the smooth surface of the worn paper.

He looks at the door no one's there he's scared fucking terrified he'll die.

He takes out the stack it's too big for his pocket he puts it in the waist of his pants tightens his belt to secure.

No one will know.

He closes the panel, leaves it exactly as he found it. He picks up the black trash bag. He walks to the back door makes sure it's locked. He leaves through the front door, locks it behind him, double-checks it, triple-checks it. He walks to the garage door makes sure it's locked, double-checks it, triple-checks it. He starts walking down the street with the garbage bag. He'll find a dumpster away from the shop.

The cash is his waistline, secured by his belt.

His life just changed.

In 1895, all twenty-three of the incorporated banks in Los Angeles County are robbed at least once. Twenty-one of them are robbed more than once. One of them is robbed fourteen times.

Freeways! Highways! EXPRESSWAYS!! AN EIGHTEEN-RAMP INTERSTATE EXCHANGE!!!! Is there anything more fun than sitting in a vehicle on a hot, crowded, slow-moving stretch of concrete and blacktop? Is there anything more fun than driving at four miles per hour? Is there anything more fun than a twelve-car pileup? No, there's nothing, no way, it's impossible, there's absolutely nothing. CO_2 and exhaust! Horns that never end! ROAD RAGE!!!! Fun fun fun, it's so much fucking fun!!!!

***

There are 27 million cars in Los Angeles County, nearly two for every human being. On any given day, approximately 18 million of them are on the 20,771 miles of state, county and city roads that stretch across its every inch. In an average year, 800 people die on the roads of Los Angeles, and an additional 90,000 are injured. There are 29 state freeways, 8 interstate highways, and one US highway. All of them are named. There's the Pearblossom Highway, the Future Chino Hills Parkway, the Antelope Valley Freeway. There's the Magic Mountain Parkway, Rim of the World Freeway, the Kellogg Hill Interchange. There's Stinkin' Lincoln (a nickname), Johnny Carson's Slauson Cutoff (highway with a sense of humor), Ronald Reagan Freeway (very conservative, very presidential), the Eastern Transportation Corridor (booorrrinnng), and the Terminal Island Freeway (oh my, don't want to end up there). Despite the fact that many of the highways, freeways, parkways and expressways of Los Angeles have strange and wonderful names, no one uses them. Every state, interstate and federal road in the county also has a numerical designation, the lowest of them is 1, the highest is 710. When discussing roads, the citizens of Los Angeles almost always use the numbers, immediately preceded by the word *the*. The roads above are better known as the 138, the 71, and the 14. The 126, the 18, the intersection of the 10, the 57, the 71 and the 210. The 1, the 90. The 118, the 261, and the 47/103.

***

Interstate 10, the Santa Monica/San Bernardino Freeway, or, the 10. The 10 is the largest and most heavily traveled east/west thoroughfare in Los Angeles. It is an ugly, stinking brute of a road, huge and gray, hulking and dirty. It creates massive amounts of noise and smog, and makes everything around it uglier and significantly less pleasant. It's the school bully of LA highways, it is hated, dreaded, people cringe at the thought of it, try to avoid it, plan their day around trying to avoid it, plan their life around trying to avoid it, but to no avail, absolutely none, because it's always there, always looming, ever present, fucking up traffic and ruining people's days, whether it wants to or not. Like the school bully, who is also very occasionally nice and cool and occasionally does something to make life easier or better, every now and then one drives onto the 10 and sees a massive, empty, open stretch of road that provides an incredibly fast and easy way to cross the most congested city in America. It's a wonderful sight, that open road, and it stays in one's mind the 99 percent of the time that the 10 is a nightmare.

The 10 starts at an intersection with the Pacific Coast Highway in Santa Monica, runs coast to coast for 2,460 miles along the entire southern span of the United States, and ends (or starts, if you want to look at it that way) at an intersection with I-95 in Jacksonville, Florida. It was originally part of the Atlantic and Pacific Highway, a transcontinental trail that pioneers and settlers followed during the westward migration of the 1800s. Starting around 1920, it became a series of paved roads interrupted by unpaved patches of desert in California, Arizona, New Mexico and Texas, and swamp in Louisiana, Mississippi, Alabama and Florida. In 1940 the project to turn all of them into one road began, and in 1957, it was fully integrated, finished and officially christened as Interstate 10.

The 10 has a humble beginning, two lanes angling left and moving quickly upwards from the PCH at the base of the Santa Monica Pier. It looks like the entrance to a parking garage or the route for people who aren't wealthy or attractive enough to go to the beach. It rolls through an underpass and spreads into eight lanes, four on each side, with thirty-foot concrete walls on both sides. Everything is hard and gray, there are chunks of concrete missing and scrape marks on the walls, it looks, and is, extremely unforgiving. It continues straight east and continues spreading and within a mile it becomes twelve lanes, within another mile it becomes sixteen. Along most of the west side of Los Angeles, the 10 is either elevated or lined with sound-reducing walls. Traffic is thick and often clogged all day every day, it is only clear late at night and early in the morning. Without traffic, it takes fifteen to twenty minutes to get from Santa Monica to downtown Los Angeles. With traffic, it can take two hours. As it moves east, and into neighborhoods that are not as economically healthy as those farther west, the 10 levels out and the walls disappear. When it hits downtown, it intersects with the 110, which runs from Long Beach to Pasadena, and just east of downtown, and it intersects with Interstate 5, which runs from Mexico to Canada. From there it continues east into San Bernardino County and the desert. Just outside of Palm Springs, it becomes the Sonny Bono Memorial Freeway.

***

US 101, the Santa Ana/Hollywood/Ventura Highway, or, the 101. The highway that is so damn cool it has five names. And yes yes yes, this is the highway that the song "Ventura Highway" by the supergroup America is named after, that song from the '70s with the great vocal harmony, the first time you hear it it's great, the second time it's okay, the third time it's annoying, and the fourth time it makes you want to find a grenade and stick it in the goddamn stereo.
The 101 starts in East LA, at the five-level East Los Angeles Interchange, where the 5 and the 10 and the 60 intersect, and it moves north and west through downtown. From there, it curves around the northern edge of Hollywood and through

the Cahuenga Pass until it reaches the Hollywood Split, where two other freeways cut away from it and head north (the 170) and east (the 134). After the split, the 101 moves into the Valley, where it heads straight west, running parallel to Ventura Boulevard, the Hollywood Hills and Beverly Hills. It then moves north into Ventura County. It follows the Pacific coastline through California, Oregon and Washington, where it once again merges with Highway 5 (Washingtonians don't call it the 5). The 101 was originally part of a trail that connected the missions, settlements and forts of early Spanish California. It ran from the border of Mexico to San Francisco. When the larger and more efficient Highway 5 was constructed, the southern section of the 101 was redesignated as San Diego County Route S-21.

The 101 is LA's hometown freeway, most akin to the outside world's image of the city. It's referenced in dozens of songs, video games are made and named after it, it frequently appears in television shows and films. People all over the globe equate the 101 with good times, fast cars, hot chicks, warm weather, movie stars and money. As is also the case with its Hollywood namesake, the reality of the 101 is very different from the outside view of it. It's crowded. It's dirty. It's run-down. It's dangerous. Runaway kids and homeless crack and heroin addicts live in cardboard-box encampments beneath its underpasses. Garbage lines its shoulders. Deserted tires, and occasionally dead bodies, are dumped on it. Driving on the 101 can be a terrible experience. It's either at a standstill, with drivers and passengers glaring at each other, threatening each other and sometimes attacking each other, or it's like the world's largest, most crowded, most dangerous racetrack, with cars weaving in and out of lanes, cutting each other off, running into the cement walls and barriers that line it. Once it moves out of downtown and Hollywood, the 101 becomes a drab, boring stretch of gray cement lined with housing developments and apartment complexes and gas stations and mini-malls. It's a dramatically different place than it was when the big hit, THE BIG HIT!!!, was written about it. It's going to be interesting to hear the words to the next one.

**

Interstate 405, the San Diego Freeway, or, **the 405**. Someone in the State of California's naming office was smoking weed when they named this road because it doesn't run within forty miles of San Diego. It's almost as if they felt sorry for San Diego for not having any big famous roads on the scale of the roads in LA, so they decided to throw them a bone and give them the 405. Lucky for them, no one in Los Angeles gives a shit, and no one in Los Angeles even bothers with the misleading and entirely inaccurate given name. The big sixteen-lane north/south artery, infamous as the scene of the OJ Simpson slow-speed car chase of June 17, 1994, is and always will be known as the 405. As a proud citizen of Mar Vista, which borders the route of the 405, once uttered—Fuck that silly San Diego bullshit, it's our road and we'll call it whatever the fuck we want.

Certified as an interstate in 1955, and completed in 1969, the 405 runs for seventy-five miles between Mission Hills in the northern end of the San Fernando Valley and the city of Irvine, which is part of Orange County. The 405 runs parallel to the Pacific coastline, but lies several miles inland. It merges with Interstate 5 at both of its ends.

The 405 is one of the most heavily traveled and congested roads in the world. When shots of the massive traffic jams of LA appear in films and television shows, they're usually taken in the ten-mile stretch of freeway between the junctions of the 405 and the 10 in Santa Monica, and the 405 and the 101 in Sherman Oaks, which are two of the five busiest highway interchanges in the country. During that stretch, the 405 moves through the Sepulveda Pass, which cuts through the Santa Monica Mountains and is one of the primary thoroughfares between the Westside of LA and the Valley. It's also home to the Getty Museum and the Skirball Cultural Center (couldn't they have come up with a better name, like maybe the San Diego Cultural Center?).

Driving on the 405 is like standing in line for a roller coaster. You dread the line, you know you have to deal with it, you get in it, and then you slowly inch your way forward for what seems like an eternity. It's always hot, something always smells, you always regret having decided to get in the line. Unlike a roller-coaster line, however, there is usually no payoff when you get off the 405. Whether you're getting on another highway, freeway or interstate, or getting on one of Los Angeles's larger surface streets, the only thing you get is more traffic. More traffic. More fucking traffic. Fuck.

***

Interstate 5, the Santa Ana Freeway, or, **the** 5. The Old Man. The Graybeard. The Granddaddy. The 5 is the oldest of the major roads in Los Angeles, tracing back to times before Europeans had landed on the continental United States, when it was part of a series of trails and trade routes, later known as the Siskiyou Trail, that were used by Native Americans. In the 1800s it was co-opted by the Pacific Railroad. In the early 1900s it became the Pacific Highway, and in the 1930s it was redesignated US Highway 99. In the 1950s it became Interstate 5, and about two hours later, the citizens of Los Angeles started calling it the 5.

The 5 runs for 1,400 miles, from the border of the US and Mexico to the border of the US and Canada. It connects most of the major cities of the western seaboard: San Diego, Los Angeles, Sacramento, Portland, Seattle, Tijuana in Mexico and Vancouver in Canada. It is usually eight lanes wide, though in certain short sections around LA, it expands out to ten. All of them are usually jammed with traffic. Because of the 5's route, which runs along the heavily populated Eastside of LA, there is no room for it to expand. Because of the rapidly growing population of southern California, and Los Angeles specifically, the traffic on it is getting worse every year. Maintenance of the

5 is incredibly difficult. If a lane, or two lanes, is shut down or blocked, it affects traffic on every other highway in Los Angeles in a negative fashion, creating giant citywide traffic jams. Maintenance has to be done in the middle of the night, between the hours of 11:00 PM and 5:00 AM. Projects take years, and by the time they're finished, there is often a need to start doing repairs on the original work. There's no way to solve the problem. It's getting worse, and will continue to get worse.

Like an Old Man, a Graybeard, a Granddaddy, the 5 is breaking down physically, wearing out. It was once glorious, the biggest and most important of the LA highways, now old age and a changing world are making it into something sad and beaten, unfixable and in a state of degradation. In a perfect world, the 5 could gracefully retire and wait for the day when it received a call from Highway Heaven. It could relax and look back on its own history and accomplishments with pride and a sense of achievement. Instead, it carries on, no way to change, no way to get better, no way to be what it once was. It carries on, it carries on.

**

California State Route 1, Highway 1, the Pacific Coast Highway, or, **the PCH**. In lieu of a standard description, a stanza from the work of a great poet may be most appropriate here:

She walks in beauty, like the night
Of cloudless climes and starry skies;
And all that's best of dark and bright
Meet in her aspect and her eyes:
Thus mellow'd to that tender light
Which heaven to gaudy day denies.
    —LORD BYRON (1788–1824)

Yes, she is a beauty, some say the most beautiful highway in the world. She inspires songs, films, paintings, photographs, people come from all over the world to see her, spend time on her, to drive her. Even in Los Angeles, a land populated with many of the most beautiful people in the world, she is considered extraordinary. So extraordinary that the unique numerical naming system used for every major road in LA County is discarded, and she is given letters instead. *The PCH*, how many times have those words brought a tear to someone's eye, *the PCH*, better charge up the calculator.

The PCH was initially the vision of a country doctor named John Roberts, who lived in the northern California town of Monterey. Most of his patients lived up and down the coast, and there were no reliable roads for him to travel on when he needed to reach them. He sent his proposal, which was for a 140-mile two-lane road running between Monterey and San Luis Obispo, to his local state congressman, who put it before the state legislature, where it was approved in 1919 with a budget of $1.5 million. Within two months it was over budget, and prisoners from San Quentin State Prison were used as a labor force in exchange for reduced sentences. Ten million cubic feet of rock were blown away and as late as 1945, sticks of dynamite were found along the side of the PCH. Over the course of the next thirty years, the legislature authorized more construction, and certified more sections of other roads to be included as part of the PCH, and it now runs from Dana Point in Orange County to a small town in northern California called Leggett.

As is often the case with things of great beauty, not all is as it may initially seem. The PCH in LA County can be a mean, ugly, humongous pain in the ass. It enters LA County in Long Beach and runs north through San Pedro and Torrance, Redondo Beach and Hermosa Beach. Through most of this section of it, it is a four-lane road lined with mini-malls and fast-food restaurants, discount chains and car lots. The only true sign that the road is on the Pacific Coast is the air, which is heavy, salty, wet sea air. The PCH then passes by Los Angeles Airport, also known as LAX, and becomes part of Lincoln Boulevard, which is fondly known by its nickname,

Stinkin' Lincoln. Because of all the traffic lights, traffic is stop-and-go, and can be incredibly jammed. The road doesn't become what one might think of as the PCH until it reaches Santa Monica, where it intersects with the 10.

Like the awkward, ugly-duckling teenager who blossoms into an elegant young supermodel, or the unsightly actress who emerges from the makeup trailer as a dazzling, magnificent movie star, the PCH leaves the surface streets of LA, strikes out on its own, and becomes immediately gorgeous. It spreads out to six lanes and runs directly alongside a 300-foot-wide beach, the waves of the Pacific crash to the shore and can be easily heard, for nine months a year there are sunbathers in bikinis, and for twelve months a year there are runners, rollerbladers and bikers on a thin, serpentine path that parallels the road. On the other side there are 200-foot limestone bluffs with white, pink and purple streaks that shimmer in the sun, that seem to glow as it falls, seem like they've been delicately painted. As the PCH moves north it continues along the coast, it curves with the inlets and coves of the Santa Monica Bay the bluffs are broken by canyons lush green overgrown canyons with houses built into their steep forested walls, the beach is thin at points thick at points there are volleyball nets with leaping players, surfers bobbing in waves, boats in the distance sailing, cruising, sitting, resting. Santa Monica becomes the Pacific Palisades the Palisades becomes Malibu. In the summer and on weekends traffic between Santa Monica and Malibu can be horrendous, wall-to-wall at three miles per hour. Beyond Malibu, the PCH thins to four lanes to two lanes there are fewer houses more trees less people bigger waves the curves more extreme the bluffs become mountains and aside from the concrete of the road, the land is as it has been since the dawn of the world blue hitting beige fading into sloping green broken large gray stone crags. For thirty miles it continues north each turn each slope each beach can take your breath away, make you question man god society your life your existence, it's so beautiful it takes your breath, your breath, it's so beautiful it can take your heart.

***

There are twelve men asked to participate each year. The Racemaster chooses them. Sometimes they know each other and sometimes they don't, sometimes they have raced before and sometimes they haven't. Each of them has a spectacular car, it is one of the reasons they are chosen. Each of them drives the car in a way that defies federal, state, county and city laws it is one of the reasons they are chosen. Each of them has access to ten thousand dollars in cash for the pot, it is one of the reasons they are chosen. No one knows the other reasons except for the Racemaster, and he doesn't share them with anyone.

They meet at 2:00 AM on April 1 of every year. The meeting place is in the parking lot of a fast-food restaurant on Olympic Boulevard near the entrance ramp to the 405, just north of the junction with the 10. There are twelve parking spots along the back of the parking lot. Each car is given a number that corresponds with a number in front of one of the spots. The cars, which are high-end European sports cars, rebuilt and modified American muscle cars, and Japanese sedans tricked out for drag-racing on the long straight empty streets of the Valley, all park with their front ends facing out. The drivers are varied in age, race, religion and socioeconomic status. None of those things matter to the Racemaster. All that matters to him are their cars, their skills, and their cash.

At 2:10 they are given the route and the rules. The route is more or less a complete circle around the city of Los Angeles. It goes from the 405 North to the 101 East to East Los Angeles Interchange to the 5 Bypass to the 10 West to the PCH North to the intersection of the PCH and Malibu Road. There is a grocery store in the Malibu Colony Plaza called Ralph's there are twelve spots in front of Ralph's with numbers identical to the ones in the fast-food restaurant. The first car to park face

162

out within the lines of the same numbered spot it started in, wins the race. The winner takes the entire pot. There are no rules.

At 2:15, the Racemaster blows a whistle and the race begins. The cars blow out of the lot, on more than one occasion there have been wrecks in the lot and cars haven't made it out of it. If they do make it out, and make it up the ramp and onto the 405, they fly, absolutely fucking fly. All of the cars, with rare exception, can move at speeds above 200 mph, and at this time of night, the roads are almost empty. The cars usually travel in fairly close proximity to each other, and the race is won or lost in the transitions from highway to highway, when the cars need to slow down to make it up and down the ramps. There is always at least one major accident, and every couple years, one, and sometimes more, of the accidents is fatal. On more than one occasion cars have been pulled over, or have led highway patrol cruisers on high-speed chases, though at this point, most of the cars have military-grade radar detectors and laser jammers that allow them to avoid problems with law enforcement. The total distance of the race is approximately sixty-five miles. The winning time is usually around 25 minutes. The fastest winning time in the history of the race was 19 minutes 22 seconds. The slowest was 31 minutes 11 seconds.

After the race starts the Racemaster drives directly from the starting point to the finish line. He loves the drive, it is his favorite time of the year. He thinks about the cars, the drivers, tries to imagine where they are, who's winning, who's wrecked, who's been pulled over, what's going through their minds. He places bets with himself as to who will win, and if he has done his job, and chosen the drivers well, with care and precision, he will be unable to guess. When he reaches the parking lot of Ralph's in Malibu, he parks his own car, a rather pedestrian Chevy that he has owned since 1983, and he sets up a lawn chair, cracks a beer and lights a cigar. As he sits and waits, and drinks his beer and smokes his cigar, he smiles and he thinks about what's happening. They're out there on the road, moving at speeds somewhere above 180 mph and most likely somewhere around 210, those fast cars and those crazy fucking drivers, they're out there. He smiles, and he thinks, and he waits.

**

If the population grows at current rates, and the ratio of cars to people remains at the current levels, it is estimated that sometime around the year 2025, Los Angeles will experience something resembling permanent gridlock.

By 1895 there are 135,000 people living in Los Angeles. In an effort to sustain the Los Angeles River as the city's primary source of water, William Mulholland, the commissioner of the Los Angeles Water Department, institutes a metering system to regulate overall water use. By 1903, there are 235,000 people living in Los Angeles and the Los Angeles River is failing. A search for other renewable water resources within Los Angeles County finds nothing.

Esperanza gets up every morning at 6:00 AM. She takes a shower and does her hair, which Mrs. Chase requires her to keep in a bun. Before she gets dressed, she spends fifteen minutes rubbing oil from the prickly pear cactus of southeastern Mexico on her thighs, one of her cousins buys it from a shaman, who claims to use the oil to shrink himself so that he can spy on his enemies, and sends it to her. Esperanza uses it with the hope that someday she'll be able to wear normal pants.

When her thigh-rubs are over, she puts on her travel outfit, a gray skirt and white blouse, Mrs. Campbell requires her to present herself in a respectable way as she comes to and from work. When she's dressed she walks to the bus stop, gets on the bus to Pasadena, gets off the bus and walks to the Campbell residence. She enters the grounds through a gate in the back of the property. She enters the house through an entrance near the back door that leads directly to the basement. She is required to be dressed and ready for work at 8:00 AM, she usually arrives around 7:45. She changes into her work uniform and walks to the kitchen, where she puts on a pot of coffee. Mrs. Campbell is very particular about her coffee. It must be a specific type (she only buys American products, so it's Hawaiian) made in a specific way (two and a quarter scoops in a size 4 filter) and served at a specific temperature (warm but not hot) mixed in a specific way (two tablespoons of milk, one teaspoon of sugar). If it is not exactly to her liking, she either dumps it on the floor, and Esperanza is required to clean it up, or, if she's in a bad mood, she throws it on her, and Esperanza is required to go back into the basement and change into a clean uniform. Esperanza serves the coffee at exactly 8:10, along with a copy of the day's *Los Angeles Times*, on a saucer which sits on a tray that rests carefully, and in a stable manner, on Mrs. Campbell's bed. While Mrs. Campbell drinks the coffee and skims the headlines of the paper, Esperanza draws her bath, which also must be a precise temperature. After having hot water splashed at her, and after being pushed into the tub twice, Esperanza set the temperature for herself by scratching minute, almost invisible, marks into the porcelain that indicate the place to where the faucets should be turned. While Mrs. Campbell relaxes in the bath, Esperanza cleans away her tray and makes her bed. If the bed is not perfectly made, with stiff corners and no wrinkles, Mrs. Campbell pulls the covers and sheets from the bed and throws them on the floor and Esperanza must remake the bed from scratch. When the bed is made to Mrs. Campbell's satisfaction, Esperanza goes back to the kitchen, where she makes two pieces of bran toast with tangerine jam and sets them on a plate at the kitchen table. Mrs. Campbell never eats them, but likes them to be there just in case. When the toast is properly made and placed, Esperanza goes back into the basement and gets her supplies, window cleaner, floor polish, a mop, a vacuum cleaner, rags, a feather duster. The cleaning of the entire house is spread out over the course of five days, each day is devoted to a specific section of it. Mondays are devoted to the living room, dining room and library. Tuesdays are for the kitchen, the breakfast room, the gallery, and the men's card room (which hasn't been used since her husband died). Wednesdays are for the guest bedrooms and bathrooms, Thursdays for Mrs. Campbell's bedrooms and the bedrooms of her children (who tend not to visit). Fridays are for the guest house and touch-up work that might be needed for the weekend. If Mrs. Campbell isn't busy, or doesn't have plans, she follows Esperanza as she works and points out mistakes she's making, or areas that might need more work, she'll often make Esperanza do something, such as dust a lamp, over and over and over, until it is done to her satisfaction. If Mrs. Campbell is busy, or she has plans, she checks on the work when she returns, and she always finds something wrong with it. If she's in a good mood, she will calmly point out what bothers her or what she thinks hasn't been properly finished, if she's in a bad mood, she'll yell, scream, throw things and break things, the cost of which she removes from Esperanza's pay. At noon, Esperanza is given fifteen minutes for lunch, which she takes in her area of the basement, and at 3:00, she is given a five-minute break, which she often spends crying in one of the bathrooms. Aside from her cleaning duties, she helps coordinate deliveries of flowers and groceries, and helps Mrs. Campbell communicate with two Mexican gardeners who work on the grounds, and who both speak perfect English, but don't want Mrs. Campbell to know so that they can ignore almost everything she says to them. Esperanza leaves at around 6:00 PM. She takes the bus home.

When she gets home, she has dinner with some portion of her family. Because most of them are illegal, and find work when they can, often standing outside home-supply superstores and picking up day jobs from contractors, she never knows who she will or will not have dinner with. They usually have Mexican food, made by the women in the house who aren't working, though every couple of weeks they pool their money and buy a mammoth bucket of fried chicken with sides of baked beans and mac and cheese. After dinner, while the rest of the family migrates towards the television, Esperanza goes to her room, where she spends her nights reading or studying. She reads romance novels, often set in Europe, where lovely women fall in love with rich handsome men, where their love is troubled and tortured, where there are always seemingly insurmountable obstacles to overcome in order to be together, and where love, deep true eternal love, always triumphs. When she isn't reading, she's studying for college entrance exams, which she has already taken once, and scored highly on, but wants to take again in order to score higher. She focuses on the math section of the test, spends hours poring over numbers, charts, graphs and formulas. It's boring and awful, and sometimes she feels like throwing the books out the window or stuffing them into the trash, but she wants to go to college and needs the higher score to try and get another scholarship. Before she goes to sleep, she applies the prickly pear cactus oil again, and then she gets on her knees and prays, she prays for her mother and father, for her family, for all the Mexicans in LA, she prays for the ability to do well on her test, for her future, for some sense of contentment. Her last prayer is always for Mrs. Campbell, she asks God to open her heart, to set her free from her hatred, to make her a kinder, better person, to give her a period of happiness before he takes her. After she prays, she turns off her light and gets into bed. When he sees her light is off, her father often comes in and kisses her on the forehead and tells her he loves her. She loves it when he does, and at twenty-one, it means more to her than it did when she was eight, ten, twelve or any other age.

It's another sunny day she applies her cactus oil gets ready takes the bus walks towards the house. There are other domestics walking the same route, maids and cooks and nannies, many of them are friends with each other. As they walk towards the back entrances of the homes where they work, they laugh and chat, smoke and tell stories. The stories are always about their employers, about their demands their routines, about their cheating husbands and spoiled children, about their lack of consideration and their sense of entitlement, about their superiority, their cruelty. Most of the women are significantly older than Esperanza, in their thirties forties fifties sixties, and in a couple cases, their seventies. They have husbands and children, grandchildren, they have lives away from their jobs. Most of them are not residents or citizens of the United States, which limits their ability to work in any other capacity. In one sense, Esperanza feels like she's one of them, or is destined to be one of them. In another sense, the idea that she's making this walk, wearing the same clothes, and working the same type of job when she's older, so profoundly depresses her that it makes her want to die. Her parents brought her to this country to give her opportunities that they never had, and so that she could have a life that wasn't possible for them. They didn't come here so that she could spend her life cleaning the mansion of a nasty old lady.

She turns into the grounds walks into the basement changes into

her uniform. As she walks up the stairs she smells coffee
someone's already made it she panics looks at her watch, it's 7:53
she's early. She stops takes a deep breath, wonders if she was
supposed to start earlier, if Mrs. Campbell told her something
that she forgot. She prepares to get screamed at, to have things
thrown at her, to be called names. Whatever's going on in the
kitchen is not going to be good. She thinks about going back
downstairs and changing and sneaking out through the back
entrance and going home. She takes a deep breath. She can smell
the coffee. She wants to go home. She thinks about her mother
and father all of the indignities they have endured over the years
working jobs like this her father always told her a job is a job
and it's your job to do it, even if you don't like it. She takes a
deep breath, she opens the door and steps into the kitchen.
A small, chubby man sits at the table. He's wearing plaid boxer
shorts and a white T-shirt with food stains on it. His hair is
red, it's thick on the sides and thin on top, he has a patchy red
mustache. He's drinking a large cup of coffee and eating some
toast with jam, he has Mrs. Campbell's paper spread out in
front of him. Esperanza doesn't know him, has never seen him,
and despite his appearance, she's scared of him. He turns to
her, speaks.
Hola. (Hi.)
She stares at him.
Mi nombre es Doug. (My name is Doug.)
Stares.
Cual es su nombre? (What's your name?)
She stares at him. He stares back, speaks.
Usted tiene un nombre? (Do you have a name?)
She speaks, because she doesn't know him, she uses a Mexican
accent.
I speak English. My name is Esperanza.
He smiles.
Nice to meet you, Esperanza.
He licks some jam from his fingers, wipes his fingers on his
shirt, picks up a piece of toast.

Would you like some toast?

Where is Mrs. Campbell?

Probably upstairs.

What have you done to her?

He takes a bite of the toast. Some jam gets caught in his mustache. He speaks as he chews.

What are you talking about?

I'm going to call the police.

She steps towards the phone. He takes another bite, speaks.

She forgot to tell you, didn't she.

Esperanza hesitates.

Tell me what?

Keeps chewing, speaking.

That I was coming.

Who are you?

Doug Campbell. I'm Mrs. Campbell's youngest son.

I don't believe you.

I've heard that one before.

You don't look like her.

Heard that one too. My brother calls me the family troll.

He wipes his hands on his shirt, leaves a streak of jam across its front, continues chewing and speaking.

Though I'm not sure why exactly he calls me a troll. I've always thought of myself as more of a prince than a troll. An unconventional prince, but a prince nonetheless.

Esperanza smiles. The man she sees in front of her is definitely not a prince. Not a prince of men, not a prince of toast-eating mustachioed slobs, not even a prince of trolls. She speaks.

Do you mind if I take the coffeepot?

You gonna have a cup?

No. I need to prepare Mrs. Campbell's coffee.

Don't worry about that.

It is part of my job. Every day I must prepare her coffee.

Breakfast in bed with the paper and then a bath, that whole thing?

Yes.

I talked to her a little while ago. She's skipping it today.

She looks at him. He smiles, there's food caught between his teeth.

Until she tells me no, I must do it.

She reaches for the coffeepot. As she does, Mrs. Campbell, in her bathrobe and slippers, walks into the kitchen. She speaks.

Good morning, Dougie.

Hi, Mom.

Did you find everything you need?

Sure did.

She walks over, kisses his cheek.

How's your coffee?

Great.

She sits down across from him.

It smells wonderful.

You want a cup?

She starts looking at the paper.

I'd love one.

He starts to get up, without looking at or acknowledging Esperanza, Mrs. Campbell speaks.

My maid will get it for me.

Doug looks at Esperanza, shrugs. She turns around walks to the cabinet, takes out a porcelain cup and a saucer. As she walks back towards the table, Mrs. Campbell looks at Doug, speaks.

It's so nice to have you home.

It's good to be here.

I almost can't believe it.

It's true, Mom. I'm right here.

Esperanza sets the cup and saucer down in front of her. Doug reaches for the pot, Mrs. Campbell stops him.

She will pour my coffee, Doug. It's part of her job.

Esperanza picks up the pot, pours a cup for Mrs. Campbell. Doug speaks.

Thank you, Esperanza.

Mrs. Campbell looks surprised.

172

I guess you've met?

Yeah, we were chatting before you came down.

Mrs. Campbell turns to Esperanza, looks incredibly angry.

What are the rules of this house, young lady?

Esperanza recoils.

I did nothing wrong, Mrs. Campbell.

I will determine what is right or wrong here. Now what are the rules of this house?

Doug speaks.

Mom, you're making too big a deal of this.

Mrs. Campbell turns to him.

I love you, Doug, and I'm incredibly pleased to have you home, but please let me run my household as I see fit.

She turns back to Esperanza, who looks terrified.

Young lady. The rules?

I didn't do anything wrong.

One of the rules of this house is that you are not to speak to anyone but me, and you are to speak to me only when spoken to. Correct?

Esperanza stares at the floor.

It seems you violated this rule by speaking to my son. Correct?

Doug speaks.

Mom, I spoke to her first and . . .

She interrupts him.

This is not your business, Doug.

She turns back to Esperanza.

You are not to speak to him again. Is that understood?

Esperanza stares at the floor, nods.

Young lady, please show me at least a small amount of respect and look at me while I speak to you.

Esperanza looks up.

You are not to speak to my son, or to anyone else in this home, unless given my permission first. Do you understand me?

Yes.

Are you sure?

Yes.

Please say, in a clear voice—Yes, I understand you, Mrs.
Campbell.
Yes, I understand you, Mrs. Campbell.
A little louder please.
Yes, I understand you, Mrs. Campbell.
I can't hear you.
Yes, I understand you, Mrs. Campbell.
Mrs. Campbell glares at Esperanza, whose hands are
trembling, whose eyes are tearing.
Normally I would dismiss someone like you for disobeying me.
This is my home and you are my employee and while you are
here you will do as I say. While my son is here, and he may be
here for an extended period of time, the same policies will
apply to him. Do you understand me?
Yes, I understand you, Mrs. Campbell.
Instead of dismissing you, I will be docking your pay. You will
receive half of your pay this week if you can make it through
the week without any further problems.
Doug speaks.
Mom, you really don't . . .
She interrupts him.
You have to be firm with these people, Doug. Please trust me.
She turns back to Esperanza.
Have you understood everything I've told you?
Yes, I understand you, Mrs. Campbell.
Good, because I am going to hold you to it. Now, please leave
us. And I do not want to see you again today, so please stay
away from areas of the house where we might be.
Yes, Mrs. Campbell.
Esperanza turns and walks out of the kitchen starts down the
stairs to the basement. Her hands are trembling, lips trembling,
tears start coming she hates herself, hates herself. She reaches
the bottom of the stairs sits down on the last step puts her face
in her hands hates herself, hates her job, hates this house and
yard, hates the street and town, hates that she's here five days a
week, hates cleaning doing laundry washing dishes dusting.

Her face is in her hands she hates that she has no confidence. Her face is in her hands she hates that she allows Mrs. Campbell to humiliate her. Her face is in her hands she hates that her life is not what it could have been. Her face, her hands. Hates.

In 1893, a mammoth crowd in downtown Los Angeles waits for hours to see San Francisco photographer Eadweard Muybridge present his zoopraxiscope and Animal Locomotion, which marks the first time a motion picture is shown in the city. In 1894, Abraham Kornheiser purchases three Kinetoscopes, machines that allow a viewer to watch a motion picture through a peephole, from Thomas Edison. His intention was to open the first movie theater in Los Angeles, which was to be called Kornheiser's Peep Show Palace. The kinetoscopes were damaged en route, and Edison refused to fix them or refund Kornheiser's money. In 1895, Edison sells Elijah Nachman a Vitascope, which was the first functional motion picture projector. Nachman opens Nachman's Magical Vitascope Theater, the first movie theater in Los Angeles County.

Joe sits behind the dumpster for an hour, two three four, the blond girl is asleep on the concrete next to him. She is breathing steadily, she appears to have stopped bleeding. Once or twice an hour she stirs or mumbles, her hands twitch or she sighs, her position changes slightly. Ugly Tom comes back twice he brings Joe a piece of day-old pizza, half of a bean-and-cheese burrito. Four Toes Tito, commonly known as Four, a tall, bearded El Salvadoran with waist-length hair who sleeps behind a hot dog stand and who was born with only four toes on each foot, comes by to see the girl he thinks he knows her but when he sees her it's not who he thinks it is. Jenny A., a thirty-eight-year-old mother of three from Phoenix, who lost her family, friends, future and life because she couldn't stop drinking, comes by to say hello and hang out and chat and see if Old Man Joe will give her a bottle of wine from his stash in the bathroom. Joe knows if he gives her his keys to the bathroom she'll drink everything he's got so he says maybe later, Jenny, maybe later, she says she understands says she's going over to the liquor store to try to bum some cash, and if she's lucky something to drink, from exiting customers.

Around noon, after almost six hours of waiting with her, the girl wakes up. She lifts her head a few inches from the ground, looks at Old Man Joe, speaks.

Who the fuck are you?

He laughs.

My name is Joe.

Where the fuck am I?

Venice, California.

No shit.

She coughs.

Where in Venice?

You're on Speedway behind an ice cream shop on the boardwalk.

She starts to slowly sit up. There is dried blood caked on her face and in her hair, one eye swollen almost shut, a gash on her cheek, a bruised lip, a missing lower tooth.

An ice cream shop on the boardwalk?

Yes.

There are fifty ice cream shops on the boardwalk.

She coughs again.

There are a bunch of them, but probably not fifty.

Fine, there are a bunch of them. Which one am I fucking
sitting behind?

Joe laughs again, looks at the girl, who is now leaning against
the dumpster. She's young, very young, maybe fifteen, too
young to be homeless, too young to be living on the
boardwalk, too young. He speaks.

What's your name?

Why do you care?

I'm trying to help you.

I don't need your help.

What's your name?

Where the fuck am I?

Behind an ice cream store near the paddle tennis courts.

How the fuck did I end up down here?

I have no idea. A friend of mine found you.

If you try to fuck me, or make me suck your dick, I'll bite it
off.

Old Man Joe laughs again. The girl speaks.

I'm serious. I'll bite your dick right the fuck off.

You're a bit young for me.

That's why most guys want to fuck me, 'cause I'm young.

Not me.

She reaches up, touches her face. Her knuckles are bruised, cut.

This is fucked.

You need help.

I'm fucked, but I'll be fine.

We should call an ambulance.

If there's an ambulance there's usually cops. I don't need no
ambulance, and definitely don't need no cops.

Then we should go to the hospital.

I ain't going to no fucking hospital either.

You need a doctor.
Unless you know one who lives behind one of these dumpsters,
I ain't seeing one.
Why?
Because.
You got warrants?
Do I look like some kinda criminal?
Yeah.
Well I ain't.
Where'd you run away from?
Why you think I'm a runaway?
You ain't fooling anybody.
It ain't none of your business.
She tries to stand, has trouble. Sits back down. Old Man Joe
stands, offers his hand, speaks.
Let's at least get you cleaned up.
Where we gonna do that?
I got a bathroom.
Where?
Down Speedway a bit.
You look homeless.
I am. Sort of. I live in a bathroom.
He holds his hand closer. She slaps it away.
I'll use your bathroom, but I ain't touching you.
She slowly stands, when she's up, he sees that she's tiny, maybe
five feet tall, maybe a hundred pounds. It makes her wounds
look worse. Joe speaks.
Can you walk?
She takes a step, winces.
Yeah.
She takes another step, winces again.
You sure?
Yeah. I'm fine.
You want some food?
You got a good dumpster?
I'll get you something fresh.

From where?

Wherever you want.

You got money?

I got friends.

He motions towards the street section of the alley.

Let's get you cleaned up, and I'll find you something good.

If you try to fuck me, you'll be sorry.

He laughs again, steps around the dumpster, walks into the street. She follows him slowly, she's walking carefully, gingerly, she has other wounds that Joe can't see. He walks a few feet in front of her, frequently turns to check on her, she stares at the ground, winces, occasionally looks up, occasionally stops and feels her face, carefully touches spots on her legs, on her torso. It's three blocks to Joe's bathroom. It normally takes Joe five minutes to make the walk, it takes them twenty. When they reach the bathroom, Joe stops, looks at her, speaks.

This is my bathroom. Let me go in for a minute, then it's all yours.

You got shit you need to hide?

Something like that.

And you don't trust me to go in first?

No.

Fuck you then.

He goes in, takes two bottles of wine from the toilet tank, looks around for anything else, there's nothing. He steps out holding the bottles. The girl sees them, speaks.

You were worried I was gonna steal your fucking wine?

Just making sure I keep what's mine.

I don't drink, and I could give a shit about your crappy wine.

He laughs again, turns towards the bathroom.

There's hot water and soap and paper towels. You gotta clean your face and hands, and clean your cuts so they don't get infected. Do it as quick as you can, and if you need help, just call.

She looks at him for a minute.

Why you doing this?

He looks at her.

I don't know.

She steps around him, closes the door. He steps away from the door, looks at the eating area that's part of the taco stand, hopes none of the tourists have to use the bathroom. If they do he'll have to get the girl out. If she resists, it might anger the owner. If the owner gets angry, there's a chance he'll lose the bathroom, and he doesn't want to have to find a new place to sleep, and he definitely doesn't want to have to find a new place to take a shit. He can hear the sink running can hear the girl swearing saying fuck, shit, goddamnit, motherfucker. He hears the sink stop running he doesn't hear anything. He waits for a minute two maybe she's drying herself off he waits another minute two he knocks on the door. No response. He knocks again, waits, no response. He knocks again. Nothing. He takes out his key opens the door she's sitting on the floor her knees at her chest. She looks up at him. He speaks.

You okay?

She nods.

Why you sitting on the floor?

Just am.

No reason?

There's a reason.

What is it?

'Cause it feels good.

The bathroom floor?

I ain't slept inside for almost a year. I ain't been in a bathroom where I had any privacy for longer than that. I ain't been in a place where I could lock the door and feel safe, for even a second, since I was a little kid. That door's got a lock, and I knew you wouldn't open it right away, so I got to sit here for a couple minutes and know I was safe, that no one could fuck with me, and that no one could hurt me. It don't matter if it's a bathroom floor. It could be a bathroom floor covered with fucking nails. It felt good.

Joe stares at her, she stares at him.

Let's get you some food.

She nods, stands, he watches her, looks at her. The blood is gone, her face and hair reasonably clean, her hands are clean. Beneath the cuts, the swelling, the anger, the pain, she looks like a pretty teenage girl. If she had makeup and decent clothes, she might be more than pretty. Limping, hurt and damaged, she's just sad and lonely and beaten. A fucked-up kid in some kind of fucked-up situation.

They walk around the corner of the building the tourists in their shorts, sandals and T-shirts are enjoying their food, enjoying the sun, enjoying their day. The girl avoids them, walks away from them, around them, as if she'll become invisible if she's more than ten feet away from them. They walk out to the boardwalk it's packed the girl scoots quickly across and through the crowd, she carefully avoids touching anyone. Joe follows bumps into three or four people, stands next to her, speaks.

What do you want?

Can you get me a cheeseburger and French fries and a milkshake.

Probably.

That would be fucking awesome.

What kind of milkshake?

Any kind.

You don't have a preference?

I like vanilla, but I don't really care.

Okay.

He walks back into the mass, steps into one of the currents of people moving south he starts moving south with them. He knows the manager of a food place a few blocks away called Big and Big that makes everything ever known, invented or eaten that can be made with fat, grease, meat and cheese. The girl follows him, but not among the people she walks at the edge of the boardwalk along the patch of worn grass lined with benches and overflowing garbage cans, she limps as quickly as she can. When Joe reaches the restaurant there's a massive crowd waiting for food, ordering food, arguing about food, paying for food. He walks to the side of Big and Big there's a steel mesh door with a giant lock he bangs on it, waits. A Mexican man wearing a dirty apron comes to the door, in a Mexican accent he speaks.

Old Man Joe. You motherfucker.

What's up, Paco?

Cooking shit, man. That's it.

The boss around?

Naw, he stayed home today. There was a big fight on TV last night and he got too fucking drunk to come in today.

I need your help with something.

What you got?

I need a burger and fries and a milkshake.

For who?

A friend of mine who ain't eaten in a while.

A friend of yours is okay with me, you old motherfucker.

Thanks.

You want cheese on the burger?

Yeah.

What kind of milkshake?

Vanilla, if you can.

Okay motherfucker, give me a couple minutes.

Thanks, man.

Next time my wife throw me out, I'm gonna come get drunk with you.

I'll supply the good stuff.

You sure as fuck will.

Paco turns away disappears into the kitchen. Joe sits on the concrete leans against the side of the building. He looks across the boardwalk the girl is looking through a garbage can. He yells—hey girl—she doesn't hear him he yells again—HEY GIRL—she looks up he motions for her to join him.

She waits for a break in the crowd limps across the boardwalk she avoids touching anyone. She stands in front of him, he speaks.

You find anything good in the trash?
No, but I didn't go down very far. There's always something in there somewhere.
You want to sit down?
You got a reason for me to sit down?
If you sit down you're gonna get some food.
You ain't fucking with me?
No.
She stares at him for a moment, slowly sits down Joe can tell it hurts her. When she's down she looks at him again, moves a couple feet away from him. He laughs.
Don't worry, I'm not gonna touch you.
Damn straight you're not.
He laughs again, she does not respond. They sit there, against the wall, don't speak, just stare at the endless stream of tourists marching by they're talking, smiling, laughing, taking pictures, checking their wallets, drinking sodas, eating cotton candy, looking around somewhat shocked and amazed and delighted by the scene before them, they're at the world-famous Venice Boardwalk. Joe is amused by them. Enjoys watching them. Is amused by their happiness, enjoys their happiness. He doesn't have any ambition to be one of them, and wouldn't trade what little he has for whatever they have, he's made a decision about his life and how he leads it, and he is at peace with those decisions. The girl glares at them, hate and bitterness written across her face, it ages her makes her look forty instead of somewhere in her teens. Sometimes she looks down at the ground clenches her jaw and shakes her head. Sometimes she mumbles to herself Joe can't hear what she's saying but the tone is nasty, unpleasant. Though she would never admit it, she wishes she were one of them, wishes she had a home bedroom a safe place of her own, wishes she had friends, wishes she went to school, had parents, wishes she had some form of happiness, wishes she had love. Whatever decisions she's made to end up here bloody, beaten, hungry and homeless weren't made for any reason other than necessity, in order for her to

survive the events of her life. She spits on the ground, stares at it, spits again.

After fifteen minutes, she looks at Old Man Joe, speaks.

I think I've had enough of this shit.

Just be patient.

Why?

Because sometimes it pays off.

Bullshit, you're a fucking con.

He laughs, doesn't respond in any other way. They sit there for a few more minutes he can tell she's getting restless a few more minutes the steel mesh door opens and Paco steps out holding a cardboard box. He looks at Old Man Joe, speaks.

Motherfucker.

My man, Paco.

He looks at the girl.

Food for her?

Yeah.

Oh little girl, you motherfucker, I have got some tasties for you.

She sits up looks surprised, truly surprised, and almost happy. Paco leans over and hands her the box.

What is it?

Special Paco Burger, Special Paco Fries, Special Paco Shake, and some packets of American-made ketchup.

She takes the box.

Thank you.

There are the faint beginnings of a smile. Joe stands, speaks.

Thanks, man.

Anything for you, motherfucker. Or maybe not anything, but some tasties every now and then ain't no big deal.

Joe laughs. Paco opens the door to the kitchen, steps inside, disappears. Joe looks down at the girl, who is staring at the burger and fries. He speaks.

You can eat it.

She looks up at him. He sits back down, leans against the wall.

It looks good.

Bet it tastes good too.

He stares at her, she looks down at the food, stares at it. She speaks.

I ain't had a meal like this in a long time.

Yeah.

Long time.

Yeah.

She picks up the burger. Looks at it. It's a thick burger, the cheese is melted over the rounded edges, it sits between the two halves of a sesame seed bun. She takes a bite of it, starts to chew takes another, chews. She sets the burger down in the box, picks up a couple fries, stuffs them into her already full mouth, chews, picks up the milkshake, puts the straw into her mouth sucks. She chews takes a pause swallows once, chews some more swallows again. She looks at Joe, speaks.

That was good.

He looks at the box there is still part of the burger and the fries sitting inside.

There's more.

I'm gonna save it.

You can get it cold and half-eaten from the garbage can whenever you want. Hot off the grill ain't happening again soon.

She looks at the food, thinks about it, starts eating again, the food disappears quickly, when she's done she licks her fingers, wipes ketchup and mustard from her face, licks her fingers again. She stands, puts the unopened ketchup packets in her pocket, throws the box, burger wrapper and cup away. Joe sits and watches her, watches the tourists, closes his eyes and thinks about Chablis. After the trash is gone, the girl comes back, sits down next to him, speaks.

That was good.

Glad you liked it.

Can you get me more?

You gonna say thank you for what I already got you?

Thank you.

You're welcome.

You know how to get anything else?

Like what?

Meth.

How old are you?

None of your business.

You're too young to be on that shit.

I'm too young to have done a lot of shit I've done.

Why you do it?

Same reason you drink.

Doubt it.

It's true.

Why you do it?

I just do. You know where I can get some?

I don't. I try to avoid it. Everyone I ever knew who did it ended up dead.

We all die sooner or later.

They died sooner.

She stands.

I gotta find some.

I'm guessing you're gonna go try to talk to whoever kicked your ass last night.

It's none of your business what I do.

Don't.

I need what I need.

Don't.

I have to.

She starts to limp away. Joe stands.

You never told me your name, girl.

She turns around.

Beatrice.

Seriously?

Yeah. Seriously.

She turns back around and walks away. Joe watches her walk away part of him is happy to see her go another wants her to stay another part just wants her to smile and say goodbye.

When she's gone Joe walks out to the boardwalk and spends three hours panhandling he makes $36. He buys a piece of pizza and sits on the beach and drinks two bottles of Chablis. When it's dark he walks back to his bathroom and lies down and goes to sleep he wakes an hour before dawn, as he does every day. He goes to the bathroom brushes his teeth washes his face. He opens the door steps outside Beatrice is lying on the cement a few feet away. A few feet away.

In 1899 there are seventy police officers trying to control a populace of well over 150,000 people. Opium dens, brothels, gambling establishments, and gin mills are spread throughout the entire city, and exist in every racial and ethnic enclave. Over the course of the next two years, the city hires 200 additional officers. The crime rate rises.

While it might be appropriate here to once again quote from the work of a great poet, it is not going to happen. Instead, a few words from Mr. Amberton Parker, socialite, heir, thespian, international superstar: *Being in love is like getting a twenty-million-dollar check for the starring role in a hot new action film, you think it's going to be great, but when it comes, it's even GREATER!*

Yes, yes, yes, Amberton is in love, deeply in love, truly in love, head-over-heels in love, so in love that he has stopped wearing shoes with laces because he's worried that he can't tie them.

Though he hasn't seen or spoken to Kevin since that fateful three-minute make-out session in Kevin's office, he is absolutely sure of his love. It's deep, it's true, and it's real real real, as real as it gets in this world.

He sits with his beautiful wife Casey in stylish, yet comfortable, chaise longues by the side of their pool. They are both wearing thongs and neither of them are wearing tops (she has a spectacular, if somewhat artificial body), he is drinking a glass of chilled rosé. Their kids are at the other end of the pool with their nannies. Amberton speaks.

It's crazy. I go to bed thinking about him, I wake up thinking about him, I think about him all day. My sense of longing is so great that it's very literally, physically, painful.

He takes a sip of the rosé. Casey speaks.

I'm happy for you.

Thank you.

Just be careful.

I will. I know the drill.

Nothing in public, no discussion of this with anyone outside of our closest friends who have signed nondisclosure agreements, nothing around the kids.

I know the drill, sweetheart, I invented the drill.

And make sure it's real before you go full-blown ga-ga.

It's real. It's as real as it gets in this world.

She laughs. He smiles, speaks.

It is. I'm telling you.

When are you going to see him again?

Not sure.

Is he playing hard-to-get?

No. I am.

You?

Yes.

Do you know how?

Of course. I'm the master of hard-to-get.

She laughs again, speaks.

You're the master of I-am-a-famous-movie-star-come-sleep-with-me-now, and sometimes the I-am-a-famous-movie-star-come-sleep-with-me-now-or-I'll-have-you-fired.

I've never done that.

Yes, you have.

Have not.

Have.

He laughs.

Okay, I have. And it was fun.

And you've definitely never had to play hard-to-get.

I did it twice in films.

Does that count?

Yes. I played a blind concert pianist who could see an individual's future by touching their fingertips.

And you won an Actors Guild Award and a Freedom Spirit Medallion for it.

I did. But it doesn't mean I can do it in real life.

He feigns shock.

You can't?

She smiles, playfully hits him, they both laugh. She speaks.

What's your next step?

Well, I'm going to see him tomorrow.

Where?

I have a meeting with my team at the agency.

He's on your team?

He is now.

Your call or their call?

I called Andrew and asked him to include Kevin.

Does Andrew know why you asked?

No one knows except you, me, and my beloved.

What was your reason?

That you told me he was an impressive young man.

They both laugh.

Don't you think you should have told me?

I'm telling you now.

Their yoga teacher arrives, they go into their studio, and, as is the case from time to time, they do their yoga session in their thongs. When they're finished they shower get dressed meet in the kitchen, where they have lunch with their children and their children's nannies. After lunch they see their respective therapists (she has issues with her father, he has issues with his mother) and then they see a therapist together (they both have issues with fame and adulation). When they're done with their therapy (twice a week, three times if it's a bad week), they go back to their rooms change back into their thongs Casey wears a top because the afternoon sun tends to be more powerful they meet at the pool. They each have a stack of scripts they are supposed to read. Because the scripts, even by their standards, are so awful, they rarely make it through the first ten pages. When a script is considered bad, or at least bad enough so that no amount of money could convince one of the two of them to star in it, they throw it backwards over their heads with a big laugh, knowing that at some point in the near future, one of their staff will come pick it up and throw it away. After an hour, and five scripts thrown over his head, Amberton gives up. He looks at Casey, speaks.

I think I'm going to go shopping.

Where?

Beverly Hills.

Why?

Maybe get a suit for tomorrow.

Don't you have a couple hundred suits?

I want a new one. A nice new perfect expensive suit that makes

me look so hot that even hetero men would want to fuck me.
Have fun.
Do you want to come with?
No.
What are you gonna do?
She smiles.
I'm not sure.
Why are you giving me your naughty look?
She smiles again.
Maybe I've been a naughty girl.
With who?
You know the new nanny?
The young one?
Oh yeah.
How old is she?
Just turned eighteen.
Oh my.
Oh yeah.
Where are the kids?
Going to a friend's house.
Has she signed the documents?
Of course.
He stands, smiles, speaks.
I don't want or need to know any more.
She smiles, speaks.
Have fun, and good luck.
He curtsies, walks into the house up to his room, takes a quick shower and gets dressed he wears jeans and a T-shirt and sandals. He gets into his car decides to drive a black Porsche with blackened windows pulls out of the garage down the driveway through the gate. As is always the case, there are paparazzi waiting on the street outside of his house a small group of men wearing cameras around their neck, SUVs and scooters waiting nearby, Amberton went to driving school to learn how to lose them in the Porsche he makes them disappear quickly in the roads that wind through the hills of Bel-Air.

He drives down to Sunset heads east towards Beverly Hills.
He passes the mansions, estates, manor homes of moguls
movie stars porn barons rock stars TV producers heirs and
heiresses that line both sides when he passes the most famous
of them owned by the playboy founder of a men's magazine
he smiles, remembers the parties he's attended there, the
women were so hot they almost made him want to be
straight. He crosses into Beverly Hills turns south onto the
surface streets they are long and straight he accelerates gets
the Porsche up to 100 mph quickly and easily hits a speed
bump and goes airborne there's fun to be had everywhere for
Mr. Amberton Parker fun fun fun. He drives down Rodeo
Drive tries to decide where he wants to shop the street is
lined with the most expensive and most exclusive boutiques in
the world. None suit his fancy today, he decides to go to the
Beverly Hills branch of a famous New York clothing store
that is on Wilshire he can see more there, have many more
options.
He pulls behind the back of the store pulls up to a gate that
leads to VIP parking in a small garage beneath the store. A
guard comes out Amberton rolls down his window the guard
motions into a camera mounted above the gate and the gate
rises. Amberton pulls in, parks, gets out of his car. He walks
towards a secure door it's about fifteen feet away. By the time
he reaches the door, it is open and a store representative, an
extremely attractive woman in her early thirties, is waiting for
him. She smiles, speaks.
Hello, Mr. Parker. Nice to see you again.
He smiles, speaks in his public voice.
Hello, Veronica.
What can we help you with today?
He steps into the store, the door closes behind him. He's in a
small private waiting room, there are couches and chairs,
tasteful prints on the walls, flowers. He speaks.
I have a big meeting tomorrow and want to get a new suit for
it. A perfect suit.

I assume you'd like to do this privately?

Yes.

Do you have a particular person you would like to work with?

You're my favorite, Veronica, if you're available.

Of course I am, Mr. Parker.

They step into a private elevator it takes them up they step into a small hallway decorated in a manner similar to the waiting room. They walk down the hall, which is lined with doors. Veronica stops in front of one of the doors, opens it with a security card they step into a medium-sized room with a large suede sofa, two matching chairs, a glass table covered with fashion magazines. There is a small refrigerator in a corner two crystal drinking glasses and a basket of fruit sit on top of it. There is an empty clothing rack. A door that leads to a dressing room. A full-length mirror.

Amberton sits on the couch Veronica sits in one of the chairs. They talk about what he's looking for he tells her a beautiful perfect suit. She asks him about brand he doesn't care he just wants beautiful and perfect. She asks about budget he says there isn't one. She asks when he needs it he says tomorrow morning.

She stands tells him she'll be back in a few minutes with some selections for him she asks him if he needs anything he says no. She leaves. He picks up one of the fashion magazines flips through it he's better-looking than all of the men, Casey is better-looking than all of the women, he puts it down. He picks up another one. Same thing. Another one, same thing. He wonders what his life would be like if he wasn't so good-looking. He would probably be a world-renowned professor at a prestigious eastern university. Or maybe an English university.

There's a knock at the door Amberton says come in. Veronica opens the door there are two assistants with her both holding dark suits in each arm there is a tailor standing behind them. They enter the room Amberton stands smiles he's excited, excited. He starts looking at the suits most of them are Italian a couple English runs his hands along their materials hand-brushed worsted, vicuna, lightweight gabardine, none of them costs less than five thousand dollars. He tries a couple of them on, he looks carefully at how they hang on his body, how their colors enhance his skin. He likes two but can't decide between them, one is black, one gray, they're both made of vicuna (the fabric of a rare Peruvian llama). He decides to buy both of them he'll decide which to wear in the morning. The tailor takes measurements marks the adjustments rushes from the room to get to work. Amberton thanks Veronica and her assistants she tells him they'll deliver the suits later this evening he says thank you. He generously tips everyone. He leaves, drives back to Bel-Air traffic on Sunset is bad so it takes forty minutes. He doesn't mind the traffic, he listens to love songs and he dreams, love songs and dreams.

He pulls up to his gate the paparazzi are still there the gate closes behind him he parks the car goes inside. He has dinner with Casey and the kids. They have fresh grouper and Asian vegetables. The nannies put the kids to bed and Amberton and Casey watch a film in their screening room. The film is a new drama starring two of their friends (though they don't actually like them). It's about a doctor and a photographer who fall in love while working in a third-world war zone. Just after they consummate their relationship during a mortar attack, the doctor (the woman) contracts a rare disease and dies. The photographer publishes a book of photos documenting her work and wins a Pulitzer. Shortly thereafter, he returns to the war zone and also dies. It's a heartbreaking film that makes both of them cry. When it's over they both sit and stare at the screen and talk about how depressed they are that they didn't do the film (it was offered to them first, but the money wasn't right). They kiss each other goodnight (on the cheek) and go to their respective wings of the house.

At some point while they were watching the film, Amberton's suits were delivered. They are in hanging bags on his bed. He takes them out runs his hands along them, very nice, extremely nice. He tries each of them on, they fit him perfectly, he spends thirty minutes looking at himself in each of them looking at himself from a multitude of angles, he can't decide which one to wear. He hangs them in the closet. He runs his hands along them one more time. Very nice, extremely nice.

He gets into bed can't sleep. He turns on a sixty-inch plasma TV mounted on the far wall, puts in a DVD of highlights from Kevin's football career that he bought off the Internet. He watches Kevin running, throwing, scoring touchdowns, giving locker-room interviews, sets the DVD so it will loop, watches it over and over again. He lies sideways on his bed so he can watch it as he falls asleep (he can't, for some reason, sleep on his back), he wants Kevin to be the last image in his mind when he drifts away, he drifts away.

He wakes and the DVD is still playing. He smiles what a wonderful way to start a day, a new day, a fine Los Angeles day, the sun is streaming through the windows it's a day that promises to be terrific.

He gets out of bed and brushes his teeth. He checks his closet the suits are still there. He walks downstairs Casey and the children are in the backyard with the nannies. He eats breakfast kiwis, tangelos, granola and pomegranate juice. He goes outside what a beautiful day. He plays hide-and-seek with the kids and he always hides behind the same tree and they always find him and when they do they laugh laugh laugh. After an hour, it's time for him to get ready.

He takes a shower soaps shampoos conditions. He shaves, puts lotion on his skin, a dab of cologne on his neck, he uses his signature scent, it's called—Ahhh, Amberton—and it's a huge seller in Korea and Japan. He goes to the closet and looks at the suits and touches them both. He knows he's going to a wear a periwinkle shirt, he puts the shirt on and tries each of the jackets with it, he stands in light he thinks will approximate the light of the agency conference room.

The black radiates strength. The gray has a certain

sophistication to it, and works beautifully with the periwinkle.
The black denotes power and virility. The gray is indicative of
a man with a heart and feelings. The black makes his body
look angular, the gray makes him look lithe. He debates the
merits of each in his mind black or gray he flips a coin and
black wins. Amberton likes to think of himself as one who
runs against the wind, so he decides on the gray. When he's
dressed he looks in the mirror and he's pleased, more than
pleased he's overwhelmed. He takes a deep breath and inhales
his scent, or, as he likes to call it, his musk, and he thinks—
Ahhh, Amberton.

He walks out to the entrance of his house there is a car waiting
for him, a black Mercedes limousine, the driver is holding the
back door open for him. He slips inside leans back against the
soft leather, it's cool, clean. The driver closes the door, and as
he walks to the driver's door, Amberton leans forward and
opens a small cabinet, where there is a bottle of champagne
sitting in an ice bucket. He picks up the bottle and removes the
cork and as he pours himself a glass, the driver sits behind the
wheel. He turns and speaks.

Good afternoon, Mr. Parker.

Hi.

Are you comfortable, sir?

I am.

Do you need anything?

I'm great, thank you.

We are going to the agency, sir.

In a jiffy.

If you need anything, sir, please let me know.

The driver turns back around, a black glass partition rises.
Amberton takes a sip of the champagne, it's perfectly chilled,
sweet with a mature taste that hints of spring daffodil and
summer cherry.

The drive is quick and easy. Amberton sips and savors the
champagne, and runs a variety of strategies and scenarios
through his head. Should he be warm and gracious, humorous

and high-energy, distant and serious, cold and clinical? He tries
to decide how he'll greet Kevin, will he shake his hand, if he
does will he use both hands and cover the first with the
second, should he kiss him on the cheek (No No No No No)?
Once they're sitting at the conference table (there are usually
four or five agents in the room with him), should he look at
him, acknowledge him, pay special attention to him, completely
ignore him? He decides to play it by ear, improvise, trust his
instincts. He sips his champagne, he turns up the air-
conditioning.

They pull into the agency's private garage. Amberton steps out
and walks towards the door. His primary agent, whose name is
Gordon, and who is also the CEO of the agency, is waiting for
him with two of his assistants (he has six). Gordon is tall and
handsome, his black hair is slicked back like a banker, he
wears a perfect black suit (it might even be nicer than
Amberton's, which Amberton briefly considers, but dismisses).
He is incredibly smart, incredibly savvy, incredibly smooth,
incredibly successful, and incredibly rich. Many people consider
him the most powerful person in Hollywood, though that is
not something he would ever say, and when asked about it, he
laughs and changes the subject. Unlike many agents, he truly
cares for the well-being of his clients, and he works incredibly
hard to further and protect their careers. He is the one person,
aside from his wife, that Amberton trusts and with whom he
shares most of his secrets. Gordon smiles, speaks.

Amberton.

Amberton does the same.

Gordon.

Nice suit.

Thank you. You too.

Thank you. It's vicuna.

So's mine.

They both laugh, shake hands.

How are Casey and the kids?

They're well.

We've got some exciting things for you today.

I'm sure you do.

They turn into the agency. The assistants follow three steps behind them. They walk along a wide, white, art-lined hallway, step into a private elevator (the assistants take the stairs). They step out of the elevator and walk through another wide, white, art-lined hallway, at the end of the hallway they walk through a set of double glass doors. They step into a large conference room. The room is long, wide, three walls are white, the other glass. There is a large, polished ebony conference table in the middle of the room, black leather Eames chairs are arranged around it. A matching ebony cabinet sits along the long wall, on the top of one end of the cabinet there are bottles of French water, ceramic coffee cups, and a silver coffee service. There are four agents in the room, two men and two women, all of them wear black suits, Kevin is not with them. They stand when Amberton and Gordon enter, all are smiling, they greet Amberton and shake his hand. When the greetings are finished, everyone sits, Amberton speaks.

Is this everyone?

Gordon speaks.

A couple of the agents couldn't make it.

Where are they?

I'm not sure.

The meeting starts, no Kevin. Amberton wants to leave, wants to cry, wants to yell and scream wants to throw his coffee mug no Kevin. He wants to tell everyone in the room why he set the meeting up, tell them all he's in love, desperately in love, and that they can go back to their jobs this was all a ruse he's sorry for wasting their time. They talk to him about a new action franchise where he would play a scientist whose job it is to save the world from environmental ruin. They tell him about a prestigious cable network that wants to make a ten-hour miniseries about Michelangelo. They pitch him a drama about a politician with hepatitis C. He hardly hears a word of any of it. He has trouble focusing, his head is spinning, it feels like there's a hole in his chest and his heart is pounding and it physically hurts him. He wants to cry. He wants to climb under the table and curl up in a ball and cry. He hasn't felt this way since he was a teenager, when his first love, a basketball player two years older than him, cut off their affair because he was worried his teammates would find out. He hasn't been denied anything since he was a teenager. His money and fame have always been enough to get him anything, everything and anyone he's ever wanted. He wants to ask Gordon to hug him, to hold his hand. He wants to call his mother and have her sing him a lullaby.

The meeting lasts an hour it feels like three days. When it's over he thanks everyone and shakes their hands again, he tells Gordon to messenger him the scripts he'll read them at home. When he gets in the elevator he starts shaking. When he gets in the car he starts crying. His crying quickly degenerates into loud, messy bawling, and as the car pulls through his gate his shirt is wet with tears and he's howling. As the car pulls to his door he sees another car, a black Lexus, which is exactly like Kevin's car, sitting near his garage. He stops howling. He starts to panic in a different way. He pulls down a mirror that's built into a flap in the ceiling. He wipes his face tries to clean himself up tries to regain his composure. He looks at his shirt there's nothing he can do. He tries to think of a reason for his appearance if Kevin's really inside he'll tell him he was so moved by the story of the politician with hep C that he broke down. He taps on the glass partition and the driver gets out and walks around to his door and opens it. He steps out of the car and he hands the driver a $100 bill and he thanks him. The sun is high and it's hot. He looks at his house it's gigantic and beautiful. Kevin's car is in his driveway. His wife and children are somewhere where they won't bother him. What a day. What a day!

In 1901, Harrison Otis, the publisher of the *Los Angeles Times* newspaper, and his son-in-law, Harry Chandler, purchase large chunks of land in Owens Valley, which is on and just beyond the northeastern edges of Los Angeles County. City Water Commissioner William Mulholland hires J.B. Lippincott, who works for the U.S. Land Reclamation Department, and also secretly works for Otis and Chandler, to survey the land, and it is determined that the Owens River and Owens Lake would be able to provide Los Angeles with a sufficient water supply. Otis and Chandler then purchase large sections of the San Fernando Valley, which would be suitable for development with a proper water supply, and also purchase the water rights to the Owens Valley from a cooperative of local farmers and landowners. They then use the newspaper to create hysteria in regard to the dwindling water supply, and to promote a bond initiative that would finance the design and construction of a new water system. When the bond initiative passes, they sell the Owens Valley water rights to the city of Los Angeles at a huge profit. Mulholland begins designing the Los Angeles aqueduct, which will bring the water of the Owens Valley to the city of LA, and which becomes the longest aqueduct in the world, with a distance of just over 223 miles.

Dylan hasn't been to work in three days. Tiny called him and told him not to come in for a while, that he would call him again when he needed him. When Dylan answered the phone and heard Tiny's voice he started shaking. When he hung up he kept shaking. An hour later he was still shaking. The money was in a stack on the table a few feet away. When he stopped shaking he put it in a drawer with his pants and T-shirts. Then he started shaking again, so he moved it to a drawer with Maddie's pants and T-shirts.

He takes Maddie to work in the morning, spends the days riding his bike aimlessly around the city. He goes into areas he doesn't know Sherman Oaks with its manicured lawns and columned mansions, Reseda and Winnetka flat dense and monotonous housing development after housing devolopment, Brentwood wide leafy streets it almost looks like Ohio he finds the former home of a famous murderer and stops and stares all he sees is a gate and tall sycamores he pulls up to the gate and spits on it. He moves into West LA it has long straight streets with orderly homes and speed bumps into West Hollywood the wide boulevards are lined with palms and the cafés are crowded in the middle of the day with beautiful men and beautiful women the men hold hands, kiss each other, the women hold hands, kiss each other. He drives down Melrose, lined with clothing shops and record stores and head shops and restaurants that go in and out of business all of the buildings covered with graffiti it's ahead of the curve in the rest of the country fashion comes over from Japan moves onto Melrose gets picked up by New York and three years later you can buy it in Wal-Mart. He drives through Hollywood. The Streets of Dreams are worn, dirty, dangerous, decrepit, they're crowded with tourists staring in shock at what isn't like any dream they've ever had of Hollywood glamour, aggressive panhandlers some as old as ninety some as young as ten harass them for money, barkers yell at them to come see wax superstars, world records, the you-can-believe-it, they yell for them to come see strippers, dancers, girls on poles. Crumbling motels are filled with addicts and dealers. Legendary restaurants have rats in the corners and roaches on the walls. Run-down houses have dirt yards cars and cracked driveways, cars on blocks, couches on the sidewalk with the stuffing torn out. Gangbangers stand on corners some are lookouts some are salesmen some are killers. Cops cruise up and down Hollywood Boulevard their presence is not a deterrent in any way at all. When he leaves Hollywood, the only film Dylan can imagine being made there would be a horror film. He goes east into Los Feliz the canyons lined with bungalows the Hills dotted with mansions secondhand shops and diners filled with actors directors musicians artists some have made it some haven't all of them hyper-aware of themselves of each other of their clothes the food they eat everything carefully chosen to project an image of seriousness, of thought, of style, of irony, of carelessness. Out of Los Feliz and into LA proper he goes through ethnic neighborhoods where the signs are in languages he can't read and no one speaks English they're Russian, Korean, Japanese, they're Armenian, Lithuanian, Somalian, they're from El Salvador and Nicaragua and Mexico, India, Iran, China, Samoa. He is often the only white face amongst the crowds of color he is often the only native-born amongst the crowds of immigrants. He knew one African-American kid in his town in Ohio, though no one there called him an African-American. He had seen Mexicans, or what he assumed were Mexicans, working on construction crews. He rides into Watts he's the minority, he rides into East LA he's the minority, he rides through Downtown he's the minority. His color used to allow him to be part of the power structure, or at least the status quo. Here it is meaningless. He is just another human being in a roiling, sun-baked mass of humanity all trying to make it through the day with food on the table a roof overhead some money in the bank. He's just another one.

At the end of each day he buys dinner somewhere a burger shack a taco stand a pizza parlor. He picks up Maddie from the 99 cent store and they go back to the hotel and they take a shower together and they eat dinner at their table in the nude. He bought pizza tonight, and because of the cash he splurged and got extra cheese, extra sauce, pepperoni, mushrooms and onions, double extra cheese. They use paper towels as napkins. He speaks.

I hope they never call back.

She speaks.

You think that'll happen?

I don't know.

You should give it back.

I can't do that.

Why?

If I tell them I took it they'll fuck me up, probably kill me.

Even if you're giving it back?

Yeah.

Then why don't we just take the money and go somewhere else?

Where?

Anywhere.

Where do you want to go?

Beverly Hills?

It's not that much money.

I know, I was just kidding. But we could go to San Francisco or San Diego.

If I just bolt they'll figure out why. And they have clubs in cities all over the country.

What about calling another that doesn't like them.

Like who?

Call the Hells Angels.

Dylan laughs.

The Hells Angels?

Yeah.

I have no idea how to call the Hells Angels. If I did they wouldn't talk to me. If for some reason they did talk to me, they'd laugh.

Why?

The Hells Angels are the Kings of the Biker World. They wouldn't waste their time with these guys. These guys actually all wish they were Hells Angels.

So what do you want to do?

I don't know. Maybe I should go to church and pray.

Didn't you do that through your entire childhood?

Yeah.

What'd it get you?

A mean-ass father and a mother who left us.

Maybe you should just stay here with me.

He laughs.

Yeah, you're probably right.

The phone rings. They look at each other, look at the phone, look back. Maddie speaks.

You want to answer it?

No.

Did you give this number to anyone?

No.

They know where we live?

I don't know.

Did you tell them?

Probably.

The phone's still ringing. They look back at it. It rings, rings, rings. It stops. They look at it, wait for it to ring again. It doesn't. They look back at each other. Maddie picks up another slice of the pizza pie, speaks.

This pizza is good.

Double extra cheese.

And all sorts of other shit. Gotta love it.

Maybe we should just spend all the dough on pizza.

Twenty-three thousand bucks' worth? We won't be eating in the nude anymore, that's for sure.

We'll need a bigger room and a bigger bed.

And a truck instead of the bike.

They both laugh. As Dylan reaches for another piece of the pizza pie, someone starts pounding on the door. They look

back at each other. Pounding on the door. Stare at each other. Pounding. Maddie shakes her head. Pounding. Pounding. Pounding. Dylan stands he's shaking again. Pounding on the door. He walks towards it. Pounding. Maddie watches him she's biting her lip shaking her head she wants to hide somewhere anywhere but she can't move pounding. Dylan stands in front of the door, looks back at Maddie there's pounding on the door on the door on the door there's pounding on the motherfucking door. Dylan speaks.
Hello?

In 1874, Judge Robert Widney builds a two-and-a-half-mile horse-drawn railcar line leading from his Hill Street neighborhood to Downtown Los Angeles. Within two years there are similar lines in Santa Monica, Pasadena, and San Bernardino, and six more lines leading through and around Downtown LA. In 1887 the Pico Street line is electrified. In 1894, the Los Angeles Consolidated Electric Railway Corporation is formed and begins buying the local horse-drawn rail lines and electrifying them. It also paints all the cars red and begins referring to itself as the Red Car Line. In 1898, the Southern Pacific Railroad buys the Los Angeles Consolidated Electric Railway Corporation. It also buys up large parcels of undeveloped land on the outskirts of Los Angeles. It rapidly and greatly expands the LA rail system into these areas and subsequently sells the land to developers. In 1901, Pacific Electric is spun off to run the Los Angeles Railway System. By 1914, it is the largest public rail system in the world, with more than 900 Red Cars on over 1,150 miles of track running into every populated area of Los Angeles County, and also into San Bernardino County and Orange County.

Esperanza's routine changes. Mrs. Campbell and Doug eat breakfast together every morning, so she doesn't have to serve Mrs. Campbell breakfast in bed anymore. Doug also likes to make the morning coffee, so she's also relieved of that duty. Because the morning service tended to be so awful, and Mrs. Campbell, before she had had her morning coffee, tended to be more abusive than she usually was, the change allows Esperanza to start her day in a calmer, easier and more peaceful fashion, which makes the rest of the day, regardless of how awful Mrs. Campbell may become, calmer, easier and more peaceful.

Doug leaves every morning just after he and his mother finish their breakfast. He always wears a white oxford shirt, often put on over whatever T-shirt he's stained at breakfast, and khaki pants and topsiders. He wears a blue nylon backpack stuffed with books that looks like the backpack Esperanza used in junior high school. He carries a brown leather briefcase stenciled with the letters DC—and he rides a small motorized scooter, which has a basket for the briefcase. She has no idea where he goes or what he does, and he usually returns after she's gone. When he first arrived, she assumed he would be gone in a short period of time, but every day he seems more entrenched. His clothes, which were initially kept in his suitcase, are now kept in drawers. His pictures, which are of rockets and spaceships and satellites and orbiting stations, and which he kept spread out on a desk in his room, have been taped to the wall. His toothbrushes (for some reason he has six of them) are in a cup on the sink, his razor is in the medicine cabinet, his soap is in the shower. He does not appear to use deodorant.

Though they never speak, Esperanza likes Doug. Sometimes during the morning, when she's attending to his mother or walking through the kitchen on her way to some other part of the house, she catches him looking at her, occasionally he smiles, and though she doesn't want to, and tries not to, she always smiles back. Though he never directly contradicts his mother, he often tells her she's being silly or acting like a tyrant, and he constantly tells her that her political views are outdated and absurd (Mrs. Campbell likes the current president, Doug calls him a buffoon). While she was initially repulsed by his manners and eating habits, Esperanza now finds them amusing and endearing, thinking that he is the way he is because he doesn't care how he eats or looks as long as it gets to his mouth, where he joyfully chews and swallows. And for someone as self-conscious as she is, his utter indifference to his appearance is refreshing. Every time she looks at her thighs she thinks about him and his stained shirts and the food on his hands and face and she tries to forget her own feelings about how she looks. It doesn't help her much, doesn't make her hate her thighs any less, but it does give her hope, it does give her some small bit of hope. At night when she's home, after she's studied and as she lies in bed before falling asleep, Esperanza thinks about Doug, wonders what he's doing. He has a TV and a video game console in his room, Esperanza has heard Mrs. Campbell scold him for staying up late and playing his silly games, he laughs and says the universe needs saving and dragons need slaying and since someone has to do it, it might as well be him. She imagines him sitting on the floor, a pizza or some potato chips on the floor next to him, staring at the TV with his controller in hand, saving the universe, slaying dragons, doing whatever it is he does, climbing into bed later with his food and a book, falling asleep with both spread out around him.

It's a day like any other day she wakes up gets ready takes the bus walks to the house enters through the back. She goes into the basement and changes into her uniform, she walks up the stairs to the kitchen and just before she steps through the door she takes a deep breath and prepares herself for whatever Mrs. Campbell's latest bit of nastiness might be, she's under the doorframe and Mrs. Campbell isn't there, just Doug, sitting at the table drinking coffee and eating a cinnamon bun. He looks up at Esperanza and smiles and speaks.

Hello, Esperanza.

She nods, he speaks.

It's okay. You can talk to me. My mother isn't here.

Where is she?

I'm not sure. She either went golfing in Palm Springs or to a spa in Laguna or to an equestrian event in Santa Barbara. I tune her out most of the time, so I don't know what she said exactly.

Esperanza smiles. Doug motions to another chair at the table.

You want to sit?

She does, but she's still scared Mrs. Campbell will appear from behind the doorway.

No thank you.

Have some coffee with me.

Esperanza glances at the door.

No, thank you.

Doug laughs.

You're worried this is some kind of test and she's hiding behind the door and is going to jump out and scream at you if you agree to sit with me for a few minutes?

Esperanza tries not to, but she smiles. Doug laughs.

My mother is so fucked up. I mean, I love her and all, she is my mom and she bore me and raised me, but it's fucked up that you're so scared of her that you won't sit here and have coffee with me.

Esperanza shrugs. Doug speaks.

She's not here I promise.

Esperanza smiles again, looks at the door, walks over to it and opens it and looks into the dining room and around the back of the door there is nothing there, no one there. She comes back around, Doug is smiling he speaks.

That was a good one.

Esperanza speaks.

Thank you.

You gonna sit now?

Sure.

She sits down across from him.

You want some coffee?

Sure.

She starts to stand, he motions her back down.

I'll get it.

He stands, steps over to the counter, grabs a cup and fills it with nice, black, steaming hot coffee.

Milk or sugar?

She shakes her head, he steps back to the table and hands her the cup and sits down. He speaks.

I have an important question.

She takes a sip of the nice, black, steaming hot coffee and looks up at him.

How much of what I say do you understand?

She smiles.

I think you understand me, but I don't really even know.

She continues to smile.

The last time I was home there was a girl working who spoke enough to be able to react to me, so I talked to her all the time, and then the guys who work in the garden, who speak English but pretend not to so they don't have to deal with my mother, told me she didn't understand anything I was saying. I felt like a total dick.

Esperanza laughs, speaks. She uses her Mexican accent.

I speak English. I understand everything you say.

He smiles.

Fantastic!

You keep a secret?

He nods.

I'm Mr. Keep-A-Secret. Nobody can keep a secret like me.

She speaks drops the Mexican accent, speaks without one.

I'm American. I was born in Arizona and grew up in LA. I speak perfect English. The immigrant thing is an act to deal with your mom. She wouldn't hire me if she thought I was legal.

He laughs.

Holy shit!

Esperanza laughs. He continues to speak.

That's awesome. You're getting one over on Old Lady Campbell. I gotta tell the guys outside, they're gonna think it's hilarious.

They already know.

He laughs harder. Esperanza speaks.

You promised to keep it a secret.

Doug speaks.

I will. Don't worry about that. I think it's great. And it'll make it easier for us to be friends. It gets shitty around here with just me and her. It'll be cool to have a friend in the house with me.

Esperanza smiles, takes a sip of her coffee.

Yeah, it will.

I can't imagine it's much fun working here?

No, it's not.

Why do you do it?

I need the money.

There must be better jobs?

The hours are regular, and not so bad. I don't work weekends. I get paid in cash and I don't pay any taxes. It could be worse.

You seem smart.

I think I am.

Did you finish high school?

With honors.

Why didn't you go to college?

I got a scholarship, but something happened and I didn't end up going.

What happened?

It's a long story.

I got nothing to do.

I don't really want to talk about it.

Okay.

What do you do?

Research at Caltech.

What kind of research?

It's sort of complicated.

Try me.

The field is quantum information science. We're trying to apply the theoretical laws of quantum mechanics to the practical world of information systems. One of the questions my research group is focusing on is figuring out nature's maximum computation power.

Esperanza laughs, speaks.

Sounds a bit beyond me.

Doug laughs.

It's beyond me too. It's beyond everyone I know. That's why
we're working on it, so that it's not beyond us anymore, which is
ultimately the goal of any research or applied science. Making
the unknowable, knowable.

Sounds exciting.

The possibilities are. Day-to-day it's grueling.

Grueling?

Yeah.

You want to try my job for a week or two?

He laughs.

Doing my mother's laundry is beyond grueling. It'd be some
form of torture for me, even going near whatever her
undergarments are would probably send me into seizure.

They both laugh. Esperanza stands.

Been nice chatting with you, but I need to get to work.

Doug nods, smiles.

Me too.

Thanks for the coffee.

My pleasure.

Guess I'll see you tomorrow.

My mom might still be away.

Really?

Yeah. Maybe we could do this again?

She smiles.

Maybe.

He smiles. She turns and walks away, he watches her go. Just
before she's through the door he speaks. Buen día.

She stops turns around and smiles again.

You too.

In 1900, Burton Green buys a large chunk of land located fifteen miles west of Los Angeles for oil exploration. After drilling hundreds of wells, none of which produce significant amounts of oil, he subdivides the land into five-acre building parcels and hires a landscape architect to design a town. His wife had spent time during her childhood in Beverly Farms, Massachusetts, and the couple decide to name their new town Beverly Hills.

Beatrice comes back two days later she's so tweaked on meth that Old Man Joe can see her eyelids shaking. She asks for some food he finds her some day-old pizza she takes two bites and she's done.

He has three days of peace. He follows his normal routine he wakes before dawn and lies on the beach and watches the sun rise and waits for answers nothing comes. He panhandles on the boardwalk and drinks the Chablis and eats day-old food and sleeps on the floor of his bathroom.

She returns. It's night he's half-drunk and happy. She needs somewhere to sleep he lets her use the bathroom he stays outside next to a dumpster when he wakes up she's gone.

Two more days not a sign of her he's sleeping on the third someone bangs on the door he wakes. He stands and asks who it is she says it's me, I need help, it's me. He opens the door and she's standing there tweaked and shaking she looks scared and helpless, scared and alone. He speaks.

What's wrong?

They're after me.

Who?

I need to hide.

Who's after you?

Please.

She turns around looks down the street looks both ways turns back to him scared and helpless, scared and alone.

They're coming. They're coming for me.

He steps aside.

Come in.

She steps inside, he closes the door behind her. He's not sure if she's paranoid because of the meth or paranoid because whoever beat the shit out of her before is trying to beat the shit out of her again or paranoid because she's fucked in the head. He locks the door. The bathroom is small they're standing inches away from each other.

Thank you.

Who's after you?

216

That lock is strong, right?

Yeah.

They're strong.

Who.

If that lock's not strong they'll fuck it up and knock it right the fuck off. I've seen 'em do it before. That's how strong they are, it's fucking crazy how strong they are.

Who?

She shakes her head, looks like she's going to cry. He carefully steps around her, sits down on the toilet seat, she stands over him.

Do you want to sit down?

Where?

On the floor.

What if I have to run?

Then you stand up and run.

They're stronger than me but I'm faster.

That's good.

I'm really fast when I want to be. Super fucking fast.

That's good.

She looks at the floor.

This floor's kind of nasty.

He shrugs.

Looks okay to me.

You have a toothbrush? I'll clean it for you.

He laughs.

No, thanks. Just sit.

A toothbrush is good for cleaning teeth, but it's better for floors and shit.

Maybe some other time.

She looks at the floor again, slowly lowers herself, as if she's not sure what will happen when she touches it. When she's all the way down, she looks up at him, speaks.

It's okay.

I told you it would be.

For now it's okay.

For now.

She looks back at the floor, shakes, twitches, has small
convulsions. Joe watches her, she focuses on a small fleck of
paint on the floor she reaches down with her index finger and
she carefully and hesitantly touches it. She jerks her finger
back, stares at the paint, does it again and again and again.
She looks back at Joe.

It's not gonna hurt me.

No.

It's just a little dot.

Yeah.

I think I'll be okay in here.

It's safe.

They're strong, but I'm fast.

Fast is good.

I'm super fucking fast.

That's real good.

Joe sits with her for the next three hours. She continues to
shake and twitch and convulse and talk about the men who are
after her. She doesn't say who they are or why they want her
and Joe isn't sure if they're real or not and it doesn't matter
anyway because she believes they're real and she believes
they're after her. When his interior clock tells him it's time to
go to the beach he asks her to come with him she's scared to
leave the bathroom. He tells her that they'll be fine. She shakes
her head no no no. He reaches for her hand she pulls it away.
He asks her if she wants to stay in the bathroom while he's
gone she says no, please don't leave me alone, that's what
they're waiting for, they want me alone, they'll take me if I'm
alone, please don't leave me, please don't leave, please. As the
time for him to go to the beach draws near he starts to get
annoyed, starts to wonder why he's taking care of this girl,
why he's letting her take over his bathroom, take over his life.
He stands, speaks.

I have to leave.

She looks up at him, scared and desperate, scared and alone.

Why?

Because it's what I do.

No.

Yes.

Stay with me.

You can come along if you want, or you can stay here, but I'm going.

Please, please, please.

No.

She begs.

Please.

He shakes his head.

No.

Once we leave, they'll get me.

He shakes his head.

There's no one out there. There's no one searching for you. There's no one following you. If there was they'd have pounded on this door.

They don't know about this place.

There is no they.

She stares at him. He stares back.

You'll protect me.

He chuckles.

Yes.

Promise?

I promise.

He reaches for the door, she stands and moves out of the way. He opens the door and steps out, waits for her to follow. She sticks her head out, looks up and down the alley, it's deserted. She cautiously steps out, her hands on the doorframe in case she needs to pull herself back into the room looks up and down again there is no one around just cars and dumpsters and empty bike racks and cans and bottles and food wrappers and newspapers. Old Man Joe smiles at her. She steps all the way out of the bathroom. He locks the door. They start walking away she's glancing around her eyes darting her hands quivering her nostrils flaring as if she'll be able to smell whomever is after her before she'll see them. They walk down to the beach, Joe leads Beatrice follows him she stays three or four steps behind. When they reach his spot, Joe lies down. She sits a few feet away, speaks.

What are you doing?

Lying down.

Why?

Because.

Because why?

Just because.

You just lie here?

Yeah.

Every day.

Yeah.

Are you stupid?

He chuckles.

Some people probably think so.

Yeah, I believe that.

He chuckles again, closes his eyes. Beatrice finds a small shell in the sand, stares at it, starts looking at it from different angles, brings it close to her eyes and examines it. Joe waits for her to start talking again is relieved when she doesn't. He takes a deep breath, another, he opens his eyes the sky is gray with fog as is often the case in the morning at the beach the sun rises and it becomes white the sun burns it off it becomes blue. He forgets Beatrice is a few feet away whatever she's found in the seashell has calmed her, contented her, silenced her. Time moves the morning starts to show itself shafts of light start to penetrate the gray and patches of white emerge another deep breath, another, another. Joe opens his eyes, closes his eyes, waits breathes, opens, closes, waits. He hears Beatrice say something he ignores her. She says it again he ignores her. Again louder again she speaks she says.

No.

No.

No.

He opens his eyes the sky is gray becoming white.

She starts to scream he sits up starts to turn around. She's screaming there's no longer a word no she's just screaming. He starts to turn the sky is gray becoming white he gets kicked in the face and it's black. She screams and Joe crumbles into the sand and it's black.

Howard Caughy buys the first automobile in Los Angeles, a Ford Model A, in 1904. He dies three weeks later when, after a night of drinking and smoking opium in a Chinatown brothel, he drives it into a tree. His son, Howard Caughy Jr., buys the second automobile in Los Angeles, also a Ford Model A. Two weeks after receiving the automobile, he tries to jump it across a ravine in the hills of Los Feliz. The jump is not successful, and he also dies.

Amberton and Kevin are in Amberton's room. Amberton lies in bed. Kevin is getting dressed. Amberton's children are in the pool, which is outside his room, he can hear them laughing and playing with their nannies. Amberton speaks.

That was great.

Kevin pulls on his shirt, ignores him. Amberton keeps speaking.

I mean, that was mind-blowing great.

Kevin starts buttoning the shirt, continues to ignore Amberton.

On a scale of one to ten, I'd give it a fourteen. Maybe a fifteen.

He buttons the top button, starts working his tie, ignores Amberton.

Do you feel what I feel?

He ties a nice double Windsor.

I mean is this for real?

Checks it in a mirror.

I can't believe how real this feels for me.

Kevin looks for his suit jacket. Amberton sits up.

Are you gonna say anything?

Kevin keeps looking for his jacket, speaks.

What do you want me to say?

That you just had the best hour of your life.

You mean fifteen minutes?

Amberton laughs.

That you just had the best fifteen minutes of your life?

I'm not going to say that.

That you think I'm gorgeous.

You say that enough already.

That I rocked your world.

Kevin finds his jacket, half under the bed.

You sound like some bad Top 40 love song.

He puts on the jacket.

I love bad Top 40 love songs.

He adjusts the jacket.

Why does that not surprise me?

Amberton smiles.

I feel like you know me. Like you've always known me.

Kevin chuckles.

I gotta go back to work.

He starts walking towards the door. Amberton speaks.

Take the rest of the day off.

Can't do that.

Why?

Because I have to work.

I'll call your boss.

He stops at the door.

No you won't.

He'll do whatever I want.

That's what he likes you to think.

I'll pay you for the day.

I'm not a whore.

I want you again.

No.

Kevin walks out. Amberton sits on his bed, watches him go.

The children are playing in the pool with their nannies.

In 1906, the first large-scale gang war breaks out between the Dragon Boys (Chinese), the Shamrocks (white, predominantly Irish), the Chainbreakers (black) and the Rancheros (Mexican). The Los Angeles Police Department, which is undermanned and outgunned, is unable to stop it. Over the course of eighteen months, thirty-six people are killed, mostly using knives, clubs, and broken bottles. In 1907, the Shamrocks commit the first drive-by shooting when they gun down two Chainbreakers from a passing railcar. The war ends when leaders of the four gangs agree not to encroach on each other's territory.

Two men come into the room they're both members of the bike club they're both huge and intimidating as hell. They tell Dylan that he needs to come with them he asks why they just stand and stare at him. He walks over to Maddie, who is sitting in a chair she is so scared she can't move. He leans down, softly speaks, so that the men can't hear him.

I guess I gotta go with them.

What do they want?

No idea.

What if they hurt you?

If I *don't* go with them they're gonna hurt me.

What should I do?

Wait here.

What if you don't come back?

Come on.

They could kill you.

If they were gonna kill me, they'd have already done it.

I guess so.

I mean, look at 'em, they look like nice guys.

She looks over at them. They look like mean-ass motherfuckers. She laughs. Dylan stands, kisses her.

Save me some pizza, I'll see you soon.

He turns around, walks out, the two men follow him. They leave the door open Maddie hears them walk away she stands walks to the door watches the men get into a pickup they make Dylan get into the back and as they pull out of the parking lot he looks up at her and waves.

She waits he doesn't come back. She eats pizza watches TV waits he doesn't come back. She falls asleep wakes up he's still not back. She gets dressed and goes to work where she sells hundreds and hundreds of items priced at or below 99 cents and when she comes home he's still not back. She walks down the street and buys some fried chicken and some baked beans. She comes home and watches TV and wants to eat, but can't. He doesn't come home.

He's gone for two more days. She hardly eats or sleeps while

226

he's gone. At the end of the second day, she comes home with a bag of chips and some pudding he's asleep in their bed. She drops the chips and pudding and the pudding breaks on the floor she doesn't care. She lies down next to him and starts kissing him kissing his cheeks his forehead his nose his ears neck arms hands she kisses him and cries. He wakes up, smiles, speaks.

Hi.

She smiles.

Hi.

How you doing?

She smiles.

Where have you been?

Driving around.

She smiles.

Driving around?

Yeah.

She smiles.

Were you in the bed of that pickup the entire time?

No, most of the time I was on the back of a motorcycle.

She can't stop smiling.

That sounds fun.

Not fun. My back fucking kills.

You want a rub?

Yeah.

He smiles, flips over.

Why were you on the back of a motorcycle for three days?

She straddles him, starts rubbing his back.

They were looking for the guys that killed their friends. I saw them and know what they look like. We rode around trying to find them.

Did you?

No, but someone else in their club did.

What'd they do to them?

No idea.

Really?

I guess I have some idea. And it's probably the same thing you're thinking, but I don't know any specifics, and I don't want to know any.

I was really worried.

He laughs.

I hope so.

I didn't know if you were coming back.

I know I shoulda called. They just watched me all the time.

Why?

They're paranoid guys.

Where'd you sleep?

At the shop, but we'd only sleep a couple hours a day. They were obsessed with finding those guys.

Eat?

Fast-food. Drive-throughs. It's sort of funny going through a drive-through on a Harley.

They ask about the money?

No.

They didn't notice?

I don't know. I didn't hear them talking about it and I didn't bring it up.

It's still here.

Good.

What do you want to do with it?

Use it to get out of here.

What about our jobs?

I already quit mine.

They let you?

As long as I never talk to anyone about them. You should quit yours tomorrow.

Can I kick Dale in the nuts before I leave?

He laughs.

Sure.

Where we gonna go?

Somewhere better than this.

Can we go back to the beach?

We can go as close as we can afford.

I want a white house with a picket fence near the beach.

He laughs. She speaks again.

I do. Seriously. That's my dream now.

We're a long way from being able to afford that.

Let's just get close.

Okay.

She starts kissing him again, he's awake now and he kisses her back. They spend the night releasing three days of tension, stress and fear on each other's bodies in each other on top of each other beneath each other. When they wake up they pack their things they fit into two small backpacks they get on the bike and ride over to the 99 cent store. Maddie quits her job. Dale asks her to stay tells her she's the heart and soul of the store she laughs at him. He gives her a slip of paper with his numbers, his office, home and cell, and tells her to call if she changes her mind. She throws it away on her way out.

They ride over to the shop. Dylan wants to leave the bike. Although they love the old piece of shit bike, and it is their only means of transportation in a city where, because of the lack of suitable public options, some form of transportation is essential, they want to sever the link between them and the shop as fully and completely as they can. The gates are closed and no one is around. There is traffic on the street, but it's quiet. There is menace in the air, death, violence. They park the bike in front of the gates. Dylan and Maddie walk away they are the only pedestrians in sight. And once again, they head west.

West.

They walk west.

The first feature-length film, *The Story of the Kelly Gang*, is produced in Australia in 1906. The second, *L'Enfant Prodigue*, is produced in France in 1907. In 1908, nine American film companies, all but one based on the East Coast, form the Motion Picture Patents Company, also known as the Edison Trust, the purpose of which is to keep non-American and independent interests out of the film business by pooling technological resources and hoarding filmstock. In 1909, the Los Angeles Chamber of Commerce begins offering incentives to filmmakers willing to shoot in the city, and promotes the abundance of sunshine (electrical lighting is expensive), the weather, and the variety of landscapes available. In 1911, the first film studio in LA, Christie-Nestor Studios, opens its doors. By 1914, there are fifteen studios. In 1915, William Fox, the founder and owner of Fox Film Corporation, files antitrust litigation against the Motion Picture Patents Company, which is declared a monopoly by the U.S. Federal Court and broken up. By 1917, Los Angeles is the film production capital of the world.

A conversation in Los Angeles. Its participants are males
between the ages of fourteen and thirty. They could be
members of any race, nationality, ethnic group, from almost
any part of the city or county:

You gotta get us a scalp.

A scalp?

Yeah, a motherfucking scalp.

Like what the Indians did?

Just like what the motherfucking Indians did.

How the fuck do I get a scalp?

You kill a motherfucker and then chop the top of his head off.
Or you just beat his ass real good and then chop the top of his
head off. It's almost worse that way 'cause then the
motherfucker gotta walk around his whole life with a fucked-
up head.

Who you want me to do this to?

Anybody wearing colors.

Any particular colors?

Don't matter to us.

Then I'm in?

That's the way it works.

How long I got to do it?

A week.

And there ain't no other initiation?

Ain't that enough?

It's pretty serious.

Supposed to be. Supposed to show us that you serious too.

I am.

We'll see.

I am.

Like the motherfucker said, we'll see.

I'll show you.

Then shut the fuck up and go do it.

You gotta gun I can use?

Laughter from multiple males. One speaks.

Yeah, we got guns.

You got a machete or some shit?
You gotta get that yourself.
Alright.

***

There are more than 1,500 street gangs in Los Angeles with an estimated 200,000 members.

***

A few of the Asian gangs in and around Los Angeles: Westside Islanders, Asian Killa Boys, Black Dragon, Tropang Hudas, Vietnamese Gangster Boys, Tiny Rascal Gang, Sons of Samoa, Asian Boyz, Crazy Brothers Clan, Exotic Foreign Creation Coterie, Korat Boys, Silly Boys, Temple Street, Tau Gamma Pinoy, Korea Town Mobsters, Last Generation Korean Killers, Maplewood Jefrox, LA Oriental Boys, Lost Boys, Mental BoyZ, Oriental Lazy Boys, Rebel Boys, Korean Pride, Asian Criminals, Avenue Oxford Boys, Born to Kill Gang, Cambodian Boyz, China Town Boyz, Crazyies, Fliptown Mob, Flipside Trece, Ken Side Wah Ching, Korean Play Boys, Sarzanas, Satanas, Temple Street, Red Door, Real Pinoy Brothers, Scout Royal Brotherhood, The Boys, United Brotherhood, Bahalana Gang, Black Dragons, Original Genoside, Four Seas Mafia.

***

Fifty to sixty percent of all murders committed in Los Angeles County are gang-related, approximately 700 each year.

***

He grew up with his mother and three brothers, two of whom had different fathers than he did. The four boys shared a bedroom, his mother slept on a couch in the living room. She worked at a movie theater at night and they got public assistance and there was enough money for food and rent and secondhand clothes, but nothing else.

He never did well in school. From the first day he went, as a six-year-old, he felt like the teachers were scared of him. Maybe not scared, but apprehensive, and they certainly didn't care about him. There were never enough textbooks, and hardly any supplies. He tried for a few years, but then gave up. He went every day, but mostly he wanted to have fun and goof around. When teachers yelled at him, he thought it was cool. The only people in his neighborhood that seemed to have any money were gangsters. They wore nice clothes and drove nice cars and had diamond watches. When they told people what to do, they did it. They had friends who loved them and respected them and fought for them and fought with them.

He got recruited when he was twelve. He was walking home and some slightly older boys surrounded him and told him he was going to be one of them and then they beat him. The next day, as he walked to school, he saw the boys on a street corner. He walked over to them and sat with them and laughed with them. He didn't make it to school that day, or any day after. He started wearing colors after his first murder. He was thirteen. He was riding in a car with other boys. None of them were old enough to drive. They saw another boy wearing a color they didn't like, the colors of their enemy. They gave him a gun. He opened the window and started firing. The boy fell. He kept firing. They drove away. They ditched the car and went back to their corner and spent the rest of the day smoking weed and drinking beer and celebrating. He saw the boy's mother on the news when he went home later that night. She was screaming, wailing, her neighbors were holding her up. He watched it with his own mother, who had no idea that he was involved. She just shook her head, waited for the next story. Day after day, they stood on the corner and smoked weed and drank beer and talked and laughed and when people in nice cars from better neighborhoods pulled up, they sold them drugs. They went out after their enemies a couple times a week, or when one of their own had been shot and they needed to seek retribution, vengeance.

His three brothers, all of whom were younger than him, followed him in. One of them died three days after joining, he got shot in the head during a drive-by. Another was paralyzed in a different drive-by. The youngest was hesitant, but realized he didn't have any other options. They were together when he did his first killing, shooting someone wearing a different color and two of the boy's sisters, one of whom was four years old. They watched a piece about the murder on the news that night with their mother, who had no idea they were involved. She just shook her head and waited for the next story.

***

A few of the white gangs in and around Los Angeles: Armenian Power, the Nazi Low Riders, Aryan Nation, the Peckerwoods, the United Skinhead Brotherhood, the Crackers, the Front, StormFront, Heil Boys, Westside White Boys, Honky, the Spook Hunters, Dog Patch Winos, the Soviet Bloc, Russian Roulette, the Georgian Pack, Aryan National Front, East Side White Pride, the Fourth Reich, New Dawn Hammerskins, American Skinheads, Blitz, the Berzerkers.

***

There were more than 30,000 confirmed violent crimes, including murders, rapes, assaults and robberies, committed by gang members within the city limits of Los Angeles between the years 2000 and 2005. It is estimated that one-fifth of the crimes actually committed are reported and confirmed.

***

Nobody knows him. Nobody has ever met him. Nobody has ever seen him. He calls twice a day, at noon and at five, to discuss whatever business is at hand. During the conversations he issues orders, reviews cash flows, checks on incoming shipments, passes judgment on friends and foes, delivers their sentences. He speaks to two people. They run the operation for him. One of them has been doing it for three years, the other for six. They are extremely well paid. Their families will be taken care of when they're gone. They are each the fourth person to hold the position. The first pair disappeared after he had the operation running smoothly enough to bring in other people, and they disappeared because they knew his identity. The others have disappeared because they made mistakes. It is inevitable that mistakes will be made. It is inevitable that they will disappear. They knew of the inevitability when they took the job. They took it because they are extremely well paid, and they are given whatever they want, drugs, money, girls, boys, whenever they want it. And their families will be taken care of when they're gone. After they make their mistake.

They work on the fifth floor of a ten-floor building owned by a shell company owned by a shell company owned by a shell company owned by him. The rest of the building is filled with other members of their organization, some of whom do work that is considered legal, most of whom do not. The fifth floor is the safest floor because it cannot be directly approached. If the LAPD, the DEA, the FBI, the ATF, the IRS, or any other rival, opposing organization tries to get to them, and get information related to what they do, they have to approach from either above or below, and by the time they reach the fifth floor, whatever they wanted or needed would be gone. The two men rarely leave the floor, which is heavily guarded, and whatever they want or need is brought to them. The one time an approach to the floor was made, and it was made by a rival criminal organization, the guards killed thirty-two men. Eight of the men were shot and killed immediately. The others were captured and taken to a warehouse. Before they died, every single one of them wished they had been shot and killed immediately.

The organization has approximately 50,000 members, though no one really knows. It controls most of Spanish-speaking Los Angeles, though there are a few remaining pockets of resistance and independence. It also controls most of the drug traffic into the city. Other groups or organizations involved in the distribution and sale of cocaine, heroin, methamphetamine and marijuana purchase most of it, wholesale, from them. Those that don't usually end up being taken to the warehouse, where they quickly wish they had purchased it from them.

Aside from drug trafficking, the organization is also involved in gun sales, prostitution, extortion, and the transportation and sale of illegal immigrant labor. With its profits from these ventures, it is buying real estate, both residential and commercial, and setting up infrastructure, including its own stores, restaurants, shipping companies, banks and schools. Unlike most, if not all, organizations of its type, it has long-term goals and plans. From its beginnings, he, from wherever he is, had a vision. It is nearing some type of reality. He wants to completely and totally control southern California.

Most of the members do not know of or about him. They are recruited the same way other gangs recruit members. Young, angry men, often without stable homes, are given money, guns, a sense of respect, a sense of belonging, and turned loose to buy, sell, rob and kill. They stand on street corners in pressed chinos and flannel shirts and their necks, arms and backs are covered in tattoos. They threaten, menace, occasionally strike out. They love being part of something and they are all willing to kill for it and die for it. Occasionally they are asked to kill for it and die for it. They recruit other members who recruit other members who recruit other members. They have become an army that is impregnable, nearly invincible, unstoppable, and growing, every day it gets larger and they control more, every day it's growing. There is little the police, or anyone, can do about it. Arrest one and there are ten more, twenty more, fifty more. Lock one up and the vacuum, if there was one, is immediately filled. Put one in prison and they fuse into the parallel organization that they have there, that controls most of California's prisons. The leaders are protected, literally and figuratively, by everyone below them, and can also be immediately replaced. The command structure was built to resemble the ones used by military organizations, which are designed to sustain damage and persevere through adversity. When asked recently what he planned to do about the group, an elected city official laughed said—I might join them if this gig doesn't work out. When he was asked what he planned to do to try and control them he stared straight ahead and said—Nothing. There is nothing I can do. The war with them is over and they won. There's nothing I can do.

***

Ninety percent of the hate crimes in Los Angeles County are committed by gang members, approximately 800 a year.

***

A few of the black gangs in and around Los Angeles: Be-Bopp Watts Bishops, Squiggly Lane Gangsters, Kabbage Patch Piru, Straight Ballers Society, Perverts, Pimp Town Murder Squad, Project Gangster Bloods, Blunt Smoking Only Gang, Most Valuable Pimp Gangster Crips, Crenshaw Mafia Gang, Fruit Town Pirus, Fudge Town Mafia Crip, Family Swan Blood, Compton Avenue Crips, East Coast Crips, Gangster Crips, Samoan Warriors Bounty Hunters, Watergate Crips, 706 Blood, Harvard Gangster Crips, Sex Symbols, Venice Shore Line, Queen Street Bloods, Big Daddyz, Eight Trey Gangster Crips, Weirdoz Blood, Palm & Oak Gangsters, Tiny Hoodsta Crips, Rollin 50s Brims, Dodge City Crips, East Side Ridas, Lettin Niggas Have It, Down Hood Mob, Athens Park Boys, Avalon Garden Crips, Boulevard Mafia Crips, Gundry Blocc Paramount Crips, Dawgs, the Dirty Old Man Gang.

***

In 2007, the Los Angeles Police Department and the Office of the Mayor of Los Angeles released a list of the most dangerous gangs in Los Angeles. In order, and with their ethnic makeup and area of operation, they are:
1. 18th Street Westside. Latino/Mexican. Throughout most of the city.
2. 204th Street. Latino/Mexican. Harbor area/Torrance.

3. **Avenues.** Latino/Mexican. Highland Park.
4. **Black P-Stones.** African American. Baldwin Village.
5. **Canoga Park Alabama.** Latino/Mexican. Canoga Park/West Valley.
6. **Grape Street Crips.** African American. Watts.
7. **La Mirada Locos.** Latino/Mexican. Echo Park.
8. **Mara Salvatrucha, also known as MS-13.** Latino/El Salvadoran. Throughout most of the city.
9. **Rollin' 40s NHC.** African American. South Central.
10. **Rollin' 30s Original Harlem Crips.** African American. Jefferson Park.
11. **Rollin' 60s Neighborhood Crips.** African American. Hyde Park.

***

The eleven gangs listed above accounted for approximately 7 percent of all reported violent crime in the city of Los Angeles.

***

A conversation between a young man and a reporter. The reporter is visiting from Europe and is writing a piece on life in American cities. It takes place in the backyard of a small run-down house.
So why do you have all of these dogs?
'Cause that's what I do. I raise fucking dogs.
How many do you have?
Right now I got about fifteen. Sometimes I got more, sometimes I got less.
They're all pit bulls?
American pit bull terriers. Every single one of them.
Why pit bulls?
'Cause they're the baddest motherfuckers there are.
Is that why you love them?
I don't love them fuckers. I just fucking raise 'em and sell 'em.
You don't love them at all?
I love 'em a little bit when they're small and shit. They're nice

and cute and happy, and they like giving licks, but then I make 'em mean.

You make them mean?

You gotta train these motherfuckers. They got it in 'em, but you gotta bring it out. You gotta beat 'em up and starve 'em and make 'em fight over food. Then they get the taste of it, the taste of blood, and they start getting mean.

You beat them as puppies?

I'll kick their ass no matter how old they are.

What if they don't get mean?

I let the other ones practice on 'em.

Who buys these dogs?

Gangsters.

Gangsters? Like Al Capone or John Gotti.

No, not like them. Like the motherfuckers out on every goddamn street corner in this city.

Gang members?

Yeah.

What do they do with them?

They fight 'em for money, have tournaments and shit. They use 'em to protect their houses. Sometimes they sic 'em on motherfuckers they got beef with.

On other people?

Yeah.

What happens?

What the fuck you think happens? Ain't no man can fuck with a pit bull.

You've seen this?

I ain't seen it happen, but I've seen it afterwards, motherfuckers with their arms or legs bit off, parts of their face bit off, and I heard about some other motherfuckers that got some real sensitive downtown shit bit off. And I heard worse than that too.

What?

I heard about these warehouses.

What do they do there?

239

They keep dogs there and they make those motherfuckers real nasty and they never feed 'em. They got a pit in the middle of the warehouse, and when motherfuckers fuck up, they throw 'em in the pit with a couple pissed-off dogs. There ain't no escape from that kinda shit.
Do you think it's true?
I ain't got no reason to doubt it.

***

Ninety-five percent of all gang members are male. Fifty percent are under the age of eighteen. Thirty percent of those over eighteen are in prison. Ninety percent will spend time in prison at some point. Fifteen percent finish high school. Less than one percent will go to college. Eighty percent grow up in single-family households. Eighty-eight percent of the children of gang members also ultimately end up in gangs.

***

A few of the Hispanic gangs in and around Los Angeles: 18th Street, Clicka Los Primos, Big Top Locos, Diamond Street, Head Hunters, East LA Dukes, Krazy Ass Mexicans, Primera Flats, Varrio Nuevo Estrada, the Magician Club, Astoria Garden Locos, High Times Familia, Pacas Knock Knock Boys, Sol Valle Diablos, Brown Pride Surenos, Alley Tiny Criminals, King Boulevard Stoners, Washington Locos, Mexican Klan, Barrio Mojados, Street Saints, V13, 42nd Street Locos, Tiny Insane Kriminals, Unos Sin Verguenza, Bear Street Crazies, Midget Locos, Barrio Small Town, Villa Pasa La Rifa, Forty Ounce Posse, Compton Varrio Vatos Locos, Big Hazard, Varrio Nuevo Estrada, Michigan Chicano Force, Brown Pride Raza, Pacoima Humphrey Boyz, San Fers 13, Burlington Street Locos, Van Owen Street Locos 13, Big Top Locos, La Eme.

***

Lying on a bunk. Staring at the ceiling. It's the middle of the night. The bunk is in a cell meant to hold one man three are living there. It's worse than he thought it would be. Much much worse. More tense, more frightening, more violent, more boring. Minutes are hours, hours are days, days are a lifetime. Tense endless moments he could die at any one of them, he could kill at any one of them. He's a killer, as are both of the other men in the cell, as are almost all of the men in the prison. Hundreds of killers living together, divided by race, hating each other, with absolutely nothing to do but wait for time to pass. It's worse than he thought it would be.

Sleep is never easy. He's up five or six times a night. Before he got here he never had trouble with sleep. Before he got here he never thought about what he did out there. They run through his mind. Every one of them. What they looked like, where he got them, who he was with, what he used, how they fell and how they bled, the screams of the witnesses who saw but would never testify. He didn't know any of them, had never spoken to any of them, had never seen a couple of them before he did it. And it didn't matter. Who they were what their families were like the dreams they may or may not have had, none of it fucking mattered. He did what he was supposed to do and he did it without thinking about it. Just got in the car and went, leaned out the car, pulled. He never regretted any of them because he never had time for any regrets. Now it's all he has. Time. Minutes are hours, hours are days, days are a lifetime. He lies in bed and stares at the ceiling. He can't sleep.

***

She's twenty-four years old. Two of her brothers were shot, one died and one is paralyzed from the neck down, another brother was beaten to death. One of her three sisters was killed. The other two have children whose fathers are either dead or in jail. She has four children with three men. One is dead, one is in prison life no parole, the third spends most of his time playing cards on the front porch of a nearby house. Her oldest child is ten. He's already wearing colors.

***

As the gang population and the related violent crime rates in Los Angeles City and County rise, state and federal programs to combat the problem through both community outreach programs and law-enforcement initiatives are being cut due to budget constraints.

***

A conversation between a father and a son. The father is twenty-six and the son is five.
What do you want to be when you grow up?
A gangbanger.
What else?
A dope-slanger?
What else?
A cold-blooded killer.
Why do you want to do that?
Because that's where the money is, and I want money.
How much money?
All the money in the world.
You're my boy. I'm proud of you. You're my boy.

***

The average gang member makes less money each year than the average cashier at the average fast-food restaurant.

In 1904, a tobacco baron named Abbot Kinney buys a large marsh west of Los Angeles and hires architects and builders to construct a "Venice of America." More than fifteen miles of canals are dug and flooded with water from the Pacific Ocean, and three entertainment piers are built on the beach, along with a boardwalk that is lined with restaurants and bars. Residential housing is built on the edges of canals. Within five years, Venice Beach is the largest tourist attraction on the West Coast, and one of the largest in the nation. In 1929, oil is discovered just south of Venice, on the Marina del Rey Peninsula. The City of Los Angeles subsequently annexes both areas and fills in the canals with concrete.

Kelly. Born in Alabama, raised in Tennessee. Competed in her first beauty pageant at age four, winning second runner-up in the Little Miss Chattanooga Jr. Princess division. Performed in her first play, an American version of *The Nutcracker* set on a hog farm, at seven. Started working with a singing coach at nine. Modeled for local department store catalogs between the ages of ten and fourteen, won the Junior Miss Middle-Tennessee Pageant at fifteen, became Homecoming Maiden at sixteen, Homecoming Princess at seventeen, Homecoming Queen at eighteen. Voted Most Beautiful, Most Talented and Most Likely to Succeed by her high school class. Received full cheerleading scholarship to the University of Tennessee. Varsity cheerleader for four years, including Head Cheerleader her senior year. Graduated with honors and a double major in theater/elementary education. Moved to Los Angeles at twenty-three to pursue a singing career. She is five foot nine, has blond hair and blue eyes, weighs 115 pounds. She is a waitress at a '50s-themed restaurant, where she also sings the ballads from a popular Broadway show, over and over and over again. She is now twenty-nine.

***

Eric. High school heartthrob. Rode, and still rides, a motorcycle. Didn't win any awards for anything, but slept with all the girls who did. Moved to Los Angeles at age eighteen to become an actor. Six foot two, long brown hair, brown eyes, 185 pounds. Works as a busboy at a high-end Beverly Hills restaurant. He is now thirty-two.

***

Timmy. The class clown. The laugh-a-minute buddy boy. The funniest kid on the block, and I mean funny funny. I'm talking absolutely the funniest fucking kid the block has ever seen!!!! Short and chubby. Black hair. Rosy cheeks. His father was an alcoholic who hit his mother. His mother was depressed and rarely spoke. They lived in a fourth-floor walk-up in Astoria,

Queens. His parents tried to have other children, but were unable to conceive. Almost from the day of his birth, Timmy loved two things: making people laugh, and eating. They fed each other. The more he ate, the worse he felt, the worse he felt the more he needed to make people laugh so that he could feel a little better. He started writing comedy routines at age twelve. He'd practice them in front of the mirror and do an act every Saturday at 5:00 PM on the street corner. He started drawing crowds, and for the first time in his life, people liked him, and people admired him. He put on his Saturday shows for two years, at which point his father made him get a job working weekends in a local butcher shop. When he graduated from high school he went to college to study engineering. He started working at comedy clubs and doing open-mic nights. He quit college three months before graduating and moved to Los Angeles. He was twenty-two. He now works the door at a comedy club and still does open-mic nights. He is forty-four.

***

John. Guitar virtuoso. Originally from Cleveland. Moved to Los Angeles with his band at age 20. Works at the counter of a car-rental office. Age 29.

Amy. Model. Originally from New York. Moved to Los Angeles to become an actress at age 23. Works as a cocktail waitress in a high-end hotel bar. Age 27.

Andrew. Self-declared genius. Originally from Boston, went to college at Harvard. Moved to Los Angeles to be a screenwriter, and further down the line, a director, at age 23. Works behind the counter at a video store. Age 30.

Jennifer. Triple threat. From Chicago. Was considered a singing, dancing and acting prodigy. Attended Northwestern on a full scholarship. Moved to Los Angeles, with visions of taking the town by storm and basking in triple-threat glory, at age 22. Works as the assistant manager of a clothing store. Age 27.

Greg. Started making short films at age 10. Graduated from

prestigious film school with honors. Moved to Los Angeles to be a director. Works as a ticket-taker at a wax museum.

Ron. Bodybuilder. Wants to be an action star. Works at a gym.

Jeff. Actor. Works in a duck costume at an amusement park.

Megan. Actress/model. Exotic dancer.

Susie. Actress. Waitress.

Mike. Actor. Waiter.

Sloane. Actress. Waitress.

Desiree. Actress/singer. Waitress.

Erin. Actress. Works at a shoe store.

Elliot. Screenwriter. Works in a bar.

Tom. Screenwriter. Makes pizzas.

Kurt. Actor. Delivers pizzas.

Carla. Singer/dancer. Serves wings in a T-shirt and a pair of short-shorts.

Jeremy. Identical twin. Actor. Works behind the counter at a coffee shop.

James. The other identical twin. Actor. Works behind the counter at a different coffee shop (they tried working at the same shop but it confused the customers).

Heather. Actress. Better body than Carla. Serves wings in a bikini top and a pair of short-shorts. Gets bigger tips than Carla.

Holly. Petite actress. Wears an *E.T. the Extra-Terrestrial* costume at an amusement park.

***

Kevin's parents always considered him odd. As a child he liked speaking in strange voices and making up accents, which he would attribute to imaginary countries. They tried to get him to stop, but he wouldn't. They offered him incentives: money, trips to the local go-kart track, books, new sneakers, as much ice cream as he wanted but nothing worked. He spoke in strange voices with made-up accents. It got to the point where they weren't sure what his real voice sounded like.

When he was fourteen, he read *King Lear*. He was a bit young to try and digest such a profound piece of classic English literature, but he did it anyway, and boy oh boy, did he do it. He was overwhelmed, blown away. The words hit him, penetrated him, affected him, in a way unlike anything he had ever experienced. From that day forward, he devoted himself to the theater. When he wasn't in school, he was in his room reading plays, starting with the Greeks and moving forward, and reciting monologues to himself. He switched permanently to a stiff, upper-class British accent, and started wearing medieval clothing both at home and at school, where dismayed officials initially tried to stop him, but gave up when he threatened to sue them for violating his rights under the First Amendment. Needless to say, he got teased, got his ass kicked by football players, he was shunned by everyone, even the most unpopular of the kids at his school. He didn't care. The words of the masters flowed through him, fulfilled him, and comforted him in a way none of them could or would ever understand. They had each other; their classes and games and parties and dances and all the petty dramas that ruled and governed their days. He had the masters, the giants of theatrical history, the titans of stage. He had drama on a grand scale.

He left school at sixteen and went to England, where he was recognized as a prodigy. He spent two years as an understudy on the stages of the West End before returning to America, to New York, where the heart of American Theater beats so soundly and so loudly, and he enrolled in Juilliard, the most prestigious acting school in the country.

It was more of the same at Juilliard. He dazzled his professors. He outperformed his peers. He took on the biggest, most challenging roles and he made them look easy. Broadway, just a few blocks away, started taking notice. Talent scouts came to see everything he did, agents offered to represent him, producers wanted to stage plays around him. He enjoyed the attention, but had bigger plans, bigger dreams, Broadway would always be there, he wanted HOLLYWOOD! He graduated at the top of his class, as expected, and as valedictorian, he gave the class commencement speech, which he did in the style of Molière, the great French playwright of the 1600s. He moved to Los Angeles the next day. He was twenty-two.

There is a curious phenomenon in Los Angeles that occurs when non-film and TV artists, such as theater actors, playwrights, novelists, painters, and theater directors, come to town. Industry people, generally executives and agents, want to work with them and be seen with them, regardless of whether they are actually talented or not, because there is a perception that because they are from the East, or from Europe, and because they are established in what could be considered the *Fine Arts*, that they are smarter, more prestigious and somehow better than their counterparts in California. Many a career has been ruined by the phenomenon, many a promising playwright turned into a TV hack, novelist into mumbling screenwriter, stage actor into preening sitcom star, and theater director into director of soap commercials. Well aware of the phenomenon, Kevin came to town with a vision, a vision that he was determined to stick with and never sell out, a vision of a glorious and innovative future: he was going to bring the works of the ancient Greeks, Aeschylus, Sophocles, Euripides, to the multiplex screens of America.

Agents and producers were initially seduced by his idea. He signed with a prestigious agency and had signed a development deal (an arrangement where he got paid to try and write a script) with a big-time producer at a major studio. When he started turning in drafts of the scripts, which were actually just transcriptions of the plays, the producer and the studio were shocked. They told him they couldn't justify spending tens of millions of dollars on a film about a violent young man who murders his father and impregnates his mother. They asked him to do some rewrites and he refused. He was quietly shown the door.

That was seven years ago. Despite setback after setback after setback, Kevin has not given up on his dream. He works nights at a medieval-themed restaurant, where he continues to polish his vast array of accents and personas, and where he acts as the master of ceremonies for jousting matches and swordfights, and he spends his days making phone calls and setting up meetings in an effort to find investors for his films. The offers for work have stopped coming in, and the agents no longer want to represent him, and most of his classmates at Juilliard are now enjoying successful careers, but none of that matters. He has a dream. Los Angeles is where dreams become reality. He'll never give up. Or as he might say, with subtle inflections of Manchester General circa 1545, *Ye not will yield for further on the battle lies and ye night is dark but thy lord willeth provideth thy light!!!!*

***

Allison. Model. Moved to Los Angeles at 18 to become a Playboy Bunny. Now 19, she works in porn.
Katy. Actress. Left her husband and three children to become a star. Works at a grocery store. Cries herself to sleep every night.
Jay Jay. Actor. Moved to LA with his mother at age 4. He is now 9. He lives in a motel and is home-schooled. His mother is a waitress.
Karl. Hometown daredevil. Moved to Los Angeles at 18 to become a stuntman. Teaches karate. He is now 30.
Lee. Actor/model. Moved to Los Angeles at 21. Waiter, and occasionally a bartender. He is now 27.
Brad. Actor. Moved at 20. Works as a bouncer. He is now 30.
Barry. Singer. Moved at 18. Works in the ticket window at the Wax Museum. He is now 31.
Bert. Writer. Moved at 24. Bartender. He is now 50.

***

When Samantha was born, at a hospital in Cleveland, the doctor held her up, looked at her, and said—Wow, *that* is a beautiful baby. As an infant, and a toddler, people often stopped her mother and asked to look at her, and occasionally they asked to take her picture. Boys started fighting over her in kindergarten, though they were also all scared of her. In fifth grade a model scout saw her and had a meeting with her parents and told them she could make millions as a teenager if they were willing to send her to New York. They thought it was an interesting idea, but cared much more about their daughter's happiness than her ability to earn money. In eighth grade the model scout, who was now an agent and had always kept a picture of Samantha on a blackboard in front of his desk, came to see her again. If anything, she was more beautiful than the first time he saw her. He met with her parents again and he told them the same thing, Samantha could make millions if they would allow her to become a model. Samantha, who had always tried to downplay her beauty, and was extremely shy and humble about it, was indifferent to the idea. She liked her friends, she liked school, she liked watching Browns games and Indians games with her father, she liked going to the mall with her mother. She was looking forward to high school, looking forward to her first date, her first homecoming dance, her prom. The man was convincing, though, so she agreed to give it a chance.

That summer during her vacation, they went, as a family, to New York. The agency put them up in a fancy hotel, and for two weeks, Samantha gave modeling a shot. She had pictures taken, went on casting calls, booked every job she went for, caused a big stir in the fashion world. Her parents went with her to the shoots, where she was fawned over by makeup artists, hairdressers and stylists, where photographers told her she was beautiful, where the clients told her how proud they were to have her represent their brands. While she enjoyed the attention, and was amused by the compliments, she was extremely bored, and found the long hours of waiting for a few minutes of work (the actual picture-taking part of the process) intolerable. The one thing, however, that she did love was a television commercial she shot for a shampoo company. She only had one line—This is my hair, this is your hair—but she loved delivering it. Before the audition she practiced it a couple hundred times, saying it differently each time, changing her tone, her delivery, changing the pose she held while she said it. She was well aware that what she was doing was sort of silly, and somewhat banal, but the process was fun for her, and she practiced until she felt she had it down perfectly. When the cameras were rolling, she smiled and delivered it in a happy, friendly, accessible way meant to convey to the casual viewer, and the hair product consumer, that this is my hair and I love it, it could be your hair too, just smile and use this shampoo. It was perfect. The director started clapping, and the CEO of the shampoo company beamed.

When their time in New York was over, Samantha and her parents returned to Cleveland, and Samantha knew that she didn't want to be a model, or didn't care enough about it to sacrifice her adolescence to it, but that she did want to be an actress. She started high school, joined the drama club, started taking acting classes on the weekends. She had her first date, at sixteen, with a boy she'd known her entire life, she did not kiss him that night, or on many nights after, but did kiss him at homecoming, and also went to the prom with him. He was the captain of the baseball team his senior year, an All-Ohio and All-American pitcher, and got drafted by a professional team. She had straight A's and high test scores and decided to go back to New York to study drama, where she could pay for school by doing modeling jobs on the side. They broke up over the summer. They had never, despite an incredible, almost superhuman effort on his part, had sex.

Her college years were easy, fun. She modeled, studied acting, worked in the theater. Her beauty stayed with her, expanded as she grew older, as she grew into her body. She became a woman, a traffic-stopping, head-shaking, heartbreakingly gorgeous woman. Men pursued her, and occasionally she'd date them, but she was focused on acting, and focused on what she was going to do when she left school, which was move to Los Angeles and become a serious actress.

When she arrived in LA, at twenty-two, she was noticed immediately. A producer approached her in a coffee shop and asked her out, she said yes and they went to dinner. When dinner was over, he said he'd find her an agent and put her in a film if she would go home with him, though he said it in a much more direct, and less polite manner. She had never fully been with a man, and was saving herself for whomever became her first love, and when propositioned by the producer, she stood up and left him at the table without answering him. She went home, which at the time was a run-down studio apartment in an area of LA called the Film Ghetto, where many young aspiring actors, writers, directors and musicians live before they begin working, and cried herself to sleep. She, like everyone else in the world, knew that this type of thing happened, she just never believed anyone would try it with her. Welcome to Los Angeles. She cried herself to sleep.

It happened again and again. She said no, again and again. She got a job waitressing at a fancy restaurant and took acting classes and tried to get an agent. She auditioned for roles at open calls and did plays at small alternative theaters in Culver City and Silver Lake. She got an agent, a young ambitious agent at a big agency, and got a couple bit parts in teen films and one-hour dramas. She always played the beautiful but elusive ingénue, and she knew that doing it was part of the process of building a career. She did an episode of a sitcom, she played the comic star's dreamgirl. She did a medical drama. She played a damaged accident victim.

She was on a date when she got the call, a date with a lawyer she had been seeing, and who she thought she might love. Her mother was on the phone. Her father was sick. He had stomach cancer, potentially treatable, but usually terminal. She broke down at the table. The lawyer took her home and helped her make travel arrangements. He stayed with her that night, and he held her as she wept, and he helped her pack in the morning, and he drove her to the airport that afternoon. When she kissed him goodbye, she knew she loved him, but she also knew that he would have to wait a little longer. Her father had cancer. It was potentially treatable, but usually terminal.

When she got off the plane she went straight to the hospital. Her father was in bed, wires, tubes and machines everywhere, a stapled incision across the front of his stomach. He was asleep, and her mother was sitting by his side, her eyes were red and swollen. Samantha immediately started crying. She didn't stop for a week. Her father tried to be positive about the situation, and reassure Samantha and her mother, but they all knew it was bad, worse than bad, they knew how it was going to end. There was blood seeping out of the incision, and they knew how it was going to end.

She went back to Los Angeles. Her father started chemo and radiation. His insurance covered most of the treatment, but the bills started piling up. There was a hospital bed in their bedroom, a wheelchair, there were home nurses, additional medicines, it all cost money, extraordinary amounts of money. Samantha chipped in what she could, which wasn't much, and tortured herself over the millions she could have made and didn't, the millions that would take care of her father now, the millions she convinced herself could save his life, if only, if only.

She was sitting in a coffee shop when approached. A young woman asked where she got the skirt she was wearing they started chatting and shared a cup of tea together. The woman was tall and blond and beautiful, she said she was an actress as well, though lately had been focusing on other things, they got along and exchanged numbers when they left. They met again two days later, again two days after that. Samantha told her about her father about the mounting bills. The woman said she might know how to help, if Samantha was interested.

Samantha said she was, the woman asked what experience Samantha had with men. Samantha told her she was a virgin. The woman smiled and said your father will be just fine.

Samantha sold her virginity a week later. She was paid $50,000 for it. The buyer was an Arab prince who lived in Bel-Air and would only have sex with virgins. She cried before, during and after. The prince told her that most of the girls cried, and that the ones who didn't weren't satisfying for him. When she left his house, she thought about driving her car into a tree, or off the side of an overpass. When she got home, she got in the shower and stayed there for the rest of the day. When the lawyer called that night, she broke up with him, told him to never call her back. When he asked why she said she didn't want to talk about it. When he pressed her, she started crying again and hung up the phone.

That was three years ago. Her father is gone, but he went in comfort and in peace. When her parents asked her how she was earning the money that she gave to them, she told them she had started modeling again. When they asked to see the work, she told them she was doing most of it in Japan, where older American models could still make money. She slept with one or two men a week. She was paid between $2,000 and $10,000 a session, depending on what they wanted her to do, or what they wanted to do to her. She stopped dating, or dating in any conventional way, and didn't go out with men unless they were prepared to pay her fee. She stopped acting, though she had heard of, and knew of, a couple of other women who had worked in her profession and had eventually achieved some form of success in the acting world, including one who had won an Academy Award, and another who had her own TV show. She hoped at some point she might meet a director or a producer, someone who would pay for her services but see her as something more than what she was, and that they would give her a break or help her get her career back on track. If she didn't, she hoped, simply, to meet someone with enough money to take care of her. She knew they would have to be a client, because if they weren't, and they found out what she did, or what she was, they would either leave her or cut ties with her.

At night, when she was in her apartment, in bed, alone, she thought about that first audition, years ago, for the shampoo commercial, and the thrill she felt delivering it. She thought about all of the work she did to prepare herself to come to Los Angeles, she thought about her mother and what she would think if she knew, she thought about the lawyer. In a way she was still acting, though that didn't bring her any comfort or satisfaction. In a way, what she did was acting that was more difficult than anything on a stage or a screen. She thought about the prince. She thought about the men, all of the men, and the way they looked at her just before they started in on her. She thought about her father. At least he died in peace.

***

It is estimated that 100,000 people a year move to Los Angeles to pursue careers in the entertainment industry. They come from all over America, all over the world. They were stars at home, they were smart or funny or talented or beautiful. When they arrive, they join the 100,000 that came the year before they did, and they await the 100,000 that will arrive the year after, the year after, the year after, the year after.

***

David. Actor. Bartender. Arrived at 23, he is now 40.
Ellen. Singer. Waitress. Arrived at 18, she is now 21.
Jamie. Actress. Wears a mouse costume. Moved at 28, she is now 38.
John. Guitarist. Busboy. Arrived at 22, he is now 26.
Sarah.
Tom.
Stephanie.
Lindsay.
Jarrod.
Danika.
Jose.
Bianca.

Eric.
Karen.
Edie.
Sam.
Matt.
Terry.
Rupert.
Brady.
Alexandra.
Meredith.
Connie.
Lynne.
Laura.
Jimmy.
Johnny.
Carl.

In 1913, the completed Los Angeles Aqueduct opens and is able to provide the city with five times as much water as it needs. Unincorporated areas of Los Angeles County, including almost all of the San Fernando Valley, and several smaller cities, such as San Pedro, Watts, Hollywood, Venice and Eagle Rock, none of which have an independent water supply, are annexed into the city. Over the next decade, its boundaries continue to expand until it encompasses almost 500 square miles.

Mrs. Campbell extends her trip. Doug and Esperanza have coffee together for three straight mornings. They talk and laugh. Doug would make the coffee and clean up when they were finished. A typical conversation between them. Esperanza speaks.

How was your day yesterday?

It was good. Nice and quiet. I sat in front of a computer all day. At the end of the day, my eyeballs hurt, but I never mind that.

What were you doing?

Staring at numbers and equations and pretending that they made some kind of sense to me. How was your day?

Fantastic. I did the guest rooms and the upstairs bathrooms. I tried out a new tile cleaner, but I didn't like it.

Why not?

Not enough sheen when I wiped it away.

Is sheen important?

All-important. Tile without sheen is like a tire without rubber. It just isn't right.

Exactly.

Have you ever thought about marketing your own brand of tile cleaner?

I have not.

Maybe you should.

It's an interesting idea. Maybe I could specifically target the illegal-immigrant-maid demographic.

Why limit yourself? You should think big. You should think HUGE!

Into the white suburban homemaker market?

It would probably be a moneymaker.

Lord knows there's a dearth of quality product out there.

You could call it—*Esperanza's Sheen*.

That's actually a good name.

Good? *GOOD?* It's a fucking great name.

She laughs.

It is, it's a great name. It's so great you could probably just fill up bottles with colored water and stick that name on it and within a few months you'd be so rich that my mom would be cleaning your sinks.

She laughs again.

You might be right.

Might be right, my ass. I am right, Esperanza, I am right.

And on and on it would go between them, until one of them decided they needed to go to work. Once that happened, and Doug was gone, Esperanza spent the rest of the day thinking about him, thinking about what he might be doing, thinking about whatever it was they had talked about that morning, thinking about what might happen between them if they had met somewhere else. Once or twice a day she would go to his room, open the door, stand beneath the doorframe and stare. The room was always a mess: clothes strewn about, books lying in small piles, a stack of video game cartridges, posters of spaceships and planets and astronauts on the walls. Esperanza is tempted to go inside the room. Not to snoop, but because she wants to feel what it's like to be in his space, to be amongst his belongings, to touch things that he touches. Despite their morning conversations, and their close proximity to each other, she has never actually touched him. Every time she has wanted to touch him, or could have touched him, she's gotten scared, scared of what he'll feel like, or what he'll make her feel, scared that maybe they won't feel the same way, scared that whatever she feels might eventually hurt her. If she touches his belongings, she can control the outcome. His belongings will never laugh at her or leave her, never look away from her, never judge her. She stands at the doorframe they're a few feet away. She stares at them.

On the morning after Mrs. Campbell's return, Esperanza wakes up dreading the upcoming day, and already missing her morning coffee with Doug. As she gets ready she thinks about quitting, about walking into the house and telling Mrs. Campbell to fuck off (over the course of her entire life, Esperanza has never told anyone to fuck off, but would be willing to end that streak for Mrs. Campbell). After she told Mrs. Campbell to fuck off, she would kiss Doug, kiss him right on his delicious little lips (and she might go after his tongue too!) for as long as he would allow her to do so. When finished, she would turn and walk out, leaving them both stunned and dizzy.

During the ride into Pasadena, and the walk to the house, she loses her nerve. Telling Mrs. Campbell to fuck off, while fun and immensely satisfying, would go against everything her parents had taught her, and would embarrass her more than Mrs. Campbell. Kissing Doug would be the bravest and boldest act of her life, but she possesses neither the nerve nor the bravery to actually do it. Each step closer to the basement is harder, more depressing, each step feels like another step closer to misery. As she walks through the gates she sees Doug in the kitchen fixing coffee and she hopes that maybe Mrs. Campbell hasn't come home and they will continue as they had for the last few days. Then she hears her voice, that wicked cackle. She says damnit Doug, making the coffee is Esperanza's job, not yours, please dump that pot out so she can make one when she gets here, if she gets here at a reasonable time. Doug says no Mom this is fine I like doing it myself. Mrs. Campbell says Doug, right now, dump it right now, or I will do it myself. Esperanza shakes her head. Oh how sweet it would be. Fuck off you mean old lady. Oh how sweet it would be.

She opens the basement door walks down the stairs Mrs. Campbell is still cackling above her something about the sugar being too lumpy. At the bottom of the stairs she takes a deep breath and walks towards the area designated as hers a small cot her uniforms hanging on a rack a small table. There is a flower on the table, a single red rose in a simple glass vase. There is a note beneath the vase she picks up the vase, picks up the note, there are no words on it just a big smiley-face drawn in red pen. She stares at it for a moment, smiles, sets it down. She stares at the rose, smiles, takes it from the vase and smells it. Upstairs Mrs. Campbell is still cackling, saying Doug, we have her to do these things for us. Esperanza puts the rose back into the vase and starts changing into her uniform. Doug is upstairs. The fuck off is out, she's reconsidering the kiss.

The Panama Canal opens in 1914. The Port of Los Angeles is the closest major American port, and becomes the primary destination for cargo ships traveling west to the United States. By 1920, it is the largest port on the west coast, surpassing Seattle and San Francisco, and is the second-largest in the country after New York.

Joe wakes up he feels sand beneath him his eyes are closed his head is pounding. He hears voices they're voices he knows Ugly Tom, Al from Denver, and Hoot. Al is an alcoholic panhandler in his fifties who sleeps under the Venice Pier, and Hoot is an alcoholic in his thirties who sleeps on the beach during the day and sits on top of a jungle gym at night drinking Ripple and making owl sounds. Ugly Tom speaks.

Should we get the cops?

Al from Denver speaks.

No fucking way.

Why not?

Because they'll arrest us.

We ain't done nothing.

That don't matter.

We gotta do something to get arrested.

No we don't.

So what do we do?

Wait for him to wake up.

When's that gonna happen?

How should I know.

It could be a while.

Yeah, it could.

You got anything to drink?

No.

You got any money?

No.

How about you, Hoot, you got anything to drink?

Hoot nods.

What do you got?

Hoot reaches into his pocket, pulls out a half-pint of cheap whiskey.

Can I have some?

Hoot nods, passes it to Al, who takes a slug.

Wow. That's awful.

Hoot nods. Al passes the bottle to Ugly Tom, who takes a slug. He smiles after he swallows.

Awful my ass. That's wonderful.

He passes the bottle to Hoot, who takes a slug and doesn't say anything. Al looks at Tom, speaks.

You got bad taste, Tom. That shit is awful.

Fuck off.

No need to get nasty.

I like what I like. And if it's got alcohol in it, I like it. If it don't got no alcohol, I don't like it. That's just me.

That's probably not a healthy policy.

I don't care.

I'll revise my statement then: you don't have bad taste, you have unhealthy taste.

Fuck off.

No need to get nasty, Tom.

Fuck off.

When he can't take it anymore, Old Man Joe opens his eyes, speaks.

Please stop.

Ugly Tom speaks.

Holy shit, he's awake.

Al from Denver speaks.

Now we don't have to call the cops.

Joe sits up.

What happened?

Ugly Tom speaks.

I didn't see it.

Al from Denver speaks.

Me neither.

Ugly Tom speaks.

But Hoot did.

Al from Denver speaks.

He came and got us after it happened.

Ugly Tom speaks.

He was sitting on his jungle gym.

Al from Denver.

Just like he always is when he ain't sleeping off being drunk.

Old Man Joe looks at Hoot, speaks.

What happened?

Hoot takes another sip from the half-pint, speaks. He has a soft voice, a child's voice, and he rarely speaks. When he does, he is careful with his words and difficult to hear. Old Man Joe, Ugly Tom and Al from Denver all lean towards him.

You was the same as you is every day, except the girl was with you and she was making circles in the sand. Three of them in black hoodies come right up on you and when you sit up one of 'em kicks you in the head.

What'd they do with the girl?

They hit her in the face and took her away and one of 'em was walking behind her and he'd smack her in the back of the head if she slowed down and she was crying and asking them to leave her alone.

You ever seen these guys before?

I seen 'em around. Sometimes they prowling on the boardwalk late at night, robbing people and hitting people.

They live on the boardwalk?

Somewhere up that way.

He points north.

You remember anything else?

Hoot takes another slug.

I was scared. I was scared real bad. I wanted to get off the gym and come help but I was too scared.

It's okay, Hoot.

I'm sorry.

Don't be sorry, you did great getting these guys to come help when it was over. That was what you should have done. You did great. I owe you one.

Hoot nods.

Is it okay if I go sleep now?

Joe smiles.

Yeah. Go sleep.

Hoot smiles and stands and leaves. When he's gone, Ugly Tom speaks.

What do you think?

Joe speaks.

My head hurts.

Al speaks.

My head hurts every damn morning. Once you start drinking that'll go away.

Joe speaks.

This ain't 'cause of hangover.

Al speaks.

I know, but the principle's the same: head hurts, get drunk, head don't hurt no more.

Joe speaks.

Maybe in a little while. Now we gotta figure out what we're gonna do about Beatrice.

Al speaks.

Who the fuck is Beatrice?

Joe speaks.

The girl.

Tom speaks.

That girl's trouble, man. You should just let that go away.

Joe speaks.

She's a kid.

Al speaks.

She ain't no kid.

Joe speaks.

She ain't more than seventeen.

Al speaks.

That don't mean she's still a kid.

Joe speaks.

Those guys are gonna fuck her up.

Tom speaks.

That ain't our problem.

Joe speaks.

If it's happening here it is.

Al speaks.

Plenty of shit happens around that ain't none of our business. I saw some drunk guy drive his car into the ocean a few weeks ago. Didn't have nothing to do with me so I walked away.

Joe speaks.

Shit that happens in the civilian world ain't got nothing to do with us. If it happens in our world, we got to do something about it.

Tom speaks.

My world's the liquor store, the tourists who give me money, and my sleeping bag.

Al speaks.

My world is the liquor store, the pier, and the Lord above, even though he's forsaken me.

Joe speaks.

That girl's too young to be living down here. And those motherfuckers in their hoodies ain't gonna do nothing but use her and hurt her. Don't matter how you look at it, it ain't right.

Joe stands, starts walking away. Ugly Tom speaks.

Where you going, Joe?

Without stopping or turning around, Joe speaks.

I'm gonna go try and do something about it.

In 1915, D. W. Griffith writes and directs *The Clansman*, also known as *The Birth of a Nation*. The movie, which is shot in and around Los Angeles, portrays the Ku Klux Klan as a heroic band of soldiers fighting to reconstruct the South and preserve southern heritage after the Civil War. It destroys box-office records and becomes the most successful film ever made. It also serves as a siren call to filmmakers all over the country, who rush to Los Angeles in search of the same type of success. Griffith later founds United Artists with a group of actors and directors, and dies in 1948, penniless in a Hollywood flophouse.

Esperanza walks upstairs the coffee is made but Mrs. Campbell insists she remake it. She does, and she serves it, and Mrs. Campbell doesn't like it, and she makes her do it again. Doug tries to object Mrs. Campbell tells him to mind his own business. Esperanza makes the second pot and the second pot is better, but not perfect, and Mrs. Campbell makes her do it again. When Doug objects again, Mrs. Campbell tells him he can have an opinion when he starts paying the bills. Esperanza makes a third pot and serves it and Mrs. Campbell deems it suitable, but just barely. Doug stares at the table. Esperanza wipes down the counters. Mrs. Campbell drinks her coffee and reads the paper. When Doug leaves, Esperanza watches him and hopes that he'll look at her, acknowledge her, maybe smile at her if he can. His face is red, his head is down, he walks away.

For the rest of the day, Mrs. Campbell follows Esperanza around the house as she works, criticizes her, makes her redo almost everything she does, purposefully messes things up after Esperanza has cleaned them so that Esperanza will have to clean them again. When Esperanza asks for lunch, Mrs. Campbell tells her that she doesn't deserve a lunch, and isn't going to get one. The two times Esperanza needs to use the bathroom, Mrs. Campbell stands outside the door, staring at her watch and knocking every thirty seconds until Esperanza is finished. When she is, Mrs. Campbell makes her scrub the toilet.

It's an endless day. Esperanza thinks about quitting, about just walking away. She thinks about Doug appreciates his attempt to stand up for her and feels embarrassed for the way his mother humiliated him, the shame he radiated as he left the room. She thinks about the flower in the basement. It's the only thing that keeps her going. Doug left her a flower, a flower, for the first time in her life a man left her a flower, a rose, a red rose, a perfect beautiful red rose in a simple clear glass vase. It wasn't a joke and it wasn't left in jest and it wasn't a mistake and it wasn't for someone else. It's hers, her flower, a perfect beautiful red rose in a simple clear glass vase. If he laughed when he left it, it was because he was happy about doing it. There was no mistake.

Esperanza finishes the last bathroom Mrs. Campbell tells her she's disappointed in her and hopes she will work harder and better tomorrow. Esperanza smiles and nods and waits to be dismissed when she is she walks to the basement walks down the stairs when she reaches the bottom she sees Doug sitting on the edge of her cot. He looks up, his face is still red he looks tired and worn, he speaks.

Hi.

She smiles.

Hi.

How was your day?

It was awful.

I thought it might be.

What are you doing down here?

I wanted to talk to you.

Aren't you supposed to be at work?

I told them I wasn't feeling well, which is actually true, and took the afternoon off.

You don't look so good.

Physically I'm fine. I just feel like an ass.

Don't.

I do.

Don't.

I'm sorry.

It's okay.

It's not.

It is.

She's been doing this to me my whole life.

I can imagine.

I fucking hate her.

You should feel sorry for her.

No.

I do.

You're a better person than I am.

She smiles.

I'm not.

He smiles.

It's okay to admit it. Most people are better people than me.

She laughs.

I like you.

He keeps smiling.

Good. I like you too.

I have a question.

What?

How long have you been down here?

A couple hours.

Just sitting there?

Yeah.

You like it down here?

He laughs.

No.

She looks at her flower, which is still in its vase.

Thank you for the flower.

He smiles again.

I was hoping the moments we spent together after you found it were going to be a bit different than they were.

None of the moments in my life that I thought would be great ever have been. That's just the way it goes.

I don't like that.

Nothing you can do about it.

He stands, smiles, she's a few feet away.

I'm nervous.

She smiles.

Why?

I want you to think that this is a great moment, a great day.

She laughs. He speaks.

I'm serious.

He takes a step forward. She speaks.

What are you doing?

He takes another step forward.

I'm a nerd, so I'm not good at this.

Another step.

What?

Another step, he's a few inches away, she can see him shaking, he smiles his lips shaking, he reaches for her, his hands shaking.

The population of Los Angeles grows from 175,000 people to 1,750,000 people between the years 1900 and 1925.

Joe walks back to the bathroom by the time he gets there his head hurts so much that he knows his new job as Boardwalk Hero won't start today. When he reaches the bathroom, he finds his stuff has been removed and set against the dumpster. He looks through it to see if anything is gone his extra clothes are there his sleeping bag is there his toiletries are there. He reaches for the door he wants to get his secret Chablis from the toilet tank but the door is locked he puts his ear to the door he can hear some tourist who's doubtlessly had too many tacos and too much cotton candy and too many mocha delights moving around he hopes they finish soon his head fucking hurts. He sits down, leans against the dumpster, closes his eyes. As soon as he starts to relax, he hears a voice.

Joe.

He opens his eyes, Larry, who is the manager of the taco stand, and who, for marketing reasons, goes by the name Ricardo while he's at work, stands in front of him. Larry is short and fat, has long blond hair and blue eyes.

What's up, Larry?

It's Ricardo during business hours.

What's up, Ricardo?

You know the rules, right.

Yeah.

You gotta be outta the bathroom by the time we open.

I know.

Your shit was in there this morning. You were nowhere to be found.

I got mugged.

What?

Not really mugged, because I got nothing to steal. But I got kicked in the head while I was on the beach this morning and I got knocked out.

Seriously?

Yeah.

Who the fuck would kick you in the head? You're an old man.

I'm not that old.

Larry laughs.
I know you say you're not old, but I don't believe that shit.
You're seventy at least.
I'm thirty-nine.
Seventy-five.
Thirty-nine.
Seventy-five.
It doesn't matter.
You shouldn't drink so much.
I'm sorry about this morning.
Don't do it again. If Roberto catches you he'll freak out.
Roberto?
The owner.
I thought his name was Tom.
Roberto. Marketing. Same as me.
Okay.
Your head okay?
It hurts.
You want some aspirin?
No. I'm gonna get drunk.
The toilet flushes. The door opens. Before they see the tourist, the smell overwhelms them, it is some combination of death, cheese, and sour milk. The tourist follows the smell he is an obese, sunburned white man wearing a tight Muscle Beach T-shirt, Bermuda shorts and neon sunglasses. He says excuse me, and steps around Larry. As soon as he's gone, Larry holds his hand over his nose, speaks.
Bet that makes you forget about your headache.
Old Man Joe, who also has his hand over his nose, laughs.
See you later, Ricardo.
See you later.
Larry leaves. Old Man Joe stands and walks into the bathroom. He lifts the lid of the tank there are two bottles there he pulls one of them out and leaves as quickly as he can. He walks back towards the beach. He finds a nice shaded spot on the grass at the edge of the beach, directly beneath a palm

tree. His head is fucking pounding. He drinks the bottle and his head starts to feel better. When he finishes his first bottle he goes to the dumpster of his favorite pizza place and finds a couple nice slices of day-old pepperoni, which he eats while sitting on the cement next to the dumpster. He goes back to the bathroom, gets his second bottle, goes back to the tree, slowly drinks the bottle, watches the swarms of tourists, a few of whom drop coins at his feet, watches the police watching the tourists, watches the locals watch the police. When he finishes the second bottle, his head is fine. He lies down and takes a nap. Before he falls asleep he thinks about Beatrice, hopes that she's okay, even though he knows she's not, thinks about what he could do to help her, get her away from here, find somewhere safe for her. He was going to do it today, all of it, get her out and be her hero. Today didn't work. Maybe tomorrow.

In 1923, local tennis champion and real-estate developer Alphonzo Bell Sr. purchases 600 acres of land and starts building what he calls the Bel-Air Estates, which later becomes the town of Bel-Air. It is conceived as a refuge from the city of Los Angeles for wealthy, white businessmen and their families.

Every city can be fun, and every city has certain elements, or facts, about it that are fun. Learning fun facts is really an enjoyable, and sometimes enlightening process. And, of course, it's fun too!!! Here is Fun Facts Los Angeles, Volume 1.

After serving as a fighter pilot for the navy in World War II, George Herbert Walker Bush, the forty-third vice president of the United States, and the forty-first president of the United States, was a drill-bit salesman in Los Angeles during the late 1940s.

It is illegal to manufacture pickles in the industrial zone of downtown Los Angeles.

A small portion of Mahatma Gandhi's ashes are enshrined at the Self Realization Fellowship Lake Shrine Temple in Pacific Palisades. They are the only portion of Gandhi's remains that are kept anywhere outside of India.

The economy of the County of Los Angeles is larger than that of forty-six of the fifty states in the United States of America.

The City of Los Angeles moves approximately one-quarter of an inch to the east every year.

It is illegal to lick a toad within the city limits of Los Angeles.

Herding flocks of more than 2,000 sheep on Hollywood Boulevard is illegal; flocks less than 2,000 are legal as long as the owner has a permit.

It is legal for human beings to marry rocks in the City of Los Angeles. The first such marriage occurred in 1950, when a secretary at an auto-parts factory named Jannene Swift married a large piece of granite.

The Port of Los Angeles handles almost 200 million tons of cargo every year.

For some reason that, despite extensive scientific research, remains unknown, potato chips weigh more in Los Angeles than in any other part of America.

There are sixty-five people in Los Angeles who have the legal name Jesus Christ.

There is more pornography produced in Los Angeles than in the rest of the world combined.

Every year, approximately 100,000 women in Los Angeles County have their breasts enhanced.

Fun fun fun, everyone knows that facts like these are tons and tons and tons of fun.

Every year, approximately 75,000 people undergo rhinoplasty procedures in Los Angeles (rhinoplasty is the fancy word for a nose job).

The Safely Surrendered Baby Law of Los Angeles County states that parents are permitted to bring any baby within three days of birth to any designated hospital or fire station and give the baby up without fear of arrest or prosecution.

Fifty-four percent of the citizens of Los Angeles County take vitamins on a daily basis, compared with twenty-two percent of the citizens in the rest of the country.

In 1886, the official slogan of the Los Angeles Travel Bureau was—Los Angeles is the Chicago of California!

The largest concrete donut in the world, which is 40 feet high and weighs 25 tons, is in Los Angeles.

It is illegal in the City of Los Angeles to provide or administer snuff to children under the age of sixteen.

There are four times more hamburgers eaten in Los Angeles County than in the rest of California combined.

In 1976 the physicians at all of the public hospitals in Los Angeles County went on strike and the average number of daily fatalities fell by 20 percent.

In 1955 the complete skeleton of an 80-foot-long, 120-ton blue whale was found buried in East Los Angeles, approximately thirty-five miles from the Pacific Ocean.

It is illegal within the city limits of Los Angeles to place two children under the age of two in a bathtub at the same time.

A little more fun, and then it's time to go! But don't worry, there will be at least one more, and possibly two or three more, volumes of Los Angeles Fun Facts!!!!!!!!

The average citizen of Los Angeles consumes 250 tacos a year.

The average citizen of Los Angeles consumes 80 gallons of carbonated, caffeinated cola every year.

Los Angeles is the only major city in the world with an active population of wild mountain lions. An average of three people each year within the city limits are killed and eaten by the mountain lions.

The average citizen of Los Angeles eats 28 pounds of fried chicken, 50 pounds of French fries, 22 gallons of ice cream, 12 pounds of tortilla chips and drinks 325 bottles of beer every year.

A contest was held in 1993 to rename the Los Angeles Convention and Exhibition Center after an extensive renovation and expansion. The winning name, chosen from over ten thousand entries, was the *Los Angeles Convention Center.*

In 1909, Glenn Martin becomes the fourth person to design, build and fly an aircraft when he takes off from the edge of an orange grove in southwest Los Angeles. In 1910, Los Angeles holds the world's first air show at Dominguez Field, which draws 250,000 spectators. In 1914 Caltech opens its first aeronautics lab. In 1917, Woodrow Wilson announces a federally funded program to build 20,000 planes for the United States military. In 1921, Donald Douglas founds Douglas Aircraft in Santa Monica, which produces the first plane to circumnavigate the earth in 1924. It becomes the world's largest aircraft manufacturer, and the DC designation of its planes an iconic representation of American aviation technology.

Amberton and Casey are in the back of a Mercedes limousine. There are four SUVs with paparazzi behind them. There are three paparazzi on the backs of motorcycles that take turns pulling up to the side of them. The windows in the limo are darkened beyond what is technically allowed by law, so it is impossible to take pictures of anything other than a darkened window. The paparazzi are undeterred.

They are going to a film premiere. The film is an action movie about four people who have alien DNA in their bodies which gives them special powers. One of them has eyes in the back of her head, and the ability to see for miles. Another has the power to melt anything he touches. The third has the strength of a thousand men, the fourth can harness the rays of the sun using lenses that grow in her fingernails. They each have premonitions that the aliens, whose DNA is in their bodies, are coming back to Earth to destroy it. They band together and engage the aliens in furious combat. They become great heroes, and the only defenders of life on Earth. At the end of the film, two of them die, but a fifth human/alien is discovered who has the power of miraculous healing, and they are brought back to life (sequels, it's all about the motherfucking sequels). One of Casey's close friends plays the woman with lensed fingers, and Amberton has done two films with the husband/wife producing team that made the movie. Amberton and Casey are both decked out in designer clothes (which were given to them for free), and had stylists come to the house to do their hair and makeup. There is a bodyguard in the front seat, next to the driver, and the partition between them is up. Casey speaks.

How many messages have you left?

Amberton speaks.

Fifteen.

Have you ever left fifteen messages for someone without getting a return call?

In tenth grade.

For who?

A girl named Laurel Anders Whitmore.

Fancy name.

Yeah. She was a blond-haired, blue-eyed socialite. The hottest girl on the Upper East Side. I was obsessed with her. I actually probably left fifty messages for her without getting a return.

Where is she now?

Last I heard she was still living in New York, on Fifth and Eighty-fifth, with a hedge fund manager husband and three perfect WASP children in private schools. I also heard she has Mom-butt.

Mom-butt?

Yeah. She became a mom and with each kid her butt size doubled.

So what, it's like sixteen times bigger than it was when she started?

Yeah. About that.

Casey laughs.

Even though I knew I liked boys, it took me years to get over her. I finally worked it out with a shrink, and we decided I was obsessed with her because she reminded me of my mother.

Oh my.

Indeed. Very very dark.

The car slows down, there is a tap on the partition, and it drops a few inches. The bodyguard, who is humongous, and before he went into private security, worked for an unnamed government agency, speaks.

We'll be there in five minutes.

Casey and Amberton speak at the same time.

Thank you.

The partition rises, shuts. Without speaking, they both lean forward and pull down mirrors that are built into the ceiling of the Mercedes. They check their hair, makeup. They each have kits with them that contain touch-up cosmetics and hair products. Casey adds some powder, Amberton adds some blush. Casey puts some extra conditioner on what she believes are split ends, Amberton adds hair spray to the bulletproof helmet of hair constructed by his stylists. The car slows down again, enters the line for the Red Carpet. They've been through this enough times to know that there is nothing more they can change, or improve, or somehow make more beautiful or perfect than it already is. They put away their kits, and close the mirrors. They look at each other. Amberton speaks.

You are so goddamned hot that if I was inclined in that way, I would take you, with gusto, right here, on this seat, right now.

She smiles, laughs.

Right back at you.

They high-five. The car stops, the partition drops the guard looks at them, speaks.

Ready.

They both respond.

Yes.

The guard gets out of the car, steps towards the back door. Amberton takes Casey's hand, they look out the window, where a horde of photographers and reporters wait for them. Behind the photographers and reporters, there are bleachers filled with screaming fans, many of whom also have cameras. The guard reaches for the door, Amberton and Casey take deep breaths. The door opens.

No matter how many times it's happened, there is nothing that can prepare a person for the experience of stepping out of a car into a swarm of people who are screaming your name and popping flashbulbs in your face. It's terrifying, confusing, exhilarating. Amberton and Casey step out, Casey first, Amberton closely behind, the guard's long heavy arms are stretched in front of them, functioning as some kind of barrier. There are hands reaching for them, flailing at them, people try to shove pictures magazines posters and pens towards them. The flashbulbs are like some kind of strobe light gone insane, an endless blinding disorienting wall of exploding white. Amberton holds Casey's hand holds it tight the guard yells step back pushes through the mass Amberton and Casey stay directly behind him both are smiling and, with their free hand, waving. They are actors. They are acting like they are unfazed, unflustered, unaffected. They both have stalkers who may be somewhere amongst the crowd they both have maniacs who send them disturbing letters, pictures, they may be somewhere amongst the crowd. They hold each other's hand and smile and wave and act and hope that they make it to the tent where the press with approved credentials will take pictures of them in a more civilized, but only slightly so, manner.

They see their publicists, they each have one, standing together near the entrance to the tent. Both of the publicists are women, both are in their mid-thirties, both are attractive, wear black designer suits, carry clipboards, wear headsets in their left ears. They are partners in a Beverly Hills PR firm that caters exclusively to film and television stars. Their names are Sara (who works with Amberton) and Dara (Casey), and they have been best friends since high school. Amberton and Casey don't speak publicly, give interviews or do photo shoots, or have any interaction with the media in any way, without speaking to them first.

The guard sees the publicists bulls his way through the crowd Amberton and Casey are right behind him still smiling and waving, still acting. When they reach Sara and Dara kisses are exchanged petite little kisses on each cheek. Sara looks at their outfits, speaks.

You guys look awesome!

Amberton and Casey both speak.

Thanks. You too.

Dara speaks.

You'll make the best-dressed lists for sure.

They both smile.

Sara looks at Casey's dress, speaks.

Is that Valentino?

Casey and Dara both speak.

Chanel.

Sara looks at Amberton, speaks.

Armani?

Amberton speaks.

Of course.

It's really nice.

Custom-tailored.

It looks like it.

Casey speaks.

How's it looking tonight?

Dara speaks.

The usual. Maybe a little worse.

Sara speaks.

We were thinking pictures and no interviews.

Dara speaks.

All of the shows asked, but we like to make them sweat every
now and then.

Amberton speaks.

Sounds good to me.

Casey speaks.

Me too.

They walk towards the red carpet, which is actually more like
stiff red Astroturf, and they start walking down the aisle. They
follow the unwritten rules of the red carpet: do not step into
someone else's picture, do not be exclusive (if one photographer
gets to shoot you, they all get to shoot you), smile, pose,
engage in playful banter with the photographers, keep moving
so that everyone gets their turn, don't pass people or steal their
limelight, pretend you know and are friends with everyone else
on the red carpet (a big happy club of famous people who are
great friends and hang out all the time). Although Amberton is
distracted, and is trying to watch for Kevin in the noncelebrity
line of premiere attendees, which runs behind the
photographers and reporters (one of his spies at the agency told
him Kevin was coming), he plays his part well, smiles (he has a
megawatt smile, IT'S MEGAWATT!!!!!), poses, kisses his wife
(no tongue), waves, acts. Sara and Dara are always a few feet
away, acting as shields, answering questions so that Amberton
and Casey don't have to answer them, ushering them along so
that the line on the carpet keeps moving. When they're

finished, they exchange kisses again, lots of fucking kisses on the red carpet, and Sara and Dara go back to the head of the red carpet to wait for their other arriving clients (though Amberton and Casey are their biggest and most important clients so sometimes the others work the carpet, temporarily, with a subordinate). Once they're done with the red carpet, Amberton and Casey make their way towards the entrance of the theater. The footprints, handprints, and in one case, the face print, of past, and a couple current, cinematic superstars are pressed into concrete blocks. Amberton doesn't look at them because he's annoyed he isn't among them, and after attending dozens of premieres at the venue over the years, he always goes out of his way, and he knows exactly where they are without having to look, to step on and grind his feet into the blocks containing the prints of the living superstars, none of whom he considers his equal. When he isn't grinding and stomping, he and Casey are shaking hands, hugging, exchanging more kisses. They see a studio boss they hate, Casey gives him a kiss Amberton shakes his hand they ask about each other's children. They see a director that Amberton got fired from a film they were doing together they exchange hugs, smiles, pats on the back. Casey sees a couple of her rivals chatting with each other (she regularly prays for one or both of them to be struck by lightning) she walks over says hello to them takes a couple pictures with them exchanges kisses with them, they look like they're best friends (and if not lightning, maybe a car crash). Amberton sees another action star they shake hands, and they shake 'em like fucking men, laugh at each other's jokes, check out each other's suits, talk about having a beer together, both mumble—you fucking asshole—under their breath when they part ways. They see producers, agents, managers, writers, other actors and actresses, studio executives, moguls. Despite the fact that many of these people absolutely despise each other, it looks like they are all in love, deeply, truly and wildly in love. Kiss on the cheek, pat on the back, give me a hug, buddy, let's take a picture. And then,

please please please, go straight to the restroom and fuck
yourself.

The lights, both in the theater and outside of it, flash a couple
times the universal sign that the show, or in this case film, is
about to start. Amberton and Casey, along with everyone else,
make their way inside. They walk down the center aisle
towards the middle, which is where there are roped-off VIP
sections for celebrities and the people who made and star in
the film. Aside from the VIP sections, seating in premieres is
usually first come, first serve. Small bags of popcorn and sodas
are offered as refreshment. Amberton and Casey avoid both
(popcorn has carbs goddamnit), and find their seats, which are
with the seats of several other universally recognized worldwide
entertainment superstars. They settle into the seats. Casey gives
Amberton a smile and a nice kiss (still acting!!!) and they wait
for the film to start. Amberton says hi to a producer he once
threatened to run out of town.

When the lights are down, and the film running, Amberton
leans back and closes his eyes. He did not see Kevin, wonders
if he's here. Despite the fact there are explosions, action
sequences, intergalactic combat, and forty-foot-tall aliens on a
giant screen in front of him, he loses himself in his love, lust
and longing, he loses himself in memories of the times, though
they have been short and fleeting, that he has spent with
Kevin, loses himself in his dreams of a future, of the idea that
someday he'll leave all of this behind and set off on a new
course of life with a real, true, 100 percent all-the-way soul
mate. He thinks it might be Kevin. The football star and the
movie star. Maybe they could open a bed-and-breakfast, maybe
they could go to Europe and spend the rest of their lives
looking at art, maybe they could buy an island.

After a particularly loud explosion, Casey nudges Amberton,
who opens his eyes and turns to her. She speaks, very quietly
(you never know who's listening), she speaks.

Are you watching?

No?

Have you seen any of it?
No.
What are you doing?
Dreaming about Kevin.
You gonna buy an island with him?
Amberton smiles.
Maybe.
You should watch some of it.
Is it good?
No.
Not at all?
No, it's awful.
Will it be a hit?
Yeah, it's gonna be huge.
I don't want to watch, I'd rather dream.
We're going to the party afterwards. You're going to have to talk about it.
I'll be fine.
You sure?
Yeah.
Amberton turns away, closes his eyes again. He wonders if Kevin has ever been to the South of France, to Buenos Aires, Fiji. On the screen, the aliens are launching a furious assault. The heroic humans with strands of alien DNA are preparing a counterattack. Half of Miami disappears in a flash. Green lasers rain down on London Bridge. Flying saucers blast away at the peak of Mt. Fuji. It's going to be a huge hit.
When the film ends everyone claps. As is customary, and considered appropriate and respectful in the film industry, the crowd sits through all of the credits, even the ones at the end for people who have jobs with strange and unexplainable names. When the credits finish running, the lights come on and everyone stands and starts to filter out of the theater. This is the only time when being a VIP means nothing. There are no VIP aisles, no special exits. There is no way to use VIP status to avoid the other people who are also trying to leave. Because

it is an industry crowd, and thus considered safe, the guards usually wait outside for the stars, unless there are special circumstances, such as a particularly nasty stalker or a bad situation with the press (reporters have been known to ambush people in premieres because it is wrongly assumed they are safe among their peers). Once outside, the guard immediately takes up a position with the star, or the exceedingly rich and important person who is worthy of a guard, and guides them to their car. As Amberton and Casey make their way slowly up the aisle, Amberton scans the theater for Kevin. He knows he'll be wearing a black suit, but so is almost every other man in attendance. He knows he's probably taller than most of the men in the room, the average height of the average movie star, producer, director or entertainment industry businessman is five foot six. He also knows he's black, and though there are plenty of black actors and actresses, and a few black directors, there are almost no black agents, managers, producers or executives. He looks through the crowd but doesn't see him he keeps looking. Oh Kevin where art thou, dear Kevin? He looks through the crowd and he holds his wife's hand and he walks slowly up the aisle, where art thou?

They come out of the theater most of the crowd is gone all of the paparazzi are still there. They find their guard flashbulbs popping everywhere they go to their car, the party is four blocks away and it's safer to drive. It takes forty minutes to get there. Casey calls home to check on the kids Amberton stares out the window, all he wants is a glimpse, for a second maybe two, he just wants to see him. All he gets are short white guys in black suits who have incredibly hot women with them and fans in T-shirts and shorts who scream and yell and behind the protection of the car's windows, look like they're insane.

When they get to the party they go to the VIP entrance (thank God they're getting VIP treatment again) and they are immediately ushered to the VIP section, which is roped off and guarded. Theoretically, everyone in the room is a VIP, or would be outside of Los Angeles, so this VIP section is actually a VVIP section, or maybe even a VVVIP section, or if every one of the superstars shows up, a VVVVIP section. It consists of ten or twelve booths, there is a waitress for each of them. In the middle of each of the booth's tables, there is a bottle of chilled champagne. Food is available, though movie stars, both male and female, are always watching their figures, and if the champagne isn't wanted, just about anything else, including any number of substances and chemicals that are against the law, is available. Amberton and Casey are among the last of the stars to arrive (not enough showed to make it VVVVIP), and as they head to their table, they stop and say hello to the stars of the film, whom they compliment on their work, to the director, whom they congratulate and declare to be a genius, and to the producers, whom they hug and kiss on the cheek and offer true and sincere congratulations for making a great, great film. When they sit down, they're exhausted. Casey speaks.

Think the food is any good?

Amberton speaks.

Are you gonna eat any of it?

I might.

Are you going to keep it down?

Depends on how much I eat.

Usually the food is themed around the movie. What kind of food do aliens eat?

They eat humans.

Do you think they're serving human?

It would be cool if they were.

Amberton motions for the waitress, who steps over, speaks.

How can I help you, sir?

What kind of food are they serving tonight?

Chicken fingers in the shape of human fingers, chicken legs shaped like human legs, mini-hamburgers in the shape of a human heart, and the drink of the evening is a Bloody Mary.

Amberton and Casey both laugh. Casey speaks.

Can you bring me a plate with a little bit of everything?

The waitress speaks.
Of course.
Amberton speaks.
And two Bloody Marys, please.
Certainly.
The waitress leaves. Casey and Amberton look out into the
party. A strong indicator of how much a studio does or does not
like, or does or does not believe in, a film is the amount of
money they spend on a premiere party. If they expect a big hit,
or are beholden in some way to one of the stars or principals of
the film, expect a big party. And big can mean a three-million-
dollar party, a five-million-dollar party, in at least one case, ten
million dollars was spent on a premiere party. This one is big,
probably in the four-to-five-million-dollar range. There are
multiple bars, multiple food stations, all of the waiters and
waitresses (except for the ones in the VVVIP section who are in
black) are dressed as aliens, there is a famous English DJ who
has been flown in to provide the music, different sections of the
room are designed to look like the different cities in the film.
There are two or three hundred people in attendance, not
everyone who gets to go to the film gets to go to the party, all of
them are taking advantage of the studio's generosity. And no
matter how awful a film might be, people rarely say anything
bad about it at a premiere party, especially if the studio has
spent money on it. Part of the reason is because it's impolite,
another is that people don't want to say something that might
later be held against them, another is if for some reason they are
proven wrong, and the film is a hit, they will look like an idiot.
In a business full of treachery and ruthlessness, it's a strange
phenomenon. It's also one of the reasons executives, producers,
directors and stars are shocked and confused when something
that carries high expectations, and something they haven't heard
a single negative thing about, bombs when released to the public.
The waitress brings the food back to Amberton and Casey.
Casey picks up one of the chicken fingers, which does indeed
look like a human finger. She smiles, speaks.

Creepy.
Amberton speaks.
I think it's hot.
Oh yeah?
Love fingers in my mouth.
She laughs, holds it up.
You want it?
He smiles.
Not those.
She laughs again, takes a bite, chews. She nods, says—it's good—with a mouth full of it, takes another bite. Amberton takes a sip of his drink, scans the room, he can't see much, the room is too crowded and there's too much going on, all seven cities are packed with revelers filling their gullets with free food and drink. Out of the corner of his eye, he sees the guards step out of the way, he turns to see who it is, his agent Gordon waves to him, following directly behind Gordon is Kevin, they are both wearing black suits. Amberton smiles, waves them over. When they arrive, he shakes each of their hands, invites them to sit down. Gordon sits next to him, Kevin sits next to Casey. Amberton speaks.
We were looking for you guys.
Gordon speaks.
We were making the rounds.
Casey speaks.
See anyone interesting?
Gordon speaks.
Same people that are always at these things. Kevin doesn't know them all yet, so I was making some introductions.
Amberton speaks.
How did it go?
Kevin speaks.
Well, I guess. It was just shaking hands and saying hello.
Casey speaks.
And collecting business cards.
Kevin pats the pocket of his coat, speaks.

Got a few of those.

Gordon speaks.

Because of his exploits on the football field Kevin has the advantage of being well known outside of the business. Most people, men at least, already know who he is and are anxious to talk to him.

Amberton smiles, speaks.

Most straight men.

Gordon speaks.

You'd be surprised.

He and Gordon both laugh, Kevin appears embarrassed. Casey speaks.

What'd you think of the movie?

Kevin speaks.

It was great. Gonna be a huge hit.

Gordon speaks.

Kevin actually represents one of the aliens.

Casey speaks.

One of the hybrids, or one of the true aliens?

Kevin speaks.

The lead female true alien. The one with the big appetite.

Amberton speaks.

She was great.

Kevin speaks.

I'll tell her you said so, it'll mean a lot to her.

Casey speaks.

How'd you find her?

Kevin speaks.

I knew her in college. She was a cheerleader.

Amberton speaks.

And did you ever once think that someday you'd be her agent?

Kevin speaks.

No, but a lot of things have happened that I never thought would have or could have. Amberton smiles. Casey takes a bite of a chicken finger. Gordon, who does not know what is going on between Amberton and Kevin, nods, and speaks.

And plenty more is going to happen. You have a huge career in front of you.

Kevin speaks.

Thank you.

Gordon sees another client, stands and excuses himself.

Amberton looks at Kevin, smiles, speaks.

Just so you know, you don't have to feel weird. Casey knows everything.

Kevin speaks.

What?

Casey speaks.

I know all about the two of you. Amberton and I share everything with each other. You don't need to feel weird around me. I think it's great that you're sleeping with my husband.

Kevin speaks.

I'm not sure what to say.

Amberton speaks.

You could tell me you love me.

Casey speaks.

Or you could say—Thanks Casey, that's pretty cool.

Kevin speaks.

Or I could say I think I made a mistake and I think this conversation is incredibly inappropriate.

Amberton laughs.

Don't say that. That's no fun.

Casey speaks.

And even if that is what you think, it's too late now. The train is running down the tracks, and it isn't stopping.

Kevin speaks.

What's that supposed to mean?

Amberton, who is sitting across from Kevin, slides his foot up the side of Kevin's leg, speaks.

Let's just enjoy the evening, Kevin.

Casey speaks.

We have food, champagne, each other's company, our own

waitress, a couple hundred of our best friends and worst
enemies, and a car is waiting for us when we're ready to leave.
Kevin looks at Amberton, speaks.

Could you move your foot, please?

Amberton smiles, speaks.

Higher up?

Away.

You sure?

Yes, I'm sure.

Amberton smiles, moves his foot slightly higher. Kevin reaches
below the table, forcibly moves the foot away. Amberton
pretends to be hurt, speaks.

Ouch.

Kevin speaks.

That didn't hurt.

It did.

Kevin stands.

I think it's time for me to go.

Casey speaks.

That would be a big mistake.

Kevin speaks.

I don't think so.

Casey smiles.

You don't understand, do you, Kevin?

Understand what?

Sit down.

As I said, I'm going to leave.

If you leave, by the time you're out of this section, you'll be
unemployed. Now sit down.

Kevin looks at Casey she's smiling, he looks at Amberton he's
smiling. He sits down. She speaks.

My husband is in love with you. You may think that notion is
ridiculous, but it's not to him. His feelings are very real, and
are absolutely true to his heart. For whatever reason, because
you're on the down-low, because you're actually gay, or because
you thought it might help your career, you decided to sleep

with him. You didn't have to do it. Eventually, his obsession would have dissipated. But you did do it. You decided to allow the relationship to become physical. Now you have to deal with it. That may mean allowing him to rub your thigh under the table at a premiere. That may mean sleeping with him again. That may mean something else, like going away with him, or visiting him in his trailer on his next film, or closing the door to your office when he stops by to visit. What it doesn't mean is that you can walk away when you feel like it, or that you can go about your day without returning his phone calls, or that you can hurt him in any way without expecting there to be consequences. We may have an unconventional marriage, but I love my husband. He's my best friend and my soul mate. We have a beautiful life together and a beautiful family. I will not allow you to hurt him in any way, or endanger his well-being or our family's well-being. If you do, I will make you pay.

Kevin stares at her. She stares back. He speaks.

So you expect me to do whatever he wants, whenever he wants?

Yes, I do. Until he doesn't want it anymore.

It's not gonna happen.

Yes, it is.

No fucking way.

She smiles.

You're new to the business. I understand your ignorance, your naïveté. Let this be a lesson to you. Movie stars get what they want, when they want it, because we're the reason people pay money to go to the movies. Nobody goes to the theater to see an agent, or a producer, or a writer, or some silly studio executive, they go to see us. Amberton and I are two of the biggest movie stars in the world. You work for the agency that represents us. That agency makes millions of dollars, tens of millions of dollars, off of us. Their job, and your job, is to service us. Your past as some sort of college football superhero, while interesting and sort of cute, is meaningless to people who are as famous as we are. If we want you fired, it can be done with a phone call. If we want to set up a situation where you can never get another job in this business, it can be done with a phone call. If we want you run out of town, it can be done with a phone call. That's the reality of this situation, and it's that way because people all over the world will pay money to see us. If you want to test it, be my guest. But I would advise you to shut your mouth and let my husband love you.

Kevin stares at her. She stares back. Gordon walks back to the table, he's finished with his other clients, his other business, he's smiling, he speaks.

Everything good here?

Casey looks up, speaks.

We're having a great time.

Gordon sits, speaks to Casey.

I just heard we're getting an offer for you tomorrow.

Really, what?

Eight million for a drama about an adulterous housewife in Connecticut.

Have you read the script?

No, but it's by a really hot writer. I'll messenger it over tomorrow.

I'll read it right away.

Casey and Gordon keep talking. Kevin looks at Amberton. Amberton smiles, puts his foot back on Kevin's thigh, moves it higher.

In 1924, Hollywood film studios produce 960 feature-length films, and for the years between 1920 and 1927, they make somewhere between 700 and 900 films a year. In 1927, Warner Brothers produces and releases *The Jazz Singer*, starring Al Jolson, which is the first film in history with synchronized dialogue, sound effects, and music.

Dylan and Maddie get a room in a cheap motel on Lincoln Boulevard in Venice. Lincoln is known by locals as Stinkin' Lincoln. It is lined with cheap motels, thrift shops, fast-food restaurants, discount stores, used-car lots. Along certain areas of it, homes that are a block or two away sell for millions of dollars. In other areas, homes that are a block or two away are used as crackhouses and filled with squatters. Regardless of the neighborhood, Lincoln stays the same. It stinks.

The motel is more or less the same as the last one: two stories, small run-down rooms, tenants who are unemployed and troubled. Dylan and Maddie don't plan on staying long, because of the money, they don't have to stay long. They spend their days looking for a house or an apartment. Somewhere to live that won't make them feel dirty. Maddie wants a house with a white picket fence by the beach. Dylan wants to make Maddie happy. They search real estate listings in the paper, go to an Internet café and look for them online. There are very few houses with white picket fences by the beach. Those that exist are expensive, three or four thousand dollars a month. They have twenty thousand dollars. They know they need to make it last. In other parts of the country it might be considered a sizable sum. Not here.

They move their search inland. The farther from the ocean, the less expensive the rents. They look in Palms, Mar Vista, West Los Angeles, Culver City. They buy an old yellow moped for two hundred dollars. It's not a car, or a truck, or a Harley, and it only goes twenty-five miles per hour, but it runs, and they can both ride on it, and they laugh about it, and they have fun with it. They take turns driving, and they both wear helmets that look like World War II military helmets. They call the moped "the agent" because it functions as their real estate agent, shuttling them from one appointment to another, and after being overtaken by a bicycle while riding along San Vincente, a busy east/west boulevard with a center divide lined with cypress trees, Dylan paints some bright red flames on the side of it. When they go out for the first time after the flames are done, they notice people laughing at them when they see them. They smile and wave. They're young and free and have some money in their pockets and they know that this is what they left home for, that this may be their California dream. After five days they find an apartment. It's a large one-bedroom with a faux stainless refrigerator and a faux marble bathroom and blue faux-finish blend-and-glaze on the walls and faux berber carpets on the faux pine floors. It's in a condo development on a street lined with condo developments near the Westside Pavilion (a large shopping mall with two department stores and a food court) in West LA. It has a gym in the basement and a pool in the courtyard. Because there are so many condos like it in the area, the rent is reasonable. Maddie loves the apartment. Dylan initially thinks it might be too fancy, if he gets another job as a mechanic he doesn't want to get grease and oil on everything. Maddie tells him she'll do the cleaning, that she did it at the motel, but the place was so dirty it was hard to notice. They agree to try and get it. They don't have any real credit history, so the property manager requires an extra deposit. They pay for the first month and the last month and the deposit in cash, and they sign the lease. When they walk out of the property manager's office with the keys, Maddie starts crying.

They sleep there for the first time that night. They sleep on the floor in each other's arms. The next day they go to a discount furniture store and buy a couch and a table and a floor lamp and a bed and a nightstand and a table lamp. They go to a discount superstore and buy a set of pots and a set of cutlery and a set of plates and dishes and glasses. They go to a discount hardware store and buy a mop and a broom and some lightbulbs and some cleaning supplies. They go back to their apartment and spend the rest of the day and night on each other and inside of each other, in the bedroom, living room, kitchen, on the bathroom floor, in the shower, on each other, inside of each other.

Next day Dylan starts looking for a job Maddie stays home

and organizes their new belongings puts them away and waits
for the furniture to be delivered. Dylan walks into every garage
he sees, every shop where he might be qualified to do
something, every gas station. He walks into the parking lot of
a large public golf course, looks for the office. When he finds
it, the door is slightly open, he knocks. A male voice speaks.
Who is it?
Name's Dylan.
Do I know you?
No, sir.
What do you want?
A job, sir. Any kind of job.
Dylan hears a chair slide across the floor, the door opens. A
bald man with a mustache and giant stomach sits in a battered
wooden chair that looks like it might collapse beneath his
weight. He looks at Dylan for a moment, speaks.
You're white.
Yes, sir.
I never get white kids coming in here looking for jobs.
I'm not a kid, sir.
How old are you?
Nineteen.
The man laughs.
You're a fucking baby.
Whatever you say, sir.
What kind of job you looking for?
Anything, sir.
You been to college?
No, sir.
First thing, if we're going to go any further, you gotta stop
fucking calling me sir.
Okay.
My name is Dan.
Okay, Dan.
Most people call me Fat Dan. A few others call me Asshole
Dan.

I'll just call you Dan.

Whatever, I don't really give a shit, just not sir.

Understood.

You got any skills?

I can fix things.

What kind of things?

Just about anything, but I'm best with engines.

Lawn mower engines?

Sure.

You ever caddied?

No.

You know what it is?

Carrying golf bags for rich dudes.

Rich dudes belong to private clubs. This is a public course. We get dudes who wish they were rich.

Guess they need their bags carried too.

Yeah, and they can be dicks just like the rich dudes.

I can carry bags.

You mind blacks?

No.

You mind Mex?

Nope.

All the other caddies are blacks and Mex.

Fine with me.

They'll probably give you shit for being a white boy.

That's fine too.

You get ten bucks an hour plus tips. Don't tell anyone out there what I'm paying you. I don't pay the Mex anything but tips because they're all illegal, and I pay the blacks minimum wage plus tips.

Thank you.

Go out there and ask for Shaka. He's the big black who runs the caddie shack. Tell him I said you're hired.

Okay.

The only other white who works here is the club pro. He thinks he's fucking Tiger Woods or some shit. If he was really any good he'd be on tour or be working at a real club. They call me Asshole Dan, but he's more of an asshole than I am. What's his name?

Tom. Call him Tommy Boy, though, he hates it.

Dylan laughs. Dan motions towards the course.

It's busy, so get out there. You might be able to squeeze in a round today.

Okay.

And if you got any problems, come back and tell me, and I'll whip those fuckers in line.

I'll be fine.

And I'll need you to come back at the end of the day and fill out some paperwork for me.

Okay.

Get out there.

Thanks again, Dan.

Don't sweat it.

Dan closes the door, Dylan hears the chair slide back across the floor. Dylan smiles, can't believe how easily he just got a job, thinks being a caddie might be cool. He saw a movie about being a caddie on cable a few years ago, and the caddies sat around, got drunk, made fun of the golfers, and occasionally got to sleep with the wives and daughters of the golfers. While he would not indulge in the last of the activities, the rest of it would be great, and he'd definitely enjoy hearing stories about caddies who slept with the wives and daughters of the golfers. In the film, one of the caddies became a great golfer and won a huge bet, big enough so that he and his girlfriend had enough to set themselves up. He wonders how hard it could be: swing the club, hit the ball, ball goes in the hole. Maybe he'll give it a try, maybe that's the future.

He turns and walks through the parking lot towards a set of three small buildings clustered around a giant putting green. One of the buildings is a snack bar, another the pro shop, the third is surrounded by golf carts and young men drinking sodas and smoking. He assumes the one with carts and the

smokers is the caddie shack he heads towards it. When he
arrives he asks one of the young men for Shaka, he motions to
an open door at the back of the building. Dylan walks over to
it looks inside a tall thick man in his fifties sits at a desk
covered with time slips and scorecards. He's wearing a golf
outfit, tan slacks a striped shirt and a hat. He has dark skin
and short hair, before Dylan knocks, he looks over his
shoulder, speaks.

Help you?

I'm Dylan. Dan sent me over. He told me I was hired as a
caddie.

He did, did he?

Yes.

Shaka spins around on his chair.

Step in here.

Dylan steps into the office the walls are covered with calendars
and pictures cut from golf magazines. Shaka looks him up and
down, smiles.

A motherfucking white boy.

Dylan smiles. Doesn't speak. Shaka laughs to himself, speaks
again.

A skinny-ass motherfucking white boy.

Yes, sir.

Don't call me sir. You can call Asshole Dan sir if you want to
call someone sir, but not me.

Okay.

You know how long he's been wanting to get a white-boy
caddie in here?

No.

A long fucking time, man, a long-ass fucking time.

Dylan laughs.

Don't get me wrong, I'm fine with having a white boy working
here, but before we get you started, I gotta know one thing
from you, and you gotta know one thing from me.

Okay.

How much he paying you?

I'm not sure I should tell you.

Shaka laughs.

You wanna fucking work here, you're gonna tell me. He can send you over, but I can say no.

What if you think it's too much?

He laughs again.

Ain't nobody at this course getting paid too much. I just want to see how much of a discriminating cracker Asshole Dan really is.

He said ten bucks an hour plus tips.

Shaka whistles.

Goddamn, Asshole Dan is a supercracker.

Dylan laughs.

I'm gonna get him a motherfucking T-shirt with a big SC on it.

Dylan laughs again.

Now that I know that, you ready to know what you gotta know?

Sure.

You know what Shaka is?

Your name?

Yeah, but you know where it comes from?

No.

Shaka Zulu was a king in Africa in the 1800s. He was a great king who united the Zulu Nation and trained an army that was so fearsome that his enemies would desert their land rather than fight 'em. I was named after Shaka Zulu, the king. Now obviously I'm not the king of no great nation, and I ain't got no army, but I am still Shaka, and this here, this Caddie HQ, this is my kingdom. Whatever I say goes. There ain't no debating involved. If you got a problem with another caddie, you bring it to me and I make a decision. There ain't no democracy, and there ain't no revolution. The one time there tried to be a revolution, I took the revolutionator and picked him up by the back of his pants and literally tossed him in the street. That's how it goes here. That's the way it is. You understand me?

Dylan nods, speaks.

You are Shaka, you are king.

Shaka smiles.

Well said, white boy. I am Shaka. I am king.

And I am Dylan. From Ohio.

Shaka laughs.

Welcome to my kingdom, Dylan.

What time should I be here tomorrow?

Tomorrow? You're starting right now.

Okay.

You ever caddie before?

Nope.

Then come on in and have a seat. I'll train your skinny ass
right now.

Dylan walks in sits down on a fold-up chair to the side of
Shaka's desk. Shaka reaches into a drawer and pulls out a
pamphlet called the Caddie Manual.

Being a caddie ain't brain surgery. Read this if you want. Don't
really matter. But if Asshole Dan asks, tell him you read it.

Dylan takes the pamphlet, puts it in his pocket.

Okay.

The job is simple. You carry the bag, you kiss the player's ass.
You hand 'em clubs, and if they ask, agree with whatever club
they say, and you kiss their ass. You wipe off the club if it's
dirty, you kiss the player's ass. If they ask how far they are
from the pin, you take a guess, and you kiss their ass. You
hold the pin while they're putting, you kiss their ass, you
replace the divots they make, you kiss their ass. Most of the
players here aren't very good, so you make them think they are
by kissing their ass. The ones that are good, you make 'em feel
like Jack fucking Nicklaus by kissing their ass. When they
cheat, and all of 'em cheat, let 'em and agree with them, and
kiss their ass, and when they're pricks, and plenty of them are,
and you wanna hit 'em in the head with a fucking club, you
kiss their ass. Like I said, it isn't brain surgery.

That was an extraordinary explanation, Shaka.

You kissing my ass?

Yeah.

Shaka laughs.

You're gonna be just fucking fine.

Thanks.

Go out there and introduce yourself to whoever's around. They probably won't like you, but if you don't act like some white supremacist motherfucker, they'll get over it. And don't ever tell 'em how much you're getting paid.

Okay.

I'll see you tomorrow at 6:00 AM.

Thanks.

Shaka nods, Dylan stands and leaves. He walks out there are a few men, some his age and a couple in their thirties and early forties, lounging around. He introduces himself to each of them, some of them don't acknowledge him at all, a couple say hello, a couple say what's up. When he's finished he sits down, leans against the wall of the shack. He watches the men, the Mexicans stay together, speak and argue in Spanish, the African Americans stay together, play cards, speak in low voices. No one speaks to him, pays any attention to him. After half an hour or so, he stands and leaves. It's a twenty-minute walk down Pico Boulevard back to the apartment. In one direction, in the distance, he sees the walled, guarded, heavily fortified grounds of Fox Studios. In the other direction, the street is lined with mini-malls, fast-food restaurants and gas stations. Dreams one way, reality the other. He lives in reality. The walk is easy, simple, the sun is out the sky is blue it's 75 degrees there is a slight breeze another day in Los Angeles. Dylan walks along the street enjoys the weather stops at a grocery store buys some chocolate cupcakes with vanilla ice Maddie likes cupcakes has since she was a little girl. When he reaches the complex there are people sitting by the pool takes the elevator to their floor it's clean he walks down the hall he can't believe how nice it is he opens the door to their apartment it smells like hamburger. Maddie is standing in the

kitchen, she's wearing an apron. There are pots, pans, boxes
and utensils everywhere. She smiles, speaks.
Hi.
Hi.
How'd it go?
I got a job.
Awesome. Doing what?
I'm a caddie.
Golf?
Yeah.
Do you know anything about golf?
Nope.
She laughs.
How'd you get it?
Because I'm a white boy.
She laughs again.
What's that supposed to mean?
They hired me because I'm white.
I thought that was illegal or something.
I guess not.
I made you a special dinner.
What?
Hamburger, macaroni, and Frosted Flakes casserole.
Holy shit.
Our first home-cooked meal since we've been here.
Fucking A, let's eat.
Maddie pulls a casserole dish out of the oven it's macaroni and
cheese mixed with hamburger meat covered with grated cheese
and cereal flakes. She scoops humongous spoonfuls of it onto
plates the cheese comes off in long hot strings. They sit down
at the table she has a bottle of regular cola for Dylan and a
bottle of diet cola for herself. She turns out the lights (though
it is still light outside) and lights two candles that sit in the
middle of the table. She speaks.
I love our place.
Me too.

And I love our new life here.
Me too.
And I love you.
Me too.
She raises her glass.
We did it.
He smiles, raises his glass.
We did it.
They toast and kiss their kissing becomes more they don't eat right away they don't stay at the table. When they come back, they're hungry Maddie has two helpings Dylan has four. When they finish Maddie clears the dishes away and puts the casserole in the fridge Dylan takes a shower she joins him they laugh about the four settings on the showerhead love the water that never runs out, never stops. They fall into bed into each other again stay up even though Dylan has work early. They don't read. They don't miss watching television.

Dylan gets up the next morning walks to work the streets are empty, the sky is gray blue glowing. It's quiet and still. Neon shop-window signs send glimmering shadows red, blue and yellow across the concrete. Cars line the curb silent and unmoving, stoplights blink they don't matter now. There are no birds, bugs, no animals. Lonely palms set in squares of dirt surrounded by blocks of cement are the only living things in sight. There is a low, elusive, almost inaudible hum in the air, it's coming off wires, the signs, lights that line the streets. In the distance Dylan sees the rings of mountains that surround the city, can see the lights of houses that dot the hills. Beyond them, more sky, the gray blue glowing. As he approaches the course he sees activity, the grounds crew is finishing up the caddies are getting ready. Asshole Dan is standing in the middle of the parking lot talking on a cell phone and smoking a cigarette, Shaka is in his office he's sitting at his desk reading a newspaper. Dylan goes to Shaka's office, knocks on the door. Shaka turns around, speaks.

Good morning.

You too.

What do you need?

I'm not sure what to do?

You're the new guy. You're at the end of the line.

How do I know what the line is?

It goes by seniority. We don't write it down or anything, everyone just knows. If there are any disputes, I come out and settle them.

Cool. Thanks.

Have a good day.

Dylan turns away, walks to the back of the shack, sits down on a small patch of grass at the edge of the parking lot, where a number of the other caddies are sitting. He says hello to a couple, nods to a couple others, and though they are all looking at him, none of them acknowledge him. At 5:45 AM the first golfers arrive. The first tee time is at 6:00. Every eight minutes, at least according to the schedule, another group of four golfers tees off. Many of them don't use caddies. They ride golf carts, use hand carts, or carry their own bags. Those that do use caddies often have caddies they have used before and specifically request them. Dylan sits and waits. Early morning becomes morning becomes late morning he sits and waits. Late morning becomes noon. Noon becomes early afternoon. The first few caddies to go out come back, and because of their seniority, he gets bumped back to the end of the line. He waits. He tries to talk to the other waiting caddies, but no one is interested. The day passes. The only times he gets off his ass are when he gets up for food or goes to the bathroom. The last tee time, which is only for nine holes of the eighteen-hole course, is at 6:00. At 6:10, he gets up and punches out and walks home. It's rush hour the streets are packed (though the sidewalks are empty). Drivers blare their horns, yell at each other, give each other the finger, he sees one throw a cup of cola at another. When he gets back to the apartment, Maddie has tuna noodle casserole waiting for him. They eat and take a shower and get into bed. There is no reading, no TV. They go to sleep three hours later.

311

When he shows up for work the next day, it's the same routine. When he gets home Maddie has hamburgers and Tater Tots waiting for him they eat dinner get into bed same. The next day at work it's the same dinner is fish sticks and a Jell-O dessert bed same. The next day the other caddies are openly hostile to Dylan they tell him to go home, get another job, that white boys aren't welcome, that he shouldn't come back. When he gets home Maddie has boiled hot dogs and frozen fries ready for dinner they eat get into bed same. The next day the Mexicans start calling him Guerro and the blacks start calling him Cracker, the Mexicans flick cigarette butts at him and two of the young black men sit on either side of him with golf clubs. When he goes home Maddie has corn dogs and onion rings and Fudgsicles for dessert when they get into bed Dylan goes straight to sleep. The next day, he gets pushed around and threatened the cigarette butts start hitting him and the clubs are swung near him he sits and waits and hopes that at some point he'll get to carry a bag and walk the course, he still hasn't done either, his turn never comes he gets hit by cigarette butts and he's scared of the clubs. At the end of the day, Shaka calls him into his office. Dylan sits in the chair next to his desk, Shaka speaks.

How's it going?

Fine.

Including the day you were hired, you've been here a week.

Best week of my life.

Shaka laughs.

You learn anything?

That nobody likes a white boy.

You never knew that before?

I grew up in a town where it was all white boys.

And did everybody like each other?

No.

See.

See what?

Nobody likes white boys, and white boys don't even like each other.

Dylan laughs.

It's true, man. All over the world, people hate American white boys. Probably the most hated species on the planet.

I'm just trying to get by, trying to make my life a little better.

Yeah, I know the feeling. What we're all trying to do. And to be honest, you seem alright.

Thanks.

This past week has been a test. It's something we do to every new caddie here. Do it to see if they really want the job, and if they're willing to put up with some bullshit to get it.

Seriously?

Yeah. It's a grind, man. Every day at 6:00 AM, sometimes twelve or fourteen hours a day. And the golfers can be assholes. You think the treatment you got waiting for a turn was bad, wait till you see how some of those motherfuckers behave.

So what would have happened if I had tried to defend myself.

Against what?

People calling me names, flicking butts at me, following me around with clubs.

I'd have told you not to come back.

That's fucked up.

I can understand you thinking that way, but it's what we do here. It weeds out unreliable, unstable potential employees. Big difference between you and the rest of the guys who've done it is you were getting paid ten an hour. Most of them sat here for a week getting shit and went home empty-handed. I also wanted to see if you could handle being around a bunch of men of color. Whether you know it or not, there are differences between all of us, and some of 'em have to do with the color of our skin. A troublesome white boy would cause a lot of problems for me.

It's still fucked up.

Life is fucked up, deal with it.

So what now?

Now you get to carry bags and make tips and deal with assholes.

Dylan laughs.

You make it sound great.

That's what it is. And as far as jobs, I think it's a pretty good one. You ain't gonna get rich doing it, but you can make a living. It's sunny every day, so every day there's golfers, and every day they need someone to carry their bags. Be cool, just like you've been, and you'll settle in just fine.

Okay.

No hard feelings?

Nope.

See you tomorrow.

See you tomorrow.

Dylan stands walks out of the office. There are two groups of caddies, one Mexican group and one black group, who are getting ready to leave for the day. The groups intermingle, but not much, members from both walk over, say hello, introduce themselves, shake his hand, offer him cigarettes, offer him beer. He smiles, says thanks, has a beer and though he doesn't smoke, he takes a drag from a cigarette. He immediately starts hacking and the other caddies start laughing and whatever happened over the course of the previous seven days disappears with the laughs. He stays for another beer, another, he knows he's going to be late for dinner he stays for another. White Boy has some new friends, the first nonwhite friends he's ever had, he stays for another.

The walk home takes twice as long it's hotter the colors brighter sounds louder, he sits down and takes a rest in front of a mattress store, he takes a second rest in front of a tropical fish store. He opens the door, Maddie is sitting at the table there's a bucket of fried chicken mashed potatoes and baked beans. There is an apple pie on the counter, ice cream in the freezer. She stands speaks.

Are you okay?

He smiles, speaks.

Yeah.

You're drunk.

Sorta.

She laughs.

Who'd you get drunk with?

My coworkers.

I thought they hated you.

It was some kind of test kind of thing. They do it to everybody
I guess they told me or something.

She laughs again.

I guess they told you or something?

Yeah, like that.

I got your favorite.

I can smell it.

He inhales, smiles.

Fried chicken and taters and beans. It smells really good, super
good.

And pie.

I love pie.

I know.

Can we eat it now if that's okay with you?

Congratulations on your first week.

Thanks, sweetie.

He smiles, it's a half-drunk idiot smile. Maddie doesn't mind,
sort of thinks it's funny. She takes him by the hand leads him
to the table helps him sit down. She tucks a napkin into his
shirt so it functions as a bib she makes him a big plate of
chicken, taters and beans when she sets it in front of him he
looks up at her and smiles and speaks.

I love you so much.

She smiles.

I love you too.

They kiss and he tries to make it more than a kiss she playfully
pushes him away back into his chair tucks his bib back in he
smiles again, speaks again.

I love you so much.

She laughs.

Just eat your damn meal.

He starts eating, within a few bites there's food on his hands and on his face and on the bib and on his shirt and on his pants, there's food spread across the table. Maddie watches him more than she eats, he's like a child who doesn't know any better taking bites while there's still food in his mouth, wiping the food away with his hands and streaking it across his face, holding the fork incorrectly picking up scraps with his fingers, he looks unbelievably happy and content. When he finishes his first helping he gets another, he finishes that gets another. While he's working on the third she puts the pie in the oven warms it up. By the time he's finished with his fourth, and the bucket of chicken is empty, she has a piece of warm apple pie with vanilla ice cream ready for him. He eats most of it with his hands when he's done he licks the plate clean he has another does the same thing. When he's finished he leans back in his chair, rubs his stomach, speaks.

That was the best meal of my life.

Maddie smiles.

Good.

I think I'm gonna vomit.

He stands and runs to the bathroom. Maddie watches him go he disappears from view she hears the bathroom door fly open hears him lift the toilet seat hears him, hears him. While he's busy, she clears the table, puts the leftover food, some potatoes and some beans, about half the pie and half the ice cream, in the refrigerator. She closes the door hears him breathing walks to the bathroom. He is sitting on the floor next to the toilet. There are new streaks on his chin and shirt. She speaks.

You okay?

I think I need to go to bed.

Yeah, that would be a good idea.

He starts to stand she helps him. She washes his face helps brush his teeth takes off his shirt walks him to their bedroom puts him to bed. He wants to fool around she laughs and says no he says he wants a kiss she offers him a cheek he kisses it gently then tries to lick it. She laughs and pushes him away he falls asleep almost immediately. She walks back to the kitchen gets a couple magazines she bought at the grocery store more stories about the rich and famous their clothes and cars, their houses and vacations, their love lives. They're still a few miles away. They feel a little closer.

Dylan wakes up the next day goes to work carries his first bag gets a thirty-dollar tip. Maddie has dinner, frozen hot wings and blue cheese dressing, waiting for him. They get into bed stay up late. He goes to work the next day carries two bags gets a twenty-dollar tip and another thirty dinner is waiting tuna noodle casserole again they get into bed. Their life falls into an easy routine. Dylan works, Maddie cleans does laundry cooks, when she's not doing those things, she watches talk shows or sits by the pool and reads magazines. Dylan becomes a real caddie, learns how to advise golfers on distance to the pin, which club to use, how the conditions might affect their play. He learns to kiss ass like a champion he learns how to work for bigger tips he watches men make fools of themselves yelling, screaming, throwing clubs, breaking clubs, getting into fights with each other, betting stupid sums on a game they're supposed to enjoy. Maddie expands her kitchen repertoire she learns to cook things that don't come frozen or in boxes she makes her own fried chicken, ham and cheese omelettes, rib eyes in the broiler, catfish in a pan, she makes her own apple pie. They go to bed early stay up late.

Though they try to save their money, and live as cheaply as they can, they slowly move through the windfall from the bikers. It dwindles to fifteen grand, to twelve, to ten, to eight. Dylan's income, on a good month, barely covers the rent, they talk about moving somewhere less expensive neither wants to do it they love their apartment, their home, their dream, the reason they ran away. Maddie starts looking for a job something part-time during the day she applies to grocery stores, coffee shops, clothing stores, restaurants. She has a couple of interviews doesn't get any phone calls. She applies to a beauty shop, to a pet store, there's an opening for a cashier at the drive-through of their favorite burger joint, interview, no call. The money is dwindling they're still fine but won't be soon. Dwindling.

Dylan comes home after a long day two bags one was a doctor who blamed Dylan for most of his bad shots and only tipped him ten bucks the other a pen salesman who got drunk and yelled. Maddie has dinner on the table chicken parmigiana and pasta Dylan can smell a pie maybe cherry. There are candles on the table. The napkins are folded. They sit down before they start eating he speaks.

What's the occasion?

Why do you think there's an occasion?

Is that a cherry pie?

Blueberry.

He smiles.

Candles, napkins, a new dish and a new pie. It's an occasion.

She smiles.

What do you think it is, Sherlock Holmes.

You get a job?

No.

Had a good interview?

No.

Is it an anniversary of some kind that I've forgotten?

No.

A birthday?

She laughs.

No.

What is it?

I've decided something.

What?

You know how I read all the gossip magazines while I'm at the pool?

Yeah.

And they're all about these famous people, actresses and singers and models and stuff.

Yeah.

Well, I think that I want to be an actress.
An actress?
Yeah, I want to be a movie star.
Really?
What do you think?
If that's what you want, give it a shot.
She smiles.
It's not what I really want.
No?
I got what I really want.
What's that?
I'm pregnant.

On October 17, 1929, construction begins on the Los Angeles Stock Exchange. The founders of the exchange intend to make it a rival to, and ultimately replace, the New York Stock Exchange. On October 24, 1929, a day commonly known as Black Thursday, the stock market in the New York Stock Exchange sees the largest one-day drop in its history. On October 29, 1929, a day commonly known as Black Tuesday, the equities markets in the United States collapse. Three weeks later the Los Angeles Stock Exchange goes bankrupt.

The city center. The bustling downtown. The urban core, the central business district, the immense skyline. The beating, beating heart of a major metropolitan area. The view from a distant highway it is usually signaled by a wall of steel, glass and concrete towers a beacon to those drawn to the hope of something more with dreams of greater lives those with outsized ambitions too large for small towns. As is the case with most of the world's megacities, the City of Los Angeles was founded by a major water source. As it grew, the water disappeared, was drawn beyond its capacity and vanished. Smaller cities in, around and on the outskirts of Los Angeles were initially folded into the city to provide water, and later because they needed the water that Los Angeles brought in via the aqueducts. Instead of starting in a central point and naturally, over a long period of time, growing outward, multiple central points, the Port of Los Angeles, Santa Monica, Burbank, Century City, Hollywood, East Los Angeles, Pasadena, San Gabriel and South Central Los Angeles, were placed into competition with each other. Some thrived, while others did not. Central government and cultural institutions based in downtown Los Angeles remained, but business and industry moved to safer, less crowded areas where commutes for workers were shorter and more convenient. Residents of downtown moved out of the area because the jobs were elsewhere. Highways originally built to provide access to downtown became hubs that led travelers to other destinations. The real estate market collapsed. Buildings and land were purchased at cut-rate prices by developers who put up skyscrapers that sat empty. The vacuum created by fleeing residents was filled by massive populations of homeless addicts and alcoholics. Established immigrant communities became small islands that more closely resembled the immigrant countries of origin than they did southern California. During daylight hours many of the streets of downtown were empty, after dark they were filled by the addicts and alcoholics. And so it remained for forty years. There are changes afoot now, slow changes, but so it remains. Here is an examination of downtown, where it has been, where it is now, and where it is going.

***

No one knows who came up with the expression *Skid Row*, or where it originated. Might have been Seattle, maybe San Francisco, some say Vancouver and others say New York. And while all of those cities have Skid Row neighborhoods, and continue to argue over and claim title to the term, downtown Los Angeles has, without debate, the largest, most settled and most dangerous Skid Row neighborhood in the country. Though it has always been there, in some way, in the early '70s the City of Los Angeles formally adapted what they called a policy of *containment*. Containment meant taking the worst of the city's transient and homeless population, and containing them in a single area. It was believed, and some still believe, that by containing this population, it would be easier to police them, easier to monitor them, easier to help them. For thirty years, many of the worst, most addicted and most violent men and women in the city were taken to Skid Row, sometimes by police, sometimes by court officials, sometimes by employees of shelters and missions in other parts of the city, and left there. Once there, without money shelter or help, they had to fend for themselves, which usually meant fighting, stealing, using, and often killing.

Spread across fifty square blocks on the eastern side of downtown, Skid Row has somewhere between ten and fifteen thousand residents. Thirty percent of the residents are HIV positive, 40 percent are mentally ill, 50 percent have STDs of some kind. Sixty-five percent have felony records and 70 percent of them have drug and/or alcohol addictions. Seventy-five percent are African American, 80 percent are men, 98 percent are unemployed. There are missions and transient hotels on the edges of Skid Row, they ring it, surround it. They feed and house almost 6,000 people a day. The rest live on streets covered with grime, which, according to tests conducted by the health department, is twenty-five times more toxic than raw sewage. They live in cardbox encampments, tin shacks, they live in tents and sleeping bags, they live on the ground. They yell at each other, scream at each other, sleep with each other, do drugs and drink with each other, fuck each other, kill each other. They live amongst garbage, rats, excrement. There is no running water and no electricity. The only available jobs, and they are always available, involve selling drugs and selling flesh. The local police department is the busiest in California. The local fire department is the busiest in the country. Ninety percent of the people who live on Skid Row, die on Skid Row. City Hall is less than a mile away.

***

In 1885, a Japanese sailor named Hamonosuke Shigeta opened the first Japanese restaurant in the United States in downtown Los Angeles. Over the course of the next ten years three more opened, as did a Japanese gambling parlor and two Japanese brothels, one of which featured geisha girls imported from Japan. In 1905, after four more restaurants, two markets, another gambling house and three more brothels opened, the area between First Street and San Pedro Street in downtown started being called Little Tokyo. In 1906, 4,000 Japanese immigrants moved south from San Francisco after the earthquake decimated the city. In 1907, just before the Federal Gentleman's Agreement banned foreign immigration, 15,000 Japanese moved to Los Angeles. Almost all of them lived in or around Little Tokyo.

For the next thirty years, Little Tokyo grew expanded thrived, it became the largest of three established Japanese communities in the United States, with almost 40,000 residents. Anti-Japanese sentiment, which was strong all over the country, but particularly strong in California, forced Little Tokyo to become self-sustaining and highly insular. And although Japanese immigrants were prevented by federal law from owning property, temples were built, markets expanded, Japanese schools established. At the time of the attacks on Pearl Harbor, it encompassed sixty square blocks of downtown Los Angeles. Just after Pearl Harbor, Executive Order 9066 was issued, which granted the federal government the power to incarcerate anyone of Japanese descent living within sixty miles of the west coast of the United States. One hundred and forty thousand Japanese Americans living in California, Oregon and Washington were rounded up and interned at what were called Assembly Centers, but were essentially jails. Little Tokyo vanished. The buildings, owned by white Americans, but inhabited by the Japanese for two or three generations, were empty, and the streets, once filled with Japanese immigrants, were silent.

When the war ended, and the citizens interned at camps were freed, around 3,000 resettled in Little Tokyo. Laws that had prevented ownership of land were lifted, but buildings remained empty, and what was once a vibrant, dynamic community more or less died.

In 1970, with the hope that a revitalized area could become a point of access for Japanese investment and businesses, the City of Los Angeles officially designated a seven-block area as Little Tokyo, and started the Little Tokyo Redevelopment Project. The Japanese did not come back in large numbers, but a number of Japanese companies opened their first American offices in the area, one opened a hotel, and the community that still existed was consolidated. Today, Little Tokyo remains contained within the area designated by the city. There are markets, restaurants, temples, the hotel is still there, there are shops that sell Japanese clothing, furniture, art. Unlike times past, there is no worry that it's going to disappear.

***

Need jeans? Got 'em. Actually got 600 different brands. Need a skirt? Tens of thousands of choices. Need shoes? Hundreds of thousands of choices. Need a bag, a belt, a hat, jewelry, a watch, a scarf, luggage? Got it all, got it fucking all. Need sunglasses, perfume, cosmetics? Need sportswear, formal wear, maternity clothes? Need a bathing suit, a tie, some underwear? Maybe you need a lacy pair of panties, or a corset, or some thigh-highs? It's all there. That and so much more, so very much more. It's called the Downtown Fashion District, and it's ninety blocks of fashion. It can be overwhelming to think about, and it's absolutely mind-blowing!!! Ninety fucking blocks of fashion. Yes, it's true. All in one place. Ninety blocks.

The Downtown Fashion District began its life as the Depravity District. In the 1800s its streets were lined with bars, brothels, opium dens and gambling houses, local hotels rented rooms by the day, the hour or in fifteen-minute increments, gunfights were common. One of the main thoroughfares of the district, called Santee Alley, which is now noted for its counterfeit bags, belts and DVDs, was named after a prostitute known to have sex with as many as fifty men a day. Many other less industrious women would take twenty to thirty men a day. Opium, and later cocaine, were openly sold and openly used, alcohol flowed like water (and because it's LA, at times there was actually probably more alcohol than water), pickpockets and thieves flooded the streets. It is believed, though not confirmed, that the first *Donkey Show* was staged in the district, and it is believed, though not confirmed, that the first bondage and S&M dungeon in America opened in the district. If it could be done, regardless of how disgusting, perverted, ridiculous or Satanic, it was done somewhere in the district.

Because of the number of working women, and sometimes men or young boys dressed as women, that were in the area, clothing shops started opening. Most of them specialized in what might be called evening wear, others sold fake police uniforms, nun's habits and priest's vestments, animal costumes, clown costumes. At the turn of the century, when opium and cocaine were outlawed (yeah, they both used to be legal, woohoo, woohoo), and alcohol and prostitution became the area's primary businesses, the number of clothing stores grew. In 1920, when Prohibition was instituted, almost all of the bars and brothels were closed, or moved to less obvious and more discreet locations. The clothing stores remained. Others moved in, and clothing factories were set up in empty buildings. Many of the women who had worked in other capacities in the buildings became seamstresses, cutters, or did laundry. Labor was cheap and available, property was cheap and available. Within a few years, the district acquired a new name.

Today there are more than 2,000 clothing wholesalers and 4,000 retail shops in the area. It is considered the West Coast center of clothing manufacturing and wholesale fashion. It has its own brands, its own celebrity designers, its own fashion shows. And while the industry is shrinking in the rest of the country, because of the continued availability of cheap property and cheap, often illegal, labor, it is growing in LA. You need a pair of socks? They've got 'em. Rubber boots? Absolutely. Are you a plus-size shopper? No problem, and the same goes for petites, and every size in between. And if you need a costume, something you don't want your friends, neighbors or coworkers to know about, well, you can still get that as well.

***

The Downtown Toy District. Twelve square blocks of fun, fun, fun. Bright colors, loud noises, flashing lights. No description should be needed for this part of the city. Imagine a humongous toy store. Imagine cars occasionally driving down the aisles. Every now and then there might be a police chase or a mugging. That's the Los Angeles Toy District.

***

The only area of downtown Los Angeles that truly resembles the core of a major metropolitan area is Bunker Hill. It is, geographically, the highest point in downtown Los Angeles. It is also covered with skyscrapers, which can be seen, on a clear day, fifty miles away. It is crowded, the sidewalks are packed, there are cars parked on every curb. It's noisy and dirty, but not foul. There are people awake twenty-four hours a day.

It was initially developed, in the late 1800s, as a high-end residential neighborhood. At the time, the primary business and banking districts of Los Angeles sat just below, and the Los Angeles River ran along its base. Victorian mansions were built and sold to wealthy businessmen and their families, and a private train ran up and down the hill. As immigrants began coming into the city, and the rail system made traveling into it easier and more convenient, many of the residents left Bunker Hill for Pasadena, Beverly Hills and Bel-Air. By the end of World War I, most of the mansions had been converted to apartment buildings. When business began leaving the area, the apartment buildings became flophouses. During the 1930s, when the ring of highways, freeways and interstates that surround downtown Los Angeles was being built, the neighborhood was cut off and isolated. Many of the flophouses became uninhabitable. They were often used as sets for horror or crime films. More often, real scenes of horror and crime occurred in them.

In 1955, the City of Los Angeles authorized the Bunker Hill Redevelopment Project. Every building on Bunker Hill was destroyed and the ground was leveled. Developers were given tax incentives to put up new buildings, and height restrictions, which had kept most buildings within the city limits at heights less than 150 feet, were lifted. For almost a decade, nothing happened. Bunker Hill just sat there, a humongous mound of brown dirt, with a couple of small trees, surrounded by highways, freeways and interstates. Then for no specific reason, other than someone decided to be the first and a number of others followed, buildings started to be built, tall buildings, really tall buildings, culminating, in 1990, with the US Bank Tower, which is the eighth-tallest building in the United States, and the tallest building west of the Mississippi. It didn't matter that no one wanted to rent space in the buildings (vacancy rates were and are among the highest in the country), and it didn't matter that they sat square in the middle of an active earthquake zone. Up they went, one after another, after another. In the early 1990s, after the completion of a number of major cultural projects, including the Walt Disney Concert Hall and the Museum of Contemporary Art, a number of the buildings were converted from commercial to residential, and a number of new residential buildings broke ground. Coupled with the rise of the nearby Arts District, and the redevelopment of the Staples Center (home of the Los Angeles Lakers), Bunker Hill has become a desirable address again. Apartments sell for millions of dollars, and there are new markets, boutiques and spas opening in the area. People are moving from areas outside of downtown Los Angeles, back into it. And now, after waiting fifty years for gentrification, and doing everything they could to encourage it, the city is thinking about instituting measures that, via the Fair Housing Act, will slow it down, by requiring a percentage of all new housing developments to be sold at below-market prices to low-income residents of the city. If their new plan works, maybe it will slow it down enough so they'll have to level it again.

***

Ohhhh the glory of the railroads, oh the glory. They came and they moved shit around and they ruled the rails and they ruled the nation and they faded away. It was glorious while it lasted, supremely glorious. But like all things and all people, their time ended. And when it did, in the late 1940s, once truck and air travel became cheap and easy, there were rail buildings, once used to store the many products that the railroads moved, that were left empty. Empty buildings all over America. Including Los Angeles.

Many of these empty buildings (once filled with railway glory) were grouped together between Alameda Street and the Los Angeles River (now a giant concrete channel used primarily for drag racing and the dumping of bodies). In the '70s, artists, who often need large spaces in order to work, and who are almost always broke, found the buildings, which had large open loft spaces, and they moved into them. In the early '80s, the city designated the area, and the buildings in it, an Artist-in-Residence Zone, which meant that in order to live there, you had to apply, and be certified, as a working artist of some kind. The AIR Zone became a self-sustaining community. It had a convenience store, a coffee shop, a couple of bars. The streets surrounding it were dangerous, filled with vacant lots and empty buildings used by drug dealers, drug addicts and prostitutes. It was an island of sophistication in an urban wasteland. Artists repulsed by the commercialism of the entertainment industry felt comfortable there, artists with no money were comfortable there, artists who wanted to live amongst other artists felt comfortable there.

But all good things come to an end, often a sad angry miserable end. The cause for such an end can usually be whittled down to one of three things: money, sickness, love lost. Artists have always had an uncomfortable relationship with money. They need it, but are often repulsed by those who have it. For as long as there has been money, and art, and people willing to spend money on art, communities initially set up by artists have been overrun with people with money who want a taste of the artist's lifestyle, despite the fact that the reality of the lifestyle is far harder, lonelier, and more boring than can be imagined. As the rest of Downtown became safer, and more gentrified, and more acceptable, the AIR Zone became a more attractive place for people to live. As zoning laws in the rest of Downtown were altered or lifted to promote development, so they were in the AIR. In 2001, the Southern California Institute of Architecture (SCI-arc), an avant-garde architecture school that has produced some of the prominent architects in the country, relocated to the Artists District, renovating and moving into an old warehouse. This was followed by a number of residential developments, also in old warehouse buildings. The artists, most of whom rented, found themselves unable to afford their rents, and started moving out. Galleries, which initially existed in the area for the same reasons as the artists, consolidated themselves and opened

Gallery Row, which services collectors more than it does the artists themselves. The original market closed, the bars closed, they were replaced by more upscale versions or chains. Everything the artists sought to escape arrived at their doorsteps. And so they moved on, or are moving on.

***

The Jewelry District. Encompassing nine square blocks, it is smaller than the Toy and Fashion districts. But boy, oh boy, does it sparkle. It is the largest, by volume of sales, jewelry district in the United States, with over three billion dollars in transactions every year. There are over 3,000 wholesale jewelry dealers in the district, their primary business is diamonds, and there are enough armed guards in the area to form an army. Like the Toy District, it resembles a giant jewelry store with cars in the aisles, and the occasional vehicular police chase. Unlike the Toy District, there are no muggings. Muggers are assumed to also be jewelry thieves and they are shot on sight.

***

You can smell the food from a mile away: crispy Peking duck and General Tso's chicken, BBQ spareribs, fried rice with everything. Chow mein noodles and roast pig and chopped beef congee, fried beef chow fun and moo goo gai pan and Szechuan-style bean curd. It drifts for miles from the steaming kitchens, it overwhelms everything in its path. For some, the smell is awful and sickening. For others it is a siren's song, drawing them in to a neighborhood full of culinary delights. Indeed, it is Chinatown.

Chinatown is the oldest ethnic neighborhood in the city (though it can be argued that the entire city is and always has been a series of ethnic neighborhoods connected by a government and a police force). Sometime in the late 1840s or early 1850s Chinese nationals working on the construction of railroad lines and roads started living in Los Angeles. By 1865, Chinatown had been established as a safe haven for the workers and their families. By 1870 it had several hundred residents. In 1871, a gang war between rival Chinese gangs resulted in a white male being caught in the crossfire of a gunfight and killed, his female companion injured. A mob of 500 white men came to Chinatown seeking revenge and murdered 20 Chinese men. They also destroyed the main street of Chinatown, called Calle de Los Negros (it was originally an African-American neighborhood) and burned the shops on it, and hung the bodies of three Chinese on posts in other parts of the city as warnings to other ethnic groups about the consequences of hurting white men and women. Chinatown was rebuilt and began flourishing, with several thousand new residents, and it established dominant positions in the city's laundry and gambling industries. In 1882, the Chinese Exclusion Act, which prevented the ownership of property by foreign or American-born Chinese, was passed and the land on which Chinatown sat became the property of the city government, which sold it to developers and private landholders.

Despite this, Chinatown continued to grow. Between 1885 and 1910 it boomed, fueled by both legal and illegal economies. The population rose to almost 10,000, and it became fully self-sustaining. In 1913 the leases many of the Chinese business owners held on their stores and residences expired and, when the landlords refused to renew them, they left en masse. The landowners sold the property to railroad companies (oh the glory!), who leveled most of the buildings. Those that weren't sold to the railroads were sold to the city, who also leveled them (they love bulldozers at City Hall), and put up Union Station. Most of the Chinese dispersed into surrounding communities such as Monterey Park and San Gabriel, or left the city entirely. Those that stayed lived in a community that was both literally and figuratively destroyed. Chinatown was reduced to a couple blocks of restaurants, a single Buddhist temple, and a store that sold kites and toy dragons.

In the 1930s, a local Chinese man named Peter SooHoo started organizing a bid and lobbying for a new Chinatown. He developed plans for a community that would be built in the style of classic Chinese architecture with modern American touches, it would include schools, markets, temples, restaurants, a huge gate welcoming visitors, all built around a central mall. In 1937, a site a few blocks from Old Chinatown was chosen and land was purchased through a fund raised entirely within the Chinese community. In 1938, a partially built New Chinatown opened. Within a year, tens of thousands of visitors were walking through the gate.

New Chinatown aged and, when it wasn't new anymore, became Chinatown. It has remained in the same place, with more or less the same borders, for the past seventy years. A restaurant may close, but another is always opening, a shop may move, but it doesn't move far. The gates are still there, the mall is still there, there is a memorial to the Chinese men murdered in 1871. It is a stable community, several generations old, and this time it isn't going anywhere. And you can smell the food, the glorious food, mu shu pork, spring rolls, fish maw thick soup, snow pea tips with garlic from a mile away.

***

Civic Center is an area on the northern side of downtown Los Angeles where most of the governmental and administrative offices of the City of Los Angeles are located. City Hall is there, the Parker Center (LAPD headquarters) is there, city county state and federal court buildings are there, the Hall of Records is there, the Kenneth Hahn Hall of Administration, where the nonexecutive offices of the city bureaucracy are located, is there. No one, absolutely no one, really has any idea what goes on in this neighborhood. It is always busy, and crowded, and there are people who appear to be working, but no one knows what, if anything, they actually do all day. It has been a mystery for over two hundred years.

In 1932, the City of Los Angeles hosts the Summer Olympic Games of the tenth Olympiad. Los Angeles is the only city in the world to bid for the games, and because of the collapse of the world economy and the Great Depression, many countries did not attend.

Dylan and Maddie lie in bed. Dylan is staring at the ceiling, Maddie has her head on his chest. Dylan speaks.

I'm still waiting for you to tell me you're joking.

Not going to happen.

What are we gonna do?

Be better parents than our parents were.

We're young. Might be too young.

My mom had me when she was sixteen.

My point exactly.

I'll never be like her.

You'll be a great mom. For sure. I'm just worried.

About what?

Money, the future, how we're going to do this, money, the future.

She laughs.

We'll be fine.

There's not going to be another windfall.

I'll get a job.

Who'll take care of the baby?

We'll figure it out.

I'd rather you be home.

Then I'll stay home.

But we won't be able to afford it.

So what do you want to do?

I don't know.

I'm not getting rid of it.

I didn't say you should.

We can handle it, Dylan.

I just want you to think about it.

I don't want to think about it.

Please.

In 1933, a fire in Santa Monica Canyon destroys forty homes and kills sixty people, and an earthquake in San Gabriel destroys thirty homes and kills fifteen people. In 1934, a fire in Mandeville Canyon destroys twenty homes and kills ten firefighters, and an earthquake in Long Beach destroys seventy buildings and kills one hundred and fifty people. In 1935, a flood in San Fernando kills twenty people. In 1936, a mudslide in Eagle Rock kills forty people.

Amberton and Kevin on Amberton's bed it's the middle of the afternoon. Amberton speaks.

Do you love me?

Are you kidding?

Do you love me?

You're not kidding.

I want to know if you love me.

I don't.

Do you love being with me?

No.

Do you love making love with me?

No.

Do you at least love my body?

No.

My face?

No.

My hair?

No.

Why are you here?

You gave me no choice.

There's always a choice.

I support my girlfriend, my mother, my aunt and uncle, six cousins.

I'll support them for you.

I don't want you anywhere near them.

You're hot when you're angry.

Are you done?

No.

When will you be done?

I'm just getting started.

In 1935, the Los Angeles Police Department, via mayoral directive, sends a battalion of police officers to the Nevada border to stop hitchhikers, primarily Mexican nationals, from entering the state of California. They return after four days and report that they were unable to stem the flow of immigration.

It's late and it's dark Old Man Joe and Ugly Tom are crouched behind a car. Old Man Joe speaks.

There they are.

What are they doing?

What's it look like they're doing?

Getting high.

That's what they're doing.

What are we gonna do?

Watch them.

Then what?

Watch them more. Learn their habits.

Then what?

Go to war.

They're bad dudes. You sure about this?

They're bad dudes, but I'm Old Man fucking Joe.

My point exactly.

They're in deep, deep trouble.

You're fucking crazy.

Look at the girl.

She don't look too good.

Two black eyes.

You can see from here?

I saw her earlier today.

She know what you're doing?

No.

She might not want you to do this.

She don't know any better.

Even if she did, she might not want you to do it.

I ain't doing it for her.

Who you doing it for?

Me.

In 1937, land is purchased by the City of Los Angeles and construction begins on what will become Los Angeles International Airport, otherwise known as LAX.

Esperanza and Doug on the cot in the basement. Esperanza speaks.
No.
My mom isn't coming home for three or four hours.
It doesn't have anything to do with that.
Then what?
I'm scared.
Why?
I just am.
Why?
You won't like me anymore.
That's crazy.
You don't know.
I know everything I need to know.
You don't.
I do.
It's happened before. Men thought they liked me. And they
learned more.
I don't think about it, I know about it.
You don't know.
What could be so bad?
I don't want to talk about it.
I'm not perfect either, you know. I'm sort of fat and going bald
and I'm terrible at cocktail parties and I act like a twelve-year-
old most of the time.
I like that about you.
And I like your imperfections. All of them.
You don't know all of them yet.
I actually probably think what you might think are
imperfections, are perfect.
Like what?
You have a mole on your neck. I think it's cool. Your hands are
rough from working, but working women are sexy. And your
thighs. You probably think they're too big. I think they're the
most beautiful things I've ever seen. They were the first things
I noticed after your eyes and your shy little smile. They're
awesome. They totally rock.

In 1939, despite being the fourth most populous city in the United States, Los Angeles ranks eleventh among major American metropolitan areas in auto sales, and fourteenth in gasoline consumption.

Not all facts are fun. Some are, some are really fucking fun, but not all of them. **Volume 1 of Facts Not So Fun Los Angeles.**

Los Angeles is the most polluted city in the United States of America.

There are approximately 6,000 crimes against the elderly every year, 1,000 hate crimes every year, and 60,000 domestic disputes every year, 10,000 of which involve weapons.

Sewage and medical waste often wash up on the beaches in Venice, Santa Monica, the Pacific Palisades and Malibu.

Los Angeles County landfills receive approximately 20,000 tons of garbage every day.

There are more storage facilities in Los Angeles than in any other county in America. They offer over 40 million square feet of storage space in more than 1,500 facilities.

There are more than 12,000 people who describe their job as *bill collector* in the City of Los Angeles.

There are more than 60,000 people working in pornography.

There are approximately 7,500 people working in agriculture (probably surprised there are any).

Twenty-one thousand students a year drop out of high schools in Los Angeles County.

There are 240 strip joints in Los Angeles County (could also be filed under fun).

The 24th through the 39th Congressional Districts of the

United States Congress are located in Los Angeles County. Seven hundred thousand people a year in Los Angeles receive food stamps.

More than 1.6 million people live below the poverty line.

Approximately 2.7 million people live without health insurance.

Seventy-five thousand people a year die in Los Angeles (really not fun). Coronary heart disease is the leading cause of death, cancer is second.

Twenty-nine cents of every tax dollar collected is spent on law enforcement. Fifteen cents of every tax dollar collected is spent on sewage collection and treatment. Eight cents of every tax dollar collected is spent on road maintenance. One-point-five cents of every tax dollar collected is spent on education.

One hundred and twenty-five thousand animals are impounded every year. Ninety-five thousand are euthanized.

Ninety thousand people are injured in automobile accidents.

Four hundred and twenty-five thousand people a year contract sexually transmitted diseases.

There are 750,000 alcoholics and drug addicts.

There are approximately 1,500 suicides every year.

The average daily population of all jail facilities in Los Angeles County is 33,000 people.

There are approximately 150,000 felony arrests every year.

Fifty-three percent of all high school students in Los Angeles have smoked marijuana (MISTAKE, MISTAKE, MISTAKE. SHOULD BE FILED UNDER FUN OR REALLY FUN OR REALLY REALLY REALLY FUN).

In 1937, Clifford Clinton, a leading critic of LA mayor Frank Shaw, has his house bombed. Harry Raymond, an investigator looking into Clinton's claims of corruption in the mayor's office, has his car bombed. Both men survive, but are gravely wounded. LAPD officers later confess to the bombings, which were carried out at the behest of the mayor.

He kisses her lips her neck runs his hands through her hair down her back along her side his hands go up her shirt, up her shirt. He fumbles she laughs he's embarrassed up her shirt he fumbles she takes off his shirt kisses his neck his chest she takes his hands in her hands kisses them she kisses his hands.

They're in his room. His mother is away. She went to visit a friend in Palm Springs who lives on a golf course and belongs to a tennis club and has a cook and a maid and four gardeners all Mexican. She left an hour after breakfast, Doug left just after breakfast, he went to a comic book store and spent two hours in the new releases section and came back when he was sure his mother was gone. Esperanza didn't know he was coming back. She was dusting a dresser getting ready to wipe down the windowsills when he walked in with a bouquet of roses, perfect blooming deep red roses, dew on the petals, perfect red. He offered them to her and she smiled and walked to him and put her arms around him and started kissing him and he dropped the flowers and they kissed, kissed and he pulled away and he smiled and he spoke.

We have two days.

She smiled, spoke.

You sure?

Yeah.

What do you want to do?

What do you want to do?

Don't answer my question with a question.

We could pretend this is our house. Pretend we live here.

You do.

I mean, like, live here as a couple.

I can't stay the night.

We'll pretend during the day.

If your mother comes home and the house isn't clean she'll go crazy on me.

I'll hire someone to do the house.

They won't know the routine.

Are you scared?

Yes.
I'm not going to hurt you.
I know.
You don't have to be scared.
I am.
Want to know something?
What?
I'm scared too. I'm really scared.
You don't have to be.
I have a hot chick that actually likes me. I don't want to fuck it up.
I'm not a hot chick.
Sure are.
No.
Yeah you are, and now I gotta figure out how not to fuck it up.
You won't.
She kissed him again it was a long deep kiss, his hands started running along her back, the sides of her body, they were both awkward, inexperienced, insecure. He pulled away, smiled, spoke.
You wanna go somewhere else?
The basement.
We've been making out in the basement for a month.
It's safe.
Let's go to my room.
Why?
It's my room. We'll have a bed.
If I say stop you have to promise me you will.
I promise.
She kissed him again pulled away picked up the flowers. He took her hand and led her to his room. She went to his bathroom filled the sink with lukewarm water and set the stems of the roses in the water, leaving the blossoms out. She walked back into his room and he was fiddling with the CD player. He turned and smiled and spoke.

What kind of music do you like?

I like traditional Mexican music and I like light hits.

I love light hits. And I love metal too, really loud, really fast and really heavy.

She smiled.

Light hits, please.

I'll play the metal later.

She laughed and he put on James Taylor and she walked towards him and they fell to his bed, they fell. They kissed, their teeth banging, they fumbled with each other's shirts. They rolled awkwardly across the mass of sheets and blankets, her on top, him on top, her again. She took off his glasses dropped them on the floor. He unbuttoned her uniform she stopped him when he tried to take it off. He reached for the hooks of her bra she stopped him. He grunted as he kissed her he was nervous, anxious. She wanted him but couldn't let herself go she vacillated between dominating him and timidity. He kissed her neck she pushed him away any mark and she'd lose her job. She kissed his neck when she started to move away he pulled her back and said more, more. They kept kissing, the edges of their lips chafed he ran his hands up her legs she stopped him. Kissing. He tried again she stopped him again. Kissing. Again she stops him. For an hour they have been kissing. He tries again, she stops him, pulls away, speaks.

No.

Why?

Because.

I love them.

No.

Please.

I won't go higher.

No.

He moves to the edge of the bed, puts his feet on the floor.

Come here.

Why?

He reaches out to her.

Come here.

She takes his hand, moves to the edge of the bed, sits next to him. He gets off the bed and on his knees in front of her. Her gray dress is at her knees her black socks are on he looks in her eyes deep brown and he puts his hands on her ankles. He smiles, speaks.

They're nice.

She smiles. He moves his hands up to her calves, speaks.

Very nice.

She smiles again he moves his hands to her knees, his fingers around the front, his thumbs in the hollow behind, he speaks.

Beautiful knees.

She keeps smiling. He rubs the back of her knees and tickles her and speaks.

Really beautiful.

She laughs, he's still looking into her eyes.

These are the type of knees that could ruin a man.

Oh yeah?

Definitely.

He moves his hands up.

And these.

Up.

These are the most beautiful lower thighs in the world.

He smiles eyes locked.

Unbelievable.

She's scared, his hands on them, around them.

Unbelievable.

They stare at each other she puts her hands on top of his hands. They're just below her skirt-line at the point where her flesh flares out, where her thighs begin to take shape. Their hands together their eyes locked. She's scared. He speaks.

You can trust me.

I know.

I'm not going to hurt you.

I know.

I love them.

I know.

Into each other's eyes. Their hands start to move slowly up. He smiles, she breathes deeply, a nervous timid smile. Skirt starts to rise, flesh reveals itself. Into each other's eyes hands slowly moving, going where no one has gone before, where she has never allowed anyone to go. In this house in Pasadena. A rich white man from a prominent family on his knees in front of a lower-middle-class Mexican-American girl who pretends she's an immigrant so she can take the bus to clean his mother's house. Her hands on his hands. They are staring into each other's eyes. He's smiling and she breathes deeply, deeply, breathes. The skirt is rising the flesh showing itself the skin is lighter than the skin on her hands, arms, feet, lighter than the skin on her face. He spreads his fingers across presses them into, he smiles and she breathes deeply, he speaks.

You're beautiful.

She smiles.

They're beautiful.

Hands moving up, into flesh.

You're the greatest most wonderful best-looking woman I've ever met.

They stare into each other's eyes.

I love you.

She smiles.

I love you and them and I love kissing you and I love holding you and I love our time together, it's been the best time of my life.

Hands moving up skirt rising exposed she smiles and breathes deeply fully exposed she smiles and she speaks.

I love you too.

Their hands together.

I love you too.

Where no one, no one, their hands, her flesh, no one, staring, smiling. As he starts to stand, the door behind him opens. Their eyes move apart he turns around his mother is standing there she's holding her purse in one hand the other open. She speaks.

You dirty Mexican whore.

He speaks.

What are you doing here, Mom?

She steps forward.

What are *you* doing here, Doug? That really is the question isn't it? WHAT ARE YOU DOING HERE WITH THIS DIRTY LITTLE MEXICAN WHORE.

Doug turns around, faces his mother. Esperanza quickly stands brushes her skirt down. Mrs. Campbell steps forward.

You cunt.

Be quiet, Mom.

She steps forward.

You dirty little cunt how dare you touch my son.

She steps forward and before Doug can respond Mrs. Campbell slaps Esperanza. Doug tries to intervene and she slaps her again drawing her nails across Esperanza's face. Esperanza recoils, Mrs. Campbell starts screaming.

WHORE. WHORE. WHORE.

She hits her again, Doug tries to pull her away, she slips away from him.

DIRTY WHORE.

Hits her again.

MEXICAN PIECE OF SHIT WHORE.

Esperanza breaks and starts sobbing. Doug grabs his mother's shoulders.

HOW DARE YOU, YOU LITTLE BITCH.

Doug pulls his mother away, she kicks at Esperanza, who is sobbing curled into a ball, screams at her.

YOU DIRTY LITTLE MEXICAN SLUT.

Esperanza sees her chance and runs for the door.

I'LL HAVE YOU SENT BACK TO YOUR MUDHUT YOU WHORE.

Runs.

WHORE, WHORE, WHORE.

Runs.
Through the house sobbing to the basement sobbing out of the
house sobbing she can hear Mrs. Campbell screaming.
Runs.

In 1941, Los Angeles County's second large-scale water conveyance project, the 245-mile-long Colorado River Aqueduct, is finished. It carries water from Lake Havasu in Arizona across the Mojave Desert and into southern California, and its delivery capacity is over a billion gallons a day. It replaces the Los Angeles Aqueduct as the primary supplier of water to the City and the County of Los Angeles.

Old Man Joe on the beach with Ugly Tom, Al from Denver,
Four Toes Tito and two other men, Smoothie, who sleeps
under the awning of a smoothie shack, and Lemonade, who, as
an unshakeable optimist, often uses the phrase—Making
lemonade out of lemons. Though fires are illegal on the beach,
they're sitting around a small fire made with garbage and
lumber scrounged from dumpsters, a couple are cooking cans
of food over it. Drinking and sleeping are also illegal on the
beach, they're all drinking and a couple will later sleep in the
sand, most likely by the fire, with alcohol in hand.
They're having a War Council. Joe has approached each of
them asked them to help him help Beatrice. None of them
initially wanted to help him, except Lemonade, who said hell
yes, Joe, I'm ready to help you be successful as you want to be.
In order to coax them into it, Joe has offered them all free
food and booze, which he has no idea how he will afford.
Right now he's more worried about his plan, which he is trying
to explain to them. He speaks.
We're gonna get weapons, bottles or pieces of lumber, and
we'll steal some garbage can tops to use as shields . . .
Al from Denver interrupts him.
Shields?
Joe speaks.
Yeah.
Al speaks.
This ain't the Middle Ages.
Joe speaks.
You don't have to carry one, okay?
Al speaks.
Okay.
Lemonade speaks.
I love shields, Joe. I'll carry one.
Four Toes speaks.
Me too.
Smoothie.
Me three.

354

Ugly Tom.

I'll carry one if I get more liquor.

Joe takes a deep breath.

Everyone but Al gets shields. Once we're armed. We'll get some dirt and camouflage ourselves.

Al.

Fuck that.

Lemonade.

Love camo.

Joe.

Nobody has to do it if they don't want to, but the mission will be more effective with it.

Ugly Tom.

Roger.

Smoothie.

Roger that.

Joe.

Then we'll divide into three teams of two. One team will walk along the edge of the beach, one down the boardwalk, one down the alley.

Lemonade.

I would like to be on your team, Joe.

Joe.

Sounds good.

Smoothie.

What about me, Lemonade?

Lemonade.

There are other choices, all great choices.

Ugly Tom.

I'll go with you, Smoothie.

Four Toes.

Looks like it's you and me, Al.

Al.

Fuck.

So we have the teams. We sneak down there. When someone sees those bastards, you whistle.

Al.

Don't know how.

Tito.

I do.

Smoothie.

I'm scared of whistles.

Lemonade.

How can you be scared of whistles?

Smoothie.

Childhood thing. Don't want to talk about it.

Old Man Joe.

Make some noise, a whistle, maybe a hoot, something.
Whenever someone makes the noise, the other teams move
towards them. When we meet up, we'll surround the three and
take the girl.

Al from Denver.

And do what with her?

Joe.

Get her help.

Four Toes.

What if they fight back?

Joe.

That's why we have weapons and shields.

Ugly Tom.

I don't want to actually use them.

Joe.

We might have to.

Lemonade.

I predict an easy victory. Sort of like the Shock and Awe thing
the president did.

Smoothie.

I'll take the back. In case any of them run through you guys
and try to get away.

Joe.

They're bullies. Bullies always crumble when they're
confronted. We just have to stay united, work as a team.

Ugly Tom.
Teamwork.
Al.
Teamwork.
Four Toes.
Teamwork.
Smoothie.
Teamwork.
Lemonade.
Love teamwork.
Joe.
Let's go.
They stand Joe kicks out the fire. They walk to Speedway start
looking for weapons they walk up and down the walk-streets
looking for garbage can tops. They meet at Joe's bathroom
they are all armed. They walk down to the strip of grass that
runs along the boardwalk find a palm tree with a small circle
of dirt at its base. They rub the dirt on their necks, faces,
arms, they're *camouflaged*! Joe looks everyone over, makes
sure everyone is ready, speaks.
Time for battle.
Lemonade cheers.
WOOHOO!!!
Joe.
Let's split up and start making our way down the boardwalk.
They usually hang out in the grass by the parking lot at the
end of Rose, but I've also seen them in the alley behind the
Sunshine Café and I've seen them sleeping on the sand.
Smoothie.
I'm nervous.
Joe.
We all are.
Ugly Tom.
What if they're not together?
Joe.
They're always together.

Al from Denver.
What if the girl's not with them?
Joe.
She's always with them.
Four Toes Tito.
If they have liquor can we take it?
Joe.
If there's a bottle of Chablis, I get it.
They all laugh. Joe speaks.
Let's go.
They split up Lemonade and Old Man Joe, Ugly Tom and
Smoothie, Al from Denver and Four Toes Tito and they start
making their way north making their way towards Joe's
enemies. Lemonade and Joe take the boardwalk, Ugly Tom and
Smoothie take the beach, and Al and Tito take Speedway
Alley. As they start off, Lemonade takes Joe's arm, looks him
in the eye, speaks.
I think this is a beautiful thing, Joe. It's like something John
Wayne would do. And it's going to be a huge success. I know it
is.
Joe speaks.
Thanks, Lemon.
Gimme a hug, man. I want a big hug.
Joe laughs, they hug, Lemonade pats Joe on the back, they
separate, they start slowly making their way down the
boardwalk. Except for other homeless men and women, almost
all of whom are sleeping, and the few who aren't sleeping are
drunk, the boardwalk is deserted. The beach side is lined with
streetlights casting wide arcs of yellow fluorescent light, most
of the stores, restaurants and stands along the alley side are
dark, though a few of the nicer ones have exterior lights on.
The boardwalk itself is a long gray silent and unmoving
beautifully perfectly quiet like some wide gray line stretching
into endless black. Joe and Lemonade stay along the alley side,
darting, as quickly as they can, from dark area to dark area.
Joe leads and Lemonade stays right behind him. They don't

speak, both are carrying broken pieces of two-by-fours with sharp ugly ends and battered metal garbage can lids. Both are carefully looking for the girl and the three they see a rat disappear into a building, a possum eating from a dumpster, quiet birds asleep in a nest on the branch of a palm, a stray dog wandering, a cat asleep on the stoop of a treatment center, a couple on the beach not homeless not asleep. As they near the stretch of grass where Joe believes the girl and the three will be they move slower, more carefully, they stay in the darkness longer. They head into a small parking lot squeezed between two T-shirt shops sit down next to a rusted camper van. They look towards the grass, where they see moving shadows, voices. Lemonade speaks.

Is that them?

Joe speaks.

Can't tell.

I think it's them.

Might be.

They're gonna run away when they see us.

I doubt it.

I'd run away if I saw us.

They're mean guys.

We'll save the girl and get her some help. It'll be like a fairy tale set on the beach in California. We'll get her some nice shoes.

Joe chuckles softly, watches the shadows. They move into the light it's definitely them three men in hoodies and the girl all of them have bottles in one hand cigarettes in the other. Joe looks at Lemonade, speaks.

You were right.

Lemonade smiles, speaks.

It's gonna be a beautiful night.

Can you whistle?

Like a train.

Joe chuckles again.

Give me one. But not too loud.

It'll be perfect.

Lemonade puts his fingers in his mouth blows through them and a high, abrasive shriek pierces the night. The girl and the three immediately stop and turn towards Joe and Lemonade who crouch behind the car and wait for their friends. Almost immediately, they hear Ugly Tom and Smoothie yelling and screaming. They turn towards the noise, as do the girl and the three, and they see Tom and Smoothie running up the sand, their clubs in one hand, shields in the other. Joe looks at Lemonade, speaks.

So much for the element of surprise.

Lemonade speaks.

We won't need it.

Guess we'll see.

It's gonna be perfect.

They stand and start walking towards the girl and the three who now see four men with clubs and shields walking towards them. The largest of them looks towards Joe, speaks.

Who the fuck are you guys?

Joe speaks.

We're here for Beatrice.

The man laughs.

Beatrice?

Joe.

Yeah.

She told you her name was Beatrice?

It's not?

Man laughs again.

No, it's not.

The other two laugh, the girl smiles. Ugly Tom, Smoothie, Lemonade and Joe stand in a semicircle around them, all have their clubs raised. Joe looks at the girl.

What's your name?

She shakes her head.

It doesn't matter.

Yes it does. What's your name?

Go away, Old Man.

Joe stares at her.

You need help. We want to help you.

Go away.

Joe stares at her, she looks at the ground while the three snicker. The largest of them steps forward.

Now that you know you're not wanted, it's time for you dumbfucks to go.

Joe stares at her, she won't look at him. Lemonade steps forward.

Young man, this lady is clearly distressed. I'm willing to bet she's acting under duress. We came here to take her from you and find a better place for her. We will not leave until that goal has been met.

Get the fuck out of here. She's my bitch to do what I want with, and that ain't fucking changing.

Joe stares at her, she looks at the ground.

We're taking her.

Fuck you.

Lemonade starts to step forward, the largest pulls a pistol from his belt. Lemonade stops. Largest speaks.

You ain't doing shit, motherfucker.

Lemonade steps back. Ugly Tom and Smoothie immediately turn and start running.

Unless I decide you're doing it.

The other two laugh, Lemonade and Joe start stepping backwards, Joe speaks.

We're leaving.

He raises the gun.

We're leaving.

Cocks it.

Let's go, Lemon.

Joe and Lemonade drop their clubs and shields and turn and start running away. As Joe runs he turns back he sees the gun raised it's being aimed. He yells at Lemonade they head for the lot where they were hiding he turns back gun raised, aimed, he hears the shot something like a crack, a pop, a small explosion. He sees the back of Lemonade's skull disappear. He sees him fall facedown. He stops he's out of breath, starts back, looks up, the largest is running towards him his gun raised. Joe turns and keeps running he has the body of an old man a very old man he keeps running into the lot through the lot around the edge of a building he stops, looks back. Lemonade is facedown on the edge of the boardwalk. A streetlight flickers above casting an arc of yellow across the lower half of his body. The back of his skull is gone a pool of blood is starting to slowly flow towards the sand, the sea. The largest of them stands over Lemonade with a gun. The other two and the girl walk towards him. Gun fires body jolts gun fires body jolts. Dead already so it doesn't fucking matter.

Gun fires body jolts.

Again.

Again.

Again.

During World War II, defense and aerospace companies set up large-scale manufacturing operations in Los Angeles County in order to produce planes, warships, weapons, and ammunition for use in the Pacific Theater in the war against Japan. By the end of the war, Los Angeles County is the single largest producer of defense and aerospace products in the world.

Amberton, Casey and the kids are in Malibu. Amberton is in one of his moods, a dark mood, a black mood, a profoundly fucking black mood. Their staff, nannies for the kids, a chef, two personal assistants, two housekeepers, are with them. When Amberton is in one of his moods, he tells his assistant, via a note, and the assistant tells the rest of the staff, who follow what are called *Amberton's Mood Rules*: try not to be in the same room with Amberton, if you are in a room with him leave as soon as possible, do not look at him, if you do happen to accidentally look at him absolutely do not look him in the eye, do not speak to him, if he speaks to you, look at the floor and respond as quickly and efficiently as possible, no matter what you hear or what you see, do not call the police, fire department or ambulance. The mood can last a day or last a month. There is often no rhyme or reason to its arrival, and there is often no rhyme or reason to its departure. It comes and it goes, stay the fuck out of its way.

This mood, however, this thermonuclear mix of sad, angry, confused emotions, was brought on by Kevin's refusal, once again, to see or speak to Amberton. At the end of their last meeting, which took place three weeks ago in the back of an armored SUV Amberton was test-driving, Kevin ended their affair, at least in his eyes, by telling a naked and quivering Amberton, who had just suggested introducing fuzzy animal costumes into their relationship and spending a weekend role-playing in the costumes, that he was done with Amberton and—in his own words—his crazy-ass bullshit. Amberton thought he was joking, and that he saw a flash of excitement in Kevin's eyes at the mention of the costumes. Kevin got out of the SUV as quickly as he could and, even though he was in a suit and tie, jogged away at a brisk pace.

There has been no contact since, despite between thirty and fifty phone calls a day, multiple office visits (Kevin shut and locked his door and waited Amberton out, once actually sleeping in the office and peeing in a soda bottle) and the delivery of flowers, chocolates, expensive suits and a sports car (all of which were returned) to Kevin's home. Initially Amberton thought Kevin was back to playing hard-to-get, but realized, after the overnight standoff at his office, that hard-to-get had become never-to-have-again. He spent a day at a spa getting a massage, facial, stone rub, pedicure, manicure and assorted shavings, trimmings and waxings, it didn't help. He spent a day with three high-paid teenage escorts, it didn't help. He spent part of a day shopping and bought several hundred thousand dollars' worth of clothing, jewelry and art it didn't help. The mood set in, the mood has stayed. After he climbed a tree in their yard and refused, for six hours, to come down, Casey suggested that they go to the beach, where there are no trees to climb.

Deprived of some of his more unconventional outlets for the manifestation of his mood, Amberton has settled into a routine involving exercise and food, hair coloring and smashing. When he wakes up, he goes to their home gym for two hours and works out with a personal trainer. When he's finished, he eats a mammoth breakfast, which he then forces himself to vomit by stuffing his fingers down his throat. After vomiting and brushing his teeth, he has his stylist come over and adjust his hair color, which he has changed, sometimes drastically by going full-head different color, and sometimes more subtly via highlights and streaks, every day for the past week. When his hair is done he walks around the house, causing the staff to panic and flee from whatever room he is entering, and he randomly picks something up, a vase, a television, a small table, a stereo, and he smashes it to bits, usually by throwing it onto the floor as hard as he can (one of the assistants immediately replaces the item after it has been smashed). After smashing, his trainer returns and he works out again, eats again, vomits again.

Today his routine is being broken up by a visit from his agent Gordon, an attorney from the agency, and another attorney who works for Amberton. They're coming for lunch, which the chef is preparing (sesame-encrusted ahi with uni sashimi and seaweed salad). After his morning workout breakfast and vomit, Amberton has the stylist dye his hair jet-black (serious, for the occasion, very serious), and he spends an hour choosing his shorts and a T-shirt (tight or loose, ribbed or not, crew or V-neck, sleeveless or short sleeves), and he settles on black pleated shorts and a tight, black, ribbed T-shirt with short sleeves. He is sitting by the pool when Gordon and the attorneys arrive, all of them are wearing black suits, cream-colored dress shirts and bright silk ties. He stands shakes each of their hands says hello, they sit, he speaks.

So what now?

Gordon.

How are Casey and the kids?

Who knows, I haven't seen them in a week or so.

Agency attorney, whose name is Daniel, speaks.

Aren't they here?

I'm in a mood. When I'm in a mood, they avoid me.

Amberton's attorney, whose name is David, speaks.

One of your *mood* moods?

Yes, one of those, David. A *mood* mood. A deep, depressing, profoundly fucked-up mood where I do stupid things and indulge myself simply because I am rich enough to do it. It's one of those again.

Gordon.

Can we help in any way?

Amberton.

By telling me why you're here, eating your meal quickly, and then leaving me to my self-destruction.

Gordon looks at the two attorneys, who both nod to him. He looks back at Amberton, speaks.

I had a disturbing meeting this morning.

Amberton.

With who?

Gordon.

Kevin.

Amberton.

366

Is he as torn up about this as I am?
Gordon.
In what sense?
Amberton.
When you leave someone you love, it hurts. I know I'm
hurting, so I imagine he is as well.
Gordon looks at the attorneys, who both look concerned.
Gordon speaks.
That's not exactly how he put it.
Amberton.
What did he say?
Gordon.
That you forced yourself on him and harassed him.
Amberton looks shocked, truly and genuinely shocked.
That's not what happened.
Daniel speaks.
Are you acknowledging a relationship with him?
David speaks.
This is all off the record, so technically he's not acknowledging
anything.
Daniel speaks.
Understood.
Amberton.
We fell in love. We pursued that love sexually and emotionally.
I don't think he's as comfortable or as open with his sexuality
as I am with mine, so he ended the relationship. It was a
beautiful thing, like the most perfect healthy colorful blooming
flower, while it lasted, it was like a flower from heaven. Now
it's like a bomb went off in my heart. I'll probably never be the
same.
Gordon.
I'm not trying to insult you, Amberton, but I think Kevin has a
different interpretation of what went on between you.
Amberton.
I don't believe that. I don't even think it's possible.
Gordon looks at Daniel and nods, Daniel opens a briefcase and

removes a tape recorder. He sets it on the table. Gordon speaks.

We got a call yesterday afternoon from an attorney representing Kevin, who left the office with all of his files. We met with them this morning. Among other things, many other things, Kevin had this recording of an event that took place while the two of you were together.

He nods at Daniel again, Daniel pushes play, Kevin and Amberton's voices, though slightly hollow and mixed amongst a small amount of static, can be clearly heard.

Amberton: I want it right now.
Kevin: No.
Amberton: You can't say no to me.
Kevin: This isn't right.
Amberton: What isn't right is you denying me what I want.
Kevin: Please.
Amberton. Right now. The way I like it.
Kevin: And if I don't?
Amberton: I make a few calls. You lose your job, your mother loses her house, and the future disappears.
Kevin: You wouldn't do that.
Amberton. I love you, Kevin.
Kevin: Please don't say that.
Amberton: I love you, Kevin. Please don't make me hurt you.

Daniel turns off the tape recorder. David shakes his head. Gordon stares at his untouched, but beautiful, sesame-encrusted ahi. Amberton speaks.

Amazing what one can do with technology these days.
Daniel.
Excuse me?
Amberton.
It's clearly fabricated.
Gordon.

I don't think so, Amberton.

Amberton.

That wasn't me.

David.

Let's not play games here, Amberton.

Amberton.

The only game being played here is the game of extortion.

Gordon.

Please don't do this to us again, Amberton. Please don't.

Amberton.

I'm not doing anything.

Gordon.

It's happened too many times before. We need you to give us authorization to deal with it.

Amberton.

Let me speak to him.

Daniel and David at the same time.

No.

Amberton.

Please, this is just a misunderstanding.

Daniel and David at the same time.

No.

Amberton.

Please.

Gordon.

He's asking for ten million dollars, Amberton. We think we can get him to eight. Needless to say, if any of the materials he has are made public, it will profoundly damage your career.

Amberton.

I don't care anymore. I'm ready to give it all up.

Daniel.

Once he comes, some of the others are bound to follow.

David.

They're all tied up because of the settlement agreements.

Daniel.

The ones you know about.

David.

Yes, the ones I know about.

Gordon.

Amberton, thoughts?

Amberton shakes his head, wipes a tear away. Gordon speaks.

Do you want me to get Casey so we can hear her thoughts on the matter?

Amberton.

No.

Gordon.

Are you giving us authorization to speak with him, to try to settle this?

Amberton.

I wanna see him.

Daniel and David at the same time.

No.

Amberton wipes away tears.

I want to see him.

In 1943, there is a large-scale riot in East Los Angeles when military personnel from local army, navy, and marine bases flood the area looking for Mexican men wearing what are called zoot suits. It is believed the riots began when a man in a zoot suit whistled at the sister of a marine while she walked down a street. Several hundred Mexican men are hospitalized, and three are killed. Two days after the riots are over, the Los Angeles City Council passes a motion banning zoot suits within the Los Angeles city limits.

Dylan and Maddie wait for rain. A week, two, three they wait for rain and it never comes. The weather is always the same: sunny, somewhere in the seventies or low eighties, a soft breeze, day after day the weather is the same, they wait for rain and it never comes. Dylan asks Shaka for a morning off, Shaka tells him to ask Asshole Dan, Dylan asks Asshole Dan who tells him to ask Shaka. Dylan asks Shaka again, Shaka asks him why Dylan tells him he needs to take Maddie to see a doctor Shaka says fine.

They take a cab Maddie won't ride on the moped anymore. They see the building, a nondescript two-story stucco office building, from a block away they see there are protesters at the curb. Maddie looks at Dylan she's terrified asks him to tell the cabbie to keep going he says no, we have to go, she says please, he says no, we have to go. They pull up to the curb. Protesters with signs surround the car the signs have pictures of dead bloody babies, pictures of doctors with targets around them, pictures of Christ the Almighty, they scream the words murder, killer, death, God, punishment. The cabbie turns around, speaks.

You sure you want to get out here?

The protesters surround the car, scream against the glass, hold their signs in front of Maddie's eyes. Dylan speaks.

Yes.

The protesters scream.

The fare is twelve-fifty.

Maddie takes Dylan's hand. He finds his cash with the other hands it to the cabbie, speaks.

Can you wait for us?

The signs dead babies targets Christ.

No.

A nondescript two-story stucco building Maddie speaks.

I don't want to go, Dylan.

He reaches for the door.

We have to.

Opens it. The screams are magnified, the yelling shockingly

loud, he steps out of the car holding Maddie's hand she closes
her eyes holds her other arm around her head like a shield the
protesters step away from them, but scream, yell, wave their
signs. Dylan rushes towards the door which is opened by a
young woman he's holding Maddie's hand pulling her along
with him rushes towards the door screams. They walk through
the door, it closes behind them the screaming and yelling is
muted. Maddie holds her arm above her head like a shield. Her
eyes are still closed. Young woman speaks.
How can I help you?
Dylan speaks.
We have an appointment with a counselor.
What time?
Ten.
The waiting room is down the hall.
She walks down the hall, Dylan starts to follow to pull Maddie
along with him. She resists, lowers her arm, speaks.
I don't want to do it.
We're not doing anything today.
I'm scared.
We're just going to talk to someone.
I want to go home.
We agreed we'd talk to someone. Then we'll go home and
make the decision.
Don't make me do this.
We're just talking.
The young woman has stopped she's waiting for them. The
protesters are screaming murder, killer, death, God,
punishment. Maddie is shaking. Dylan puts his arms around
her, speaks.
I love you.
Then don't make me.
We're going to be okay.
Please.
We're just going to talk.
He looks at the young woman and nods and starts guiding

Maddie down the hall. After a few steps he pulls away but keeps her hand the young woman seats them in a small room with chairs along the walls, tables in the corners, magazines on the tables and in racks above the tables. Maddie moves her chair over so that it's touching Dylan's leans against him clutches his arm if she could sit in his lap she would. There are posters on the walls advocating safe sex, responsible contraception, adoption, in them happy couples smile, laugh, hold each other's hands. None of them look like they've been called killers, murderers or sinners, none of them look like they're shaking with fear. Maddie stares at the floor, Dylan alternates between looking at her and looking at the posters. He tries to reassure her. Two minutes last fifteen hours. Their name is called they stand walk to a door they are greeted by a woman in her forties dressed simply and cleanly in a white shirt and beige skirt. They follow her through a door down a short hall into a small clean office more posters on the walls. She sits behind a clean desk they sit in chairs opposite. She speaks.

My name is Joan.

Dylan says hello Maddie tries to smile Joan speaks.

How can I help you?

Dylan tells her that Maddie is pregnant. Joan asks if they are sure she is pregnant Dylan tells her they've taken three tests all positive. Joan asks if they know what they want to do with the pregnancy, Dylan says no, that's why we're here, Maddie starts crying. The woman asks Maddie why she's crying she shakes her head she can't speak, Dylan tells the woman that Maddie doesn't want to be here, doesn't want to contemplate anything other than keeping the baby. The woman says she understands, that the decision is an incredibly difficult one, that they should consider all of their options, seriously seriously consider them, before they choose one way over another. Dylan nods. Maddie cries. The woman gives them some pamphlets. The pamphlets have information on medical procedures how they work and why they're safe, on adoption and how to give a child to someone else, on keeping the child, the financial realities, the realities of having children at a very young age, religious implications. The woman goes over the pamphlets with Dylan and Maddie Dylan reads along with her Maddie clutches at his arm and stares at the floor. When they're done the woman calls them a cab and walks them out the back door to a parking lot where the cab waits there are protesters at the edge of the lot fewer than there are in the front but enough to be heard, they yell, scream, wave their signs. As the cab moves slowly past the protesters Maddie ducks puts her head in Dylan's lap she cries for the entire ride home. Dylan tries to talk to her she can't talk just shakes her head. When they get back to their apartment she goes to their bedroom shuts the door he tries to go in and talk to her, comfort her, she asks him to leave her alone he says let me help she says leave me alone. He leaves the apartment buys her favorite dinner nachos and tacos from a Mexican fast-food restaurant he goes to a grocery store buys her favorite soda grape and new copies of six gossip magazines he goes home she's still in their room he tries to open the door it's locked. He knocks she says what he tells her about dinner and the soda and the magazines. She does not respond. He eats alone and sleeps on the couch.

The Los Angeles Air Pollution Control Board is established in 1946 in an effort to discover the cause of the brown cloud hanging over the city and decide how to combat and disperse it. In 1949, after intense lobbying from both the automobile and oil industries, and against the recommendations and position of the Los Angeles Air Pollution Control Board, the public rail system, which at one time was the largest in the world, and still serves a majority of the city's population, is decommissioned and torn out. It is replaced by a small fleet of buses.

They come to rock. They want to rock long and they want to rock hard, they want to rock all day and rock all motherfucking night. They come with long stringy hair, with Mohawks, bald, they come with clean arms, tattoos, track marks, they come in jeans, skate shorts, leather. They come because rock is in their blood and rock is in their bones, they come because they eat rock, sleep rock, shit rock, and most important, they dream of rock.

They call it Rock School, though its official name is the Academy of Popular Contemporary Music. It started in the back of a guitar store when a salesman, who also happened to rock fairly hard in a local metal band, offered to teach an accountant, who came in looking for a flying-V electric, how to play. The accountant told his friends and some of them wanted to learn the mystery of rock, they told their friends who also happened to be interested in learning how to rock so hard in the proper way. Though the salesman initially felt somewhat uncomfortable teaching nonrock citizens how to live and rock his lifestyle, or at least pretend to live it and rock it, his band wasn't doing very well and he needed the money, so he did. A year later, seeing the business his salesman was bringing due to his teachings, and seeing the opportunity to make more money by having more students to whom he could sell guitars, the owner of the shop made an offer to the salesman, and they opened, across the street from the shop, an official, or as official as something can be in the world of rock, school. It was an immediate success, and surprisingly, to both of its owners, many of the students were young, knew their rock, and just wanted to learn to play their instruments. They opened a lead guitar department, rhythm guitar department, a bass department, a drum department, and a keyboard department (sometimes keyboards rock, but usually not, so they kept it small). A band that got together at the school made a hit record, and talked about the school's influence, more students came. A second band hit, more students. They bought a building, a third band, more students, bought another, a fourth, more students. Over the next five years they bought two more buildings added academic classes, such as history of rock, theory of rock, songwriting, lyricism, the cultural impact of rock, and started different subspecialty departments such as pop-metal, classic metal, death metal, classic rock, the blues, R&B, and punk (though no self-respecting punk can actually play his instrument and all of them fucking hate school). Students started coming, and still come from all over the country, all over the world. All they want to do is rock, all day and all night, in the classroom, in practice studios, in hallways and courtyards, in school recitals, at some point in local bars and clubs, and if they're lucky and good, on the radio, TV, and in arenas and stadiums all over the world. Rock. Long live it. All day and all night, like a motherfucking hurricane. Rock.

***

They come for their families, who usually live in rural farming areas of Korea, China, Cambodia, Thailand. They are recruited by men who roam the areas looking for talent, the prettier the better, the younger the better. They are told they will have jobs, a place to live, that they'll make money for their families, that they will have better lives, that they will have a future.
They come over in groups of fifteen or twenty, in the rear sections of cargo containers with little or no light, no running water, and no electricity, that get moved through the Port of Los Angeles. One or two die on every trip, the others have to live with their bodies. Once the containers are opened, they're hustled into windowless vans taken to a windowless warehouse given showers and food and clothes, usually lingerie. They do their hair and they put on makeup. They are put on display. Buyers arrive middle-aged Asian men and women. The buyers inspect them, poke at them, prod at them, sometimes they take them into small rooms with mattresses and test them. They negotiate prices for them, anywhere from five thousand to

twenty-five thousand dollars. They put them in windowless vans. They take them to their new homes. They take them to what was supposed to be their American Dream.

They live together in a single room in nondescript buildings spread throughout the city and the county. Four five six sometimes ten young women in a single room its floor covered with old mattresses. They share a bathroom. They cook noodles on hot plates. They watch TV though they don't understand most of what is being said. They share clothes and they share makeup and they share basic necessities like soap, shampoo, toothpaste. They never leave.

Men come, drawn by the sign that says Massage or the ads in the adult-classified sections of independent newspapers and magazines. They start coming at 8:00 AM and they keep coming until midnight. None of them actually expect a massage, or if they do, it is a small part of what they seek. They want young Asian women who will do what their wives won't, their girlfriends won't, what they can't get elsewhere. They pay fifty dollars for half an hour, one hundred for an hour. They pay a man, usually a large, armed man, and they go to a small dark room with a massage table. The girls go to the room one by one until the man chooses one of them. Once the choice is made, the girl goes to a bathroom and gets a towel, some lotion, condoms, and comes back to the man's room and closes the door.

When they're done, if the girl has performed well, she is given a tip. She is allowed to keep half of the tip for herself, and has to pay the other half to the house. What goes to the house is placed against the initial cost to acquire her, plus 50 percent weekly interest. Her portion of her earnings is usually sent back to her family. On a good day a girl can see fifteen or twenty men, on a bad day none. If the girl works hard she can eventually pay herself off. If she can't, she is used until she is no longer wanted. She is then either thrown out of the house or she is dropped on a street corner.

***

They come to work. They come across on foot, in freight trucks, on trains, in tunnels. They have little or no education. They have no money. Many of them have family in the area, but their family members are in the same situation. No papers. No chance of legal work. No way to take advantage of many of the opportunities that exist in a country, and a city, of dreams. They stand on the street. They arrive at dawn. The sun is always out in the winter it's 75 degrees, in the summer it's 105. The street is lined with battered trucks, many of which they own. Some of them are in crews attached to the trucks they sit in them, on them, hang from them. A hundred yards away there is a home-improvement superstore, 100,000 square feet of plans, tools and materials. Legal citizens, many of whom own homes, and whose own families immigrated to this country at some point in the near or distant past, go into the store and purchase whatever they need for their projects. A few of them do the projects themselves. Most of them don't. They load the supplies into their cars and pull out to the street and move towards the curb.

The men crowd around the cars. Most of them don't speak English, but know a few choice words to make it seem as if they do. Regardless of whether they do or don't, whatever the driver of the car needs, carpentry, painting, plumbing, gardening they know how to do it. As the window comes down they yell I work hard, I do job right, I work all day cheap, they push each other, knee each other, kick each other, get in fights over the position closest to the window, all they want is to work, and they will work long and hard, all they want is a day's wages. They try to get the driver's attention and if they get it, try to negotiate a good situation for themselves the longer the job the better, the higher the hourly the better. If they're chosen they try to get their brothers, fathers, cousins, uncles and friends chosen. They get in the car quickly or motion to the driver of whatever truck they are attached to if a truck is needed. A good wage is ten an hour a great wage fifteen. Any wage is better than nothing.

If they are not chosen they wait. They sit and they wait they will wait all day with the hope that they might get an hour of work. When the sun drops they go home. Some have families some don't some of them sleep in their trucks or cars some of them sleep on the street. The next day, they will arrive at dawn.

***

They come to escape. Most are from small towns in the Midwest, the South, the Southwest. Though many are still children, eleven, twelve, thirteen, fourteen, fifteen, they are escaping their childhoods, escaping physical abuse, mental abuse, sexual abuse when they couldn't take it anymore they ran, ran west, ran to California, towards the lights of Hollywood Boulevard.

There are several hundred of them. They live in packs beneath bridges and overpasses. They sleep together, eat together, take care of each other, love each other, hurt each other. The packs always have a leader usually a teenage male usually someone who has lived on the streets for an extended period of time. During the day they go down to Hollywood Boulevard, sit along the stars embedded in the concrete, panhandle, beg, occasionally, if they are desperate, rob the tourists. They forage for food in dumpsters. They get their clothing at shelters. They buy and sell drugs. They buy and sell themselves. They buy and sell each other.

Most people, tourists employees at local shops and restaurants and theaters, the police, ignore them. They can be difficult to look at kids in ragged clothes usually black clothes faces dirty hair tangled fingers caked with grime. Many are skeletal from the lack of food and the abuse of drugs. When one of them dies they try to identify them and contact their families they're usually buried in paupers' graves.

They stay for as long as they can a day week month some stay for years. Some go home. Many die. A few go to shelters or treatment centers. The unlucky, though some say the opposite,

just disappear. When they enter adulthood they leave it's harder
to beg harder to garner sympathy harder to live amongst
children. They run somewhere. Though by now they know
there is no escape, no escape.

***

They come looking for waves. On bikes with saddlebags and
on foot wearing backpacks in old pickup trucks with sleeping
bags in camper vans bought from hippies. Many grew up in
landlocked states without salt water they saw surfing on TV or
in videos they read magazines filled with pictures of long-
haired men in shorts dripping wet surrounded by beautiful
girls. Some tried it on family vacations and found themselves
others have known it throughout the entirety of their lives. All
of them find peace and joy alone on the water a serenity
contentment to which they devote their lives.
They live crowded together in cheap apartments in El Segundo,
Playa del Rey, in the Marina and Venice. Some park in lots
along the ocean they move every few days some live in Malibu
campgrounds some sleep on the sand. They take jobs in
restaurants, bars, at surf shops, as cabdrivers, anything that
leaves their mornings free when the tides are high and the
beaches empty and they walk with their boards and paddle out
to where breaks start to curl. Some don't have jobs don't want
jobs would rather starve than devote time they could spend on
water doing something they despise. A few can make a living
at it they travel the world to compete in tournaments come
home when they're free. To all of them jobs are just a means
nothing more, nothing more.
How many are there two or three hundred maybe five, maybe
six hundred men and a few women. Many know each other
and are friendly some are not and avoid each other's beaches
avoid each other's waves. If someone isn't welcome they'll
break their board ride over them in the water cut them with
their fins. Out of the water they might be friends smoke weed
together drink beer on the water what is theirs is theirs and

they will fight to protect it. It's a dream their life no stress no expectations no ambition just love something they truly and dearly love that will never leave them, never forsake them. It's sand and salt, water and waves, love.

***

They come in the name of God. Silently and under assumed names fake papers with real visas students and teachers, researchers, religious men who hate. They despise America despise the decadence of Los Angeles they're revolted by the excess, the narcissism, the waste. They want to destroy it. They want to kill its residents.

They learned their craft in Afghanistan, Pakistan, Iran, Iraq. They saw their brothers die in the name and aspired to join them. They are trained in death and mayhem and how to deliver them they are trained in the words of a book they say justifies them but doesn't.

They watch. They listen. They prepare. They only speak to their own. They have plans based on their observations and they have the materials to make their plans realities. Some of the plans are small a café a restaurant a store that sells goods that revolt them. Some are larger, schools, malls, government buildings, houses of God where infidels and Jews worship false idols. Some are massive city blocks to contaminate hospitals to burn a port to annihilate an airport to raze. A hundred thousand people at a football game. Three hundred thousand at a parade.

They live on quiet streets in homes that look normal apartments like any other they drive cars that don't draw any attention they avoid notice. They miss their beards but it is sanctioned. They miss their robes but it is sanctioned. They miss their brothers but believe they will see them again when it's over. They live on quiet streets and they wait for a signal, a message, words strung together that mean more to them mean that it's their time. They live on quiet streets and they wait to die and they pray to the East that they take you with them.

In 1950, Los Angeles resident Richard Nixon is elected to represent the State of California in the United States Senate.

They come to live. They come because the help they need is unavailable in whatever town, city, state or country where they reside. If they don't get it, many of them, if not all, will die. At home they ask their doctors what they should do, where should they go the doctors say West, go West, it may be your only hope, go West.

It is the largest nonprofit medical facility on the West Coast. There are 2,000 doctors and 7,000 support staff. It is the most heavily funded medical facility on the West Coast the overwhelming majority of its funds come from private donations. It is considered the best medical facility in the western United States and one of the best in the world. Founded at the turn of the twentieth century by a wealthy family looking to provide medical care to Jews who were turned away at other hospitals. It did not discriminate so others began to come because of the quality of care. It grew expanded moved grew more expanded more moved again. In the '70s it moved to twenty acres on the edge of Beverly Hills. It grew and it expanded and there are now eighteen buildings spread across the acreage and plans for more.

Walk through its halls it is one of the few places in the city where race is irrelevant, religion is irrelevant class is irrelevant. The child of Polish immigrants living in Iowa gets chemotherapy for lymphoma. An Arab prince has heart surgery. A gangster from Watts recovers from a gunshot wound. A movie star has a child. A Japanese businessman is treated for a brain tumor. A seventy-year-old Mexican gardener who does not speak English and has never voted or paid taxes gets a new hip. An Armenian has kidney stone surgery, a Russian has eye surgery, a Jew from Syria gets a new heart. The priority is not money or the enrichment of an endowment it is health and care and recovery it is providing services that make the world a better place. A 700-pound woman from Arizona who hasn't walked in a decade has gastric bypass. A four-year-old burn victim from Oakland has a series of skin grafts. A teenage girl has reconstructive facial surgery after being hit by a drunk driver. Priority life.

***

They come to learn at the seventy-five colleges and universities in Los Angeles. Many of them are drawn by the idea of living under the sun. Many come because they think they'll spend their free time amongst movie stars and recording artists and that the life they see on TV and in magazines can be theirs while they're in school. Many come because some of the schools are the finest in the country, the finest in the world. Many come simply because they're accepted.

There are approximately 1.2 million college students in Los Angeles County. Eight percent of them are black, 20 percent Latino, 13 percent are Asian, 12 percent are from outside the United States, and 45 percent of the students who start school finish with a degree of some kind. The largest schools are University of California Los Angeles, with 37,000 students, and California State University Long Beach, with 31,000 students. Hebrew Union College has 57 students, the Rand School of Policy has 60. One of them has an operating budget of $800,000 a year. Another has an operating budget of $1.7 billion. There are ten law schools in Los Angeles, two medical schools, two dentistry schools, and thirteen seminary schools. Fifty-six schools offer education degrees. Two offer degrees in advanced theoretical astrophysics. There are departments at the schools covering more than 600 other subjects, including the production of maple syrup, queer musicology, Hitler studies, Peloponnesian dance, the phallus, nonviolent terrorism studies, solar psychology, dream failure therapy and soap opera conception and production.

When they're done, if they ever finish, some of the students return to the other 50 states and 190 countries from which they came. Sixty percent of them, however, stay in Los Angeles. They work in every type of job available, in every field, though less than 3 percent of all of the graduating students of all of the schools in Los Angeles work in their specific field of study. They join a workforce of 7 million other people with college degrees, the second-largest college-educated workforce in the world.

***

They come to fuck, suck, lick and moan. They come for single penetration, double penetration, triple penetration. They come for bondage, S&M, gangbangs. They come for interracial, anal, latex, poolside, snowballing, bodystocking, creampie and piledriving. Some of them actually enjoy it, and all of them expect to get paid for it. They go to the San Fernando Valley, also known as Porn Valley, or Silicone Valley, where 95 percent of all American pornography is produced. Though actual statistics are hard to find or verify, it is estimated that it is a business that generates between $10 and $14 billion a year in revenue.

It is a business built on the backs of women, or rather, on women on their backs, or standing, sitting, bent over, legs up, legs curled, facedown, sometimes on swings, sometimes in cages. Though men are a required aspect of it, it is not the men who bring in the money. Pornographers need girls, young hot fresh girls, girls who are willing to do whatever they ask as many times as they ask with whomever they provide and do it on camera for people around the world to see, usually on video or the Internet. There is no shortage of girls in Los Angeles. There is no shortage of girls willing to have sex on camera for cash. Though there are scouts who patrol the streets of the city looking for talent, and often approach potential talent with the simple statement—how much would it cost me to fuck you on film—thousands of girls, and women, come to LA every year hoping to break into porn. They are women of every age (yes, there is a fetish that involves watching elderly women have sex), every size (yes, there's another involving obese women), every race. They are willing to do almost anything in order to become a star. And yes, porn stars can be as famous as their less liberal counterparts in the traditional entertainment industry. A brand-name porn girl can make, via films, magazine shoots, a personal subscription-only Web site and endorsed products such as dildos vibrators and sex dolls, millions and millions of dollars a year. They have devoted fan bases, fan clubs that follow and revolve around their every move, franchise films that involve multiple sequels (and multiple orgasms!!!). Some have television shows on cable TV, a few have segued into careers in nonpornographic film and television.

For most, though, there is no fame, no fortune, no happily-ever-after. There is simply, day after day after day after day, mindless, meaningless, loveless sex. They take whatever jobs come their way, or whatever jobs their agents (yes, there are also talent agencies that only handle porn girls) can find for them. They have surgery to enhance or alter their bodies (there are also plastic surgeons whose entire practices involve surgery for the porn industry). They make enough to pay their bills but barely, and those who don't often work in that other money-for-sex industry. Alcoholism is common, drug addiction rampant. Though HIV is extremely rare, and most porn producers require HIV tests before proceeding with shoots, many of the women contract other sexually transmitted diseases such as herpes, chlamydia, hepatitis, human papillomavirus (genital warts), bacterial vaginosis. The window to become successful, with certain fetishistic exceptions, is very short, and most of those that come are no longer considered desirable after their twenty-fifth birthdays. Some go home, and hope that no one they knows sees them in anything, and try to start new, more conventional, lives. Some stay and work as strippers, escorts or try to get into the business end of porn. Some become wives and mothers and look back on their foray into filmed entertainment as a period of oats-sowing, a wild adventure that made them happy for a few years. Some are destroyed by it and die addicted, diseased and alone.

The psychological effects are more difficult to quantify, and vary from girl to girl, woman to woman. Some of the women, often the most successful of them, don't suffer any outward or obvious psychological effects, and very frankly, absolutely love their jobs and couldn't imagine doing anything else. They believe that what they do brings pleasure, literally and figuratively, to millions and millions of people around the world. It isn't illegal and nobody forces them to do it, and it is their right, their absolute right, to chase their dream, and make it a reality. Others are damaged beyond repair, feel victimized, taken advantage of, suffer from low self-esteem, depression, anxiety disorder, cannot maintain healthy relationships. Whatever the level of success, whether they are fluffers (women who, off camera, keep the male actors erect between shots), anal specialists, golden shower girls, toesuckers or world-famous brand-name porno superstars, they come ready willing and able, year after year after year, to a city that welcomes them, loves them, uses them, films them, sells them, year after year, they come.

* * *

They come to visit an endless stream of tourists 25 million a year they spend $13 billion and employ 400,000 people. Drawn by the allure of fame, fortune, glamour and sun they fill the 100,000 hotel rooms night after night the stream never ends. They come for Disneyland, Universal Studios, for the 2,500 stars embedded on the Walk of Fame on Hollywood Boulevard. They come for Venice Beach, the Santa Monica Pier. They come to shop Rodeo Drive, Robertson Boulevard, Melrose Avenue. They come for the Lakers and Clippers, the Angels and Dodgers, the Galaxy and the Kings. They come for Griffith Park the La Brea Tar Pits Huntington Gardens. They come for LegoLand, Wild Rivers Waterpark, Magic Mountain. They come to see the *Queen Mary*. They come to see the Sunset Strip. They come to the homes of movie stars, though mostly what they see are the driveways and security gates of stars. They come to sit in the seats of Mann's Chinese Theater, the Pantages Theater, the Kodak Theater, the El Capitan, the Cinerama Dome. They come to walk the halls of LACMA, MOCA, the Getty Museum, the Museum of Tolerance, the Guinness Book of World Records Museum, the Petersen Auto Museum, the Norton Simon, the Hammer. They come to sit in the sun on the twenty-seven-mile stretch of sand that starts in Manhattan Beach and ends in Malibu. They come to laugh at the Comedy Store, the Laugh Factory, the Improv. They come for Spago, the Ivy, Morton's. They come to stand outside of the Oscars, the Golden Globes, the Grammys. They come to see celebrities, though they almost never do. They come to watch the ponies at Hollywood Park Race Track. They come to wonder at the Magic Castle. They come to listen at the Hollywood Bowl and the Greek Theater and the Wiltern. They come to party at the Roxy, the Viper Room, Whisky A Go Go, at Area, Café des Artistes, Freddy's. They come to stay at Chateau Marmont, the Peninsula, the Beverly Hills Hotel, the Hotel Bel-Air, the Mondrian, Shutters. They come to see what they see on television and in films, what they hear about in songs, what they dream about when they want to forget about their lives 25 million a year spending $13 billion.

***

They come for freedom. Thirty thousand Persians fleeing the rule of ayatollahs. One hundred and twenty-five thousand Armenians escaping Turkish genocide. Forty thousand Laotians avoiding minefields. Seventy-five thousand Thais none in Bangkok sex shows. Two million Mexicans living amongst their own. Twenty thousand Bulgarians who don't want to be Russian. Fifty thousand Ethiopians who eat every night. One hundred thousand Filipinos with a stable government (sort of). Two hundred thousand Koreans neither north nor south. Thirty-five hundred thousand Hungarians who don't want to be Russian. Seventy thousand Guatemalans with a chance at real jobs. Eighty thousand Nicaraguans free from war. Ninety thousand Salvadorans with a chance at real jobs. Twenty thousand Vietnamese who came to America to avoid an American war. Fifteen thousand Samoans who crossed the ocean. Thirty thousand Cambodians living without the Khmer Rouge. All are the largest communities of people in the world outside of their native countries. Also seven hundred thousand Jews living in safety. Fifty thousand Japanese none interned. Five thousand Serbians and five thousand Croatians none at war. Eight thousand Lithuanians who don't want to be Russian. Six thousand Ukrainians who don't want to be Russian. Four hundred and fifty French who hate American coffee and hate American people. Four thousand Romanians who don't want to be Russian. Two hundred Germans who drive nice cars. Thirty thousand Native Americans to whom it belongs. Seventy-five thousand Russians who don't want to be Russian and eat McDonald's and love capitalism.

In May of 1955, the Los Angeles Police and Fire Departments lift race-based hiring restrictions and commission their first black officers. Later that month there is an earthquake, a large fire and a mudslide. Local preachers claim the disasters were God's punishment for the hirings.

Esperanza stays in her room. Her mother brings her food, her father comes in every night before he goes to bed and sits with her. She usually doesn't want to talk, she just lies in bed, he sits next to her and holds her hand.

She does not go back to the Campbell home. She does not go anywhere near Pasadena. She makes no attempt to contact Doug or his mother.

During the day she watches television, mostly Mexican soap operas. At night she stares at the wall. She tries not to think about Doug, though, as is often the case when one tries not to think about something, he is all she thinks about, hour after hour, night after night. She remembers the first time she saw him, chubby, jelly stain on his shirt (which she later got out using high-powered stain remover), something that looked like a small piece of an English muffin stuck in the corner of his mouth. She remembers the first time he made a face behind his mother's back how hard it was to keep from laughing. She remembers the smell deep and pure of the first rose he gave her, the smell of his breath not bad sort of like orange juice the first time he kissed her, the way he felt dense heavy and warm the first time they lay together on her cot. She thinks about the moments before his mother came home the moments alone in his room his hands on her thighs staring at her smiling his words I love you she believed him still believes him. Alone in her room it hurts more because it should have worked, or would have worked under different circumstances, it hurts more when the reasons are no good. His mother.

A week two three her parents understanding at first become increasingly concerned. Her mother tries talking to her when she brings in her meals many of the meals are left untouched Esperanza never responds. Her father tries talking to her as he sits beside her he tells her how much potential she has how smart and beautiful he believes she is she never responds. Her cousins knock at the door, nothing. Her aunts and uncles knock at the door, nothing. She loses weight everywhere but her thighs. She doesn't shower she smells. She stops brushing her teeth terrible breath, her hair becomes tangled. Her mother brings her food untouched, her father sits by her side and talks to her she never responds. She remembers his hands, they were soft and smooth the hands of a man who had never done manual labor, slightly pudgy, sometimes with ink stains, sometimes food stains.

On the fourth Sunday of her isolation Esperanza wakes up reaches for the remote control turns on the television. One of the Spanish channels is showing a weekend marathon of a popular show about a family in Baja that owns a hotel. The members of the family fall in love and out of love with the staff and the guests, there are marriages and divorces, fights and affairs, there's an occasional murder mystery. As she watches, a young woman threatens to commit suicide by jumping into the propeller of the family's yacht, the young woman has been having an affair with the eighty-five-year-old patriarch of the family which he ended when his wife found out about it and stabbed him with a barbecue fork. The young woman screams, yells, calls the old man names, begs him to take her back, warns him that he will die with the image of her chopped up in the sea if he doesn't take her back. Esperanza laughs at her, laughs at her situation, laughs at the idea that the old man would end up with her, that their love actually had a chance. The young woman keeps screaming and yelling and when the scene ends, with the young woman hanging by her fingertips from the back rail of the yacht and the old man heading into the cabin for a cocktail and a massage, Esperanza turns off the TV, gets out of bed, takes a shower and gets dressed. She brushes her teeth (the yellow disappears quickly and easily) and does her hair (like she's going to prom) and puts on makeup and a dress and walks to the kitchen, where her parents are having coffee before they go to church. They're surprised to see her. They both smile, stand and embrace her, her father picks her up and twirls her around and says Amo a mi hija, yo falté a mi hija and she laughs it's the first time she's laughed in almost a month and it hurts a little but mostly feels great, almost perfect like something she loved and lost and found again she laughs. When her father sets her down he kisses her cheeks and tells her she looks wonderful, she smiles and asks if it would be okay if she went to church with them. Her father claps his hands together and says sí, mi hija perfecta hermosa, and her mother bursts into tears, and five minutes later they walk out of the house together.

They sit in the front row. Jorge sings every hymn at the top of his lungs. They take communion together. Graciella (who controls the family's finances) empties her wallet into the offering plate. At the end of the service, they mingle with the other parishioners in front of the church until everyone is gone, and on their way home, Jorge suggests they stop for brunch at a restaurant that makes Mexican French toast, which uses tortillas instead of regular bread, and is topped with brown sugar and cinnamon. Midway through the meal, Jorge looks at Graciella and raises his eyebrows slightly she shakes her head slightly he does it again with more emphasis she shakes her head again. Esperanza notices what he's doing knows he wants to say something that he feels is important, she speaks.

What is it, Papa?

He feigns surprise.

What do you mean?

She laughs.

You have something you want to talk to me about?

Why do you think that?

You're not so subtle, Papa.

I am very subtle.

She laughs again.

Am I right?

Maybe.

Esperanza looks at her mother.

Am I right, Mama?

Graciella nods.

Yes, you are right.

Esperanza looks back at her father.

What is it, Papa?

Jorge reaches over, takes Graciella's hand.

We love you very much, Esperanza.

I know you do.

We want you to be happy. To have a happy life.

I know you do, Papa.

When you came home last month we knew something was wrong. When you won't come out of your room or eat or talk to us, we know something is really wrong. We think . . .

Graciella interrupts him.

Your papa especially.

Jorge nods.

Me especially thinks that if you had someone in your life, like your mama and me have each other, you would be happier.

I don't want you to set me up, Papa.

Of course you don't. What girl wants her father doing that? No girl wants it. But we, and especially me, were very worried about you. You are so shy and so humble, you don't even know how beautiful you are, how wonderful you are. When I see you sad it crushes me. For the last month, every night after I leave your room, I go in my bed and cry myself to sleep.

Graciella speaks.

Every night, Esperanza. Like a little baby.

Esperanza speaks.

I'm sorry, Papa.

Jorge speaks.

You don't need to be sorry. You were feeling your own pain. My pain was because I couldn't help you. So I decided to figure out how to help you when you started being better, and I knew you would be better, because everyone, until the very end, which is a long ways away for you, always gets better. So what did I do?

Graciella speaks.

Wait till you hear this.

Jorge smiles.

I joined a singles group for young Mexican professionals.

Esperanza starts laughing.

I had your cousin Miguel find it for me on the computer. It is called Talk and Tequila, a mixer for young Mexican professionals in East LA.

Graciella speaks.

And he went. I tried to stop him, but he was very stubborn.

Jorge.

I did. I went. I paid twenty dollars to go to their Birthday of Benito Júarez Mixer. Everyone stared at me and one of the group members asked me why I was there.

Esperanza.

What did you say?

Jorge.

That I felt young and I was a professional father.

And what did he say?

He asked me if I was there making sure it was safe for my daughter.

They all laugh.

And I told him yes, that was why I was there, that my daughter is the flower of East LA and I wanted to see if there were men in attendance who were worthy of her.

Esperanza.

Were there?

Jorge.

Yes. Lawyers and doctors, teachers and salesmen. All worthy young Mexican professionals.

Esperanza.

There's a problem, though, Papa.

What is that?

I'm a maid, not a professional.

Graciella.

He has a solution for that.

Jorge.

A wonderful solution.

Esperanza.

What is it?

Jorge.
Students who are studying to be professionals can be part of the group.
Esperanza.
I'm a maid. An unemployed maid.
Graciella.
Stop saying that.
Jorge.
You are the flower of East LA.
Esperanza.
I lost my scholarship. I don't think I can get it back.
Jorge.
Your mother and I went to the bank. They told us to talk to a lawyer. We talked to a lawyer who sent us to the offices of the city. The offices of the city sent us to three other offices and they finally sent us back to the lawyer who made us fill out lots of papers. We put your name on the deed of the house. We own the house with no bank mortgage. It is no mansion but it is a house with a yard and it is worth some money after all these years. The bank said they will give you a loan, a special education loan with the house as collateral, for you to go back to school. When you are in school, you are a professional and can go to mixers and I will wait out front for you.
Esperanza smiles.
Thank you, Papa.
Jorge.
It was your mother's idea.
Esperanza.
Thank you, Mama.
Graciella.
We love you, Esperanza.
Jorge.
Yes. More than anything. The only time I cry again is at your wedding.
Esperanza laughs.
I love you too.

By 1958, Los Angeles is the largest automobile market in the country and its six million residents consume more gasoline per capita than the residents of any other city in the world.

Joe runs away from the boardwalk, though for him, running is more like walking quickly in a stilted, awkward manner. He takes an alley that runs east/west, he's going inland, east, away from Lemonade, who is lying dead on the concrete somewhere behind him. He doesn't know where he's going. He doesn't know where any of his other friends are, what they're doing. He's scared to go back to his bathroom the girl knows where he lives and they could come to kill him. They may be killing his friends or trying to find them so they can kill them. His friends may be fine, sitting together getting drunk or eating pizza from a dumpster, they may be with the police, he doesn't know, doesn't know what to do or where to go, he just wants to get away from what he saw, from the body of his friend lying dead on the concrete.

He crosses Pacific Avenue. Homes are in the same style as on the walk-streets along the beach, small California bungalows with three-stair stoops and front porches, some are painted bright colors red, blue yellow there's one that's purple and pink. They're in good shape European cars sit in the driveways and line the curbs furniture on the porches costs more than he can panhandle in a year, maybe two, he keeps walking east. He crosses Main St., which runs through Santa Monica and Venice, in Santa Monica it's lined with cafés and bars and stores that sell designer clothes and special hand creams, face creams, creams for everything imaginable. In Venice there's one huge building with a fifty-foot pair of steel binoculars at the entrance it used to hold a fancy advertising agency now they're gone, the rest of the street is desolate, empty parking lots, warehouses, a gym.

He crosses Main Street still walking east he enters another residential neighborhood. The houses are the same style though not as well cared for, paint is chipping, furniture is broken, cars are older some don't run. And while the rest of Venice sleeps there is life here, people sitting on porches listening to music and drinking, cars moving slowly up and down long narrow streets, cars parked in alleys with illuminated brake lights, teenagers on corners hands in their pockets hats pulled low pretending to be indifferent they see everything around them in teams of three or four they service the drivers of the cars, provide them with whatever they want, whatever they need. Everyone has the same color skin there are no whites no Asians no Hispanics, and unless they're coming in to do business, none are welcome. Occasionally a police cruiser will roll slowly down one of the streets no one looks no one watches no one cares nothing changes it's just another car with an unwelcome white man behind the wheel he'll leave soon enough.

Joe walks no one pays much attention to him he looks like what he is a homeless man in ragged clothes with no money and nowhere to go. Now and then someone on a corner will offer him smoke or rock when he walks past liquor stores men standing at their entrance say we got good shit cheap but it's not cheap enough. He wants to sleep, though there's nowhere for him to lie down he doesn't want the concrete of an alley or the rats and smell of a dumpster or a line of garbage cans, if he goes into someone's yard it would most likely end badly for him. He keeps walking, playing the events of the night the planning dividing into groups of two creeping down the boardwalk the gunshots again and again the gunshots and the body convulsing. He hears the distinct pop/crack at first he's not sure if it's his mind or if they're real hears them again three in a burst followed by a scream followed by four more in a burst more screaming. He's seen enough tonight he turns south away from the shots away from the screams away from the cars and the corners he wants to walk away from more but can't just turns south.

The change comes quickly. He crosses a street and though the houses are the same and the yards are the same and the cars are the same and the business is the same, the music is different, the skin color is different, the language is different. On one side he found indifference, on the other open hostility. As he approaches corners teenage men step into his path he lowers his head and steps around them they spit at his feet at the back of his head. No one offers to sell him anything and when he's spoken to he can't understand the words though he knows the intentions. There are fewer liquor stores they are just as crowded. Police are less common but treated in the same manner no one cares no one stops no one acknowledges. He doesn't hear any gunfire but leaves quickly he knows the rules this is not somewhere he is welcome he keeps walking south. The change comes quickly. He crosses a street and though the houses are the same and the yards the same all built in the same style at the same time on lots with the same amount of land on one side they are worth far less than on the other side. There is no one outside. Porches are empty but for their expensive furniture. Cars are new, clean, have single red lights blinking on their dashes (though the alarms really don't do anything but make noise). It is quiet, still, peaceful. Beds of flowers line one edge of the sidewalks, healthy palms the other. The few houses that are empty have for sale signs in front of them with seven-figure price tags. Empty lots are cared for flat and green no garbage no car parts no cardboard boxes. Joe walks up and down these streets he wonders what it would be like to live among these people, if he had the money would they even let him. Police cruisers are highly common and highly visible though there is nothing for them to do except be seen keep the residents calm and happy let them know that if interlopers from the other areas intrude they will be dealt with quickly. One of them stops alongside Joe a black officer in the white car asks him what he's doing he says leaving the officer says good. On his way out he passes through a crowd of paparazzi camping outside the house of a movie star who recently had twins, the first pictures of the children will sell for hundreds of thousands of dollars. Joe asks how long they've been there one of them says fuck off another says a week a third calls him a drunk homeless fuck and tells him to go away. Joe asks how long they will wait the singular answer is as long as it takes and somewhere inside the house five-day-old children sleep under siege because their mother has a nice smile and beautiful hair and can recite lines on camera.

Joe walks to Venice Boulevard divided by a median that used to hold a railcar and is now mostly grass dead without rain. Half a mile one way is home the beginning of the boardwalk and a hundred yards farther the Pacific Ocean. Half a mile the other way he has no idea because he's never been there and he usually gets scared when he walks inland. He crosses Venice Blvd. there is a small church sitting between two mini-malls it's beige stucco a cross above its doors they're open even though it's the middle of the night. Joe walks to the door, stands below the cross looks inside there are two rows of pews fifteen or twenty on each side a humble altar behind it. On the wall a man hangs from a cross his hands are bleeding, his feet are bleeding. Joe stares at the man. He may be wood or plaster the blood red paint, he may be salvation, he may be nothing more than a doll for adults. Joe steps into the church. He walks to the first pew a few feet from the altar a few more from the man. He sits down he stares he thinks about his friend is he still on the ground where he died have they taken him away is he lying in the back of an ambulance or a van, is he lying on a cold steel slab? He sits and he stares there's a dim light above the altar it casts shadows across the racked body of the man Joe sits and he stares and he tries to remember if he ever knew Lemonade's real name, if he ever knew his dead friend's real name.

He sits for an hour two.

The shadows move as the sun starts to rise it is the first morning in a decade that Old Man Joe aged thirty-nine but looks seventy-five isn't lying on the beach watching the sky turn gray white pink blue isn't waiting for answers but seeking them.

Streaks of light come through the door he sits and stares. Parrots wild in Venice they were brought here in the early 1900s and never caged they never left start singing in the palms.

Traffic behind him.

Sits.

Stares.

Blood on his hands blood on his feet.

Light moving up the aisle, streaks, slowly.

His friend somewhere in the city dead.

A priest walks in lights candles smiles at Joe nods priest leaves candles burn.

Joe picks up a book it's simple black in the carrel of the pew a gold cross embossed he looks at the face of the man he doesn't look like he's in pain he speaks.

Why'd you take my friend?

His eyes are open they're deep blue, calm, at rest.

Why did you take my friend and leave those pieces of shit who killed him?

His hands open not clenched in pain fingers extended inviting.

Why?

Why?

Why you let men with different-colored skin hate each other for no reason. Why you let one man have more than another man when they both deserve it. Why you let children die in the streets killing each other over a corner or some white powder or the color of a bandana. Why you make my friends eat out of dumpsters and drink their fucking lives away when they ain't done nothing to hurt nobody their whole damn lives.

His mouth is open slightly his teeth white he's not grimacing calm.

Why you make me spend my life chasing yellow, make another man spend his life chasing green, another man spend his life spilling red. If you for real and you love everyone like they say you do then why you treat us different, why you give to some and not to others, why you take and hurt and destroy so many people that are just trying to get by and get through the day. Why you let that happen over and over and over again. Those that got, get more, and those that don't get nothing over and over and over again. If you for real it don't make no sense to me.

He wears no clothes just a white sheet tied loosely at waist.

You want worship for what? For what you give? For how you treat us? For what you allow to happen? For the hatred that exists that you don't stop? For the violence that you don't stop? For the death that you don't stop? Man killing man killing women killing children that you don't stop. And you want worship? You want us on our knees? You want devotion? You want exaltation? You want faith?

A crown of thorns pressed into the skull bleeding at the tips.

I walk down the street and men hate me not love me, hate my skin, my smell, the clothes I wear, the way my hair is, what they think I am and who they think I am not one motherfucker looks at me and sees love they just hate, every single one of them, and you call yourself all-knowing, all-powerful, say you sit in judgment.

Thick streaks in his hair, on his chin, running down his chest.

You want and say you deserve and we must or we are condemned and all you give us is this, this world where children get burned alive and men spend their money blowing each other up and women sell themselves to feed and all we see is destruction and war and mayhem in your name and it never gets better and you never stop all-knowing and all-powerful it never ends. It never ends. And it never will.

Head hanging but not in defeat.

Why'd you take my friend? He didn't deserve it. None of us deserve it.

Lit from above.

Joe stands and walks out.

In August 1965, a white Highway Patrol officer pulls over a black motorist for driving erratically on a street in Watts. The driver and two family members are arrested, and riots erupt that last a week. Fifteen thousand National Guard troops are sent in to contain the riots. Thirty-four people are killed by police, and three others die. Over a thousand are injured and almost 4,000 are arrested. Six hundred buildings, almost none of which were private residences inhabited by African Americans, are damaged or destroyed by looting and fire.

Amberton is in a battered white van with a man named Kurchenko. Kurchenko is a short, tense, wiry man, veins are visible all over his body. And though he is not more than thirty-five, he looks fifty, he has thin gray hair and a thin gray mustache and he is missing one of his front teeth, his other teeth are the same gray as his hair. He has forty or fifty small black Xs tattooed all over his forearms, he will not discuss where he got them, what they represent, or what he did to deserve them. Amberton met Kurchenko through a private investigator who refused to continue to work for Amberton. The PI gave Amberton Kurchenko's number and said call this guy, and please don't ever call me again. They have been following Kevin's mother for the past three days. They follow her to work, they follow her to the grocery store, to Kevin's apartment, the hair salon, friends' houses, restaurants, church. Amberton has a camera and takes pictures of her, Kurchenko stares at her and mumbles to himself in Russian.

Amberton gives Kurchenko a day off. He goes home. He hasn't spoken to Casey since he left with Kurchenko, hasn't seen or spoken to his children. He goes to his wing of the house, takes a shower, shaves his entire body, except for his head, masturbates. He leaves without seeing or speaking to Casey or the children.

He goes to a hotel in Beverly Hills known for its discretion. He takes a suite spends the first twelve hours in the suite ordering room service, eating, making himself vomit. He orders some porn on pay-per-view starts watching it decides he'd rather have the real thing he calls an escort service orders four boys the younger the better. Thirty minutes later they're in the suite. They might be fifteen, sixteen, seventeen, none are older than eighteen, he's happy with them and spends the next six hours doing things to them that could send him to prison for many, many years. When he's finished he gives them large tips goes to sleep.

He wakes the next day his phone keeps ringing over and over it keeps fucking ringing. Only three people have the number

Casey Gordon and his attorney he picks up the phone answers it.

Hello?

Casey speaks.

Where are you, Amberton?

Out.

Out where?

Just out.

We had an interview this morning?

What?

An interview. With that family magazine. They're doing a feature about us, about how you can be famous and still have a happy, stable family. I told you about it about two hundred times.

I forgot.

Can you get home?

Tell them I had to go away.

Away?

Yeah, tell them I went down to New Orleans to do charity work.

Who's gonna back that up?

Gordon and the publicists.

I'm pissed, Amberton. This really meant a lot to me.

It's a bad time, Casey.

He hangs up, goes back to sleep. He sleeps for twelve more hours. He wakes up, orders a cheeseburger, eats it, throws some of it up, checks out, leaves.

He meets Kurchenko. They're in a maroon minivan. They sit outside Kevin's grandmother's house. Using binoculars, they watch her eat, sit in front of the TV, go to the bathroom. Amberton takes some pictures. They spend a day outside of her house. They decide she isn't going to leave, isn't going to go anywhere. They go to Kevin's sister's house. She has four children, all girls, between the ages of four and twelve. Using binoculars, they take pictures of them eating, watching TV, going to the bathroom. They follow them to and from school.

They follow them to and from dance class. They follow them to and from church. They take pictures of them.

They go to Kevin's girlfriend's apartment. Using binoculars, they watch her eat, sit in a recliner and read, cook. Amberton alternates between crying and calling her names dirty fucking cunt, disease-ridden whore, cum-guzzling bitch. Kevin pulls up Amberton starts sobbing tries to get out of the minivan Kurchenko stops him. Amberton keeps trying Kurchenko restrains his arms and legs with duct tape, puts a strip of the tape over his mouth. He watches Kevin and his girlfriend, takes a few pictures, drives away. An hour later he takes the tape off of Amberton's mouth. Amberton starts sobbing again Kurchenko asks him where he wants to go Amberton gives him the name of the hotel in Beverly Hills.

In 1968, Robert Kennedy is shot and killed at the Ambassador Hotel after winning the California Democratic presidential primary.

Neither Maddie nor Dylan have insurance they want to go to a doctor to make sure Maddie is doing okay they find a walk-in clinic. A doctor looks at her, checks her pulse and blood pressure, gives her a blood test that tells them what they already know, gives her an ultrasound everything appears to be fine. It costs nine hundred dollars.

They have three thousand left. They need to move. Maddie doesn't want to move Dylan tries to make her understand they can't afford to live in the apartment anymore they need to save money for their child. They argue about it for a day, for a week. Dylan tells her they can continue to live there but she'll have to get a job and they won't be able to buy diapers for their child, Maddie tells him she'll start looking for a place in the morning.

For the week two three Dylan goes to work spends the day carrying golf bags and pretending he knows the lines of putts and making jokes and giving mediocre golfers compliments on their mediocre shots. Maddie spends the mornings looking through classified ads makes lists of potential places though she doesn't know where many of them are located they're within their price range. She takes a nap has a small lunch usually macaroni and cheese and strawberries for dessert. She spends her afternoons on buses and sidewalks going from apartment building to apartment building. Once she sees them she usually moves on to the next one, they're run-down, dirty, the neighborhoods scare her, there are too many blacks, too many Mexicans. When she does go into the buildings she is always disappointed, the apartments are small, the kitchens are old, the bathrooms are dirty they remind her of her house in Ohio, make her feel like she's living with her mother again. She wants a building like the one they live in, clean and safe and white she wants an apartment like the one they live in. When she gets home every afternoon she cries she doesn't want to leave. When Dylan gets home she makes dinner and they eat silently and they watch TV silently and get into bed silently they're both too tired to do anything but go to sleep.

She starts to show. Not noticeably, at least to anyone who wasn't looking for the bump, but enough for Dylan to notice, for her pants to stop fitting, she needs new bras. They go shopping buy everything three or four sizes too big they'll only be able to do this once. Another week two three the money keeps dwindling he doesn't know how they're going to pay for their apartment, how they're going to pay their medical bills, how they're going to support their child, another week, Maddie stops looking for a new apartment says it's too tiring another week.

He goes to Shaka he arrives at work early knocks on his door Shaka is reading the paper looks up speaks.

You're here early?

I wanted to talk to you.

Come in, sit.

Dylan walks in sits, Shaka sets down his paper.

What's up?

I'm wondering if there's any way to get more hours, or do some extra work.

Shaka laughs.

More than the twelve or fourteen a day you're already getting?

Yeah.

What's wrong?

Nothing's wrong.

Why do you need more hours?

My girlfriend is pregnant.

Shaka smiles.

No shit?

Dylan nods.

No shit.

Congratulations.

Thanks.

You excited?

I'm scared shitless.

Shaka laughs.

Pretty normal, I think.

A little is probably normal. I'm truly scared shitless.

How old are you?

Nineteen.

My wife had our first when I was twenty.

What'd you do?

Worked my fucking ass off. Still doing it. We got four now, though two of 'em are out of the house and basically grown. I know how you're feeling though.

So then you know I need to make more money.

You're doing okay all things considered.

We live in an expensive apartment, we don't have insurance, my girl doesn't work.

Those are all fixable problems.

Not really.

Move to a cheaper place. Once you're here for six months, which is soon, you can apply for city benefits, and if you're married your wife is covered too. Make your soon-to-be-wife get a job. Problems all solved.

I'd rather just make more money.

Then you better start offering blow jobs to the motherfuckers whose bags you carry, 'cause there isn't another way working here. You already make more than just about every other caddie on the staff.

How many of them got kids?

Shaka laughs.

You kiddin' me? Just about all of 'em, and most of 'em got more than one. Nobody here's gonna cry for you. People will do what they can to help, but it's life, man, you gotta make it on your own.

So no more hours?

Shaka shrugs.

There aren't any to give.

How do I do the insurance?

Get married. To do that, you go to city hall and get a marriage license. I got a cousin who's a pastor who can do a ceremony and do the formalities, if you need witnesses, my wife and I will do it. Once you're married, you fill out the forms and you should be covered. And I'll ask around about a place to live. If I find something, it ain't gonna be a place like you got now, walking distance with yuppie neighbors and a pool, but it'll be safe. Once you're there, you can figure out if your woman needs a job or not.

Thank you.

No problem.

Seriously, thank you.

You're welcome.

Dylan gets up leaves the office gets in line for his first bag it's a bearded, tattooed meat salesman who looks like a biker but pulled up in a small compact American car loaded with meat samples he takes two strokes off his score on every hole. After that it's a Korean who speaks no English and throws his clubs. It's a slow day it doesn't look like there will be a third bag so he leaves the course walks home. He hopes Maddie isn't there he knows she was going to go grocery shopping. He opens the door calls Maddie's name nothing. He walks into their bedroom pulls out their remaining cash counts out five hundred dollars. He leaves the apartment walks back towards the course stops at a jewelry store it's part of a nationwide chain they call themselves the Diamond Masters. He looks at the rings he stares at the case with the most expensive, three and four carats with diamond bands they're beautiful and they make him hate himself because he loves Maddie and wants one for her but knows he'll never be able to buy her anything like them. He moves sequentially down two carats beautiful but never, one carat maybe someday, sequentially down he's surprised what he can get for $500 it's better than he expected though it's nothing compared to what he would like to get her, what he believes she deserves, what he feels is equal to his feelings for her. He motions to a woman working behind the counter who comes over shows him rings they're small and simple but beautiful in their way the woman asks him his age he tells her she says the rings he's looking at are perfect for a

young couple starting a life together and it makes him feel
slightly better though not much. After looking at ten rings,
maybe fifteen, he chooses a 1/4 carat diamond solitaire with a
simple gold band it costs $499 he pays the tax with his day's
tips. The woman puts it in a box hands it to him, smiles,
speaks.
I hope you have a long, beautiful life together.
Dylan smiles, speaks.
Thank you.
He walks home. Even though he knows she'll say yes he's
nervous, with each step closer to home he's more so. The ring
is in his front pocket. He's scared it's going to fall out, so
every few steps he checks to make sure it's still there. He
wants to look at it but he's worried someone will take it.
Twice he goes behind buildings and takes it out and looks at
it, smiles, touches the surface of the diamond with his finger,
even though it's small he's proud of it. It's better than
anything anyone they knew at home had, neither set of their
parents even bothered with rings. He tells himself it's a
beginning, their beginning, someday, somehow, he'll get her
a bigger one, for now this is perfect, it's theirs and it's
perfect.
As he walks into their complex he can feel his heart start
pounding his hands start shaking. He checks his pocket for the
seventy-fifth time the ring is still there, he stops in front of
their door and takes it out and looks at it and smiles. He puts
it back. He takes a deep breath, he opens the door.
Maddie in the kitchen she's making Hamburger Helper
Homestyle Salisbury. She turns around smiles, speaks.
Hi.
Dylan smiles, speaks, he feels like glass he's shaking.
Hi.
Good day?
Okay.
How many you get?
Two.

Big tippers?

Okay.

She turns back to the Homestyle Salisbury, stirs it, turns down the heat on the stove. He stares at her back. He's terrified. He wants to step forward can't just stares and shakes. Their life together rolls through his mind in a second or two, images flashing together meeting at elementary school the first time he saw her he felt it, he was seven and he felt it, watching her in class, on the playground, sitting with her at lunch their first kiss at eleven behind a liquor store where they both went to pick things up for their parents, the first time they went to the movies they saw *The Flintstones: Viva Las Vegas* they spent the entire time holding hands and kissing, the times they called each other because they were scared of their parents, the times they held each other after receiving a beating, all of the plans they made starting at twelve they had their dreams, their school dances, makeouts in the car, losing their virginity on a blanket in a field, graduation still dreaming, still dreaming, it passes by in a second or two.

He takes a step forward she's still stirring he feels like he's outside of himself. He steps forward puts his hand in his pocket still there. He steps forward how many times has he thought of this moment he doesn't believe it's here, now, happening, real. He steps forward he's a few feet away she hears him turns around. She looks at him he's shaking she speaks.

What's wrong?

Nothing.

You look funny.

He pulls out the ring shaking hand she smiles.

What are you doing?

He drops to one knee smiles wider.

What are you doing?

He flips the top of the box the ring sits on a satin pillow. She smiles wider he speaks.

I love you, and since I was a kid I wanted to spend my life

with you, and I love you so much, so much, and I want to
know if you'll marry me?
Smile wider, she speaks.
Yes.

On August 9, 1969, four members of Charles Manson's Family enter the Los Angeles residence of film director Roman Polanski and murder five people, including Polanski's wife, actress Sharon Tate, who was eight and a half months pregnant, and Abigail Folger, the heiress to the Folger's coffee fortune. On August 10, 1969, Manson and three members of his Family enter the home of Leno and Rosemary LaBianca and stab the couple to death, carving "War" into Mr. LaBianca's stomach and writing "Death to Pigs" and "Helter Skelter" in the couple's blood on the walls of their home. Manson and four members of the Family are arrested, convicted of murder and sentenced to death. Their sentences are later commuted to life in prison when the death penalty is outlawed.

Patience. Diligence. Hard work. The daily grind it can wear a person down, oh yes it can, that daily grind, it's a day-after-day kind of thing and it just wears a person down. One expects there to be some kind of reward, or payoff, for all of the effort, something that makes it all worth it, that puts a smile on the face, a spring in the step, a tingle on the spine, and a feeling of freedom and joy in the heart. Here is Fun Facts Los Angeles Volume II.

At no point in world history has there been a greater number of professional artists, writers and musicians living and working in a single city than there are in Los Angeles in the twenty-first century.

The word *T-shirt* was coined in Los Angeles by a Japanese man working in a clothing factory. He called the item a T-shirt because it resembled the letter T when laid out on a table, and he was in the process of learning the English alphabet.

If Los Angeles County was a country it would have the fifteenth-largest economy in the world.

In 1918, a Chinese immigrant working in a Los Angeles noodle factory invented the fortune cookie. He did so believing that a cookie with a positive message in it would raise the spirits of the city's poor.

In 1949, Frank Zamboni, who owned a local ice rink, invented the Zamboni ice-resurfacing machine. It is now used in 85 percent of the world's ice rinks.

There are three hundred wild buffalo, which are protected by law, that roam Los Angeles County.

It is illegal in the City of Los Angeles to hunt for moths beneath the arc of a streetlight.

It is illegal in the City of Los Angeles to fly balloons more than five feet above the surface of the ground.

It is illegal in the City of Los Angeles to sit on the surface of an outdoor table at a restaurant.

There are an average of twenty vehicular car chases in Los Angeles County every day.

There is a museum in Los Angeles devoted to the banana. It has almost 20,000 banana-related items.

If all of the law enforcement officers in Los Angeles County were consolidated into an army it would be the fifth-largest army in the world.

There are more support groups in Los Angeles for the victims of UFO abduction than in the rest of the country combined.

Almost half of the dogs in Los Angeles are American pit bull terriers or pit bull mixes.

It is illegal in Pasadena for a male boss to be alone in a room with a female secretary.

The world's first video graveyard, where TV screens play videos of the people buried beneath them twenty-four hours a day, every day for eternity, is in Los Angeles.

There are more businesses in Los Angeles owned by women and minorities than in any other city in the United States.

Every year, at 8:00 PM on the second Saturday of July, hundreds of people gather along a section of Los Angeles rail track to drop their pants and moon passing passenger trains.

Every Halloween, 500,000 people, most of whom are dressed in costume, gather along Santa Monica Boulevard to watch the West Hollywood Halloween Costume Carnival, which primarily consists of floats filled with men dressed as women.

ARPAnet, the first use of linked computers on a single network, was invented by the United States Defense Department in Los Angeles and became operational on January 14, 1969. ARPAnet later became more commonly known by its civilian name, the Internet.

There are, on average, sixty sightings of Sasquatch in Los Angeles every year.

There are more swimming pools in Los Angeles than in any other city in the world.

The average citizen of Los Angeles owns 7.4 pairs of shoes.

Barbie was invented (or born) in Los Angeles in 1959. Her inventor (or mother) was a woman named Ruth Handler.

The average citizen of Los Angeles owns 8.3 bathing suits.

The average citizen of Los Angeles owns 6.4 pairs of underwear.

The hot fudge sundae was invented in 1906 by an ice cream parlor on Hollywood Blvd.

The average citizen of Los Angeles eats 127.2 pieces of licorice every year.

On average, there are 333 days of sun every year in Los Angeles.

At no point in world history has there been a greater number of individuals in a single city living in mental institutions and treatment centers than there are in Los Angeles in the twenty-first century.

In 1970, a Superior Court judge issues an order forcing the desegregation of Los Angeles schools. The judge survives an assassination attempt and loses his job in the next election.

A Friday and Dylan gets the afternoon off, he and Maddie go to the courthouse in Beverly Hills. There is another one closer but Maddie wants to go to Beverly Hills because she knows it's where the stars go to get their marriage licenses and she thinks it's funny and cool and exciting. They take a cab, go inside, stand in line, get the forms and fill them out, have them notarized. They turn them back in pay the fee $45 they get their license they have ninety days to have a ceremony, at which point they will be officially married.

After they get the license, they walk around Beverly Hills. They walk up and down perfectly manicured white streets lined with shops that sell bags for more than the average American makes every year, that sell diamonds for millions, that sell clothes for enough to feed small towns, they are streets designed to lure those with money and tempt those without there is no regard for those who have nothing, it's the American way, the American way. They stop in front of windows. Dylan brought some money with him $150 to buy her a present he quickly realizes $150 won't get her anything. Maddie is dazzled by the clothes she loves the fabrics the colors it's the clothing she sees on television and in magazines and she's too intimidated to go inside any of the stores, they just look through windows. They wander for an hour two Dylan wishes he had more money Maddie deserves what they're looking at as much as any of the women they see walking in and out of the shops, women wearing more in jewelry than he'll see in twenty years, women with fake faces fake bodies women complaining on their cell phones why, what do they have to complain about, is there really anything wrong. He holds Maddie's hand. He's embarrassed by the money in his pocket ashamed that there isn't more. She's excited about their marriage and Beverly Hills and seeing her happy makes him forget himself and the money or lack in his pocket and seeing her happy breaks his heart in a small way, each smile, each laugh, every time she looks at something and gets excited about it, happy, in a small way, it breaks.

She gets tired so they walk to a hotel there's a line of cabs they get into one of them and start heading towards their apartment. Dylan tells the cabbie to stop at a mall near their place Maddie asks why he says if we're going to get married you're going to need a dress. She laughs, says we're not having that kind of wedding, he says I love you and I want you to have something special. They pull up to the front get out of the cab Dylan pays the fare. Maddie smiles and takes Dylan's hand and kisses him on the cheek and they walk into the mall. There are two department stores at either end, a couple hundred other stores in between, a food court, a parking garage, a grocery store in the basement. It is a nice mall, more upscale than down, its clientele the upper middle class of West Los Angeles and Santa Monica and Westwood. Dylan asks Maddie where she wants to start she smiles and says let's just walk.

They walk, look through windows, occasionally Maddie goes into a clothing store picks something up runs her fingers along holds it in front of her body puts it back. Many of the clothes look similar to the clothes in Beverly Hills, there are slight differences in cut or pattern or material, huge differences in price. Maddie isn't intimidated by the stores or people in them she speaks to the saleswomen smiles when they compliment her ask if Dylan is her fiancé she always puts her arms around him and says yes. After an hour maybe more she's found two dresses one simple white linen the other light blue strapless one is in a department store the other in a chain. She tries them both on asks Dylan his opinion he doesn't care, thinks she's beautiful in both, they go to the food court and get sodas and she talks about each of them, why she likes them, why she doesn't, about the stores both are national the department store more upscale, she decides on the white one because it's a wedding dress, or something close to a wedding dress, simple white linen.

They go to the department store take the dress simple white linen off the rack. Dylan was scared to check the price while

Maddie was looking at it she hands it to him and says thank
you and kisses him and he carries it to the counter where a
woman stands behind a register she smiles at him, speaks.
Hi.
He speaks.
Hi.
Did you find everything you need today?
Dylan looks at Maddie, speaks.
Yes. Thank you.
The woman takes the dress scans it. Dylan is scared to look at
the total. Woman speaks.
One hundred thirty dollars and forty-four cents.
Dylan smiles pulls out his money hands her one hundred and
forty dollars she takes it gives him his change starts wrapping
the dress. Maddie smiles and says thank you and kisses Dylan.
Woman finishes with the dress, hands it to Maddie they walk
out of the mall hand-in-hand Maddie smiling talking about
how excited she is about the dress about how she made the
right decision about how it will be perfect for their ceremony,
however they decide to do it. They leave the mall stop at a fast-
food chicken restaurant on their walk home buy a bucket and
some baked beans and some macaroni 'n cheese and three
portions of chocolate pudding, one for Dylan two for Maddie.
They get home Dylan puts the chicken on the table Maddie
goes to their room. Dylan gets plates forks knives and napkins
sets the table as best he can, as he sits down, Maddie comes
out of the room. She's wearing her new dress. Simple white
linen to just below her knees. Thin straps over both shoulders.
Cut low enough to show some cleavage, but leave more to the
imagination. She walks to the table smiling and spins around
Dylan laughs. She starts posing like the stars in magazines
Dylan laughs she starts strutting around the apartment like a
model on a catwalk Dylan laughs. She stops in front of him,
speaks.
What do you think?
You're beautiful.

It fits well, don't you think.

Perfect.

You can't even tell I'm pregnant.

Nope.

I'm happy we'll be able to show our baby pictures of our wedding day and I'll be wearing a pretty dress.

Dylan smiles.

Yeah.

She smiles.

Thank you.

I'm happy we were able to get it.

She runs her hands down its front.

Except for my ring, I think it's the nicest thing I've ever owned.

His heart breaks, just a little.

You're beautiful in it.

She smiles again.

You said that already.

You are, you're beautiful.

She sits down on his lap, kisses him, it's a long deep kiss, one that neither wants to end they stand move into the bedroom still kissing hands moving she pulls away, smiles, speaks.

I don't want to mess it up.

She carefully takes off the dress, hangs it up Dylan sits on the edge of the bed watches her she turns around walks towards him he stands meets her they kiss, hands, tongues, his clothes, her remaining clothes they fall onto the bed onto each other into each other they forget about dinner about moving about their child they forget and feel each other feel on and in, feel, again, again again.

They sleep when Dylan wakes it's automatic now it's still dark. He gets out of bed goes to the bathroom brushes his teeth, puts on his deodorant, splashes cold water on his face another day hauling fucking golf bags. He walks out of the bathroom Maddie is in bed asleep on her back covers at her waist slowly and steadily breathing. He stops and stares for a minute, two, just stares at her face a shadow across the top half of her body slight rise emerging breasts filling out at the line of her neck at her hands one falling off the side of the bed at her hair long and thick still cascades across a white pillow at her mouth open slightly trembling with every breath. He kneels next to her he's scared to touch her or wake her he just wants to be near her and he whispers you are so beautiful and I love you and he kisses her cheek and his heart breaks, just a little it breaks.

He leaves walks to the course. He gets a cup of coffee says hello to the other caddies one of them says Shaka wants to speak to him. He walks to Shaka's office knocks on the door, which is half open. Shaka asks who is it Dylan says his name Shaka says come in. Dylan opens the door, steps in, Shaka motions for him to sit, speaks.

Morning.

Morning.

Feeling good today?

Yeah.

You get the license yesterday?

Yeah.

How'd it go?

It was pretty easy, pretty simple.

You ready to get married.

Dylan smiles.

Guess so.

Seriously, you ready to get married?

Yeah, I am. I'm excited about it.

I talked to my cousin. He's free tonight. And my wife can come be a witness.

Really?

You said you were ready.

Yeah, I am.

Then it's a go?

Where will we do it?

Here.

In your office?

On the course. Under a tree or some shit. Somewhere that looks nice.

Cool.

You got a suit at home?

No.

I didn't think so, so I brought one for you. It's my son's old suit, he's about your size. It's hanging on the door behind you.

Thanks.

You got a camera?

Nope.

One of my daughters wants to be a photographer and said she'd take pictures for you.

Awesome. Thanks.

I used to think she was just crackpotting, but she showed me some of her pictures and they're actually good, real good.

Awesome.

Maybe we'll get a pizza or something after?

Aren't I supposed to take my wife home to bed?

If you're gonna do it right, you're gonna need a meal beforehand.

Dylan laughs.

I guess so.

After your first round, you call your girl and make sure she can come. If she can I'll make some calls and make sure everyone's here.

What time?

Gets dark around 8:00. Last out will be around 5:00. If she doesn't have any plans, have her here at 8:15.

I know for a fact we don't have any plans.

You never know with a woman.

We don't have any friends except each other. We never have plans.

Shaka laughs.

Well maybe your lady and my lady will get along and then your lady will have a friend and start making plans on your ass.

Dylan laughs.

I'd actually sort of like that.

Yeah, just you wait.

Thanks for everything. We don't have any family out here, and the family we got at home is awful, and it's really cool you're helping us out.

You're okay for a white boy. And you're one of us now, a caddieing motherfucker, and we take care of our own.

Thank you.

Dylan stands, offers his hand, Shaka stands and takes it and they shake and Dylan looks like he might cry. Shaka pulls his hand, motions towards the door.

Get out there and make some money. Lord knows you're gonna need it.

Dylan laughs, leaves, gets in the caddie line, his first bag is a guy in dental school who spends most of the round talking about how much he hates public golf courses and how much he's going to enjoy making enough money to join a private club. When the round is over $40 tip he goes to the pay phone and calls Maddie who is awake, eating the previous night's chicken for breakfast. He asks her if she has any plans tonight she laughs he tells her he needs her to come to meet him at the course at 8:15 she asks why he says he has something fun for them to do she asks what and he says just come, and wear your new dress. She asks why and he says please just come and she giggles and says okay. He says I love you and she says I love you and they hang up.

His next bag is an actor the man, who is tall dark and handsome in his late twenties, gets upset when Dylan doesn't recognize him and he asks Dylan if he lives in a fucking cave. Dylan asks what's he been in and the man says one of the biggest soap operas in the history of television Dylan asks why he doesn't belong to a private club the man says he does but sometimes he likes to play amongst *real* people. Dylan asks which club the man tells Dylan to stop asking questions and for the rest of the round the only time the man speaks to

Dylan is when he hits a good shot and wants Dylan to tell him how good a shot it is. When the round is finished the man gives Dylan $10 says thanks gets in a Mercedes drives away. It's 4:00 Dylan starts to get a little nervous. His chance at another bag comes up he takes it, it's a woman who works as a hairdresser and is learning to play golf because she thinks it might help her land a husband. She's playing with a friend who is also a hairdresser it is the friend's first time on a course, Dylan hopes they get frustrated and quit early. They score a nine and fourteen respectively on the first hole, a par four that is considered one of the easiest holes on the course. They score thirteen and seventeen on the second hole, a par five. They score ten and twelve on the third hole, a par three. They're laughing at themselves, and having fun, but also know that they are keeping the golfers behind them waiting, so they decide to play one more hole, it's a par four they score fifteen and seventeen, they decide to get some drinks and spend some time at the driving range. Dylan carries their bags to their cars, they tip him $50 because they know how it is to survive on tips they tell him they hope to see him again.

It's 5:15 three hours or so until he gets married. He's very nervous he wonders if he needs to get anything he goes to Shaka's office knocks on the door. Shaka speaks.

Come in.

Dylan steps in, Shaka is at his desk, he's reading a book on investing, he looks up, speaks.

Ready?

I don't know.

What time is it?

A little after five.

And you don't know if you're ready?

I'm ready, like I'm ready to do it, but I don't know if I'm ready like I have everything.

You need your woman, an officiant, a couple witnesses, rings. You got those things, you're ready.

No rings.

You don't got no fucking rings?

Dylan laughs.

No.

Goddamn, I'm less impressed with white people every day. You and Asshole Dan ain't got half a brain between you.

Dylan laughs again. Shaka stands up.

Come with me.

He walks out of the office, Dylan follows him they go to the parking lot get into Shaka's car, a ten-year-old Japanese sedan kept in perfect condition they drive a mile or two they pull into a mini-mall park in front of a pawn shop. Shaka looks at Dylan, speaks.

Now, I'm gonna tell you some shit that could get me in trouble, so you gotta promise to keep a lid on it.

No problem.

I play golf now and then. When I was younger I was good. Occasionally I play for money. People always think they're gonna beat me, but they rarely do. Because they think they're gonna beat me, they bet more than they can afford to lose, and then they gotta give me shit to cover their bet, usually watches or jewelry or something like that. I bring the shit here and hawk it. I'm friends with the guy, he'll be good to us.

Shaka opens the door gets out of the car, Dylan follows they walk into the shop it's filled with musical instruments, stereos, televisions, guns case after case of guns, jewelry case after case of jewelry. The owner, a middle-aged white man in a golf shirt, looks like a suburban banker. He says hello to Shaka they shake hands and chat while Dylan looks at the rings. After a minute or two the man comes over stands in front of Dylan, speaks.

You want new ones or used ones?

Aren't they all used?

Nope. Got people come in all the time to sell rings before they actually get married.

Really?

Sometimes they're broke, sometimes they change their minds

before they go through with it, sometimes the rings are probably stolen, though I'm not allowed to know that.
I'd rather have new ones.
Probably best.
Man opens a case and pulls out a black felt ring display puts it on the counter. He pulls four sets of rings places them on the glass, speaks.
Take your pick.
Dylan looks at them three gold one silver or platinum he can't tell two have inscriptions in them he sets those apart the other two are blank one set is wider, with an elaborate pattern engraved, the other pair simple gold the man's ring slightly wider than the woman's. Dylan picks them up speaks.
How much?
How much you make today?
A hundred bucks.
Give me fifty.
Seriously?
Shaka's a friend. You seem like a nice guy. Be sort of a wedding gift from me to you.
Dylan smiles.
Thank you.
He takes out fifty bucks, hands it to the man. The man takes it says good luck, shakes Shaka's hand says see you soon, Shaka and Dylan walk out of the store. As Dylan gets in the car he thanks Shaka who smiles says no problem they drive back to the course Dylan doesn't say a word just stares at the rings plays with them, rolls them through his fingers, holds them to the light kisses them.
They pull up it's 6:45 business day is coming to an end the parking lot is half empty. Caddies who might normally be at home are hanging around, talking on their cells, some are wearing nicer clothing than they normally wear dress shirts, slacks, sandals, belts. Dylan asks Shaka what's going on and Shaka smiles and says we're having a wedding. He walks back to his office. Dylan follows asking questions, Shaka says the

same thing over and over just wait and see, white boy, just wait and see. He gives Dylan the suit and a shirt and a tie and a pair of shoes says go to the locker room and shower and get ready.

Dylan walks to the locker room, which caddies are not normally allowed to use. It's filled with other caddies showering and putting on nice clothing. All of them shake his hand and say congratulations he's shocked and thrilled and can't really believe it's happening. There are two men in the locker who are golfers and though they have no idea what's going on they say congratulations to him as well. He takes a shower. Gets out of the shower puts on the suit it's slightly small but fits well enough to wear. He combs his hair. He puts on the shoes he becomes more nervous with each passing minute wonders what Maddie is doing, what she's thinking, if she knows, how she'll react when she arrives. It's not exactly what he expected, or thought of when he thought of their wedding, getting married at a golf course in Los Angeles with his coworkers, a bunch of black and Mexican caddies, but he's happy about it, excited, thinks it's another part of their adventure, something they'll be able to talk about when they're fifty, sixty, seventy, something their children will tell their children.

He looks at himself in the mirror. He looks good enough the suit is sort of funny. He checks his pockets the rings are inside of the jacket. He walks out of the locker room he sees chairs being set up in two sections, with an aisle between, on the grass in front of the clubhouse. It's 7:30 in forty-five minutes he's getting married he wonders what Maddie is doing, how she's feeling. He walks over offers to help with the chairs the four caddies setting them up two Mexican, one Salvadoran one black say no go to Shaka's office and relax. He walks to Shaka's office and knocks on the door.

Come in.

He opens the door, steps in, Shaka is wearing a suit, a large man, who looks like Shaka's brother, but slightly older, is sitting in the chair across from his desk. The man, who is wearing a long black robe, stands. Shaka speaks.

Dylan, meet my cousin Khama. Khama, this is him.

Dylan and Khama both laugh, shake hands. Khama speaks.

A big day for you.

Dylan smiles.

Yeah.

You excited?

Yes.

You have anything in particular you'd like to say during the ceremony?

No.

What religion are you?

I'm not, really. My parents used to go to a Baptist church, but that was so they wouldn't feel guilty about drinking and cheating and beating each other up.

I'm sorry.

Nothing to be sorry about. It was what it was. My girl's parents are the same way.

I hope you're going to avoid making the same mistakes.

It's why we left. Came here.

It wasn't so you could be married by a black man named after an African king?

Dylan laughs.

You too?

Yes. Shaka and I and every male member of our family. We often argue about whose namesake was greater.

Shaka speaks.

Mine was.

Khama speaks.

This is a joyful occasion, so I won't engage him.

They laugh. Khama speaks.

It's okay if I just use the standard vows?

Yes.

The whole thing will take about five minutes. Just follow my lead. Before it starts we'll wait for her at the end of the aisle.

Shaka speaks.

My wife is gonna wait for her in the parking lot and show her where to go.

What if she freaks out?

My wife is very good at dealing with people who freak out.

They laugh again. Khama speaks.

Any questions?

Thank you for doing this.

Is that a question?

Dylan laughs.

No, I just wanted to say thank you.

My pleasure.

Dylan looks at Shaka, speaks.

How'd you plan this so fast?

I just told everybody you were getting married, that we were gonna do it here. Usually when one of us gets married, everyone goes. In this case we didn't have to go anywhere. And who doesn't like a wedding? You can get drunk and dance and act stupid and your wife lets you do it.

They laugh.

Thank you too. For everything.

Shaka nods.

You're one of my boys here. I treat my boys well.

Thank you.

You wanna have a quick drink before we get out there?

Fuck yeah.

They all laugh again, Shaka reaches into his jacket pocket pulls out a small flask of whiskey he and Shaka each take a drink Khama passes on it. They leave the office and walk back to the grass in front of the clubhouse. The sun is down it's getting dark. The chairs are set up and most are filled, the other caddies are sitting in them with their wives and children, the aisle between them is lined with flashlights their beams shooting straight into the sky. As Dylan walks down the aisle the assembled whistle at him, say congratulations, Asshole Dan, who is there with his surprisingly attractive wife, stands and shakes his hand. He and Khama go to a small half-circle of flowers placed on the ground at the head of the area, stand in the middle of it, it's just after 8:00.

He stands for two minutes, three minutes five minutes seven. He rocks back and forth on his heels, fidgets with his suit, stares at the ground looks up and smiles looks back at the ground. He turns to Khama who is standing with his hands folded at his waist a small black book in one of his hands Khama nods. He looks at Shaka, who is standing at the foot of the aisle, there is a chair with a boom box on it next to him, Shaka smiles and gives Dylan a thumbs-up. Dylan looks towards the lot, he can't see much from where he is, he can't see the entrance or the exit, he can't see where Maddie would naturally walk into the lot, he can't see Shaka's wife waiting for her. The longer he stands the more nervous he becomes, the more he wants to see Maddie, just see her, face smile walk dress he wants her near him, he waits and smiles and his fellow caddies sitting in the chairs in front of him watch him and smile at him Shaka watches him, smiles at him, even Asshole Dan is smiling at him.

He sees her come around the corner. She looks nervous slightly confused excited, she's smiling she sees him, he smiles lifts a hand a small wave. She shrugs he motions for her to come to him she looks around and sees the chairs, the people, Shaka pushes play on the boom box she smiles and laughs and he motions for her to come to him.

Maddie starts walking towards the aisle, she's carrying a bouquet of flowers. Shaka's wife, a tall thick dark-skinned woman in a pink dress, follows a couple feet behind. She turns up the aisle and Dylan can feel his hands start shaking, she's wearing her dress, smiling, not paying attention to anything else, anyone else. Each step she's closer their eyes are locked each step his pounding heart, shaking hands, each step he feels happier, stronger, each step there's no one else in the world he loves. As she gets closer she walks quicker he's not sure what to do but he wants to touch her all he wants to do is touch her.

437

He opens his arms she runs the last few steps into them and he closes them around her. She says what is this he says our wedding she giggles he whispers in her ear I love you I love you I love you.

The assembled laugh the wedding march doesn't usually end this way. Dylan and Maddie stand there holding each other for a moment, two. Shaka, who followed his wife up the aisle, sits in the front row, she sits next to him. Khama clears his throat Dylan and Maddie both look towards him the assembled laugh again. They separate, Khama speaks.

I usually counsel young couples before they get married to make sure they are getting married for the right reasons. What I have just seen tells me no counsel is necessary here.

Everyone laughs a few clap. Khama looks at Maddie, speaks.

Young lady, my name is Khama, and before we get started I'd like to introduce myself and say congratulations.

He offers his hand she smiles and takes it and speaks.

Nice to meet you.

You as well.

He looks briefly at both of them.

Shall we get started?

They both speak.

Yes.

Khama turns to the assembled welcomes them, turns back to Maddie and Dylan, who are standing facing each other, holding both of each other's hands, he asks them if they are ready for their vows. Without looking away from each other they both say yes. Dylan goes first he repeats I Dylan take you Maddie to be your wedded husband, I promise to love comfort, honor and keep you for better or worse, for richer or poorer, in sickness and in health, forsaking all others, I will be faithful to you so long as we both shall live. As he does his voice cracks tears run down his cheeks Maddie squeezes his hands they look into each other. She follows him says the same vows, her voice cracks she happily cries Dylan squeezes her hands their eyes into each other. When they are finished Khama asks for

438

the rings Dylan reaches into his coat pocket hands shaking he fumbles the rings catches them everyone laughs. He hands them to Khama, who hands one of them back to him, speaks.

You're going to need this.

More laughs, Dylan smiles speaks.

Thanks.

Khama.

Repeat after me. With this ring, I thee wed, I give it to you as a symbol of my vows, my love and my commitment, and with all that I am, and all that I have.

Dylan repeats, places the ring on Maddie's finger both of their hands shake still smiling. Khama turns to Maddie, hands her the other ring. They repeat the process still shaking smiling Khama speaks.

In the name of the Father, the Son and the Holy Ghost, and by the power vested in me by the State of California, I now pronounce you man and wife.

He turns to Dylan.

You may kiss your bride.

Huge smiles they lean forward and their lips meet as husband and wife their lips meet and open a long deep kiss. The assembled starts clapping and whistling. They keep kissing, their arms around each other long and deep. Khama smiles, laughs, they keep going, the clapping gets louder, the whistling more frequent, they're lost in each other found with each other holding each other, kissing each other. Shaka pushes play on the boom box wedding procession music starts playing Maddie and Dylan pull apart whisper I love you to each other turn smiling to face the assembled. They start walking hand-in-hand down the aisle, everyone stands as they pass still clapping and whistling. When they reach the end of the aisle, Shaka, and his daughter, who has been taking pictures, are waiting for them. Shaka speaks.

Congratulations.

They both speak.

Thank you.

Shaka.

Surprised?

Maddie laughs.

Totally. Who are all these people?

Dylan.

The other caddies.

Shaka.

Except for me, and I used to be one, and the fat white guy,
who we call Asshole Dan, he runs the place.

Maddie laughs.

Dylan told me about him.

Shaka.

And me?

Maddie.

If you're Shaka, he told me about you too.

I am, and he better have been cool, or this wedding is over.

They laugh. Shaka speaks.

You ready for the next part?

Dylan.

What's that?

Dancing, drinking and eating. I told you you're gonna need
some sustenance if you're gonna perform like you should later.

They laugh.

Where we gonna do it?

Right here.

On the course?

Right the fuck here.

Shaka steps away, starts barking out orders, the chairs are
rearranged into something resembling a circle, the disks are
changed in the boom box, coolers full of beer are brought out
from the clubhouse. The other caddies and their wives or
girlfriends form a line, start walking up to Dylan and Maddie,
congratulating them, handing them white envelopes. When the
line is finished, everyone is dancing, drinking, pizzas have
arrived they're eating. Dylan and Maddie join them Dylan
drinks but not too much Maddie sips at a beer, but never

finishes. They separate the men make fun of Dylan, warn him about what he's gotten himself into, the women talk to Maddie about her dress, about children, about dealing with their husbands. They have a first dance to a song they don't know a slow, soul song when the dance ends they're kissing again the other couples cheering and whistling again. A cake is brought out it's white cake with white frosting from a grocery store they cut it, feed it to each other, lick it from each other's fingers. The party lasts an hour two three most of the assembled are drunk some start stumbling some of their wives take them home some of them take their wives home. Dylan and Maddie start to get tired they find Khama thank him, find Shaka and thank him. Shaka tells Dylan to take the day off tomorrow and guard the envelopes on the way home it is tradition for all of the caddies to give their day's tips to the groom on his wedding day. Dylan thanks Shaka again, hugs him, Maddie thanks him and his wife hugs them, they walk home hand-in-hand as man and wife. When they get home they get into bed Dylan's nourishment serves him well, serves Maddie well, for the first second and third time as man and wife.

Tom Bradley, an African American, is elected mayor in 1973, defeating incumbent Sam Yorty, who is white, in a campaign in which Bradley accuses Yorty of racism and Yorty questions Bradley's ability to fight crime in his own community. Bradley becomes the first minority mayor of Los Angeles, and the second African-American mayor of a major American city.

Old Man Joe walks back to the boardwalk as he approaches his bathroom he sees an LAPD cruiser sitting near it. He doesn't want to deal with the police immediately so he walks to the liquor store he doesn't have enough money for a bottle of Chablis so he buys a bottle of Thunderbird and goes behind the liquor store and starts drinking it. It's strong and tastes like grape juice mixed with gasoline, it's far more powerful than Chablis after four or five long draws he's suitably buzzed to deal with the police he hides the bottle under a dumpster and walks back to the bathroom.

The cruiser is still there, an officer is leaning against the hood, another is sitting in the driver's seat. Neither sees him until he's a few feet and he speaks.

Officers?

They both look up. The one on the hood speaks.

Yeah?

Are you waiting here for me?

The one behind the driver's seat gets out of the car, the other speaks.

What's your name?

Old Man Joe.

The one from the driver's seat speaks.

Yeah, we are. You carrying anything?

No.

You mind if we search you?

No.

Joe raises his arms, they pat him down. Joe speaks.

Am I being arrested for something?

The one from the hood.

Not at this point. You're wanted for questioning.

Did you catch them?

Driver's seat.

We're not completely sure who they are. That's why we need you.

Okay, let's go.

Driver's seat opens the rear door Joe gets inside there's a cage in front of him door closes there are no handles on the inside of it. The police get into the front seats, start the car, pull away. The drive to the station takes fifteen minutes it's six or seven miles through Venice, Mar Vista, Culver City, Joe can't remember the last time he was this far away from the ocean. He stares out the window the streets are crowded with cars the sidewalks are empty not a person to be seen. They pass minimalls, fast-food restaurants, three- and four-story apartment buildings, gas stations, discount stores. They drive under a highway it looks like a parking lot. The sun is high and hot everything's bright the signs the storefront windows with reflective glass the cars trucks the concrete the buildings painted bright colors faded into depression. They drive and he stares and no one says a word.

They pull up park behind the station the officers let him out. Though he hasn't been arrested it feels like he has they walk him into the station stand on either side of him they're close to prevent him from walking away, making any sort of quick movement. They put him in a room beige walls a table and three chairs a one-way mirrored window, they tell him someone will be in to see him. When they leave he tries the door, even though he's not under arrest, is locked.

He sits and waits stares at the wall cleans his fingernails picks at them a bit. The T-bird starts to wear off a headache starts to replace the buzz, he wants more, he wants water, he wants coffee, he wants aspirin, something. He stares at the wall picks his nose rubs the results on the bottom of the table, he sits and waits. The walls are beige. He's hungry he wants something to eat.

The door opens and two middle-aged, tired-looking men in suits come in one is white one is black both of their suits are blue, the white one has a mustache. They both have sodas with them they sit down across from him. The white one speaks.

I'm Detective Sullivan.

Black one speaks.

Detective Jackson.

Old Man Joe nods. Sullivan speaks.

Your name?

Old Man Joe.

Jackson speaks.

That your street name?

It's my name.

Sullivan.

What's your real name?

Does it matter?

Jackson.

It might.

When it does, I'll give it to you.

Jackson looks at Sullivan, who frowns. Jackson looks back at Joe.

Tell us what happened.

What do you guys know?

Sullivan.

Listen, man, we're trying to figure out what happened with this guy. We don't need any shit from you. Just tell us what the fuck happened so we can get on with it.

Can I have a soda?

Jackson.

What kind?

I don't care.

Sullivan pushes his, a diet cola, across the table.

Thank you.

Joe opens it, takes a sip, sets it down. He tells them what happened, they take notes, when he's done, they set down their pens. Jackson looks at Sullivan, who shrugs. Jackson turns back to Joe, speaks.

What the fuck were you thinking?

What do you mean?

You make fucking shields and get clubs and go marching down the fucking boardwalk like knights or some shit?

I wanted to help the girl.

Sullivan speaks.

She want your help?

I don't know. I don't think she knows.

Jackson.

Was it worth your friend's life?

No.

Sullivan.

You traded your friend's life for some fucked-up girl.

I was just trying to help.

Jackson.

You fucked up.

I know.

Sullivan.

You killed your friend.

I know.

Jackson.

One of the dumbest fucking things I've ever heard of.

Joe gets pissed.

I fucking know, okay? Now why don't you stop fucking telling me how stupid I am and go get the motherfuckers that did it.

Sullivan.

You want to go to jail?

Joe stares at the table, shakes his head.

If you want to go to jail, keep talking to us like that and that's where you'll go, you understand me?

Joe stares at the table, nods.

Jackson.

Can you identify the shooter, his friend, and the girl?

Yes.

Sullivan.

You know their names?

The girl's name is Beatrice. I don't know the guys' names.

Jackson.

Beatrice what?

No idea.

Sullivan.

You know where they are?

The boardwalk, I guess. I don't know.
Jackson.
Where on the boardwalk?
The north end of it, near Rose, near where you found the body.
Sullivan.
You wanna take a ride with us, see if we can find them?
Not really.
Sullivan.
Why not?
Because I don't.
Jackson.
Don't like cops?
No, I'm okay with cops. Like some of them. Don't like others. Just depends.
Don't like us?
You're fine.
Sullivan.
Just don't want to help us.
I just want to go home.
Sullivan.
To the bathroom?
Yeah. I want to go to my bathroom and get drunk and hate myself for a while.
You should fucking hate yourself for a long while. A good long while.
Joe nods.
I know.
Sullivan looks at Jackson, who motions towards the door. They stand and leave. Joe sits in the room for another hour. Just sits and hates himself. When the door opens a uniformed officer steps in, tells him to get up, they walk out of the station house, the officer leads him to a car, opens the back door, Joe gets back into the cage. The officer drives him back to Venice, drops him in front of the bathroom. As the car pulls away Joe walks back to the liquor store, buys another bottle of

447

Thunderbird, walks behind the liquor store, pulls his first bottle out from beneath the dumpster. He sits down and he starts drinking and spends the night getting drunk and hating himself.

In 1975 the Los Angeles Police Department admits to keeping secret files on almost 6,000 citizens of the city. The files were profiles of suspected communists, black and Mexican community leaders, potential spies, and enemies of the city government.

Los Angeles is the capital of many things. It is the entertainment capital of the world. It is the pornography capital of the world. It is the defense and aerospace capital of the world. It is the street-gang capital of the world. It is the beauty-queen-hoping-to-be-rich-and-famous capital of the world. It is the crazy-person capital of the world. It is the artist capital of the world. It is the immigration capital of the world. It is also, most unfortunately, the major-city-that-gets-tagged-by-natural-disasters capital of the world. All of the others, debatably, are good, or at least interesting, and there are cities around the world that would gladly take the titles away from them (Caracas, Venezuela, actually sued for the title of craziest and lost in court at The Hague). Nobody, repeat nobody nobody nobody, wants to take away the title of major-city-that-gets-tagged-by-natural-disasters capital of the world. Not one fucking place wants that one. No fucking thank you.

Why, one might ask, would a city be so unlucky? Does God Hate Los Angeles? Maybe. Does it have bad karma? Some think Los Angeles is too young to have any real karma. Does something about Los Angeles force the elements to conspire against it and attempt to destroy it? Don't know the answer to that one. All that can be said is that shit goes hideously wrong in Los Angeles all the time, and that nature really kicks its fucking ass. Here is a brief, brief history of natural disasters in Los Angeles from the date of its founding in 1781 until the year 2000 (after the year 2000, many people believe we entered the biblically foretold End of Days and everything that happened after that is definitely God's fucking fault).

September 8, 1781. Four days after the founding of Los Angeles, a flash flood washes away all of the settlers' building supplies.

1783. Drought lasts eleven months killing most of settlement's crops.

1790. Drought lasts fourteen months killing
most of settlement's crops.

1796. Earthquake destroys more than half of existing structures
in the settlement. Four dead, twelve injured.

1805. Drought lasts ten months destroys first orange grove in
southern California and most of settlement's crops.

1811. Massive flood wipes out large sections of the village.

1812. Earthquake kills 40 people, destroys majority of village's
buildings.

1815. Massive flood. Kills fourteen people.
Wipes away large sections of the village. The Pueblo of
Los Angeles is moved to higher ground.

1818. Series of floods wipes away large sections of town, kills
40 people. Pueblo is moved to higher ground for a second time.

1819. Wildfire destroys most of town's crops.

1820. Drought lasts ten months, destroys most of town's crops.

1827. Earthquake.
Fifty buildings destroyed, 75 people dead.

1829. Wildfire destroys 20 farms on the outskirts of city,
kills 4 people.

1832. Massive floods destroy 20 buildings, kill 20 people.

1838. Drought lasts 9 months, wipes out most of city's crops,
destroys orange groves.

1844. Flooding kills 15 people.

1850. Wildfire destroys 30 farms, 20 homes, 1 school, 11 people
dead.

1856. Earthquake.
Seven buildings destroyed, 1 dead.

1857. Earthquake.
Twenty-six buildings destroyed, 4 people dead.

1859. Massive flooding.

1862. Massive flooding.

1863. Flooding through the first part of the year,
followed by a 14-month drought that destroys all of the city's
crops and most of its livestock.

1864. Smallpox kills most of remaining Native American
population and 350 residents of the city.

1865. Tsunami destroys 30 ships in the Port of Los Angeles.

1867. Massive flooding. Rainstorm that lasts seven days,
destroys most of the city's roads and creates a lake in
downtown Los Angeles.

1869. Mudslides kill 11.

1872. Earthquake.
Ten buildings destroyed, 4 people dead.

1875. Wildfire destroys 1,000 acres.

1879. Wildfire destroys 4,000 acres, kills 3 people.

1884. Flood changes the course of the Los Angeles river so that
it flows through the center of downtown, destroys 15 buildings.

1888. Massive flooding. Six people die.

1891. Massive flooding. Eight people die.

1894. Wildfire destroys 500 acres of farmland. Mudslides close
roads in Santa Monica and kill 4 people.

1899. Drought wipes out orange groves, 2 people die.

1901. Flooding destroys four homes. Mudslides kill 6.

1904. Drought lasts 8 months.

1909. Drought lasts 10 months.

1912. Earthquake.
Seven buildings destroyed, 1 dead.

1914. Massive flooding. Destroys 30 buildings,
wipes out roads and rail tracks, shuts down Los Angeles
Harbor, $10 million in damages.

1916. Earthquake. Destroys 22 buildings, kills 6 people.

1922. Wildfire destroys 700 acres, 60 homes, kills 2 people.

1926. Flooding. Mudslides close roads throughout the western
half of the city, destroy 4 homes, kill 1 person.

1933. Earthquake. Destroys 250 buildings, kills 120 people,
$75 million in damages.

1934. Two separate floods. First kills 40 people,
second kills 45 people.

1938. Massive floods kill 80 people and cause
$35 million in damages. Mudslides kill 12 more people
and cause $5 million in damages.

1941. Earthquake registers 4.8 on the Richter scale.
Floods submerge downtown Los Angeles. Second earthquake
also registers 4.8 on Richter scale.

1942. Floods submerge downtown Los Angeles.

1943. Floods submerge downtown Los Angeles.

1944. Floods submerge downtown Los Angeles.

1947. Mudslides kill 6 in Santa Monica and Malibu.

1949. Wildfires destroy 200 acres and 12 homes.

1951. Earthquake registers 5.9 on the Richter scale.

1952. Earthquake registers 6.0 on the Richter scale.

Seven people are killed, $25 million in damages.

1954. Smog prevents airplanes from landing and ships from docking for three days.

1961. Fire destroys 484 homes and 21 other buildings in Brentwood and Bel-Air, causes $120 million in damage.

1963. Baldwin Hills Dam collapses releasing millions of gallons of water on the local community. One hundred homes destroyed, 5 dead, $60 million in damages.

1969. Massive floods and mudslides kill 93 people, destroy 105 homes, and cause $500 million in damages.

1971. Earthquake registers 6.6 on the Richter scale. It kills 70 people and causes $550 million in damages. Another fire in Bel-Air destroys 90 homes and kills 3 people and causes $80 million in damages.

1978. Wildfire destroys 40,000 acres of land and 300 homes, kills 11 people.

1979. Earthquake registers 5.2 on the Richter scale. Mudslides destroy 40 homes.

1980. Long Beach levees break and cause flooding in the area, $20 million in damages.

1981. Fruit fly infestation destroys remaining orange groves, $40 million in damages.

1987. Fruit fly reappears, destroying most of the remaining agriculture industry. Earthquake registers 5.9 on the Richter scale. Kills 10 people and causes $450 million in damages.

1988. Fruit fly appears yet again and destroys all of the remaining agriculture industry. Earthquake registers 5.0 on the Richter scale, $10 million in damages.

1989. Earthquake registers 5.1 on the Richter scale, $17 million in damages. Second earthquake registers 5.0 on the Richter scale, does $34 million in damages.

1991. Earthquake registers 5.8 on the Richter scale, 2 people are killed, $60 million in damages.

1992. Flooding causes $15 million in damages, mudslides kill 6 people.

1994. The motherfucking Big One. Earthquake registers 6.7 on the Richter scale. Seventy people die and there is $20 billion in damages.

1997. El Niño storms hit the coast, do $50 million in damages.

1998. El Niño storms continue to pound the coast, do $50 million more in damages.

In 1976, in a bicentennial effort to alleviate massive traffic jams, Los Angeles opens the nation's first carpool-only freeway lanes.

Amberton and Kurchenko sit in a fast-food restaurant in Koreatown. Amberton is wearing a disguise, sunglasses and a long black wig and a long black beard and belly suit that makes him look slightly pregnant. Kurchenko is eating a fishwich and onion rings and drinking a milkshake, Amberton refuses to eat. Everyone else in the restaurant is Korean, and no one is speaking English, so they speak openly. Kurchenko speaks.

So what do you want me to do?

Amberton speaks.

I'm not sure yet.

I'm tired of waiting. You need to decide. One of the kids, his mother or his grandmother, or him. I think the kids, but you decide.

He hurt me really bad.

I no care about that.

I'm still in pain.

Then one of the kids. That will break his heart.

I think him.

Okay. I don't like blacks, so him is fine.

Maybe break his leg.

I'll shoot him in the knee. Much worse than a breaking.

Make sure it's his good knee.

I'll shoot both knees.

That'll be good. That'll be really good.

Shotgun with a slug blows them to bits.

The worse the better.

Now we discuss payment.

Same as usual.

No, I no want money.

What do you want?

I want to get my Screen Actors Guild union card. I want role in your next film.

I'll try.

No. No try. You agree to do it and you do it or I leave and no shotgun to the knees.

Okay. Fine. I'll do it.

I want to be good guy. Someone who saves a woman or a priest. Someone I can show to my mother and say that is me, Momma, saving a woman or a priest on the big screen.

I understand.

It is the American Dream.

It's one of them.

And Screen Actors Guild has good medical insurance. It's a double win for my mother because she see her son a hero and she get to go to good doctor for her teeth.

Dentist.

What you say?

Never mind.

You understand the terms of the deal?

Yes.

I shoot out his legs to bits and I get to be in your movie.

Yes.

We shake on it.

Okay.

They shake hands, as they do it, Kurchenko stares at Amberton, looks him dead in the eye, squeezes Amberton's hand. Satisfied with whatever it is he sees, he grunts, nods, lets go, and starts eating his fishwich again. Amberton looks out the window, another sunny day just like the last one, and the one before, just like the next one, and the one after. He turns back into the restaurant sees a white man with a digital tape recorder staring at him, walking towards him. In the same way a dog can smell fear, Amberton can smell a reporter. He kicks Kurchenko under the table, motions towards the man, who arrives, stops in front of them, holds out the digital recorder, speaks.

Wondering if you have any comment on the lawsuit against you, Mr. Parker.

Kurchenko stands. The reporter takes a step back. Kurchenko speaks.

What you say?

I would like to speak with Mr. Parker?

Who?

Amberton Parker. Right there. In the disguise.

Kurchenko speaks.

That's no international superstar Amberton Parker. That's my cousin Yakov Zaionchkovsky.

No, sir. That's Amberton Parker, and he's about to get sued for sexually harassing another man.

Kurchenko swats the recorder away, yells.

Go away little man with voice machine and pencil. You disappear now.

The reporter scrambles after the recorder. Amberton stands and he and Kurchenko rush out of the restaurant. As they're getting into a small innocuous Japanese sedan from the mid-'80s, they see the reporter coming out after them. Amberton starts yelling at Kurchenko.

Go go go go.

As Kurchenko starts the car and puts it into gear, Amberton pushes the passenger's seat back and crawls into the space on the floor between the seat and dash. He's still screaming.

GO GO GO GO GO.

Kurchenko floors it and they fly out of the lot he cuts straight across traffic drives away Amberton still screaming.

GO GO GO.

Kurchenko smacks him on the top of his head, speaks.

Shut up. I go. We already away.

You don't understand, they'll follow us.

There's just one. And I have training in evasive driving. We are gone from him.

Amberton curls up.

I'm ruined.

Shut up.

I am. I'm ruined.

He's one little fellow. I'll take him out to desert and feed him to buzzards.

You can't do anything. All operations are off.

No. We shake. We look in the eyes. I still get my Screen Actors Guild union card. My mother needs a doctor.

You don't understand.

I don't care. We make deal and deal is still good.

I'll get you your part if I can. What you don't understand is I may never work again.

One reporter no big deal. They say you do bad things you just deny them. That is the way of this land.

Amberton breaks down, starts crying, sobbing into his hands. Kurchenko takes Amberton's phone, which is in the center console, and tosses it on the floor. He speaks.

I no want to hear you blubber. Call your wife. Blubber to her.

Amberton sobs. There are tears running down his face, snot running from his nose, drool running from the sides of his mouth. All of it is gathering in his fake beard. He picks up the phone, looks at it, pushes a couple buttons, reads a text message. He looks up at Kurchenko, looks slightly more composed, speaks.

You know where my agency is?

Yes, I do. It is my dream to have agent there.

Get me there as soon as you can.

Can I come in with you?

No.

Then I drop you at hotel.

I'll take you another time. I promise.

And our other deal is sealed.

Yes. Fine. Just get me there. As fast as you can.

Kurchenko starts driving towards the agency. Amberton gets off the floor and sits in the seat. He makes a call tells someone he's on his way, hangs up. He opens the visor mirror and starts taking off his disguise. As he pulls off the beard, he winces, and there are splotches on his face where the glue holding it onto his skin resisted removal. He runs his fingers through his hair, smiles, polishes his teeth with the tip of one of his fingers. Twenty minutes later, they're in

Beverly Hills, as they approach the agency building, Kurchenko speaks.

It is the most beautiful place in the world.

Amberton looks over at him.

How do I look?

Kurchenko looks at him.

Your face is red.

Red, really red, or just sort of red?

Kurchenko looks back at the building.

I like to get married in that building.

Please tell me, red or really red or just sort of red?

They pull up to the entrance.

I heard all the girl secretaries wear short skirts and no underwear.

Amberton opens the door, steps out. As he walks towards the doors, Kurchenko lowers the window, yells.

Good luck to you, my friend. See you on the set!

Amberton walks inside. He walks past the receptionists, who stare at him, and goes directly to Gordon's office. He walks past Gordon's assistants and opens the door and goes inside and closes the door behind him. Gordon is on the phone, he motions for Amberton to sit, Amberton does. Gordon says he needs to go to whomever he is speaking to, hangs up the phone, looks at Amberton, speaks.

You gain some weight?

No. I'm wearing a prosthetic stomach.

Jesus fucking Christ. Is it that bad this time?

I don't know.

Why is your face red?

How red is it?

It's really fucking red.

I was wearing a fake beard and the glue was stickier than I thought.

Goddamnit, Amberton.

What do you want to do?

Your attorneys are in the conference room waiting for us.
They got here quick.
You pay them a lot of money. For something like this, they
better get here fucking quick.
Let's go see them.
I need to talk to you, the agency's attorneys are in there with
them.
Why?
Because Kevin fucking works here. He's going after us as well.
Can he do that?
Yes, he can fucking do that.
Oh.
Gordon stares at Amberton for a moment. Amberton looks at
the picture, a million-dollar painting of three women having
sex, hanging on the wall behind him. A moment, two.
Amberton speaks.
That painting is kind of hot. Not hot, you know, in my way,
but Casey would probably like it.
Gordon speaks.
You need to focus, Amberton. It's bad this time.
I know.
We need to deal with this immediately before it becomes
something we do not want.
I know.
Go to the bathroom and wash your face and take off your
stomach and put on the spare suit in the closet in there.
What kind of suit is it?
It's nice, okay? It's a nice fucking suit.
Great.
Amberton stands walks to the bathroom, goes in closes the
door. He looks at himself in the mirror. He has what appears
to be the outline of a beard, except that instead of being dark
brown, which is the natural color of his facial hair, it is red.
He opens the medicine cabinet a toothbrush, toothpaste, a
second toothbrush still in its packaging, deodorant, six types of
cologne. He takes each of the colognes out, opens them one at

a time and smells them, he likes one called Hong Kong Silent Thunder, he applies it liberally to his wrists and neck. He closes the medicine cabinet, looks at his face, it's still red, he turns on the cold water and starts splashing it on, it feels good but doesn't change the way he looks. He runs some water through his hair, it always looks better slightly wet, takes off his clothes looks at himself in the mirror from one angle he thinks he looks perfect, from another he thinks he looks awful. He puts on the suit it is a nice suit lightweight gray gabardine with subtle white pinstripes it fits surprisingly well. He tries to decide tie or no tie he puts it on, takes it off, puts it back on, there's a knock on the door, Gordon speaks.

We need to get going, Amberton.

Amberton speaks.

Almost ready.

He looks in the mirror. For the first time since he walked into the agency, he thinks about why he's here, what he has to go deal with, he puts his hands on either side of the sink looks into his own eyes, speaks.

You dumbfuck. You stupid piece of shit motherfucker. I fucking hate you, you spineless pervert son of a bitch, you fat dumb ugly cowardly fuck. I hate you, I fucking hate you.

He stares at himself for another moment, takes a deep breath, looks down, shakes his head. He stands and turns and opens the door and walks out of the bathroom.

Gordon is sitting on a sofa reading a daily entertainment business magazine, he sets it down, speaks.

You look good, much better.

Amberton speaks.

I know.

They walk out of the office down a long hall lined with agents' offices and the cubicles of their assistants they walk into a conference room Gordon holds the door for Amberton. Five attorneys sit at the table they all stand when Gordon and Amberton enter, everyone shakes hands, sits back down. An assistant enters the room asks if anyone needs anything, no one does so the assistant leaves. Daniel, who is Amberton's primary attorney, speaks.

Tell me what you know, Amberton?

I know there's a lawsuit.

Yes there is. Do you know what it alleges?

I can imagine.

Normally I would ask if it's true, but because the agency has also been named, I would prefer that you not speak at all in relation to any of the allegations.

Okay.

David, the agency attorney, speaks.

I'm not going to coddle you, Amberton. For years we've protected you, covered for you, lied for you, backed you up. Now we may be fucked because of you. He has pictures, audio and video. He had a PI follow you while you were following members of his family. He says you raped him multiple times, and threatened him on multiple occasions. Add the fact that he's African American, and he says you used racial slurs while raping him, and we've got a massive, massive shitstorm on our hands. It's really fucked this time.

None of that is true. We were in love. We were lovers.

Daniel speaks.

Please don't say anything else, Amberton.

David speaks.

The evidence seems to indicate otherwise.

Amberton.

We really were in love.

Daniel.

Please, Amberton.

Gordon.

He has video, Amberton, he has proof that you were following his family around. Whether you thought you were in love is irrelevant. If this gets out you're done. Absolutely, completely and totally done forever.

Amberton stares at the table, takes a deep breath. No one says a word, they just wait for him. He looks up, speaks.

We were in love. It's true, and I will say it until the day I die, we were in love. I understand the situation though, and I'm willing to do whatever it takes to make it go away, and I'm willing to pay whatever he wants to keep his mouth shut. A reporter approached me a couple hours ago and asked me about this, so I think whatever we need to do, we should do it quickly.

Everyone exchanges concerned looks. One of the other attorneys, a distinguished older man, who looks like a kindly grandfather but is actually a pit-bull libel attorney, speaks.

Who was the reporter?

I don't know.

Who did he work for?

He didn't say.

Fuck.

Yeah.

Fuck.

Yeah.

David speaks.

The suit, which his attorney has shown us but hasn't filed, asks for fifty million dollars. They have told us he'll settle for twenty. The only way to stop this is to pay it. We want you to cover the entire sum.

Daniel speaks.

No fucking way.

Amberton speaks.

It's okay.

Daniel speaks.

That's a huge amount of money, Amberton. Far more than we've ever paid before. We can do better.

Amberton speaks.

I make more than that on every movie. I don't care about it. If that's what he wants, give it to him. I hope it makes him happy.

The lawyers exchange looks. Amberton stares at the table, takes a deep breath.

Can you leave me alone now, please.

They look at each other again. Amberton looks up.

I love him. I'm upset. Can you go do whatever it is you do and leave me alone, please?

They look at Gordon, who nods. They stand up and leave.

Once they're gone, Amberton starts to cry.

On September 4, 1981, Los Angeles celebrates its two hundredth anniversary. There are no riots, no deaths attributable to racial tension, no earthquakes, no floods, no mudslides.

Esperanza gets a job working at an office supply superstore. She starts as a clerk on the evening shift she rings up customers buying pens, tape, paper, printer cartridges, occasionally a shredder or a cordless phone, file cabinets, coffee machines, wastepaper baskets and envelopes. She works from 4:00 PM until midnight she makes minimum wage, after taxes it's less than she made cleaning Mrs. Campbell's house. She is, however, much happier. She likes working behind the counter, interacting with people, some of them speak English some Spanish she smiles, rings them up, asks them how they're doing some of them could care less, but enough are friendly so that the shift goes by quickly. A few men ask her name she always smiles and points to her name tag one of them comes in four times over two days and on the fourth visit asks for her number she smiles and says no, but maybe at some point down the line. He smiles and says I'll be back once a week until you say yes.

She goes to a lawyer's office with her parents they sign the appropriate forms the house is now in her name. They go to a bank and fill out the appropriate forms she now has funds at her disposal so she can go back to school. The day the bank forms are processed and approved and the family receives notice they have a party at the house, the entire extended family is there, they cook a huge meal and drink and listen to music and dance. When Esperanza is ready for bed she asks her mother and father to come to her room. When they're there she thanks them and hugs them and tells them she will do everything she can to make them proud of her and as she hugs them she starts crying which makes them start to cry. They stand in the middle of her room and hold each other and cry with joy this time cry with joy.

After six weeks at work, she gets promoted to assistant night manager. There are two other assistant night managers, one stocks the shelves, one runs the copy department, her job is to oversee the other cashiers. She never yells at anyone, if they're upset she talks to them about why and tries to help them, she's flexible with scheduling issues. At first she is slightly overwhelmed but two or three weeks later she gets used to the job, enjoys the responsibility. She becomes friends with her coworkers she becomes closest to a Mexican-American single mother with three children under six whose boyfriend is in jail for twelve years for manslaughter, and a nineteen-year-old African-American woman who is saving up for college. When the store is slow, as it often is after eight or nine o'clock, they read gossip magazines, talk about their favorite stars, talk about their coworkers, talk about men. Neither can understand why Esperanza is single she tells them she's shy. They both tell her she's hot, that she should go out with some of the men who are always flirting with her, she tells them that they probably wouldn't flirt with her if they could see her legs, they both laugh say she has great beautiful thick legs, that some men prefer a woman with some meat on her bones, Esperanza laughs and says she hasn't met any, but thinks of Doug, she doesn't want to but she thinks of Doug.

She tries to decide on schools. There are two community colleges nearby where she could go and a four-year university in Pasadena tells her they would accept her on short notice based on her high school grades and test scores. She goes to each of the campuses with her mother and father walks around meets with admissions directors speaks to professors. She doesn't know what she wants to do yet or what she wants to major in so she decides to go to one of the community colleges and get some of her basic college requirements out of the way and then transfer into a four-year school when she feels she's ready. She fills out the registration forms signs up for classes they start in a couple months she works out her schedule so she can still work. Her parents tell everyone they know how proud of her they are she will be the first person in their extended family ever to go to college.

She goes to a Talk and Tequila event held by the Young Mexican Professionals of East Los Angeles. The event is on a Saturday night she spends most of the morning trying on outfits with her mother and cousins. She doesn't like anything she has so she asks her mother to go shopping with her. They drive to a mall with designer outlets. They walk through the stores both are intimidated by them. They avoid ones with the names of fancy designers from the East Coast, they find a few others that sell nice clothing at discount prices. At an outlet for a large department store, Esperanza finds a black business suit with a skirt and a jacket. She tries it on it fits well the skirt stops just above her knees when she looks in the mirror she's terrified. Her mother steps behind her and smiles, Esperanza looks at her in the mirror, speaks.

What do you think, Mommy?

Beautiful.

Are you sure?

Yes.

What about them?

They are part of you, and you are beautiful, and you are the only one who doesn't know it.

Esperanza smiles, looks at herself, runs her hands down the front of her suit. She looks at herself for a moment, two, smiles and turns around and hugs her mother.

Thank you, Mommy.

I love you, Esperanza.

They check out. Graciella tries to pay Esperanza doesn't let her. They go home Esperanza takes a shower does her hair puts on her outfit. When she walks into the living room her entire family, all seventeen of them, are waiting for her. When they see, they burst into spontaneous, raucous applause, whistling and cheering, giving her a standing ovation. Her father, who is wearing his best and only suit, stands at the door waiting for her, smiling ear-to-ear, holding a flower that he pins on the front of her jacket. As they walk out, the family follows, and continues cheering as they drive away.

They go to the event, which is in a banquet room at a local hotel. Jorge walks in with Esperanza, stands with her as she signs in at the registration desk, tries to go into the event with her, she asks him to leave she'll call when she's ready to come home, he tells her that he'll wait for her in the parking lot. He kisses her goodbye, she walks into the room.

There are bars at both ends, a banquet along the wall with chips, salsa, guacamole, taquitos. There are tables spread throughout, a DJ at a table in the corner. There are thirty or forty people in the room, slightly more men than women. Esperanza is nervous and scared her hands are shaking slightly her heart is pounding she wonders if she looks okay if anyone is staring at her legs. She doesn't know anyone, doesn't know how she's going to meet anyone, isn't sure where to go or what to do. A man approaches her, introduces himself, she starts talking to him, he introduces her to a few of his friends they go to a table she has a lemon-lime soda, they all drink beer, people come and go she meets more men, more women, she gets a few business cards, one man asks her to lunch, she asks for his number and tells him she'll call him. When she leaves she finds her father standing just outside the door he is peeking in to watch her he smiles and hugs her and says you did great, and I'm very proud of you. She hugs him says thank you, Daddy, thank you.

She gets promoted again to shift manager she is in charge of the store when the general manager isn't there. He offers to switch her to the day shift she says no she doesn't want work to interfere with school.

School starts she takes economics, English literature, biology, American history. She never misses a class she's never late never misses an assignment. In her first semester she gets straight A's, makes the dean's list.

She goes out to lunch with the man he's an accountant for a clothing manufacturer. He's nice enough but there's nothing more. She goes out with him again, again, waits to see if something comes there's nothing. She goes out with an attorney nothing, a computer programmer nothing, an elementary school principal twice, the third time she knows, nothing. She keeps going to Talk and Tequila events. Before each she goes to the outlets with her mom and buys a new outfit. Her father always takes her, watches her from the door if he can, waits for her. She becomes part of a group who always meet at the events, a woman who works as an immigration attorney, a woman studying to be a veterinarian, two men who are partners in a video game company, a man who is a journalist for the newspaper downtown, a woman who teaches math at a local high school. She is younger than them but mature enough to fit in they all want the same thing success, stability and love, at some point children.

Second semester of school she takes theater, philosophy, computer science, chemistry. She's still not sure what she wants to do or study sometimes she thinks doctor sometimes teacher sometimes she thinks she should go into business. She likes the idea of advertising she met a copywriter at a Talk and Tequila event his job sounded fun and exciting, different every day.

She's at work gossiping with the girls, a clerk on the day shift is dating one of the men in the stock department. The clerk is only twenty-six has already been married twice, the man in the stock department is in his late thirties has never been married. As they discuss whether they think it will last or not a man approaches the counter Esperanza looks towards him it's Doug he's smiling tentatively smiling it's Doug. Her heart falls, leaps, pounds, she's tried to forget him, get over him, erase the memories the good and bad just erase them, but when she's alone they always come back. He walks up to the counter smiling, tentatively smiling he looks at her, speaks.

I've missed you.

In 1984, the City of Los Angeles hosts the Summer Olympic Games of the twenty-third Olympiad. In retaliation for the American boycott of the 1980 Moscow games, the Soviet Union and the whole of the eastern bloc countries, fourteen in all, do not participate in the games. The United States wins 174 medals, leading all countries, and the games turn a profit of almost $200 million.

Two men sit in a loft on the eastern edge of downtown Los Angeles. Both are painters. Painter1 lives in the loft, Painter2 lives near New York.

Painter1: It's just over 2,000 square feet.

Painter2: Fucking humongous.

Painter1: Costs me $1,800 a month.

Painter2: No fucking way.

Painter1: Have a five-year lease, goes up ten percent every year.

Painter2: That's nothing.

Painter1: It's not nothing.

Painter2: You know what you get for $1,800 a month in New York?

Painter1: A bathroom?

Painter2: A bathroom in a bad neighborhood.

They both laugh.

Painter1: It's why I left, why I came here. The only people still in New York are the ones who've already hit it big or have family money.

Painter2: Not me.

Painter1: You're not in New York, you live in a shitbox in a hideous neighborhood in New Jersey.

Painter2: Yeah.

Painter1: It's the new world here. We can afford to live, we can afford to work, there are good galleries, and there are tons of collectors with money. Fuck New York. If it's not dead already, it's close.

***

There are more than 500 art galleries in Los Angeles. More than $750 million a year is transacted in art purchases. There are more than 50,000 artists living in the city. If actors, writers and musicians are included, there are more than 400,000.

***

He has fourteen billion dollars. He made it in real estate, banking, insurance. He was born and raised in Los Angeles,

474

his father was a carpenter his mother stayed home and raised him and his two brothers. He started working at twelve, helping his father, carrying tools, doing odd jobs, organizing supplies. When he wasn't working he was studying. He graduated third in his high school class, earned a partial scholarship to USC, enrolled in the undergraduate business school. He kept working with his father, though he was now a fully capable carpenter, and paid for everything, including basic living expenses, that his scholarship didn't cover. He graduated near the top of his class and got multiple job offers. He said no to all of them.

He started his own company instead. It was the early 1960s Los Angeles was in the midst of another massive population surge. The city was spreading outwards, east into the desert, south into Orange County, north into the fringes of the San Fernando Valley. People needed, and wanted, well-built affordable housing in safe areas. He borrowed some money bought some land he and his father built a house sold it at a profit. They reinvested their profits hired a larger crew did it faster. They did it again. Again and again and again. They started working on multiple houses at a time. They started buying larger plots of land, building small developments. They always reinvested their profits. Again and again.

He started a mortgage company that provided mortgages for the homes his company built. He started building large developments in rapidly growing communities. His company earned a reputation for high-quality construction. Everything they built sold quickly. The mortgage company started providing financing for most of the homes. He stopped doing any actual construction work and stayed in the office, or went into the field to look for land. By the time he was thirty he was a multimillionaire. He reinvested. Expanded. Started building developments all over the West Coast. He started an insurance company that sold the new homeowners their insurance. By the time he was forty he had several hundred million dollars.

He went to France. He was thinking of expanding the company

into Europe there was land in France that was affordable and met his criteria for development. He was in Paris negotiating the deal for the land and during a break he went to the Louvre. He had an hour he started walking the halls he had never looked at art before, never even really thought of it. Art was for people who were born rich, or for crazy men who cut their ears off, or for people who had too much time on their hands, or it was the junk he needed to stick on the walls of his model homes. He was entranced. He saw the Nike of Samothrace, Aphrodite, the Mona Lisa. He saw Fra Angelico, Goya, Delacroix, Rubens, Michelangelo's *Slave*, he stood in front of Titian and wept he didn't know why. He called his attorney, said close the deal without me, spent the rest of the day wandering looking astonished devastated confused overjoyed. He went to the Orsay the next day saw Manet, Monet, Degas, Gauguin, Van Gogh, Cézanne, Picasso he knew nothing but felt everything the next day the Musée Rodin and stood in front of *The Gates of Hell* for an hour two it was the most beautiful most terrifying thing he had ever seen, he went inside and he saw *The Kiss* and he knew he was in love, he knew he was in love.

He stopped in New York on his way home. He had married several years earlier, he and his wife had two children, he told his wife he was going to be delayed a couple days. He went to the Met, MoMA, he walked the spiraling hall of the Guggenheim, he walked through the galleries of Fifty-seventh Street. He spoke to no one. Just walked and looked and felt and fell deeper. He went to an auction house he didn't know if there were any auctions there weren't so he stood in the foyer and looked at catalogs of upcoming auctions.

He went home. He told his wife she was surprised he asked her to go back to New York. They went a month later. They checked into a hotel and spent three days. He took her to all of the museums to all of the galleries he tried to explain what he saw and what he felt and why he was in love they stood outside of Warhol's Factory and stared at the people coming in and out.

He started coming to New York every couple months for a couple days sometimes his wife came sometimes their two children both girls came, sometimes he came alone. He started buying paintings a Picasso lovers shattered into multiple perspectives a Matisse flowers in a vase and a Modigliani thin young woman looking in the mirror. He had them shipped to Los Angeles and put them in their house. They did something to him every time he walked past them, made him laugh or smile, made him sad, made him think, sometimes he tried to imagine what the painter was thinking when he made a certain stroke, used a certain color. He walked by them as often as he could they did something sometimes he cried.

He started buying more and he filled the house with paintings that could hang in museums. He built a bigger house he had the architect build galleries for the paintings. He hired someone to look for art for him and manage and care for what he already owned. He bought more the new house wasn't big enough so he bought a building he filled it so he bought a bigger building filled it. He worked. He spent time with his family. He looked at art. That was his life. He decided he didn't want to work anymore he sold his companies they were worth billions. He spent time with his family. He looked and bought and spent time with his art. That was his life.

There were others like him, before him. There was Getty in Malibu his home became a museum his foundation became an institution. Norton Simon in Pasadena he left it for the public to see and love and learn. Entertainment moguls heads of studios of agencies of record companies of empires they chased the same things the same beautiful things he chased. There were others like him and before him but there was no one as obsessed, devoted, no one as wealthy, no one as much in love. He became the biggest collector in the world. He built a new house designed by the world's preeminent architect titanium, concrete and glass. He built a separate space on the same land a perfect gallery made of titanium concrete and glass and rotated masterpieces in and out. Artists came to him the most famous artists in the world and they made things for him because he loved them. He bought another building. He started a foundation. He amassed the greatest collection on the planet. He did it all for love.

His children are grown, his wife still with him. They travel the world looking at art, talking about art, thinking about art. He spends $250 million a year acquiring art. It is spread throughout the city at museums, in his building, at his home and in his gallery. Museums from around the world come to borrow it they hope he'll give it to them someday. No one knows where it will go when he's gone if his children will get it if he'll give it all away if there will be a museum with his name. For now it sits, the greatest art collection in the world, in Los Angeles. Put together by a man who understands what its financial value is but would keep it all if it wasn't worth a penny. No one knows where it's going or if it's going anywhere at all. He doesn't know. And right now he doesn't care. All he cares about is that he is in love, with everything in it, truly and deeply in love.

***

UCLA School of Art and the California Institute of Art known as CalArts, both of which are located in Los Angeles, are considered among the top five art schools in the United States. Three of the top five film schools in America, USC School of Cinema, the American Film Institute and UCLA Film School, are located in Los Angeles. One of the top five design schools, the Art Center College of Design, is located in Los Angeles, two of the top ten architecture schools, UCLA School of Architecture and the Southern California Institute of Architecture, are located in Los Angeles.

***

An interview between an art critic from France and a famous artist from Los Angeles. It takes place in Venice, at his house, on his back porch, a block from the ocean. The sun is shining.

478

They are both drinking tea.

Critic: It is nice here, no?

Artist: Always.

Critic: Always?

Artist: It's the same every day. Sunny warm. Because we're near the ocean, it's never hotter than eighty-five and never colder than sixty. And no humidity.

Critic: Does that influence your work?

Artist: It doesn't in that I don't do work that relates to weather. It does in that I like the sun and it makes me happy and I get to work outside if I feel like it. And because I also take photos, I can work pretty much whenever I want. There is always good light and easy conditions.

Critic: Your photos, the most famous ones, are of gas stations, pools, parking lots, fast-food restaurants, highways. Why?

Artist: I see them. Every day, everywhere I turn. I started thinking about them as objects, as cultural symbols, as things that are mundane and beautiful and ignored. Placing them into a different context helped me understand that there are works of art all around us. We might not see them or care about them or look twice at them, but they are there. When I take a series of photos, and place them next to each other in a gallery, people understand it.

Critic: When you came here, in the early '60s, Los Angeles was a cultural wasteland. What made you want to live here?

Artist: I wanted to learn to surf, and I wanted to live near the beach and I wanted to look at girls in bikinis every day.

Critic: Seriously?

Artist: That was part of it, for sure. But another part had to do with LA's culture and LA's place within our culture. To call LA, then or now, a cultural wasteland is, in my opinion, an incredibly ignorant remark. Los Angeles is the cultural capital of the world. No other city even comes close to it. And when I say culture, I am talking about contemporary culture, not what mattered fifty or a hundred or a hundred and fifty years ago. Contemporary culture is popular music, television, film, art, books. The other disciplines, dance, classical music, poetry, theater, they don't hold any real weight anymore, their audiences are small, and they're more like cultural oddities than the cultural institutions. More people watch TV every night than go to every ballet performance in every city of the world for a year. More rap and rock CDs are sold every year than classical CDs have sold for the last twenty years. And movies, fuck, movies are humongous. I'd be willing to bet that the highest-grossing film of the year grosses more than every show on Broadway put together, probably two or three or four times as much. And the only things that rival the influence movies have on our culture, and the world's culture, are TV and popular music. And all of it, all that product, all that entertainment, all that culture comes from here. I didn't want to be part of New York. I didn't want to be part of some stagnant preexisting art world that didn't know it was being outdated. I wanted to go to the New World, and I felt this was it, because at some point, books and art, which are still in New York, are going to follow the rest of our culture and come here. I wanted to be part of the first wave of the new, be part of something fresh instead of something that was rotting, to go to the place where others would eventually follow.

Critic: And you really think that's going to happen?

Artist: It's already happening. No one can live in New York anymore because it's too fucking expensive, so they come here where it is still relatively cheap. And the gallery system in New York is too closed. Everyone there has these huge rents for these huge spaces and needs massive amounts of money to keep their doors open. That forces them to show, and sell, what they know people will pay for in an immediate way. That discourages great new work because new artistic ground is broken by taking risks, and the galleries there can't afford to do that. If they do and the shit doesn't sell, which is usually the case for young artists doing new work, the galleries have to close their doors. Here they take the risks and show work no one else is willing to take on. That also draws the artists doing

the work because they know they can show it here. Eventually, because of that, because the newest freshest work is being created here and shown here, everything will move here. And the economics of the city will support it. There are a ton of rich motherfuckers here willing to spend money on art. People with spectacular collections that will eventually make their way into our museums, which will then rival New York's, the museums in Paris, Rome, Madrid, anywhere.
Critic: How long do you think it will take?
Artist: Could take ten years, twenty years, thirty years. It could, if New York gets flattened by terrorists, happen overnight. It will happen though. It's inevitable.
Critic: And where will you be?
Artist: Might be here on this porch. Might be down the street on a bar stool. Might be in the ground. Don't know.
Critic: And your legacy?
Artist: I was the first here. And I saw it all coming.

***

A few artists living and working in Los Angeles, the medium or mediums in which they work, and the highest price ever paid for a piece of their work in a public auction.

Ed Ruscha, painter, photographer—$3,595,500
Paul McCarthy, performance artist, sculptor—$1,496,000
John McCracken, sculptor—$358,637
Chris Burden, performance and conceptual artist—$84,000
Robert Graham, sculptor—$390,000
Edward Kienholz (deceased), sculptor—$176,000
Raymond Pettibon, painter—$744,000
Kenny Scharf, painter—$180,000
Mike Kelley, multi-media artist—$2,704,000
Mark Grotjahn, painter—$530,000
Lari Pittman, painter—$120,000
Richard Pettibone, painter—$688,000
Catherine Opie, photographer—$27,500

Sam Francis (deceased), painter—$4,048,000
Ed Moses, painter—$28,400
Jim Shaw, painter, sculptor—$656,000
Ken Price, sculptor—$228,000
John Baldessari, photographer—$4,408,000
Liz Larner, sculptor—$27,600
Joe Goode, painter—$38,400
Charles Ray, sculptor—$2,206,000
Billy Al Bengston, painter—$10,800
Jorge Pardo, painter—$156,000
RB Kitaj, painter—$569,169
Richard Diebenkorn (deceased), painter—$6,760,000
Robert Therrien, sculptor—$84,000
Nancy Rubins, sculptor—$2,280
Robert Irwin, painter—$441,600
David Hockney, painter—$5,407,407

***

Art museums in Los Angeles: Los Angeles County Museum of
Art (LACMA), Latino Art Museum, Palos Verdes Art Center,
UCLA Armand Hammer Museum of Art & Cultural Center,
Watts Towers Art Center, University Art Museum—Cal State
Long Beach, Santa Monica Museum of Art, Petterson Museum
of Intercultural Art, Museum of Contemporary Art (MOCA),
Long Beach Museum of Art, LACE—
Los Angeles Contemporary Exhibitions, Hancock Memorial
Museum, Frederick R. Weisman Museum of Art—Pepperdine
University, Downey Museum of Art, Craft & Folk Art
Museum, Geffen Contemporary at MOCA, Huntington
Library, Art Gallery, & Botanical Gardens, Museum of
African-American Art, Museum of Latin American Art,
Norton Simon Museum of Art, Museum of Neon Art
(MONA),
J. Paul Getty Museum, Getty Center.

***

She met a boy. He was really a man, but she called him a boy whatever the word she met him and fell in love with him deeply and immediately in love. It was in New York. At a party for a mutual friend a writer who was releasing a book he had grown up with the writer she knew the writer's girlfriend. They were at the bar. She asked the bartender for a beer, the bartender asked what kind she said Budweiser. He looked at her she had blond hair blue eyes a deep scratchy voice he said you like Budweiser she said yes. He smiled and said I've always dreamed of marrying a woman who loved Budweiser she smiled and said here I am, motherfucker.

She had a big job at a big gallery that was famous for taking poor, unknown artists and turning them into rich, famous artists. She lived in New York had for ten years didn't think of ever living anywhere else. He was a production manager on film shoots in Los Angeles had spent ten years working his way up he didn't think of ever living anywhere else. They hung out for the rest of the party talked about football, books, art, music, film, beer they liked most of the same things they left together and went out for late-night cheeseburgers kissed on the stoop of her apartment building when they went to sleep that night both alone he in a hotel she in her bed they both knew it was over except for the logistics, they both knew.

She didn't want to leave New York, he couldn't leave Los Angeles, logistics. For six months they alternated traveling eventually he said I want you to come here, I can't live without you, it's not gonna work if you won't come. She had just gotten a promotion to become the director of her gallery it was the only job she had wanted and the job she had worked for for a decade. He said there was art in LA she said it wasn't the same. He said she would have a better life the sun shining every day more free time less stress she said she would feel like she had wasted a decade trying to get to the major leagues only to demote herself once she got into them. He started sending her Internet links, magazines, museum schedules, gallery guides she said she knew there was cool shit happening in Los

Angeles, she just preferred the cool shit happening in New York. He kept trying talking sending he never begged but definitely pleaded she said there's production work here, just come here, he kept trying talking sending definitely pleading. Two things happened: one of her friends decided to leave New York and open a gallery in Los Angeles, the owner of the gallery where she worked made her put up a show of paintings she hated but he said would sell when she objected he told her the last three shows hadn't sold her job was to make him enough money to keep the doors open. Doors open indeed she opened the doors and walked out and didn't come back. She called her friend who was opening the gallery asked if he wanted some help he said fuck yeah. She called her boyfriend and said she had a change of heart she was willing to give it a try.

He was waiting for her at the airport. He had flowers and candy and a six-pack of beer and he was wearing a T-shirt that said LA ROCKS. She laughed and hugged him and kissed him they went straight to his apartment, which was a two-bedroom in Silverlake in New York it would have cost five thousand a month, in LA it was fourteen hundred, they spent the next twenty-four hours in bed. When she came out the sun was shining she was wearing a T-shirt it was the middle of fucking February she was thrilled. She went down to her friend's new gallery it was located in Chinatown, on a street lined with other galleries, it was one of three art districts in the city the others in Culver City and Santa Monica. She walked in the space was huge and open he smiled and he said welcome to the wild wild west she asked how in the fuck he could afford such a nice place he said LA's still cheap, still a place where people without trust funds still have a chance.

She started working with him. She thought artists and gallerists and curators would be impressed with her résumé and they were but not as much as she imagined which she took as a good sign, a sign that they were confident that they were as good as New York. She made friends people here helped each other artists gallerists and curators they were a legitimate community instead of a group of jealous, competitive warring factions. The artists themselves freed of the demands of the art market were doing things newer, fresher more groundbreaking than many in New York, risks were easier to take if they failed the consequences were not as grave. She liked the work she did and the work they showed it felt more like what dealing art should be, more pure. And at night she went home to someone who loved her and whom she loved sometimes she missed New York and wondered what might have happened if she was still in the majors but she missed it less often, cared less about it, missed it less often.

Six months after she arrived she was settled in working and living she was walking across a street when she got hit by a bus. Unlike most people in Los Angeles she walked as much as she could she was in the middle of a crosswalk when it hit her she got knocked out of her shoes and flew thirty feet through the air. When the driver got out he said he wasn't used to seeing people in the crosswalk and couldn't stop in time she had a broken back and a broken jaw. She spent two months in the hospital he slept three or four nights in a chair next to her when she got out she spent two more months at home he spent all of his free time with her he bought her burgers and beer they watched football on Saturdays and Sundays. When she was able to walk again she went to the gallery her friend had replaced her with someone else from New York. She was crushed asked him why he said the world was moving quickly changing quickly he didn't know if she was coming back and he needed to keep up. She asked if she could have her job back he said he'd have to talk to his new partner.

She went home cried he came home tried to help her she told him she wanted to go back to New York. He said they couldn't go back there was no work for him. She said she couldn't live in a city where bus drivers weren't used to seeing pedestrians and ran them the fuck over she wanted to leave to fucking leave. He asked for six months she said for what he said most people who move to Los Angeles from New York hate it for a year or two then love it and never want to leave, she laughed said fine six months and we're gone.

He kept working she tried to find curating work, thought about trying to be an art advisor, which is someone who helps other people buy and collect art. A month she still wanted to leave two the same in the third she got a phone call. It was the biggest art dealer in the world he had three galleries in New York two in London one in Rome he wanted to open another in Los Angeles would she be interested in doing it for him, running it for him. She asked where he said he had found a space in Beverly Hills she asked what he wanted to do he said the space would be a place to take risks to do shows he couldn't do in his other galleries a place he would use to gain a foothold in LA's growing market a place to show new artists. She smiled, wondered if they had buses in Beverly Hills, she was back in the big leagues.

***

More artists, writers, actors and musicians than in any other city in the history of the world. Every day more. Every day.

In 1985 there are 800 gang-related murders in the City of Los Angeles.

There are eleven Veterans Administration medical centers in Los Angeles County that provide inpatient, outpatient, physical rehabilitation and counseling services to 45,000 veterans.

US Army Staff Sergeant Andrew Jones, lost his eyes in the second Iraq War.

US Marine Corps Corporal Phillip Tamberlaine, treated for alcoholism, fought in Vietnam.

US Marine Corps Private First Class Juan Perez, lost an arm in the first Iraq War.

US Navy Seaman Harold Franks, post-traumatic stress disorder, Vietnam.

US Army Specialist Anthony Mattone, Gulf War syndrome, first Iraq War.

US Army Sergeant First Class Nikolai Egorov, lost both legs, second Iraq War.

US Air Force 2nd Lieutenant Terry Daniels, drug addiction, Vietnam.

US Marine Corps Master Gunnery Sergeant Charles Davis, lost both legs, one arm, second Iraq War.

US Army Captain Ted Bradley, gunshot wounds, second Iraq War.

US Army Command Sergeant Major James Parma, brain damage, Afghanistan.

US Navy Lieutenant Eric McDonald, drug addiction and alcoholism, Vietnam.

US Army Major Brian Jones, lost one arm, one leg, one eye, Afghanistan.

US Marine Corps Major Sean Jefferson, Gulf War syndrome, first Iraq War.

US Marine Corps Private First Class Michael Craven, gunshot wounds, second Iraq War.

US Army Private Thomas Murphy, paralyzed neck down, second Iraq War.

US Army Private Michael Crisp, paralyzed neck down, Vietnam.

US Marine Corps Private Tonya Williams, brain damage, second Iraq War.

US Navy Chief Petty Officer Samuel Jeter, alcoholism, post-traumatic stress disorder, Vietnam.

US Army Sergeant Letrelle Jackson, lost both hands, second Iraq War.

US Army Private Joseph O'Reilly, facial reconstruction, second Iraq War.

US Army Specialist Lawrence Lee, Gulf War syndrome, first Iraq War.

US Marine Corps Private First Class Tom Chin, lost one leg, gunshot wounds, Afghanistan.

US Army Private Braylon Howard, knee reconstruction, lost one hand, second Iraq War.

US Air Force 2nd Lieutenant, William Hult, burns on 90 percent of body, second Iraq War.

US Navy Ensign Joshua Feldman, alcoholism, drug addiction, post-traumatic stress disorder, Vietnam.

US Marine Corps Chief Warrant Officer Edward Winslow, brain damage, burns, first Iraq War.

US Army Lieutenant Colonel John Fitzgerald, alcoholism, depression, Vietnam.

US Navy Commander David Andrews, alcoholism, depression, Vietnam.

US Marine Corps Private First Class Eric Turner, lost one foot, second Iraq War.

US Army Private David Chung, brain damage, loss of hearing, eyesight, Bosnia.

US Army Specialist Lee Tong, gunshot wounds, second Iraq War.

US Army Specialist Pedro Morales, Gulf War syndrome, first Iraq War.

US Army Specialist Jennifer Harris, burns on 85 percent of body, Afghanistan.

US Marine Corps Sergeant Major Jonathan Martinez, paralyzed waist-down, Vietnam.

US Army Private Calvin Hart, paralyzed neck down, second Iraq War.

US Army Sergeant First Class Timothy Gould, lost one arm, Nicaragua.

US Army Private Rachel Powers, facial reconstruction, hearing and sight loss, second Iraq War.

US Army Private Jason Nichols, alcoholism, drug addiction, post-traumatic stress disorder, Vietnam.

US Air Force Colonel Brian Kennedy, alcoholism, drug addiction, post-traumatic stress disorder, Vietnam.

US Marine Corps Master Gunnery Sergeant Joseph Baldelli, Gulf War syndrome, first Iraq War.

US Army Private First Class Scott Hall, both legs, both arms, second Iraq War.

US Air Force Airman Basic Felipe Chavez, both eyes, second Iraq War.

US Navy Seaman Apprentice Orlando Weeks, alcoholism, depression, Vietnam.

US Marine Corps Lance Corporal Melvin Barfield, one arm, first Iraq War.

US Army Private Adam Drew, drug addiction, post-traumatic stress disorder, Afghanistan.

US Army Private Franklin Hernandez, both arms, second Iraq War.

US Marine Corps Major Robert Willingham, burns 85 percent of body, Afghanistan.

US Marine Corps Private First Class Chris Barret, brain damage, Vietnam.

US Army Private Marcus Durham, gunshot wounds, second Iraq War.

US Army Private Craig Duffy, Gulf War syndrome, first Iraq War.

US Marine Corps Private Andrea Collins, paralyzed neck down, second Iraq War.

US Navy Chief Petty Officer Brad Johnson, alcoholism, drug addiction, post-traumatic stress disorder, Vietnam.

US Navy Seaman Moises Rivera, brain damage, second Iraq War.

US Air Force Airman David Chang, facial reconstruction, second Iraq War.

US Army Private Andrew Fedorov, drug addiction, post-traumatic stress disorder, Afghanistan.

US Army Private LaTonda Barry, Gulf War syndrome, first Iraq War.

US Marine Corps Private Ahmed Jarrahy, one leg, second Iraq War.

US Army Specialist Frederick Marquis, alcoholism, Vietnam.

US Army Specialist Derek Quinn, both eyes, hearing loss, Afghanistan.

US Navy Senior Chief Petty Officer Tony Andrews, one arm, alcoholism, drug addiction, Vietnam.

US Army Command Sergeant Major, Gary Burnett, alcoholism, drug addiction, Vietnam.

US Air Force Captain Michael Lowry, brain damage, second Iraq War.

US Marine Corps Captain John Lulenski, both legs, both arms, second Iraq War.

US Army Captain Matt Bell, paralyzed waist down, Vietnam.

US Army Private First Class Heath Andrews, Gulf War syndrome, first Iraq War.

US Air Force Airman Basic Heath Mulder, burns on 80 percent of body, Afghanistan.

US Navy Seaman Apprentice Darren Dixon, one arm, one eye, second Iraq War.

US Army Private Francisco Sanchez, brain damage, Vietnam.

US Army Private Jeremy Franklin, elbow reconstruction, second Iraq War.

US Marine Corps Lieutenant Colonel Paul Young, alcoholism, drug addiction, Vietnam.

US Army Staff Sergeant Chad Springer, paralyzed neck down, Afghanistan.

US Navy Warrant Officer Toby Wells, dental and facial reconstruction, second Iraq War.

US Army Corporal Leroy Washington, both arms, second Iraq War.

US Marine Corps Private Allison Gomez, both eyes, Afghanistan.

US Marine Corps Chief Warrant Officer David Suzuki, one arm, one leg, one eye, second Iraq War.

US Navy Seaman Brandon Jones, both eyes, hearing loss, Afghanistan.

US Army Private Carlos Perez, Gulf War syndrome, first Iraq War.

US Army Private Adam Stern, alcoholism, drug addiction, post-traumatic stress disorder, Vietnam.

US Army Specialist Lance Konerko, burns 95 percent, second Iraq War.

US Army Specialist Sarah Bannister, Gulf War syndrome, first Iraq War.

US Air Force Airman Basic Luis Reyes, paralyzed neck down, second Iraq War.

US Navy Seaman Apprentice Steven Atkins, brain damage, dental and facial reconstruction, second Iraq War.

US Army Private Phillip Ito, paralyzed neck down, second Iraq War.

US Army Private LeCharles Jackson, paralyzed neck down, Afghanistan.

US Army Private Joe Rodriguez, both arms, both legs, dental and facial reconstruction, second Iraq War.

US Army Private Daryl Jones, both arms, both legs, Afghanistan.

In 1988, the Environmental Protection Agency determines the air in Los Angeles is the most polluted air in the nation, primarily due to fumes from the mammoth exhausts produced by its automobiles.

Scandal, motherfuckers, everybody loves a scandal. Even if you try to turn away, you can't, when you try to ignore it, you find it impossible. You know why? Because it's awesome, hilarious, awful, it's a fucking mess, and it almost always makes you feel better about yourself. So admit it, you love and your friends love and your family loves everyone you know loves a scandal, the bigger the better, the uglier the more fun, the more devastation the better you feel.

**

He was born in Miami his parents are Cuban. He grew up wanting to become an actor the biggest Latin movie star in history. As a child he dressed up and put on shows for his mother, his sister, they both loved him and his shows and they fawned over him he was a precocious child, smart and funny and entertaining.

As he grew up he didn't fit in with any of the other Cuban boys in his neighborhood they idolized boxers and baseball players he couldn't have cared less. He would skip their afterschool games and come home and read magazines and watch soap operas and listen to his mother gossip with her friends, neighbors, there was always something to talk about, a new story, someone drinking or fighting or cheating, someone creating some sort of little scandal. When he was old enough ten or eleven he started gossiping with his mother. He'd collect stories at school bring them home he loved it when they were good enough for his mother to pass them on, and he loved that he knew things other people didn't know, but wanted to know, that secrets were currency, as valuable as anything else in the world, sometimes more valuable.

He did well in school. He was on the student council, he starred in most of his school's shows and plays, he got good grades. He came out to his family in tenth grade, first to his sister, then to his mother, then to his father, none of them were surprised, all of them were supportive, they said they loved him regardless of who or how he loved, all they were interested in was his happiness. At school he was one of a very small number of gay students, and though most of the kids were cool to him, he got slurred and taunted enough so that he developed a very thick skin and very sharp tongue. And no one who disparaged him escaped without getting something back, something that was always smarter and more pointed, something that hurt significantly more. Rarely did someone come back for more, but if they did, he was always ready for them.

When he finished high school he went to New York for college. He had been accepted to one of the best theater schools in the country, and he wanted to be on Broadway. He made friends did shows went out dated lived the life of a college student, for whatever reason people confided in him, told him stories, shared their secrets with him. When he was asked, he kept them secret. When he wasn't asked, he didn't. He started a column in the school paper, a gossip column that dealt with what was going on at school, who was dating who, who might want to date who, debunked or confirmed rumors, had funny blind items. It was lighthearted and genial, well written, showed off his wit. It became the most read column at the school, students who had never bothered with the paper started picking it up, talking about it. A professor encouraged him to take a journalism class he did, he enjoyed it, journalism became his minor, acting and theater was still his first love. When he finished school he decided to stay in New York. He hadn't made it to Broadway yet and still had the dream, he decided to look for a job in journalism as a way to pay his bills and support a life in New York. He got an internship turned it into a full-time position. He became a reporter became the editor of a small gay magazine. He went on auditions when he could did plays when he had time. The magazine he worked for folded he got a job at a huge, national, weekly gossip magazine. He was a reporter he was expected to find stories, report stories, break stories. In the world of professional gossip getting stories is all about having relationships with people who have them and protecting those people as sources. He started going out more, hitting parties, clubs, premieres, meeting more people some of whom were celebrities, developing friendships. He was easy to be around, funny friendly gracious, he listened well, people trusted him. He learned about the facade of fame, that the people who lived behind the facade were no different than other people, that some were good and decent and relatively normal, that others abused their privilege, abused the gifts society bestowed upon them, treated those they thought beneath them as if they were less than human. Stories started coming. He always made sure what he wrote was accurate, that his sources were valid. Many of the stories were harmless, sometimes he passed on stories about people he liked, with those he didn't, as long as he knew it was true, he was merciless. Because he was young and new to the business, reporters more senior than him often took credit for his work. Sometimes he missed stories because he was working on his acting. Sometimes, because he was young and new, the stories went to other people first. He worked hard, though, and began to love his job.

A year into the job, the magazine's sales started to slow down. The market had become overcrowded there were new magazines every day, the Internet was drawing away a large portion of the magazine's audience. The magazine needed to make layoffs he was one of them he was crushed. He had been proud of his job and it was fun and it allowed him to pursue his dream. He cried when he left the office cried when he got back to his apartment cried when he called his mother, when he told his sister. He wasn't sure what he was going to do. He wanted to stay in New York he still hoped to get on Broadway, there was no way he'd be able to do it without a job to pay his bills. He didn't want to wait tables or serve coffee. He had been in New York for seven years. He decided to leave.

He went to Los Angeles. There were more opportunities for actors, for every one job in New York there were fifty in LA. He started a Web site with a gossip blog, he hoped he could generate enough interest to attract a couple advertisers, which would allow him to work on his own schedule, go to auditions, control how he lived his life. He named his site after a popular gossip column, used a variation of the numbers that also indicated a humorous, satanic intent. He looked at other blogs and tried to figure out what worked and what didn't, the better ones broke original stories and updated themselves more frequently, posting a few new pieces every hour. He started working his old contacts, making new ones, started linking to other gossip sites, letting them link to him. He didn't have an Internet connection in his new apartment, so he went to a local coffee shop that had free wireless Internet access, and worked from one of their tables.

He found an audience quickly, advertisers came because of the audience, money to pay his bills came because of the advertisers. He started devoting more time to the blog, getting to the coffee shop before it opened at 6:00 AM and sitting on the ground in front of the door so he could get into the wireless network, updating more regularly, sometimes four or five times an hour. People started e-mailing him, he got more scoops, better stories, the media started to notice his site, pay attention to it, get their news from it. An evening tabloid entertainment show did a piece on him and called the site *The Most Hated in Hollywood*. The next day traffic to the site shot up, two three four times more than it had ever been, and the gossip column that he had named his site after threatened to sue him. He had never been sued, didn't want to be sued, didn't have attorneys, didn't know what to do. He was worried after getting back on his feet in LA that everything he had done was going to disappear in a mammoth judgment.

He changed the name of the site. There was a socialite he loved she had a catchy recognizable name she had been involved in a sex tape scandal, an arrest scandal, she had multiple rich famous boyfriends, her every move was documented by journalists and paparazzi. He came up with a Hispanic version of her name that was also catchy, funny, smart. He took advantage of being called *The Most Hated in Hollywood* and put it right on the front of the site, he rebranded himself as the Queen of All Media. He set up the Web addresses so that traffic was directed from the old Web address to the new one. And people kept coming. More and more every day. And the stories kept coming. More and more every day.

He started breaking many of the biggest media, gossip and entertainment stories in the country. Starlet goes to rehab he knew about it first. Actor about to leave his wife he knew about it first. Socialite switching boyfriends he knew, rock star and movie star breaking up he knew, boy band member living in the closet he knew. He had advantages over traditional magazines and TV shows in that as soon as he knew something and could verify it, he could put it up on his site immediately, there was no waiting for another issue to be printed or for the evening's broadcast. People kept coming, more and more, a million a day two million a day three million a day. He started doing TV appearances and other journalists started writing stories about him. Instead of using his real name he started using the name of his site the more it was printed and repeated the more it was recognized the more people came the more people wrote about him the better the stories he got. Celebrity has a sex tape it's about to be made public he knew, a feud between the two stars of a TV show he knew. People kept coming.

He's now as famous as many of the people he writes about, the paparazzi follow him, the media cover him. Between six and eight million people a day come to his Web site, ad revenues are huge, and his brand is worth millions and millions of dollars. Beyond any of that, he loves what he does, loves meeting celebrities, loves covering them, loves breaking stories, loves being the first to know, loves the process of running the site, loves the attention he gets from it. He still works from a table at the same coffee shop where he started, he works twelve-, fourteen-, eighteen-hour days. Fans come by to see him and take his picture and shake his hand, celebrities come by to talk to him and shoot themselves with him for their reality shows. He gets sued regularly, though never for libel or defamation, but now has lawyers who deal with it he's never lost a case. He can make or break records and bands by posting their songs on his sites with links and positive reviews. And despite all of the success and attention, he's still the same, the same kid who loved to gossip, the same high schooler with a sharp tongue, the same college kid who dreams of acting. He has a TV show a talk/reality show that's going to be on cable he hopes it will lead to roles in network shows, studio films, and eventually, the place he always wanted to be but never dreamed he would find via gossip the Internet and breaking stories, Broadway.

***

A funeral. Eight people stand around a grave. The coffin is cheap the cemetery run-down the stone small the priest never met the deceased. Her parents are there, her two sisters, two people who starred in a sitcom with her when she was between the ages of twelve and fifteen, a former agent, a man who says he dated her but really sold her drugs. She drove her car into a tree. The press said it was an accident. The people gathered around her know better, every single one of them knows better, and every single one of them blames themselves in some way. She was nineteen.

***

They met on the set of a film. They are both in their twenties, both famous actors, when they met they had both recently gone through very public highly documented breakups with other actors, they had both vowed never to date an actor, or even someone famous again.
They played brother and sister. They had immediate chemistry that was absolutely contrary to any sort of acceptable brother/ sister relationship. They hung out together, ate together,

relaxed in each other's trailers. They talked about what they felt and agreed to wait until the film was over.

They couldn't wait. It happened at the end of a long day. They were in his trailer. Some of the crew members heard them. Rumors started immediately. They denied them. The rumors persisted. They were in his trailer, her trailer, his home, her home. The press got hold of the rumors, exploited the brother/sister angle, even though they were only pretending to be brother and sister.

They were on the covers of magazines. They were followed. TV shows covered them. They had no privacy, no peace. The film ended he sold his house moved into hers. Paparazzi waited outside for them. Hid in their bushes. Climbed their trees. Followed them everywhere. Waited for them everywhere. They left the country. They followed, waited. They came back. They followed, waited.

A friend had a barbecue for them. It was really a surprise wedding. It got leaked there were helicopters overhead. They couldn't hear each other saying their vows, her flowers were blown away, they had to go inside.

She got pregnant quickly. The magazines found out they were on the covers again, the worst of them called it incest baby, even though it was no such thing. She went to her doctor's appointment with bodyguards in a black SUV. He started riding a motorcycle that was fast enough to outrun them. They were scared to leave their house.

She had the baby, a little girl, in a secure wing at a hospital on the edge of Beverly Hills. There were guards at both ends of the hallways, guards outside their door. When they went home three black SUVs departed from the hospital garage one after another all of them had blackened windows two of them were decoys.

There is a reward for the first picture of their child. They have heard it's $500,000 but they don't know for sure. They have been offered a million for a photo shoot they don't want to do it. They feel like they chose their lives in the public eye their child has not. She is less than a week old. They keep all of their shades drawn, they never leave the house.

***

He lived in a small town. He was small, frail, weak. He didn't like school, hated sports. He spent most of his time watching TV. He was fascinated by the people he used to dream of somehow opening the box and stepping into it and becoming one of them. When he was old enough to understand that wasn't possible he dreamed of what their lives must be like. His mother worked at a Laundromat and his father drank and hit her. He spent a lot of time dreaming.

When he was eighteen he left home. He got on a bus heading west and got off when it stopped going. He found a job at a car wash and started trying to see some of the people he had watched on TV. He walked through Hollywood all he saw were homeless kids and drunks and drug dealers and people dressed in superhero costumes and cops. He walked through Beverly Hills he saw a movie star the host of a talk show. He walked through Santa Monica a movie star and bit player on a sitcom. He was fascinated with them they didn't seem human to him. He was scared of them. He wanted to be one of them.

He started going to premieres. He tried collecting autographs he got a few. He stood outside of nightclubs got a few more. He bought a star map and tried waiting outside of houses, the star map was wrong no one lived where it said they lived. In most of the places he went, there were men with cameras, they took pictures of the stars, they often followed them. He became friends with a couple of the men, they sold the pictures they took and made a living doing it. He saved up bought a camera. He started hanging around the men and taking pictures with them. They helped him sell a few of his pictures he made enough money to quit his job.

It becomes his life. Searching for celebrities, taking pictures of them. He learns that the other men who do it are divided, more or less, into two groups. One of the groups works with the celebrities, tries to befriend them, if the stars oblige them with pictures they leave them alone. The other group doesn't give a fuck. They believe the stars, by becoming public figures, are fair game. They go where they go. They take pictures of their spouses, their children. They believe that the price of fame and fortune is a total and complete loss of privacy. If the stars are allowed to make money, they are allowed to make money off of them. He starts in the first camp, he tries to make friends, play nice, give the celebrities some space in exchange for shots. Somewhere he hopes, and believes, that one of them might take a shine to him, become true friends with, take him in and share their life with him, even though his view of their life is an illusion. He's awkward, the jokes he makes aren't funny, he's somewhat pushy. A couple of stars, on different occasions, react badly, yell at him, curse at him, call him names, one of their bodyguards threatens him. He switches camps. He doesn't give a fuck.

He finds a partner. They agree to share whatever they make, fifty-fifty. When a particular shot of a particular celebrity is desired by a magazine or Web site, they work together to get the shot. They ride a motorcycle one drives the other rides on the back with a camera. They follow celebrities everywhere. They camp out in front of their homes. They go to their weddings, their doctors' appointments, their lunches, their dinners. They shoot pictures of them through the windows of their homes, sitting in their backyards, anywhere, everywhere. They don't give a fuck. The loss of privacy is the price of fame. There is a bounty for pictures of the kid. The parents are famous, and they choose to be famous, and they make a ton of money making movies, and the kid is an extension of the parents. Fair fucking game. He is sitting in a tree his partner is on the ground beneath him. They take turns in the tree, take turns getting food and supplies, charging the batteries for their camera. There are other photographers in other trees, and in bushes, and on hills, and in cars outside the gate, and in helicopters, but they have the best position. They got here the day the kid was born they figured everyone else would be at the hospital. They will wait until they get the shot. As soon as someone opens a curtain or a door or steps outside. They will fucking be there to get that goddamn shot. It doesn't matter how long it takes.

***

Sales are lagging. There haven't been any arrests or breakups or deaths, nothing great for a cover. The competition has been gaining and they need to break an exclusive. An exclusive on the cover will start moving them off the stands again, will hold off the competition for a few more weeks.

She started as a writer, moved up to contributing editor, became fashion editor, celebrity editor. She became editor-in-chief at a smaller magazine and built up its circulation. She wanted the editor-in-chief job at one of the big ones there were two or three depending on who you talked to and whose circulation numbers you believed. When one of the jobs came up she interviewed there were two other candidates. She made promises neither of them did, said she had raised circulation at her other magazine, she'd do it again. She got the job.

She started strong. She was aggressive and paid well for information and photos. The circulation numbers went up. Her competitors saw what she was doing started doing it themselves. Their circulation numbers went up. It went back and forth, back and forth. She spent more needed bigger numbers spent more.

It's been slow. She needs a big cover. She knows the couple and offered them $750,000 if they would cooperate. They said no. She offered again this time a million they said no again. She put out the bounty. She knows other magazines also put out the bounty. She raised hers she would go as high as she needed to go. Her husband asked her why she said she needed to get the numbers up. He asked her if she felt bad about doing it to the couple who had always been good to her, had given her interviews and pictures, had been extremely cooperative, and without hesitation, she said no.

***

He wished he hadn't said it.
She regrets taking pictures.
He shouldn't have thrown the punch.
She just couldn't stop, she tried, tried as hard as she could, she just couldn't stop.
They shouldn't have gotten married.
He should have listened when the police told him to calm down.
She wished she had worn panties.
He didn't really hate blacks.
She shouldn't have had the last four drinks.
He just couldn't stop, he tried, tried as hard as he could, he just couldn't stop.
He wasn't trying to hurt anyone.
He shouldn't have gotten behind the wheel.
She shouldn't have cheated and she regrets it.
He didn't really hate gays.
He shouldn't have cheated and he regrets it.
He didn't know anyone had a video camera.
She just couldn't stop, she tried, tried as hard as she could, she just couldn't stop.
He still loved her.
She shouldn't have trusted him.
He shouldn't have gotten behind the wheel.
She should have said no.
He regrets it.
She regrets it.
He regrets it.
She regrets it.
He didn't really hate Jews.
He just couldn't stop, he tried, tried as hard as he could, he just couldn't stop.

She didn't think anyone would care.
He thought it was his house.
They should have never gotten married.
He didn't know it was loaded.
He should have asked her how old she was.
He shouldn't have touched the boy that way.

***

She knows at some point they're going to find out and she knows that as soon as they do her life as she knows it is absolutely fucking over.

***

He doesn't understand why everyone cares so much, he just wants to work doing something he loves and live his life and be left alone.

***

One thinks all publicity is good publicity. Another knows better.

***

Some don't give a fuck.

***

Some seek it out.

***

Others build their lives around trying to avoid it.

***

No one goes through it and comes out the same, no one goes through it and comes out unscathed, no one goes through it and comes out with their innocence, no one goes through it and comes out with their trust.

***

She starred in her first film at ten. Her mother took her to an open audition and the director thought she was perfect and the studio screen-tested her thought she was adorable. She got the part and shot the film and audiences loved her and the film made $350 million.

Her mother had been a dancer worked as a secretary for a high school principal her father was an accountant at a pool supply company who only came home three or four nights a week when he did he was drunk.

She did another film got paid a million dollars her parents became her managers collected 20 percent both of them quit their jobs. She made an album of classic children's songs updated and set to rock music it sold two million copies she made another three million and her parents got their 20 percent. She went on tour and sold out small arenas she made fifty thousand a night her parents 20 percent.

She officially dropped out of normal school her parents hired a tutor. They bought a bigger house in a nicer neighborhood in their Midwestern hometown the father stayed home with their other three children. He had staff to help him with them he only came home three or four nights a week. She moved to Los Angeles with her mother.

Another hit film.

She had her first drink at thirteen.

Another hit film.

Smoked pot at fourteen.

Album.

Lost her virginity at fifteen he was a twenty-four-year-old actor.

Film.

She was making eight to ten million dollars a year her parents 20 percent.

Tour.

Her mother went home and left her with her bodyguards. The father wasn't coming home at all the other children needed someone at home with them. Cocaine at sixteen, meth at sixteen. The job of the bodyguards was to protect her, not raise her. When they tried to control her she told them to leave her alone or lose their jobs. One of them kept trying. She called home and spoke to her mother and the man lost his job. The others gave up.

Film.

Film.

There were no rules, no guidance. All of the people around her depended on her. They made money when she made money. She was seventeen. She felt too much responsibility. When she tried to talk to her mother, her mother told her to keep working, that work would take her mind off whatever pressures she felt. When she tried to talk to her father he wasn't available.

Film.

She was followed everywhere she went. By photographers, reporters, people who wanted to be near her, spend time with her. People fawned over her. Got her and gave her whatever she wanted, whenever she wanted it. All she really wanted was love. Not because of her fame and money but because of what was inside of her. No one seemed to care what was inside, when she tried to talk about how confused she was, scared she was, tired she was, overwhelmed she was, the people she tried to talk to wanted to talk about the next magazine shoot, the next album, the next film. She dated older men all of them were also famous. She thought they might understand and might love her and make her feel safe. They used her for her body, played with her, discarded her when they were done. When she called her mother heartbroken her mother couldn't talk because she was busy working on the next deal, her father wasn't around and no one knew where he was.

She drank it made her feel better. She got high it made her feel better. She went out and everywhere she went people called her names and took her picture and wanted to be near her and with her and gave her things clothes food drinks jewelry cars for free and it made her feel better.

An arrest at eighteen. The judge made her pay a fine.
A film it didn't do well.
Another man.
Her parents somewhere her bodyguards placid her friends were they really friends? She was followed everywhere and she was confused and scared and no one would tell her what she was supposed to do.
An album with disappointing sales.
Another arrest and a trip to rehab they gave her a private suite and didn't make her follow the same rules the rest of the patients followed. Three hours after she got out she was drinking her boyfriend a twenty-six-year-old singer took her out for dinner and then took her home.
Her mother came to visit. Her mother told her she needed to calm down and get to work the entire family was depending on her. Her mother told her that her father was missing and they thought he was in Florida with another woman and she shouldn't expect to hear from him. When she started to cry her mother told her to get it together the entire family was depending on her. She was nineteen.
Another film another disappointment.
On the covers of magazines in the gossip pages every day some of what they wrote was true but most of it wasn't, they said nasty things about her, called her names, mocked her, made fun of her hair, her clothes, her family, her name. She didn't understand why she had never done anything to them, it hurt her, scared her, confused. She drank and got high it made the feelings go away for her, it made her numb, it allowed her to forget, it allowed her to feel something like what she imagined normal must feel like. She drank and got high and no one tried to stop her or told her to stop it or told her she was hurting herself.
Another arrest.
Another rehab.
Headlines screaming druggie, disaster, uncontrollable menace.
Her mother screaming what are you doing you're ruining it for

everyone we need you, we need you. Her father gone maybe Florida, maybe Mexico. Her friends telling her that she's fine, she's just having fun, she's still a kid. Confused hurt and scared so she does more, and she can't stop, she does more, she can't stop, she does more.

She's twenty years old.

***

After the fifth rehab he just gave up.

Her parents saw an ad for her sex tape on TV.

He doesn't understand why other people do the same things, but no one cares.

She trusted people when they said they would stand by her and defend her.

His career was just taking off.

Thirty years in the public eye and it didn't mean anything.

No one will stop her because if they try they won't be able to make any money off of her.

At this point, he just wants to die.

At this point, she might as well be dead.

Where is everyone now?

It was supposed to be a dream come true.

***

He moved to Los Angeles when it was over. He had lived in LA before he went to New York and for some reason it felt safer to him.

He never expected any of it. Not the rise, not the fall, not the love, and not the hatred that followed.

When it started he thought it would last a few days. Everyone told him it would last a few days. After a few weeks he started getting scared. He knew, despite what they were saying, that they were turning on him. He wasn't sure what was going to happen, but his instincts told him something.

He started taping phone calls, it was legal in New York.

Taping phone calls with the agents, the editors, the PR people, the producers of the show, the executive producer of the show. None of them knew he was doing it.

He went on the show. It wasn't what he was told it was going to be. He got berated, yelled at, booed, scolded, lectured, humiliated. He knew there was no way to stop it, or defend himself, so he went along with it. Some people said he deserved it, some said he didn't, he understood both sides of the argument.

It got covered live.

It was the lead story on the evening news, ahead of the war, the political shooting, the continued disintegration of Middle-Eastern governments.

It was in every newspaper in the world.

He went home. There were reporters outside both entrances to his building. He hoped it was over.

The phone kept ringing. He got calls from the agents, the editors, the PR people, the executive producer of the show. She apologized and said they did what they needed to do and they hoped he was okay. Two days after the host called she was worried he was going to hurt himself. They talked for almost an hour. What she told him directly contradicted all of her public statements. She told him a story about her life before she was famous, about some mistakes she made. She told him a story about a book she wrote, and about what was in it, and about why she decided to halt the publication of it, and who helped her make the decision. He taped everything.

The reporters wouldn't leave, so he left. Before he did he made copies of the tapes he put one set of copies in a safe deposit box in New York, he took one set of copies with him and put them in a safe deposit box in Monaco, he sent another to a friend who put them in a safe deposit box in Washington DC. He stayed away until it passed. He came back to America and moved to Los Angeles. He didn't speak to anyone in the media, give any interviews. He kept his head down and his mouth shut.

He's working again. He's happy again. He loves what he does

and he loves his life. It comes up every now and then he tries not to let it bother him, he never comments, he tries to focus on work and friends and family.

Someday he might discuss it.

Someday he might tell his side of it.

Someday he might play the tapes.

Someday.

In 1990, the population of Los Angeles is over ten million people.

Dylan gets the day off he and Maddie have a one-day honeymoon. They take a bus to Santa Monica and have a picnic on the beach and go to the pier and eat ice cream cones he gets mint chip she gets two scoops, one strawberry and one French vanilla, she's eating for two, eating for two. When they finish their cones they go to the end of the pier there are rides and carnival games Dylan wants to win a teddy bear for the baby. He plays a game with a water pistol no luck he tries the ring-toss no luck he plays a free-throw game two-out-of-three YOU WIN! on the third try he gets it. A big brown teddy bear wearing the jersey of one of LA's basketball teams. YOU WIN!!!

They leave the pier, walk up to the Third Street Promenade five blocks of upscale shops and boutiques, the street has been paved with stones and sealed off from traffic, it is lined with booths selling perfume and jewelry, it is lined with benches palm trees and streetlights. They look through the windows of clothing stores, furniture stores, they walk past crowded outdoor cafés. They stop at a toy store they go inside and look at toys someday maybe, they go into a baby store and look at bassinets, cribs, changing tables, rocking chairs, blankets that cost as much as Dylan makes in a week, someday maybe.

They leave the store walk hand-in-hand down the promenade there are other families all around them they have two three four children Maddie watches them smiles looks at Dylan squeezes his hand maybe someday.

They walk back to the bus stop wait, the sun is starting to drop, they're both tired. Dylan sits down on a bench Maddie sits on his lap, leans in kisses him long and deep for a moment, two, three, she pulls away, smiles. He speaks.

What was that for?

She speaks.

Because I love you.

I love you too.

We're gonna be okay.

He smiles.

Yeah, we are.

We came out here and made a life for ourselves and we're gonna be okay.

Smiles again.

I told you we could do it.

Thank you.

We did it together.

It was you. If you hadn't made me do it I would have never left there. And I'd have hated myself for the rest of my life.

I would have never done it if you weren't in my life. I would have stayed too.

For the first time in my life I'm happy.

Good.

I love you.

I love you too.

The bus pulls up they get in sit down. Dylan sits next to a window, Maddie sits next to him takes his hands in hers, leans her head against his shoulder says it again I love you, says it again. The ride takes half an hour Dylan stares out the window watches the city pass by gas stations, mini-malls, fast-food restaurants, blocks of one-story Spanish-style homes, blocks of three- and four-story apartment buildings. When the bus arrives at their stop Maddie is asleep Dylan gently shakes her she smiles says what he says we're home, we're home.

They get off the bus walk hand-in-hand three blocks to their building. They walk up the stairs to their floor down the hall go into their apartment. Maddie says she's tired is going to sleep Dylan wants to watch TV. Maddie walks into the bedroom, changes into her pajamas, goes into the bathroom starts washing her face. Dylan finds a football game a team from San Francisco playing a team from New York winner is in prime position for the play-offs.

There's a knock at the door. Dylan turns towards the bathroom, speaks loudly.

You expecting anyone?

Maddie leans her head out, speaks.

Nope.

Should I see who it is?

Might as well.

Dylan stands walks to the door looks through the eyehole. A middle-aged man in a button-down stands at the door he looks vaguely familiar though he doesn't know why. The man knocks again, Dylan stares at him through the eyehole tries to remember. Man knocks again this time harder. Dylan speaks.

Who is it?

Man quickly glances down hall, speaks.

I need to speak to you.

Why?

You work at the golf course, right?

Why do you need to speak to me?

Maddie leans out again, speaks.

Who is it?

Dylan looks at her, shrugs, shakes his head. Man speaks again.

I need your help, please.

Dylan looks back at Maddie, who shrugs. As he looks back to the keyhole, and starts to unlock the door, he sees the man step aside. Someone steps in front of the man the eyehole goes black. Dylan tries to lock the door it flies open. He's knocked back three men all large, tattooed, one has beard rush into the room. One of them forces Dylan against the wall puts his forearm against Dylan's neck, one of them turns and locks the door, the other rushes towards the bedroom. All are wearing jeans, motorcycle boots, T-shirts, leather jackets. The one who locked the door turns around, pulls a sawed-off shotgun out of his jacket, speaks.

You try anything and you're fucking dead.

The one who rushed the bedroom comes out with Maddie. He's carrying her, holding one arm across both of her arms and her chest, holding one hand over her mouth. She's struggling, thrashing beneath his arm, kicking. The man with the shotgun turns to her.

Calm down, bitch, or I'll fucking shoot you.

She stops. Her eyes are wide she's terrified. The man with the
gun motions towards a chair near their table. The man with
Maddie guides her towards the chair, forces her down, starts
duct-taping her to the chair. The man with the gun turns back
to Dylan, who is still being held against the wall. He motions
to the man holding him, the man steps back. The man with the
shotgun speaks again.
You know why we're here?
Dylan shakes his head, tries to speak, his voice cracks.
No.
You sure?
I don't know.
You took something from a friend of ours.
Dylan shakes his head.
No.
The man finishes taping Maddie to the chair. Her arms are
taped, her legs are taped, there is a strip across her mouth.
Man with the shotgun motions towards the bedroom, both
men walk towards it, go into it, start going through everything
in it. Man with shotgun turns back to Dylan, looks at him for
a moment, swings the butt of the gun at him, hits him in the
face. His nose immediately breaks, blood flies against the wall,
he falls to his knees his face in his hands. Man pulls his hair
with one hand, holds the shotgun with the other. He jerks
Dylan's head back. Maddie's eyes are wide, and she's shaking.
Man puts the gun in Dylan's face.
Some money went missing from a friend of mine's shop.
Nobody but you could have taken it. He wants it back.
Dylan speaks through the blood.
Don't have it.
Man jerks Dylan's head again, jams the barrels of the gun into
his mouth.
Where is it?
The men are tearing the room apart.
Don't have it.
Man drags Dylan across the floor by his hair, sets him next to

Maddie, speaks.

On your fucking knees.

Dylan gets on his knees. Man speaks.

We've been looking for you for months. Someone associated with us saw you at that fucking golf course. We've been watching you for a couple weeks. We know this bitch is pregnant.

He puts the barrels of the shotgun against Maddie's stomach.

You want me to kill them both?

Dylan looks at Maddie, he's bleeding shaking with fear, she looks at him tries to say something against the tape tears start running. Dylan speaks.

We don't have your money. I swear to God we don't.

The men walk out of the room. Man with shotgun turns towards them. One of them has the envelope with Dylan and Maddie's wedding money in it. He holds it up, speaks.

Four or five grand in here.

Man with the shotgun turns back to Dylan, who speaks.

Don't have our money?

We got that from the guys I work with. They pooled it from their tips the day we got married. It was a wedding present. I swear to God, please, I swear to God.

Man kicks Dylan in the face, blood and teeth fly out of his mouth. He slumps to the ground, out fucking cold. Man turns to the other two.

Get him out to the van.

They step forward, pick him up, put his arms over their shoulders, start dragging him towards the door. When they reach it, one of them unlocks it, opens it. The man who originally knocked on the door is standing in the hall, the other men drag Dylan out and away, he goes with them. The man with the shotgun stares at Maddie, who is trying to look away from him. He puts the barrel of the gun beneath her chin, lifts, forces her to look at him. He speaks.

If you weren't pregnant, and I had more time, I'd fuck you. Unfortunately, things are as they are. If you call the police, or

try to do anything to help him, I'll come back and I'll cut that
fucking kid out of you and then I'll kill you.
He stares at her.
You understand?
She's shaking, crying. She nods.
Good.
He turns and walks out.

In 1991, four white LAPD patrol officers are videotaped beating a black motorist with batons after the motorist led them on a high-speed chase, resisted arrest, and attempted to take one of their weapons. The videotape is played by media outlets around the world. In 1992, the officers are put on trial for use of excessive force and acquitted by a predominantly white jury. The day the verdict is read, massive riots break out in the City of Los Angeles. The riots last for four days. Fifty-five people die, 3,000 are injured, there are more than 7,000 fires, and 3,500 businesses are destroyed. There is more than one billion dollars' worth of damage.

Old Man Joe spends three days sitting next to the dumpster behind the liquor store drinking Thunderbird and eating beef jerky and vomiting and going to the bathroom in a bush. He leaves when the owner of the liquor store, whom he has known for years, tells him he's going to call the police.

He leaves, he doesn't want to be seen by anyone he knows he goes to another dumpster a block inland it's behind a construction site, two old Venice bungalows are being torn down and replaced by a new glass and steel loft building. When it gets dark he goes to his bathroom no one sees him. He washes himself brushes his teeth. He changes into his spare set of clothes.

He walks north into Santa Monica. He walks along Ocean Avenue a block from the Pacific. It's just before dawn the street is empty, the streetlights dropping circles of light over the blacktop, the palms still, a deserted parking lot, the only sound the waves rolling, the only smell the drifting of salt of the sea. He walks a couple miles he sits on a bench. The sun rises he watches it come there is no beauty in it for him, no joy, no peace. When he feels ready he stands and starts walking again the street slopes slightly upwards as the beach becomes the bluffs. He turns inland again walks another mile he sees the line before he sees the shelter three or four hundred homeless men, women and children snaking around the block hoping to get inside and have some breakfast.

He gets in at the end of the line, it moves slowly. Many of the people in it seem to know each other they talk about how they've been, where they're sleeping, good dumpsters, new spots to sleep, who's missing, who's been arrested, who's dead. Old Man Joe doesn't speak to anyone, just stares at the sidewalk, shuffles forward. Ninety minutes later he's inside he gets a small box of cereal, a small carton of milk, an apple, he gets a weak coffee in a paper cup it's hot and tastes good. He eats the food walks to another line that's in front of a door with a sign that says counseling. The line is much much shorter, twenty or thirty people, but moves much much slower.

Three hours after he joined it he is shown into a small
cluttered office an African-American woman sits across from
him. She speaks.
How can I help you?
He speaks.
I'm trying to find a friend.
That could be difficult. Who's the friend?
He was a homeless man who lived on the boardwalk in Venice.
He died a few days ago.
He's probably in the county morgue.
Yeah, I figured. I want to go see him.
Are you related to him?
No.
Then it's probably not possible.
Why?
They don't allow anyone but relatives in to see bodies, and
then, only if they're there to claim them.
I need to see him.
Why?
Because it's my fault he's dead.
Why do you say that?
You hear about that shooting?
Yes.
It was my fault.
Did you pull the trigger?
No.
Were you with whoever pulled the trigger?
No. I was with my friend.
When he got shot?
Yes.
The person who pulled the trigger is to blame.
I have to see him.
What was his name?
Lemonade.
What was his real name?
No idea.

How long had he been on the streets?

Long time.

You know where he was from, or what he did before he was on the streets?

No.

There's no way you're going to be able to see him.

Please.

It's not my call. It's the law.

What if I just say I'm family?

If you don't know his name or anything about him, that won't work.

What's going to happen to him?

They'll keep him there for ninety days. They'll try to ID him. If they can't, and no one comes looking for him, they'll cremate the body. They keep the ashes in storage for four years and if no one has claimed them by then, the ashes will go into a grave with the ashes of the rest of the bodies that went unclaimed at the morgue this year.

They just dump them in together?

Yes.

Is there a gravestone or anything?

Just a plaque with the year they died above the grave.

He deserves better than that.

I'm sure he does.

I have to talk to him.

I'm sorry.

I have to talk to him.

I'm sorry.

Joe starts to cry.

I have to talk to him. I have to . . .

He breaks down, sobs. The woman watches him. He puts his face in his hands and sobs uncontrollably sobs. The woman watches him. A minute two three sobbing watching. There is an empty chair next to him the woman stands and comes around and sits down and puts her hand on his shoulder she says I'm sorry and he sobs, she puts her other hand on his other shoulder says I'm sorry and he sobs, she hugs him and says I'm sorry and he sobs. When he stops he pulls away there is snot and there are tears on his face he wipes them away and he looks at her and he speaks.

What do I do?

Do you want to tell me whatever you were going to tell him?

Why do that?

Sometimes it's just good to say it, even if you can't say it to the person you want to say it to.

Just pretend?

No, just say it. The same way you would if he were here.

Joe looks down, looks up.

I'm thirty-nine years old. I know I look eighty but I'm not. One day I just woke up this way, like I aged forty years overnight. I got no idea why, it just happened. Ever since that day I been waiting for an answer as to why. I figured maybe God was sending me some kind of signal or something, or that what happened was part of some greater calling, or meant I was supposed to do something with my life besides drink and beg change. Every day I woke up thinking and hoping that it was the day it would finally be revealed to me, and that once it was, I'd do something that would make me feel better about myself, or feel like I was a decent person who had done something with his life. So when I find that girl, that kid, behind a dumpster, and she's all beat to hell, and fucked up, for some reason I think that if I save her or help her or get her off the boardwalk, then maybe I'll get my answer. So I tried. I tried to do something good. And I couldn't do it. So I got you and the rest of our friends to help me. And all that happened was you ended up getting killed. For no reason. For no fucking reason. And you were the best person I ever met on the streets. Always happy, always good to people, always willing to help someone. And not because you thought you'd get something out of it, but just because it was the way you were. And you helped me, and I got you killed, and I'm so sorry. I'm so fucking sorry. I took your life and wasted it for nothing. Because I want some answer to some fucking question that's unanswerable. Why? Why? Nobody knows why? People saying they know the answers don't know shit 'cause there is no answer. Life just is what it is and you can try to change it or you can just let it be, but there ain't no why, there just is, there's just life, and I'm so fucking sorry, I'm so sorry.

Joe starts crying again, puts his head down, cries. The woman puts her hands on his shoulders and waits for a minute and he's done, he looks up, she speaks.

You better?

I don't know.

I think you are, you just might not know it.

Guess we'll see.

Can I help you in any other way?

No.

Come back if you can.

I will. Thank you.

Joe stands the woman stands. She hugs him it feels good to him better to him than anything else of the past few days he holds her until she pulls away. She steps back, opens the door, he says thank you again, leaves the office and starts walking down the hall by the time he's at the exit there's someone new in her office.

He leaves. He starts to walk back to the boardwalk it's early afternoon he's tired. He stops every twenty or thirty minutes, sits for an hour. When he's close to the ocean he walks to the bike path in Santa Monica, which becomes the boardwalk when it crosses into Venice, and he starts heading south. When it does cross it changes immediately. The pavement isn't as nice the garbage cans are overflowing there is trash along the edges of the concrete. Joe laughs to himself, as nice as Santa Monica might be, he thinks life is more interesting with a bit of garbage in it. He walks over to a trash can and picks up a discarded soda cup from a hamburger stand, and he throws it across the border. It comes to rest in the middle of the bike path. He laughs, turns and keeps walking.

He cuts across the sand, walks to the edge of the ocean. He takes off his shoes, socks, carries, walks with his feet in a few inches of water. The sun is down and it's dark and the water is cold it feels good on his feet, ankles, sharp, refreshing, makes him feel alert, alive. A hundred yards or so from the taco stand where his bathroom is he stops and he takes off his clothes and starts to walk into the waves they knock him over. He doesn't bother to get up he sits in two feet of water lets the waves pound him, roll over him, every fifteen seconds another one comes, sometimes they're over his head sometimes at head level sometimes at his chest. The water's cold the Pacific in LA never warms up very much. The salt is strong in his mouth, his nose, his ears.

He starts to shiver. It might be because he's cold it might be because he needs alcohol. He crawls out of the ocean puts his clothes back on, he picks up his shoes, and he walks across the beach towards the boardwalk. As he approaches the exercise bars near Muscle Beach he sees four men sitting in a circle passing a bottle. As he gets closer he sees it's Ugly Tom, Al from Denver, Tito and Smoothie. Tom sees him, speaks.

Old Man, where you been?

Joe walks towards them.

Around.

Al.

Around where?

Joe.

Behind the liquor store.

Ugly Tom.

Uh-oh.

Joe.

Yeah.

Joe sees they're passing a bottle. He sits down, speaks.

What's the occasion?

Smoothie.

They caught those fuckers.

Joe.

Where?

Al.

They were in Santa Monica. Under the pier.

Joe.

They in jail?

Tom.

Probably for the rest of their lives.

Joe.

What about the girl?

Tito.

Turns out she wasn't really living down here. Her father is some rich TV producer in Sherman Oaks and she'd just come down here one or two nights a week. She's only fourteen. They'll probably let her go.

Joe shakes his head.

That's fucked up.

The bottle, which is strong, decent bourbon, comes to him.

Smoothie.

Have a drink, Joe.

Joe takes the bottle, takes a long draw, shivers. He holds it towards Al, who is sitting next to him. Al takes it, speaks.

We pooled our dough for this. Out of respect for Lemon, and to show him we're thinking of him, before each draw we say something Lemonade might have said.

Al.

Welcome to the party, Joe. It's the best party we've had all year.

Al draws passes to Ugly Tom.

It's a helluva night. Warm and quiet and calm. Don't think there's a better place on the planet.

Draws passes to Smoothie.

Never had a bottle taste this good. Like they made it out of special water.

Draws passes to Tito.

To great friends, the best friends.
Draws passes to Joe. He holds it up.
To a great life, the best life.
He takes a long draw, shivers.

In 1993, approximately forty years after the public rail system of Los Angeles was shut down, during which time it became the most congested county in America, a new underground subway line, called the Red Line, opens for use.

Amberton immediately signs the settlement papers. His financial advisor has the funds wired an hour later. Kevin resigns from his position at the agency and goes out to dinner with his mother and his girlfriend. Everyone signs iron-clad nondisclosure agreements. The reporter receives a call from one of Amberton's attorneys warning him that if he prints anything insinuating any sort of gay relationship or potential sexual harassment lawsuit he will be hit with a defamation lawsuit. Gordon and the other agents on Amberton's team start looking for a big-budget film that needs a male superstar.

Amberton spends three days in Casey's bedroom. He sleeps most of the time. When he's awake he cries and watches daytime talk shows. He refuses to eat and loses six pounds. He refuses to shower. He refuses to brush his teeth.

On the fourth day Casey brings their children in to see him. They ask what's wrong with him. Doing this is Casey's last-resort tactic, and it always works. Amberton gets out of bed and has a bowl of cereal and takes a shower and brushes his teeth.

They decide to go to Hawaii. They pull the children out of school. They rent an estate on Kauai they fly over on a private jet. The estate comes staffed with two butlers, a chef, gardeners, a masseuse. There are three homes on the estate. Amberton, Casey and Casey's girlfriend stay in one. They keep one empty in case they have visitors. The kids and their nannies stay in the third.

They spend their days on the beach, in the ocean. They hire a surfing instructor they are all able to get up after a few days. They like the instructor and decide to keep him on staff for their entire stay. Amberton thinks about trying to sleep with him, wonders if he'll do it, and if not, if he'll do it for money. At night they have dinner together on a deck built at the edge of the sand. Amberton is trying to gain weight most nights he keeps his food down. After dinner Casey and Amberton walk the kids and their nannies back to their house they kiss the kids goodnight. Casey goes back to her bedroom with her girlfriend. Amberton either goes to the media room and watches a movie or goes to his bedroom and reads magazines. Scripts start arriving, they arrive with offers. The offers are usually 20/20 offers, twenty million dollars with 20 percent of the first dollar gross. There are also usually letters with the scripts, from either the director or producers or both, the letters explain why they love Amberton, why they love him for the part they are offering him, why they think the film will be the biggest blockbuster in history, and why they will be heartbroken if he doesn't take the part. Amberton loves the letters. He has accepted roles in films in the past based solely on the strength of the letters without reading the script. He tapes the best of them on the mirror of his bathroom, and reads them while he gets himself ready for the beach. After fifteen or twenty scripts, including roles as an ex-CIA agent with a kidnapped family, a doctor who, after an accident with an X-ray machine, has the power to heal with his hands, a cop with a drug problem who gets backed into a corner by the local mob, and a superhero called the Caterpillar, Gordon calls him, tells him he needs to make a decision. Amberton asks Gordon which movie will make the most money and take the shortest time to shoot. Gordon tells him it's probably the film about the detective with a rare medical condition who gets locked in the basement of a drug dealer's house, which turns out to be haunted, and the detective has to battle the dealer, his henchmen, and the poltergeists, in order to get free in time to make it to his doctor so that he can receive lifesaving medicine. Amberton tells him to accept the offer and call him back with a start date. Two days later Amberton gets the call, he has to be back in three weeks for rehearsals and wardrobe fittings. He finds Casey and tells her, she calls the nannies and asks them to call the children's school and notify them that they'll be returning. He knows he'll need to be buff for the film so he goes back to his room and starts doing push-ups.

In 1994, African-American football star O.J. Simpson is arrested for the murder of his ex-wife Nicole Brown-Simpson and Ronald Goldman after a slow-speed chase involving fifty LAPD squad cars. He is later acquitted of the crime, despite overwhelming physical evidence, by a predominantly African-American jury. There are no riots after the verdict is read.

The first time Doug came in to see Esperanza she asked him to please leave, he said okay and he turned around and he walked out of the store. The women Esperanza works with all wanted to know who he was and what he wanted and why she sent him away, she wouldn't tell them. He comes back the next day she sends him away again. Next day same thing. He comes back every day for two weeks, same thing. The women think Esperanza is crazy. A nice, polite, slightly chubby, rich-looking white boy comes in trying to fix something up and you don't talk to him, that's flat-out fucking crazy. She refuses to address it. He stops coming.

School ends, she decides not to take summer school. She's nervous about applying to a four-year school without a clear idea of what she wants to do, she wants to spend her free time focusing on it. She meets with people from Talk and Tequila tries to learn more about their jobs, a financial advisor, a marketing executive, a real estate developer. She meets a news producer at a Spanish-language TV station takes a tour of the studio. She meets a veterinarian, spends a day at a dog shelter. She meets a political consultant goes with him to a debate. She volunteers twice a week with an organization gives English lessons to new immigrants maybe she'll become a teacher, maybe not, she doesn't know.

When she doesn't have plans, she helps her mother or her cousins or her aunts and uncles around the house she feels a greater sense of attachment to it, to her family, she knows if something happens to them, it will be hers, and she will be responsible for the people who live in it. On most days she runs or exercises, not because she has any ideas about altering her appearance, or shrinking the size of her thighs, she has accepted that they are what they are and will not change, but because exercise makes her feel good, strong, healthy. Occasionally she dates, a movie, a lunch, a Saturday afternoon in the park, she goes on four dates with an LAPD officer and kisses him, but thinks of Doug while she's doing it, and doesn't feel the same way she felt when she was kissing him. She wonders where he is, what he's doing, she wonders if she made a mistake by not speaking to him, or listening to whatever he had to say to her.

Summer slows down. August is hot it never rains it's over a hundred degrees on most days, sometimes as high as 110. People do their errands in the morning before the sun is high and burning, the store is incredibly slow at night. One of the women leaves she gets a secretarial position with the city. Another starts, but she gets caught stealing cordless phones and reselling them she gets arrested. Another starts, but she gets fired because she takes two smoke breaks an hour, when Esperanza tells she can't take that many she says fuck off, I'm an addict, I gotta have my smokes. They decide not to hire anyone else the three women, Esperanza one African American one Mexican American, can easily handle however many customers are in the store. Near the end of August, at the end of a slow night, the door opens all three look up, Doug walks into the store. He looks disheveled, looks like he's been drinking. One of the women whistles, the other laughs and says white boy is back. He walks straight to the counter, looks at Esperanza, speaks.

I have to talk to you.

She speaks.

Have you been drinking?

I have.

I'm not going to talk to you if you're drunk.

I'm not drunk. I'm scared. I needed a drink or two or three to be able to come and say what I have to say to you.

They stare at each other. The women watch them. A moment, two, they stare. The women look at each other, look back at them. One of them speaks.

Get on with it, white boy, we're waiting.

He stares at Esperanza, takes a deep breath.

I love you. I miss you. When you left my mother's house, I left. I packed my things and stayed in the basement of a friend's house until I found my own apartment. As soon as I was settled, I started looking for you. You never told me your last name, you never told me where you lived. I didn't know where to go or how to find you. I hired a private detective and spent all my free time driving around East LA hoping I would find you somewhere. I always imagined I would see you walking down the street and I would jump out of the car and you would see me and come running towards me and we would kiss and go right back to the way things were. It would be like some Hollywood movie with a perfect ending and we would live happily ever after. Obviously it didn't happen. I never found you or saw you. The PI was able to find you through one of the women who used to ride the bus with you. Once he told me where you were and what you were doing, I tried to figure out what to say to you. I had it all planned and I was ready to say it when I walked in here before, but when I saw you, I froze, and when you told me to leave, I was too overwhelmed to do anything but what you asked. And it was the same every night after. I'd come prepared to tell you what I needed to tell you and you'd tell me to leave and I would be overwhelmed and walk out. I figured at some point you'd ask me what I wanted, but you never did, so I gave up. I thought maybe having you reject me would help me get over you, but it didn't. Every day, all day, all I did was think about you and hate myself for not having the guts to say what I wanted to say to you. So this time, I had a drink or two or three and I'm not leaving until I say what I have to say.

He takes another deep breath.

I love you. I miss you. You're the most beautiful woman I've ever met, inside and outside and in every way, and part of the reason you're so beautiful is because you have no idea how beautiful you are. I can't live without you. I don't want to live without you. I don't care about my mother or my family or living a life that doesn't have you in it. I should have run after you when you left, but I was scared and didn't know what to do. If I could do it over I would run after you and never let you leave me, never, never. I want you to give me another chance. I want you to give us another chance. I know you felt what I did when we were together and I want you to give it another chance. Please. I promise I'll never let you leave again, and I'll never not stand up for you again, and I'll never let anyone make you feel the way she did again. Please. I love you, and I miss you.

He stares at her, she stares at him. The women look at each other, both nod, both are impressed. Esperanza smiles, speaks.

My last name is Hernandez.

He smiles.

I know.

She smiles.

And I live in East Los Angeles.

He smiles.

I know.

She smiles.

And I've missed you too.

In 1997, after intense lobbying from the automotive and oil industries, Congress reduces funding meant for the Metropolitan Transit Authority of Los Angeles to expand the scope of construction of the new Los Angeles subway.

He had a wife. He had three children. He had a good job and a house and the respect of his neighbors. He had a life and he had a name.

There was an accident. It wasn't his fault he was hit from behind while he was coming home from work. His car got pushed off an overpass and it flipped as it was falling the roof hit the ground. They couldn't believe he was alive.

He was in a coma for eight months. When he woke up he was different. As soon as he could walk, he left the hospital. They brought him back. He left again. They brought him back he left again.

When he went home he was confused. He didn't know the children, and he didn't want them. He didn't know his wife and he didn't want to know her. He left and they brought him back. He left again they brought him back they hoped he would change. He left again they brought him back. He left again they let him go.

He has been walking for several years. He wears a backpack with a change of clothes and a toothbrush and a bar of soap. He has an ATM card each month his former wife, who is remarried but still mourns him, puts $200 in the account. He uses the money to eat, to buy new shoes, for toothpaste and soap. He has no idea where the money comes from and he doesn't care.

He sleeps where he can, when he can, sometimes during the day, sometimes at night, for three or four hours at a time. If he doesn't feel safe he will not sleep, and he'll keep walking until he finds somewhere that he feels is safe. As he walks endlessly walks he talks to himself. And as his process of walking is a process of repetition, one foot in front of the other in front of the other, his process of speech is a process of repetition, word after word, the same words in more or less the same order, word after word. He calls himself the Prophet. And so, as the Prophet walks, the Prophet speaks.

I walk through the Land of Angels, I walk through the Land of Dreams. I see the people who live here ten, twelve, someday

fifteen, twenty, twenty-five million black white yellow and
brown separate and together loving hating killing mixing
helping each other or not, they are all here and more every day,
spreading piling joining crowding crushing there are more every
day. I see them come. Come on bus and foot. In cars and
planes overhead in helicopters if they're rich in the backs of
cargo trucks and on the tops of freight trains I saw a man
come on a horse it got hit crossing the highway. They come to
live on this land more in this place than any other thousands of
square miles I walk them every day. Years of walking and I
haven't seen it all. Year after year after year I have yet to step
foot on every street on every road every boulevard and avenue,
every highway freeway expressway interchange, every beach,
every bluff, every path through hills untamed, every trail
through mountains without a house on them, every dead
stream in every empty desert, every scrub-filled field fighting to
live for a decade or more I have walked and I have yet to see it,
know it, hear it and feel it there's room for more. And so they
come. To live with Angels and chase their dreams. It ain't all
bright lights and billboards. Some dream of a roof, some
dream of a bed, some dream of a job, some dream of enough
money to eat, some dream the dream forgetting, leaving,
hiding, transforming, becoming, some dream the simple dream
of getting through a day without worrying about dying, some
dream of families here or there or wherever they left them
dream of bringing them and starting over and actually having a
fucking chance, some dream of being allowed to live, speak,
believe and dress as they please. Some dream of bright lights
and billboards but they are few to the many who dream of a
place that will accept them, nourish them, allow them to grow
into whatever flower or whatever poison they want to become,
allow them to scream yell decry pray beg discuss deal buy sell
steal give take become or not whatever the fuck they want
because it's possible, it's possible here. In gas stations and mini-
malls. In studios and stages. On the beaches in the hills. In
houses bigger than any man needs or deserves in houses so

decrepit they don't deserve to stand. In churches, temples, mosques, in caves filled with bottles and drawings on the walls. In trailers and tents under the deep blue sky. In row after row block after block of ugly motherfucking buildings, identical houses, in jail cells and towers of glass. Day after day I see them. I walk and I hear them. I walk and I feel them. I walk in the Land of Angels, I walk in the Land of Dreams.

By the year 2000, Los Angeles is the most diverse, fastest-growing major metropolitan area in the United States. If it were its own country, it would have the fifteenth-largest economy in the world. It is estimated that by the year 2030, it will be the largest metropolitan area in the country.

The sun rises in a clear sky that moves from black to gray to white to deep, pure crystal blue.

Esperanza sleeps. Her aunts uncles and cousins spread through the kitchen, dining room, living room and back patio all talking about what they think he's going to be like the first Anglo to come to their house for dinner. Esperanza says she loves him that he is the only man she has ever loved, that she believes she will spend the rest of her life with him, that he loves her, that she is the only woman he has ever loved, that he believes he will spend the rest of his life with her. Her mother and father sit together on the front porch holding hands he won't arrive for hours but they want to be the first to greet him.

Amberton walks onto the set he is greeted by the director, the producers, the other actors. They shake his hand tell him how much they admire him and how excited they are to work with him. He goes to makeup, he goes to wardrobe, he goes to his trailer and has a cup of herbal tea and an egg-white omelette and piece of multigrain toast. He brushes his teeth they shine he checks his hair it's perfect he takes a step back and looks at himself in the mirror it's smaller than he would like it to be but for now it's fine he likes what he sees, he knows he'll look good on film, that his fans will be happy. There's a knock on the door he steps over to it and opens it a tall blond blue-eyed twenty-two-year-old production assistant asks him if he's finished with breakfast and would he like his plate taken away. Amberton smiles, introduces himself, and invites him inside.

Old Man Joe lies silent and serene on the sand his eyes are closed he can hear the waves he can taste the salt his hands lie still upon his chest his breath is easy his heart beats steady. He has fourteen dollars in his pocket and two bottles of Chablis in the tank and all he needs in the world, all he needs to know, all he needs to feel, all he needs to own, all he needs to live, all he needs in the world he has he lies silent and serene in the sand, his eyes closed, hands still, heart steady.

Maddie sits staring out the window sleep never comes

anymore. Her neighbor found her and released her she left the apartment immediately ran from the building ran into the night ran. Next morning she went to the course and found Shaka she was too scared to call the police and believed they would come back for her and their child if she did. Shaka called his wife. She picked Maddie up and took her home and held her as she cried and made her eat and taught her to pray. They go to church together every morning and they get on their knees and look to the cross and try to believe that someday he'll come back. She knows at some point she'll have to find a job, Shaka offered her one working in the office at the course but it's too close, too close. She lives in their back bedroom and spends her days looking at an album of pictures that were taken at their wedding. They are the only pictures she has of him, the only pictures of the two of them together. When the child moves inside her she holds the album close and says this is your father, he loved you, he loved you.

The sun rises in a clear sky that moves from black to gray to white to deep, pure crystal blue.

One in Georgia packs his things he's going to take a bus. Four in Mexico walk across scorched earth water in packs on their back. Two in Indiana best friends coming together they pack their best clothes while their parents wait to take them to the airport. One in Canada drives south. Sixty from China in a cargo container sail east. Four in New York pool their cash and buy a car and drop out of school and drive west. Sixteen cars of a passenger train crossing the Mojave only one stop left. One in Miami doesn't know how she's going to get there. Three in Montana have a truck none of them have any idea what they're going to do once they arrive. A plane from Brazil sold out landing at LAX. Six in Chicago dreaming on shared stages they rented a van they'll see if any of them can make it. Two from Arizona hitchhiking. Four more just crossed in Texas walking. Another one in Ohio with a motorcycle and a dream. All of them with their dreams. It calls to them and they believe it and they cannot say no to it, they cannot say no.

It calls to them.

It calls.

Calls.

Thank you Maya and Maren, I love you. Thank you Mom and Dad, Bob and Laura. Thank you Peggy and Jagadish, Amar and Elizabeth, Abby and Nick. Thank you David Krintzman. Thank you Eric Simonoff. Thank you Jonathan Burnham. Thank you Tim Duggan. Thank you Jenny Meyer. Thank you Roland Philipps. Thank you Jane Friedman, Brian Murray, Michael Morrison, Kathy Schneider, Carrie Kania. Thank you Davidson Goldin and Joe Dolce. Thank you Tina Andreadis and Leslie Cohen. Thank you Richard Prince, Terry Richardson, John McWhinnie, Glenn Horowitz, Bill Powers. Thank you Ben Foster. Thank you Billy Hult. Thank you Josh Kilmer-Purcell and Brent Ridge. Thank you Jeff Dawson, Peter Nagusky, Bill Adler, Kevin Chase, Eben Strousse, Chris Wardwell, Nikki Motley, Nancy Booth, Todd Rubenstein, Susan Kirshenbaum, Kathleen Hanrahan and Ray Mirza, Geren Lockhart, Andy and Christina Phillips, Sarah Watson. Thank you Michael Craven and Warren Wibbelsman. Thank you Scott Wardrop and Jacob Niggeman. Thank you Nan Talese. Thank you Bret Easton Ellis. Thank you Norman Mailer. Thank you Eric Hanson and Danny Melnick. Thank you Colin Farrell and Shea Whigham. Thank you Sonny Barger and Fritz Clap, Bart of HAMC New York and Pee Wee of HAMC Las Vegas. Thank you Eric Lewis. Thank you Cory Brennan and Black Tide. Thank you Mark Mrdeza and 3rdrail. Thank you Stephen Elliott. Thank you Elizabeth and Philippe Faraut, Suzy and Jean Pierre Faraut. Merci beaucoup aux personnes de Beaulieu Sur-Mer, France. Thank you Pat McKibbin and Mary Schoenlein. Thank you Nils Johnson-Shelton and Suzi Jones, Jonathan Fader, Chuck and Jan Rolph, the Kansas Freys and the Brockport Freys, Gina and David and everyone in the extended Landers Family of New Jersey, Timory and Keith King, Stacy and Anne Wall, Cynthia Rowley, Tracey Jackson, David Duval, Evgenia Peretz, Donal Ward, Will Cotton. Thank you Amy Todd-Middleton and Alex Rotter. Thank you Lisa Kussell and Nanci Ryder. Thank you Marty Singer and Lynda Goldman. Thank you Kevin Huvane, Rich Green, Jack Whigman, Todd Feldman, Jay Baker. Thank you Tara Cook, Allison Lorentzen, Michael Signorelli, Eadie Klemm, Kate Taperell. Thank you James Spackman and Nikki Barrow. Thank you Job Lisman, Patrice Hoffmann, Ulrike Ostermeyer, Claudio Lopez, Sabine Schultz, Ziv Lewis. Thank you Alan Green. Thank you Preacher and Bella, I miss you both my little friends.

Thank you Joel Spencer and Joy Kasson and Jan Sayers and all the people at BJI. Thank you Dr. John Barrie, IParadigms and Ithenticate. Thank you Drivesavers for saving my ass and saving a large portion of this book. Thank you to those who wrote me letters and emails thank you. Thank you to the booksellers thank you. Thank you to the readers, the readers, the readers, thank you.

'James Frey. Born in Cleveland, Ohio, September 12, 1969. Started stealing sips from drinks at seven. Got hammered for the first time at ten. Vomited from abuse for the first time at ten. Smoked dope at twelve. By thirteen was smoking and drinking regularly. Blacked out for the first time at fourteen ... At fifteen tried cocaine, acid and crystal meth for the first time. Got arrested three more times at sixteen ... Blacked out and vomited regularly. Three more arrests at seventeen.'

a million little pieces
JAMES FREY

A Million Little Pieces tells the story of James's life before *My Friend Leonard*. Aged twenty-three, James wakes with no front teeth, no wallet and no idea where he is; his body close to collapse from over ten years of exposure to, amongst other substances, alcohol, crystal meth, crack, cocaine and glue.

What follows is the harrowing tale of his rehabilitation interspersed with the story of how he got there. Scenes from his life at the centre; his struggles with authority, self-inflicted violence and his illicit relationship with Lilly are interwoven with tales from his past; what shaped him and what brought him so close to death, all told in unflinching detail.

'Inspirational and essential' Bret Easton Ellis

'Frey really can write. Brilliantly. And if you don't think so, f*** you' *Evening Standard*

'I crack my eyes, look through the slits. My heart starts pounding. I see two pairs of leather shoes, expensive shoes. Who the fuck is here. I try to place the shoes, I can't. I try to place the voices, I can't hear them well enough to place them. I crack my eyes more, look up without moving my head. Why the fuck would someone be in my apartment. Cabinet doors start opening and closing. I look up more, more, more. I see the backs of two heads. I see a familiar bald spot. I open my eyes and I sit up and I speak. Leonard.'

my friend Leonard
JAMES FREY

Sober, and on the brink of release from jail, James is ready to start a new life with Lilly. When this new life falls dramatically apart, he is devastated. Utterly alone and struggling to stay clean, he turns to Leonard.

Before long, he is immersed in Leonard's mysterious underworld: living in an apartment with no furniture, doing errands in return for envelopes of cash, falling in love and trying not to get shot.

'Beautiful, sad, potent, irresistible' *Elle*

'Dangerously addictive' *Tatler*

'If you care about what other people think, you will always be their prisoner'
— James Frey